D1290051

BOOKS BY

Ruth Doan MacDougall

A LOVELY TIME WAS HAD BY ALL *1982*

THE FLOWERS OF THE FOREST *1981*

AUNT PLEASANTINE *1978*

WIFE AND MOTHER *1976*

THE CHEERLEADER *1973*

ONE MINUS ONE *1971*

THE COST OF LIVING *1971*

THE LILTING HOUSE *1965*

A LOVELY TIME WAS HAD BY ALL

A LOVELY TIME WAS HAD BY ALL

Ruth Doan MacDougall

New York

ATHENEUM

1982

Library of Congress Cataloging in Publication Data

MacDougall, Ruth Doan, ———

A lovely time was had by all.
I. Title.
PS3563.A292L6 1982 813'.54 82-71056
ISBN 0-689-11276-9 AACR2

Published simultaneously in Canada by McClelland and Stewart Ltd.
Composed by American-Stratford Graphic Services,
Brattleboro, Vermont
Manufactured by Fairfield Graphics, Fairfield, Pennsylvania
First Edition

TO THANE JOYAL

A LOVELY TIME WAS HAD BY ALL

I

''Then I guess that's that.'' Gently, Jacob hung up the telephone.

He was using my office, which had been a rambling-rose bedroom when we bought this house ten years ago, and from the kitchen doorway I looked across the living room at his back. His spine slumped, causing the swivel chair to squawk; he sat defeated amid gray office equipment—sleek desk, filing cabinets, typing table, electric typewriter—below bookshelf cliffs.

I said, "I've started lunch. Should I stop?"

"Yes."

So I turned off the burner under the saucepan of tomato soup. Sunshine shot across the snowbanks outside and ricocheted around the kitchen, making me wince. The white plaster walls became too dazzling, and the strange warmth chilled. January thaw was carrying the snow away.

"A letter," Jacob said, his back to me still. "I suppose I've got to toss together a letter of resignation."

We were separated by the length of the living room, its exposed beams and gleaming wideboard floor a sudden no man's land. Everything trapped there seemed watchful, the elegant knights and simple citizens in brass rubbings, the Queen Anne chairs squatting on either side of the enamel woodstove ringed with embossed woodchoppers and reindeer, even the fallen blossoms in the pattern of the oriental rug, even the thick vegetation, spider plants, prayer plants, piggyback plants, baby's tears, devil's ivy, waiting and wary.

I ventured, "A brief letter," grabbing at this project, the writer in me taking over through the shock. "Don't give them the satisfaction of a diatribe. Short and sweet. I'll do a draft."

"Short and bitter."

"Dignified."

He swiveled around, a lithe man all at once turned torpid. I realized his shaggy white hair was no longer very premature. His eyes were large and myopic, always provoking me by hinting in their blankness that they saw more than other people's did, and they were green, not the corrupt green of jealousy nor the green of Helen O'Connell's smoky song; they were pure springtime, the only pretty ringtime, hey ding a ding ding. Tinted contact lenses glowed, suggesting sunglasses. He had such a stunned look on his face that I knew he wasn't going to explode, so now it was okay to cross the living room toward him. I paused midway for a normal domestic chore, checking the fire in the Jøtul, saying, "Can we let the stove go out and save some wood? The house'll probably cool off too much, though, won't it, and we'll have trouble heating it up when the sun sets. The thaw is trying to bamboozle us."

"As usual."

He got to his feet in bleached blue slow-motion, his Levi's and sweatshirt as faded as mine, and I was instantly reminded of how he'd returned one day this December from the Granite State Craftsmen's Cooperative shop in Exmouth, where he'd gone to fetch the tall two-drawer pine blanket chest he had painstakingly built in his spare time, copying a unique antique, and had placed there to sell, an experiment to learn if he could make money woodworking and escape his high-school librarian job; too expensive, it hadn't sold, and he'd decided to give it to me for Christmas, knowing I'd coveted it all along. In just such a dazed way had he got out of the Renault in our driveway and, staring at me, walking to the utility trailer he'd hauled, touching the old mattress pads covering something inside, he'd blurted, "I don't know how to tell you but they ruined it they moved it to a spot in front of a radiator it's split apart," and he yanked back the padding to reveal the mutilated chest.

Then, I had said, feeling as sick to my stomach as at bedtime during crash diets, hollow and weak and helpless, "You can fix it. You can fix anything!" Now I said, "You always claimed you'd like to celebrate your fortieth birthday by retiring. Well, you've retired a few months early."

"I never expected a gold watch, but let's go to the Pot o' Gold."

"We'll miss *The Gong Show,* it's almost time." A silly quibble, while my mind churned with words for the letter of resignation, dismissing "incompatible" because it sounded like a divorce, as did "irreconcilable differences." Why should such words occur to me? Another word was "heartbreak." How about "the hostile and unprofessional attitude of the principal"? "Unprofessional" was a good touch; teachers and administrators were paranoid about their status. Perhaps "lack of support for reading"? No, any more tirades about something as real as three years without money to buy books would only fall again on the deaf ears of an administration now dedicated to Alternative Learning, whose principal had turned the library into a mass study hall, whose superintendent wanted Jacob to change his title from "Librarian" to "Media Generalist." I could, however, mention "a wall of indifference" and substitute the jargon which meant "wall" in educators' language: "acoustical barrier." How about plain old "stupidity"?

Jacob said, "That was *The Gong Show* on the phone, and I've been gonged. Come on."

I realized I was shaking so much my fingers would just jam the typewriter keys if I tried to draft the letter. He had the right idea. Flee the feelings in this house.

At the coat rack, he seized our blaze-orange goosedown jackets. The blanket chest stood nearby, repaired after miracles with glue and clamps, the crack a thin thread that fooled guests into thinking it really was an antique. I hugged him, squashing the jackets between us. "We'll be all right. We've got our savings."

The telephone rang.

Furniture quaked and knickknacks jingled as Jacob dashed across the living room into the office. "Steve? Oh. Hello, Dorothy."

So it was not the superintendent calling back, having reconsidered his telephone answer to the ultimatum Jacob had finally given him yesterday in a private meeting after school. Jacob had said, "Let me run a library."

It was my mother, a champion at bad timing.

"No," Jacob said, "we didn't hear about that. I'll get Ib."

I mouthed at him, "Do I tell them yet?" and he shook his head. I went into the kitchen and picked up the wall-phone extension, clumsily, rattling. Click, said Jacob's receiver.

Long-distance in Bridgeford, birdlike Dorothy was all of a twitter, but this could mean anything from a new acquisition for her collection of samplers to the latest tidbit about my forty-one-year-old only-brother Batch's marital problems. "Ib, dear," she said. "Why isn't Jacob at school, does he have a cold? This flu that's going around—flu shots or not, you're bound to get it, everyone is. Except Pris Patterson, who *wants* it. She has to give a pep talk about the zoo to the Chamber of Commerce next week and she's been visiting all her friends who have the flu, hoping to catch it so she can beg off, but naturally the perverse bug is ignoring her."

I asked, "Why doesn't she just lie and say she's sick?" Then Jacob went past, irritatedly gesturing hurry-up, and I realized that Dorothy had once more managed to distract me from an immediate problem. "I'm sorry, I'm rushed, off to the drugstore to buy some stuff for Jacob, you know how he loves patent medicines." Not protesting that observation as he usually did, Jacob disappeared out the back door to the porch which linked the house and barn.

"Dry toast," Dorothy said, "junket, juice. I won't keep you a minute. The reason I called, I thought you might have heard the news on the radio and be worried about me and the poor baby hippo."

"The poor baby what?"

"You didn't listen to your noon news? Or hasn't the report reached your area down there? No matter. I'm joining the search party now, but I won't be in any danger. Little Horace can seem a bit unnerving, I grant you, especially if you happen to step outdoors in your underwear and meet him on your porch, as that man did last night when he heard a strange noise outside and went to investigate, but Little Horace wouldn't harm a fly."

Last spring, Dorothy had gone too far, yielding to the siren song of her most trusted dealer and buying a particularly tempting sampler for four hundred bucks. GOD BLESS OUR HOME, indeed! When Sebastian, my father, had recovered enough to speak, he'd carefully suggested she get a part-time job that would help support her collecting habit. To everybody's amazement, she went right out and found a job, and it wasn't in an antique shop but as a tour guide at the Bridgeford Zoo, otherwise known as Nature-Friends Family Park. "Working with antiques," she had explained, "selling samplers to someone else, would be exquisite torture and an experience I prefer to avoid. Besides, I love animals." A few days later she added, "I do wish, however, that the animals wouldn't go to the bathroom or become romantic whenever I lead schoolchildren past."

Jacob backed the car out of the barn and turned it around in the shoveled dooryard, its black Le Car lettering on milk-chocolate sides swinging past the kitchen windows like a modest revolving billboard. He idled, his gloved fingers tapping impatiently on the steering wheel. He wasn't the sort who honked while waiting; in fact, when he rarely did punch the horn, angry at some crazy roadhog, he never hit it hard enough to produce more than a yelp. Pleased by the former trait, I was annoyed and frustrated by the latter. When *I* used the horn, I leaned on it.

I said to Dorothy, "Have I got this straight? A hippopotamus broke out of the zoo and showed up on a neighborhood porch?"

"The only reason Little Horace charged the man was sheer fright. The man jumped back indoors in time, but he didn't believe his eyes so he didn't call the police, but this morning they tracked Little Horace to that house and into the woods—"

"I really must go," I said. "How big is Little Horace?"

"—and he's still lost and probably confused and cold, though thank heavens for this thaw, isn't the weather delicious? Yes, you hurry along, buy Jacob some Contac or whatever, but remember, vitamin C, plenty of rest, tell him to pamper himself and forget about the Dewey Decimal System. Little Horace most recently tipped the scales at almost five hundred pounds, but for a baby hippo—"

I said, "Goodbye, Dorothy. Don't try any daredevil stunts."

Our driveway, twisting through the woods that had begun reclaiming cleared fields a century after the house had been built in 1794, was actually a long lane, its difficult narrowness a dandy excuse for snowplows to leave us stranded until last. Now, between snowbanks, it was January-thaw mushy, and so was the dirt road it joined.

As we drove toward town past raddled trailers displaying in their yards their cherished snowmobiles, I suspected Jacob too felt a stony lack of the rage this ugly scenery usually provoked. The Millsted rednecks had won; the Exmouth High School administration had won. He and I were, on both fronts, vanquished.

I asked, "What exactly did Steve say?"

"He said he'd considered the matter overnight. He said, 'I'm not willing or able to change anything. You'll have to go on with your duties the way they are and with no money again at least this year.' "

"I didn't think to refrigerate the soup. Damn."

"It won't breed a lethal amount of bacteria while we're gone."

I looked from his taut profile to the trailer we were passing. Its yard was full of old cars buried in the snow that covered its border of rocks painted white, and above it waved an American flag on a flagpole taller than the trailer was long.

The dirt road jolted to macadam.

In the same moment that I said, "You know how my phobia—," he said, "I realize your leftover phobia—." Our tendency to talk in unison, thoughts traveling along the same paths, seemed reasonable, considering we'd been married eleven years, yet apparently we chorused more often than most other couples, startling listeners.

I glanced at him again. Nevertheless, he was only as familiar as a walk home in the dark.

But we didn't need to finish the phobia sentence. We both were hiding from the implications of what had just happened by picturing Dorothy's kitchen and wondering how Batch and I had lived to grow up unpoisoned by the contents of her refrigerator whose shelves somehow managed not to buckle under their load of leftovers, bowls and saucers containing dribs and drabs, some limp stringbeans, cat food, a blob of mashed potatoes, bleu cheese which was really Cheddar, tuna salad which smelled too oniony from sitting too long. All were suspect. During my years at home, I had done my best to try to keep track of the age of the food—was this congealed sausage patty left over from last Sunday's breakfast or the week before?—but being on the alert didn't always save me. I still can't eat chicken-noodle soup because of the time I heated up a closely inspected portion for lunch and swallowed a spoonful only to learn I'd been fooled, it was tainted. According to Batch (whose name is short for Sebastian, Jr., and not slang for the unmarried state he was toying with), when I came out of the bathroom after throwing up I kept vowing, "I refuse to eat another leftover ever again in my whole life, from this day forward!"

Impossible; Dorothy might be extravagant about samplers, but she was Depression-thrifty about food, and leftovers were sacred. Consequently, I later insisted maniacally in my own household that leftovers not be allowed to accumulate. A midnight-snacker, Jacob obliged, his raids soft silver rustlings as he peeked under aluminum-foil covers, like an elf playing in tinsel.

He asked, "Did I hear Dorothy correctly? A baby hippopotamus?"

"Little Horace escaped from the zoo." I leaned forward and switched on the radio. No news, just the beat of synthesized boredom from WEXM, so I flipped it off. "Dorothy was leaving in hot pursuit."

We reached the Millsted Shopping Center, which consisted of an A&P, a state liquor store, an abandoned hardware store, and an empty parking lot. Beyond a sawmill and a shoe factory, Main Street also seemed deserted, as if tumbleweed should roll past the Rexall drugstore, the small grocery store, the 6 Bits Diner, the dusty dress shop, and the Millsted Savings Bank from which Jacob's father, a loan officer, was soon to retire. Children in snowsuits were tucked among shopping bags in the back seat of a car parked outside the bank; all the bright hectic sacks shouted the names of the huge supermarket and department store and various boutiques in the Exmouth Mall. Millsted was growing, swelling with trailers, matchbox houses, mock chalets, prefab log cabins, even a few geodesic domes, but most of the new population traveled to nearby Exmouth to work and to spend its money. And, until today, Jacob had earned his paycheck there.

He asked, "How did Little Horace get loose?"

"I don't know."

"Some goddamn fool will probably shoot him."

Melting snow gurgled in gutters and poured out of drainspouts. A side-street beside the Town Hall led to Jacob's parents' house; we didn't detour. At the top of Main Street stood a Southern mansion complete with pillars, built long ago so the rich mill-owning family could dwell above the town it also owned. Nowadays the house belonged to an Exmouth proctologist, a newcomer whose specialty provided old-timers with material for comments about what, instead of mill-workers' sweat, paid for all the fresh white paint, the reshingled roofs, the fabled dinner parties beneath crystal chandeliers.

Jacob said, "Maybe the thaw inspired Little Horace. Or aren't baby hippopotamuses afflicted with spring fever?"

"I wish I'd remembered the soup."

The street wormed through some decaying wooden duplex housing, past a new stucco apartment development which already looked equally dilapidated, its patio balconies sagging over trampled snow, and then the pavement stretched forward to become a two-lane highway bouncy with potholes.

Three years older than I, Jacob had been born and brought up in Millsted, had known this road in his high-school days when it was smooth enough to be used for drag racing, when the only business establishment between the outskirts of town and Skinner Pond was a lumberyard vast as a flattened forest. Since that time, speculators had discovered the pond, rechristened it Rainbow Lake, and to provide services for the sudden outbreak of seedy summer cottages there appeared along the road, in the sparse pine woods, an improbable laundromat, a boat rental and bait and tackle store, a bread-cigarettes-beer grocery store, a moccasin shop, and, inevitably, the Pot o' Gold Restaurant.

Jacob pulled into the parking lot. We sat looking at the cat's-cradle tangle of snowmobile tracks that looped the pond's surface.

He asked, "What day is today?"

"Tuesday. January twentieth. Nineteen-seventy-six, and you've just declared your independence at the start of this bicentennial year."

"When you turned the radio on, I realized what my head

feels like, it feels like someone is spinning a radio dial in my brain, all the stations flashing past, garbled." He got out of the car.

The Pot o' Gold was a low rectangular building thickly covered with dark slab siding, as if it were trying to grow a skin of giant bark. Restaurants make me nervous, my basic caution about food, thanks to Dorothy's leftovers and also to the restaurants I'd worked in during high-school summers, intensified by the horror stories Batch loved to tell me. Dismaying my parents, Batch had quit college, married his high-school sweetheart, and become a salesman, and for years now he'd traveled around from restaurant to restaurant in New England, selling food mixes; as intimate with restaurant kitchens as Orwell's *plongeur,* he passed along to me the secrets he learned. Ptomaine gossip. I, of course, was unable to inspect the kitchens in restaurants where Jacob and I dined, so instead I always checked out the ladies' room and sent Jacob on a mission to the men's, figuring there might be some sanitary correlation.

The Pot o' Gold's bathrooms hadn't deteriorated too much since its opening, and the fare hadn't yet killed us. We came here quite often, Millsted not exactly offering a variety of choices. We did, however, avoid the place on Thursday evenings after walking in one time and discovering a Kiwanis meeting, with all the members—including Phil, Jacob's father—standing at attention, reciting in a self-conscious rumble the Pledge of Allegiance, hands over hearts, some of the older men still forgetting to add "under God."

Jacob opened the storm door and the inside door, and we went through the main room, where the rainbow-striped walls were dimmed by cigarette smoke and deep-fat-fryer grease, into the shadowy coppery lounge. In the painting behind the bar a rainbow trout leaped.

The lounge seemed empty, but from the hidden nook in which she counted her tips came the sound of coins clinking, and Madeleine Guguerre yelled, "Playing hooky today?"

Jacob replied, "There's no truant officer on my tail."

We sat down at a heavy pine table smeared with varnish. I virtuously moved the amber glass ashtray to a nearby table. The room smelled of ashtrays, though, and of Saturday night still lingering.

"Well," I said, and then I surprised myself by taking a great gulp of the stale air, as if I were catching my breath after a headlong race. "Will you have to go back to the school and clean out your desk?"

"I don't care about anything in my office except my coffee mug."

"The hell with the mug."

But I had given it to him, in happier *Laugh-In* days; its gilt lettering retorted "Look That Up In Your Funk & Wagnalls!" He said, "I've got to call Gert and tell her when she gets home from school. I'll ask her to take the mug home tomorrow, and I'll stop sometime and pick it up."

"If she's still speaking to you." I'd gathered that Gert, his motherly secretary, had been frightened by and therefore angry at the increasingly likely possibility of his quitting, leaving her in charge and in the lurch.

"Yes," he said.

Madeleine startled us with her fat-person quick quiet tread, appearing suddenly, her white waitress uniform as huge as a sail. "The usual?" Onto the bar she plunked the plastic Nissen Bread bag in which she carried her tips. She'd gone to school with Louise, Jacob's forty-two-year-old sister, and as she clattered ice and poured Scotch she gave him news to pass along to Louise, not noticing that he was paying even less attention than usual. "My luck," she said. "I thought Frank—Frank Aubert, you know, he's a policeman in Exmouth—I thought I'd finally found a steady man, I mean a cop ought to be a good influence on my boys, a good example, shouldn't he? But now he's gone and got himself kicked off the force."

"Oh?" I said.

She slapped down on our table the paper coasters that always stuck to the bottoms of the chunky amber glasses that matched the ashtrays. "You'll want two BLTs and black coffees, right? It's been hushed up, but Frank's the thief who was robbing the candy counter at the movie theater. During his night patrols, while he checked the locks at the theater he'd credit-card one open and go in and help himself to the Almond Joys. What a dumb shit."

Jacob's interest had been snared. "When I was a kid, I used to think that firemen *set* fires. I'd watch the engines go howling past and figure the firemen were on their way to start an exciting blaze. Maybe I was right."

Madeleine said, "I was wrong about Frank, that's for sure. Hi there," she added, as a stranger entered the lounge. "What can I get you?"

The man was wearing an Archie Bunker plaid wool jacket, but it drooped loosely on his gaunt frame. "Any chance you're still serving breakfast?"

"Depends. What've you got in mind?"

"Two eggs. And a Bud."

"Okay," said Madeleine, launching forth. "I guess the cook won't throw a fit. How do you want your eggs?"

"I'll have them looking at me. Do I pay now?"

"Let's see if you like them first."

The man swung himself onto a stool at the far end of the bar and huddled there.

I said to Jacob, "Maybe Gert will quit, too. In protest."

"Not with kids in college and tuition bills."

It belatedly occurred to me that I, like Gert, should have been furious at Jacob during the past death-watch days. Instead, while Jacob spent this last weekend prowling around the house, whirling to me periodically and saying, "I can't keep my New Year's Resolution and go along with this crap anymore, it's getting worse and worse, I've got to make a stand," I was too numb to do more than reply lightly, "A midlife crisis, how conventional!"

I said, "Maybe some of the teachers will quit."

"Nobody will."

"You've worked with some for ten years."

"Colleagues." He was slowly peeling the coaster off his glass, the task seeming to demand as much dexterity and concentration as brain surgery. "But times are hard and jobs are scarce."

"And most of your chums are happier with microfiche."

"Software."

"Jesus Christ, I just realized. Now that it's done, we don't have to stay in Mangy Millsted. No reason to hang around this town."

"The house?"

Our pale yellow house in the woods. I said, "We've been sitting in our oasis of acres these ten years, watching the rabble and rubble creep closer. The house isn't the house we bought. Jacob, are you going to be sick?"

"I fervently hope not."

Madeleine returned from giving the order in the kitchen and squeezed herself behind the bar. "Though I should have known better," she continued, opening a Budweiser. "You can't trust a cop nowadays, you can't even expect them to *try* to do their duty. Why, this last Labor Day weekend," she told the stranger, pouring, setting the beer glass in front of him, "the guys from Brunelle's Lumberyard down the road, they got out of work early that Friday afternoon and most of them decided to stop in here for a quick one and naturally they were still here by eleven o'clock at night. When they started beating up on each other, I called Moose, our local cop, and would you believe what that big slob's reaction was? Sorry, he says, but I'm not getting mixed up in those fights ever again. And when I gave him a piece of my mind about my tax dollar, he told me what I could do with my tax dollar. So, while the chairs were flying, I called the state trooper. I have to admit the trooper did show up, but the moment he walked in here the guys grabbed him and lugged him outdoors and threw him in the pond. So I did what I should've done in the first place. I called old man Brunelle, who owns the lumberyard. He's a little bitty thing, but all he had to do was march in and look at the guys and they turned meek as lambs. I mean, they knew damn well their jobs could be gone in an instant, at a snap of his fingers. You didn't say toast but I put in an order, do you want marmalade or grape jelly? Where're you from, by the way?"

"Down-country," the man said, "passing through. Grape jelly."

Jiggling his drink now, Jacob was studying the soaring iridescent trout, and I mused upon marmalade and thought how amazing it was that although Jacob and I were from hometowns only fifty miles apart, we hadn't met here in New Hampshire. We had met an ocean away, in England.

Then my stomach plunged; not with seasickness. Maybe I was going to be the one who started puking. "Jacob," I asked urgently, "when you were a kid, what did you want to do when you grew up?"

"Get steady ass."

"Aside from that. Seriously, for once."

After a while, he said, "Be a hermit."

"Mutually exclusive?"

"Oh, Christ, I suppose some sort of artist. No encouragement from my folks, as you had, but that's no excuse. A teaching degree from UNH instead, and then I figured if I avoided teaching altogether and became a librarian—well, I'd be a hermit among bookstacks."

"Hey, Madeleine!" hollered Bill Moulton, a regular, entering the main room. "How about a chicken salad sandwich and some French fries?"

Madeleine shot back, "You can have the French fries but the cook hasn't caught today's chicken yet." She looked at the stranger, and this time she moved her Nissen Bread bag off the bar and cached it somewhere beneath before she set sail again.

I said to Jacob, "I'll never understand Bill. The chicken salad sandwiches here taste like kindergarten paste."

"Then he must enjoy eating kindergarten paste. I recall I did."

"But didn't you outgrow it? Look at his work, though, he loves driving his bulldozer as if he's playing in a sandbox. Hi, Bill."

Wearing his khaki workclothes and his cap with its CATERPILLAR insignia above the visor, Bill leaned into the lounge and said, "Well, well, Isabel and Jacob. Taking the day off, huh? Sure must be nice. Knock, knock."

I said wearily, "Who's there?"

"Isabel," said Bill.

"Isabel who?"

"Isabel necessary on a bike?" And Bill went haw-hawing off to the men's room.

All at once I wished I'd told Dorothy what had happened. And then I realized why divorce words had presented themselves. It *was* a divorce. I asked, "Remember how Batch phoned us and everybody when he decided to leave Nicole? When we get home, why don't we phone everyone and announce your divorce from Exmouth High?"

Jacob snapped, "Just phoning Gert will be more than I can handle. And anyway, Batch is only separated, he won't make up his fucking mind."

I shut up.

Madeleine brought our sandwiches and coffee. Returning to the bar, she switched on the TV framed in a serried array of liquor bottles whose colors competed for customers' attention, labels a-twinkling. She selected a soap opera, and we ate, our eyes aimed toward it.

My God, I thought, what has Jacob done?

As we drove away from the Pot o' Gold, I began worrying about the money we'd spent there. A stupid spree! How downright self-indulgent and irresponsible to go out the moment you've quit your job and blow eight dollars in a roadside restaurant on overpriced bar booze and BLTs you didn't want! Sensing I mustn't say this aloud and hating the unaccustomed curb on my tongue, I chose another subject, remarking tentatively, "Why do you suppose that stranger was passing through? People don't pass through Millsted, they bypass it."

"Maybe he was looking for a hideout. Maybe he's an escaped prisoner, like Little Horace."

"We'll never know, will we."

"Not unless he makes the news."

The afternoon sun was sinking, and Jacob turned on the car heater. Neither of us wanted to go home. He drove slowly, letting the car drag its feet, yet the trip back through unfurling shadows began to seem so fast that when, as we neared downtown, I heard a siren screaming behind us my first thought was: This is all Jacob needs, a speeding ticket, the perfect end to a perfect day.

Jacob pulled over, but the police cruiser raced past, and we continued on.

I said, "We must remember to tell Madeleine that at least Moose still endangers all our lives by chasing speeders, even though he now avoids fights."

"Mmm."

Kids walking home from school had paused only briefly to watch the cruiser and had then kept going, presumably toward the more inviting reality of their television screens.

Jacob stomped on the brake. "What the hell?"

Main Street no longer looked like a ghost town. Coatless owners and clerks were running from the stores to gawk and point before hurriedly retreating to doorways out of the paths of two stampeding snowmobiles which leaped from street to sidewalk and back again, splashing snow, their helmeted riders whooping over the snarling engines. One snowmobile caromed off the 6 Bits Diner, and the white-aproned short-order cook on the doorstep angrily brandished his spatula. Not to be outdone, the other bounced into the braking cruiser, skimmed off a fender, and flew up the high mountain of snow dwarfing the grocery store; when at the peak the rider was thrown, he undauntedly wiped his bloody nose on his jacket sleeve, jumped back in the saddle, revved up again, and hightailed it down a side-street, followed by his buddy. Then Moose, sitting hunched in the cruiser and staring slack-jawed, noticed all of us taxpayers, remembered he was wearing a badge, and screeched off after them.

I wondered how many seconds had elapsed and if I had blinked.

"Damn," Jacob said. "My father has spotted us."

"School's out, so we don't have to use the flu tale now."

Phil left the bank's Ionic-columned entrance and bustled toward us, and Jacob rolled down his window, keeping the car running, giving an appearance of haste. Phil gasped, "Wasn't that something? Did you recognize—those helmets hid—were they drunk or whatever it is kids get up to nowadays?"

The claim that men considering marriage should study the prospective bride's mother before making a final decision used to cause me to retort that I always got a good look at boyfriends' fathers, but I wasn't able to check out Jacob's father, for Jacob hadn't brought a photograph of his family to England, not even a blurry snapshot such as the one of my parents and Batch he'd wheedled out of me. I'd remembered, however, that knowing my first lover's charming self-satisfied father had not prevented me from making a fool of myself, so I decided to risk marrying Jacob, father unseen, and take the consequences. Phil had turned out to be physically a portly version of Jacob and mentally so different I would have suspected, were it not for the resemblance, Jacob's mother of a fling with that Millsted rarity, a stranger passing through, a Depression stranger, mysterious hobo.

"Glad I caught you," Phil said, pushing his clear-plastic-rimmed glasses back on his nose. "Mom was saying just this morning how much she'd like to see you. Come to supper tonight."

I expected Jacob to begin weaving excuses, because he found mealtimes at his folks' house so difficult he always went to great lengths to avoid them, but instead of inventing some urgent chore, like a cellar flooded by the thaw, he glanced at me questioningly, didn't give me time to react, and said, "Okay. Six o'clock?"

"Fine," Phil said. "Drive carefully, the roads will be getting icy."

"Yes, Dad."

As we drove on, I said, "You could have used simple short-notice. What if your mother has only two pork chops on hand?"

"She never has only two pork chops on hand."

He refrained from pointing out that I was the person who invariably had just a half-pound of hamburg thawed when unexpected guests dropped in at dinnertime. Because those of my suggestions he objected to most vehemently were often the ones he eventually followed, I wondered if his deciding to face the torture rack of his folks' dining-room table meant that he intended to tell them he was no longer employed. Did he want to announce his divorce after all? I didn't dare inquire and we drove home in silence.

The kitchen seemed deceptively cozy, now that the brilliant sun had eased up. The plaster walls were again milky, the wooden cupboards warm tea-brown. The only sign of catastrophe was the abandoned saucepan on the stove, left as though we'd fled before an erupting volcano.

Taking off my jacket, I asked, "Are you going to phone Gert?" at the same moment Jacob said, "I'll use your office," and the telephone joined in by ringing.

Jacob grabbed the extension. "Hello? Oh. Have you rounded up Little Horace?"

Although the call wasn't from a repentant superintendent imploring him to return, Jacob obviously welcomed any interruption that postponed his call to Gert, for he shrugged, didn't pass Dorothy over to me, and kept listening, while I went into the downstairs bathroom and brushed my teeth and then, in the living room, checked the woodstove fire; it was dying.

"Well," Jacob said, "thanks for letting us know. Uh—"

I froze, gripping the door-handle of the dark green Jøtul. He was going to tell Dorothy!

He said, "I guess you and Sebastian have heard me bitching about school so much lately you won't be dumbfounded to learn I've quit, as of today, no sweat about finances, we've got some savings—what? Well, um, I do have a slight touch of flu but it didn't affect my thinking—"

I went to the rescue, and as Jacob thrust the receiver at me Dorothy's twittering sorted itself out to: "I've heard, Jacob, that people running a temperature sometimes behave in the craziest fashion because of their fever, I do hope you haven't burnt all your bridges—"

"It's me," I said. Jacob went into the living room. "He

doesn't have a fever. What he certainly would have if he stayed at that school is bleeding ulcers or a heart attack or both. Didn't you notice the strain he was under when we visited at Christmastime, how he was munching Tums by the fistful?"

"He's always under a strain then, I'm well aware he hates holidays and it's perfectly understandable. But good God, Ib, I *am* dumbfounded!"

"We'll be fine, don't worry."

"But what's he going to *do?*"

"Do?" I listened to Jacob raking coals. "Get some peace and quiet. Take a break."

"Will he be able to use Exmouth for a reference if he's quit? All those years! May I tell your father—and I'll be telephoning Batch about Little Horace—may I tell them?"

"Sure. What happened to Little Horace?"

"Perhaps Jacob doesn't have a fever, but I predict Pris Patterson will, complete with the flu she's been trying to catch so she can skip that Chamber of Commerce meeting, because when our search party located Little Horace in Larned Cove she plunged right in to try to coax him out. He'd broken through the ice and was floundering around but he was also enjoying his freedom and every time Carl managed to lasso him he slipped away, until finally the rope did hold but then he balked and it took all six of us to haul him to the truck. I'll never forget the sight of his poor short legs digging into the mud. And Pris! I asked her why on earth she was more afraid of the Chamber of Commerce and public speaking than double pneumonia and a runaway hippopotamus, but she didn't even pretend to have an answer, she just stood there dripping and shivering and vastly relieved."

"I've got to rush again, we're going to the Wetherbees' for supper."

"Are you absolutely positive Jacob isn't incapacitated by the flu? I do think the old word for influenza is much more descriptive, it does 'grippe' you, and if Jacob is in its clutches—"

"Give Sebastian and Batch my love."

After I hung up, I turned on the overhead light and opened the cupboard that was our emergency larder for snowbound predicaments. Powdered milk, Spam, granola bars; a first-aid kit of food. In my childhood I'd often listened to a harrowing tale recounted by Mrs. Lyford, the mother of my best friend, a larder saga about how during their early married years Mr. and Mrs. Lyford's emergency provisions hadn't sustained the little family during a long blizzard, as intended, but instead had fed them when Mr. Lyford was suddenly laid off from the textile mill. Mrs. Lyford always concluded, "We lived out of that larder for weeks on end," her voice trembling a bit, still frightened, the memory making the present security and prosperity more precious, knock on wood.

We had this back-up supply. And the freezer down cellar was full of the vegetables we'd piously raised organically. It also contained about one hundred and fifty pounds of cow. We now bought our supposedly "organic" beef from a business farm upstate, trying to think of it in the abstract; when we'd purchased the freezer and first started buying bulk beef, we had arranged with an area vocational coordinator at Exmouth High to raise a steer for us on his back-to-the-land farm, but Jacob began to complain that in the teachers' room the coordinator kept reporting the progress of the doomed beast and suggesting we come see it—visiting privileges?—and so the hamburg and roasts and steaks which resulted made us feel as if a farmed-out illegitimate child had returned to us swaddled in freezer paper, and we dined queasily.

Vegetables. Meat. On the canning shelves in the cellar were the pickles and relishes I'd put up, although books warned they lacked any nutritive value. Sauerkraut. Our car was paid for but the house wasn't. And in our savings account we had thirty-two thousand five hundred twenty-four dollars and sixty-five cents, just sitting there, not cleverly invested, simply waiting there as if in a piggy bank handy for us to grab when at last we decided to run away from home.

Jacob went into my office. I glanced across the stretch

of living room and saw him bend to dial, then straighten to stand leaning against the bookshelves, acting casual. "Hello, Gert," he said. "Has the news of my abdication reached you yet?"

Startled, I turned back to the kitchen and poured tomato soup in a red stream down the sink. Abdication? On Dorothy's list of heroes the Duke of Windsor came in second, with Jesse Owens and Charles Lindbergh following. In first place was Sebastian, my father the CPA, who, orphaned by a train crash, had been brought up by his Boston grandparents whom I'd never known, had come to Bridgeford for a week's vacation and, meeting Bridgeford-born Dorothy through her lawyer father, had transferred his work to Bridgeford for, as he often put it, wryly but gently, "A lifetime's vacation with you, my dear Dorothy." To which Dorothy always replied, blushing, "Oh, baloney!"

As I washed out the saucepan, I thought that if I too hadn't taken a vacation I wouldn't have met Jacob Philip Wetherbee, this man who had now landed us in such a terrifying situation, who could make such a foolhardy decision, this goddamn idealist—this quitter.

Twelve years ago, in 1964, I had gone to England on a summer vacation for a very old-fashioned reason: to try to mend a broken heart.

And it was restored enough during the three weeks scheduled there to make me realize I'd become so intrigued by this glimpse of Britain that I wanted to stay and see more. Virginia Lyford, my best friend with whom I was traveling, encouraged me, as did, by cable, my parents. But a job was necessary. The U.S. Embassy directed me to the U.S. Air Force, where terms like "local hire" were used and triplicate forms were signed and I found myself with a housemother type of job at one of the high-school dormitories catering to U.S. Air Force brats, in Clopton, Suffolk. Age twenty-five, I faced a new life alone in a foreign country.

Misgivings assailed me when the day came for the departure of Virginia, who was returning to New York, to her loft apartment, her roommates, her dancing. She didn't want me to bother accompanying her to Heathrow Airport, so we said our goodbyes in Russell Square, where we often had stopped for a rest after sightseeing. A final time we sat together at a teetery table and drank ginger beer, watching pigeons waddle across the grass past people spread out on deck chairs around the fountain.

Virginia said, "I'm bound to encounter Gary sooner or later when I go back to Bridgeford to visit my folks. How should I slant the story?"

"Such a pity he's cooped up with his kiln, while I'm trotting the globe."

"Okay."

A pigeon strolled over to our table, bobbed at the cigarette butts crushed on the pavement, and skirted Virginia's suitcase and our pocketbooks set beside our wobbly chairs. The pocketbooks were both very large; Virginia's was readied for the flight home, but the open side-pockets of mine were still crammed with paper fans of city maps, bus and subway maps, magazines, plus a copy of *England on $5 a Day,* turned so that the embarrassing touristy title would not show, a vain attempt at camouflage.

I said, "You needn't add that although I'm heart-whole again, I am still praying for a bolt of lightning to strike him in the balls."

The pigeon inspected an empty straw-wrapper. I had planned to play career-girl-in-big-city after college, toiling at a menial job by day, writing by night, but during the Christmas vacation of my senior year at Connecticut College for Women, Dorothy's alma mater, I had gone home for the holidays and had run into, at an eggnog party, the man who had been the football hero of my high-school class. Gary Bates. He had done a metamorphosis from flirtatious quarterback to dedicated artisan; I'd dated him in high school and I should already have learned my lesson about him, but I fell for it. He'd returned to Bridgeford after art classes and apprenticeship to open a pottery shop in a converted ice-cream stand where he made primitive bowls and tortured vases, and when he took me into this studio and showed me the wheel on which he "threw" these treasures,

I should have known I would someday be throwing them myself, at him. But after I graduated I got a job as a typist in a Bridgeford law firm (where the memory of my grandfather had sunk so far into oblivion he wasn't even a portrait in the waiting room), and I rented a furnished apartment in a house near Gary's apartment, and for three years we lived together in the clandestine fashion demanded by a small town back then. Batch was not big-brotherly protective about this arrangement; he was amused. My parents practiced forbearance, although Dorothy did give me a birthday present of a little framed sampler on which, amid needlework flowers and birds, these words loomed darkly:

Dear Child delay no time
But with all speed amend
The longer thou dost live
The nearer to thy end.

Virginia stretched, dancer-luxurious. "I'm dawdling. The weather's been so warm and sunny, I didn't expect that." She glanced at her watch and hastily finished her beer, the startled pigeon lunged upward, and the parting quickened to a merciful rush. As she scrambled into a pompous black taxicab, she called, "Give my love to Carnaby Street! Goodbye, goodbye!"

After the taxicab had darted off spryly and disappeared in traffic, I turned and again contemplated the Square. The sunshine was indeed astonishing. The people lying insensible on the chairs beneath its rays and the people coming from the subway to this greensward and walking round and round the fountain seemed, I thought, to have found their way to a truce with the nonsense that was life; during the past weeks here I had felt at moments that someday I might.

Hurrying back to our small bed-and-breakfast guesthouse, hoping to get indoors before I started blubbering, I wondered, amazed, at the convolutions my mind must have coiled through those three years while I waited for Gary to be ready to get married, to settle down, hearth and home. Our version of domesticity had lulled me, and so it was a bone-marrow shock when I sauntered into his studio unexpected late one May afternoon and discovered, in the time-honored manner, that he was unfaithful.

The guesthouse had a jolly red door. I ran inside, up the stairs to our room stripped of Virginia's things, where on my little Travel-Maid clothesrack only my own bra and underpants now dripped over the washbasin, and safe in privacy I treated myself to one last muffled yowling bawl. Out the window, above the miniature flowergarden, the top of the guesthouse's brick wall was cemented with shards of glass.

That done, I had begun packing, and the next day I took the train to Clopton.

To Clopton and to my destiny, I thought as I dried the saucepan. The wasted tomato soup had been made from tomatoes we'd grown last summer in our vegetable garden, a garden rich with ten years' work, with wheelbarrowloads of compost, trailerloads of priceless mulch and manure. How could we move away and leave this garden?

I realized that the superintendent's phone call had made us forget the mail completely. Putting on my jacket, I jogged down the muddy lane. Our mailbox, large enough to hold manuscript boxes, today contained a glossy assortment of catalogs, not just seed catalogs but also clothes and gifts, and as I walked back toward the house I marveled at the companies' audacity. Shamelessly they pushed their wares so soon after Christmas, brazenly they offered to us punch-drunk buyers their gorgeous Turkish caftans, bentwood rockers, decorative but inefficient pepper mills, ginseng facial creams, Mexican candlesticks, even bathing suits swirling with seashells and water lilies! But this year, this moment, I preferred these to the seed catalogs, not knowing where we were going or if we'd ever plant another garden.

The delicate yellow house and barn were thickening to honey, while against the snow the woods became sharper, bare trees black. Jacob could remember the house standing empty in his youth, a farm abandoned years ago; when we returned from England in 1966 and began house-hunting he was surprised that his father suggested this place. "Oh,"

Phil had said, sucking his teeth as usual at the beginning of a story, "it was bought up since you left, a nice young couple, the Clarks, they spent a small fortune having it fixed, no wallboard but a real plasterer to do most of the walls, new floors but wideboard, and then just when Mrs. Clark finished hanging the curtains her husband's company transferred him to California. He worked for Exmouth Wire and Cable. Isn't that something? Just when she finished hanging the curtains." Edna, Jacob's mother, chimed in, "Them tab curtains." "So," Phil continued, "they're selling in a hurry and the price is right, as the saying goes, eighteen thousand. Thirty-five acres, the land alone is a good investment."

What do you do when a bank's loan officer recommends a house? We looked at it, and the Clarks' renovation suited us so well that after we bought the place and moved in the only change we made was turning the downstairs bedroom into my office. But we did have to accumulate furniture, for they took everything west, from their canopied four-poster to their pewter collection, causing us to try to imagine a New England interior waking up bewildered in a Spanish villa. When we started shopping, I'd realized that although I still believed theoretically a house should be furnished in the most contemporary manner, I simply wasn't comfortable with modern styles except in my practical office; Jacob agreed, so we avoided furniture stores, entering one only to buy a fold-out sofa, and instead we prowled secondhand stores and went to auctions where, back then, those prices were also right. A wrought-iron lamp stand for four bucks. A pine kitchen table for seven.

Now the place was filled with our possessions. As I walked through the barn to the porch whose screens were covered with winter plastic, I wondered how the hell I could have mentioned moving so glibly. I'd never packed a house and barn before. I'd hardly even packed an apartment. Garden tools and birdbaths, the washing machine and that sofa—impossible, an inconceivable task! And where would we move to?

In the kitchen I saved the seed catalogs but tossed the

others into the wastebasket so I wouldn't see anything I really wanted to buy. I must economize; the wife of an unemployed librarian, I must start practicing frugality. All at once I remembered reading an article in which English girls who had deadly dull factory jobs tried to describe to an interviewer what drifted in and out of their minds during work. They mentioned thoughts about boyfriends and where to go on dates. Mostly their paycheck daydreams were about clothes and makeup but one girl confessed that her ambition was to buy a wastepaper basket for her room even though her family would think she was putting on airs.

Jacob had disappeared. I climbed the steep old staircase and found him naked in the bedroom, damp from a quick shower, studying an open bureau drawer.

I said, "We forgot the mail, but we only got catalogs anyway." The bedroom was plain, a Boston rocker, some plants, a faded rag rug on the floor and no canopy over the fourposter because Jacob claimed it would give him claustrophobia and would also make him feel as if he were a Boy Scout again, an experience he had not enjoyed, particularly the April outing when his troop camped out atop a mountain and was awakened at midnight by a spring snowstorm suddenly embracing the pup tents. I asked, "Had Gert already heard?"

"They didn't bother to tell her. Typical. But she'd guessed. Which of my mother's sweaters did I wear the last time we went over?"

"Your green popcorn-stitch." This drawer and others were full of sweaters Edna had knitted us, nightshirts Dorothy had made Jacob, embroidered nightgowns she'd made me; on the bed was the bedspread crocheted long ago by my grandmother Dolly, Dorothy's mother, its color ecru not intentionally but from age; above the bed hung a sampler, embroidered by Dorothy when she was pregnant with me, which showed a kitten chasing a ball of optimistically pink yarn into a garlanded bower. Because of all these nimble fingers, I'd never had to get serious about learning to sew and knit, I'd never had to direct my patience toward needlework, thank God. "Was Gert furious?"

Jacob pulled on shorts and a T-shirt. "She started crying."

"Oh, hell."

"She said when she first came to work she'd been scared to death, she was afraid of the books, and then the second day I made some comment about not thinking of the place as a library but as a supermarket, businesslike, and that, she just told me, calmed her right down and she knew she'd enjoy working there. And she did, until these past couple of years. Funny, I'd suspected she was intimidated by the books, but I feared my supermarket remark was condescending."

"Will she bring your coffee mug home?"

"Yes, though I told her I wouldn't blame her if she smashed it to bits with one of our brick bookends." He heard himself. "No longer 'our,' are they. They're her bookends and the next librarian's. That is, Media Generalist. Maybe the administration is heading in the right direction, a huge study hall. Give the books to the town library."

While he talked, I swapped my sweatshirt for the black turtleneck jersey his parents had given me at Christmas, and, sucking in my cheeks, I made my Marlene Dietrich face in the bureau mirror but, as always, I failed to look high-cheekboned and sultry. I sighed and watched, reflected, Jacob put on the fisherman sweater which made him look like a British Isles travel poster.

In England, when I had got settled at Clopton—with an apartment in a stately home's cottage, a new car (really new, not secondhand), American Express checking and savings accounts (chaotically confusing at the outset, the checking account in both dollars and pounds), and pots and pans and sheets and towels from the Base department store called the Afex—I became a weekend tourist, feverishly on the move, afraid that, although I lived off-base, I might get lazy and succumb to the familiar. For me, friendly American cheeseburgers at the Officers' Club snack bar were only the most obvious bait in this trap.

Deciding I needed a hobby to give my travels a reason cluttered with paraphernalia, I chose brass-rubbing because it reminded me of how, as a kid, I'd puzzled over the mention of this peculiar English pastime in *Cakes and Ale.* After buying and studying books about monumental brasses, in my spiffy racing-green MG Midget I sped hither and thither down roads on the wrong side, hedgerows high above me, and I plucked up enough courage to ask timidly for directions at teashops, sometimes even understanding the East Anglian answers, and sooner or later I reached my destination and carried into a church my roll of architects' detail paper and lumps of hard black crayons, my dust rag and whiskbroom and roll of tape.

One wet October afternoon, a Saturday, I was crouching on the tomb of a knight and his lady (1451 A.D.) when the church door opened and I saw Jacob for the first time, although because the church was quite dark I didn't really see him but only registered a vague impression of horn-rimmed glasses, a windbreaker shiny with rain, and the short haircut that meant he too was an American.

I shivered. There was a big kerosene stove at the rear of the cold church, but it probably was only lighted for services; brass-rubbers dared the elements the way Arctic explorers did. To my relief he acknowledged my presence with nothing more than a nod, following the code of not interrupting concentration, and I went back to work on the lady's headdress. This elaborate piece of apparel was the most important part of the brass, and I had already spoiled two tries at rubbing it. I am not clever with my hands, but I am stubborn.

Then swift movement made me glance up again, annoyed. He was vaulting onto a tomb, where he had taped his paper over the only other brass (more modern: 1484 A.D.) that the church boasted. Amazed, I saw he'd taken off his shoes. American sneakers. He began walking back and forth on the tomb, pressing the paper into the lines of the engraving underneath. This trick had never occurred to me. His socks were so white in the gloom that above them he seemed to disappear, an invisible man in white wool socks treading white detail paper. He knelt and began to rub.

I got the headdress right at last, and slowly the gown emerged, and cloak, and the eerie dog at the lady's feet.

I'd not yet quit smoking; I decided I could have a cigarette break. Jumping down from the tomb, I saw the figure in the man's brass materializing as quickly and easily as if it were just the head of a penny he was rubbing. Showoff.

The narrow wooden benches on either side of the aisle were scooped shallow with all the centuries of respectable rumps sitting on them. As I walked toward the door, the small hard kneeling pads on the stone floor beneath the benches reminded me of souvenir shops in Bridgeford which sold those fat little burlap pillows that lament "For You I Pine, For You I Balsam," but I supposed these pads would smell of dust, not forest perfume. I dragged open the door. It was cold in the entryway, yet warmer than inside.

Stretching, imitating Virginia as I unkinked my spine, I told myself sternly that brasses set into church floors were more backbreaking than those on tombs, besides usually being more worn, from traffic, and harder to rub. There were no chairs out here, so I sat down amid missionary bulletins on a low table and, lighting a cigarette, enjoyed the sight of the windy rain gray on the stone shops across the lonely wet street. English rain. So wondrously unbelievable, still, that I was actually roaming around this scepter'd isle. The dim stone pubs were closed until evening. Beyond the shops the chimney pots of the village swirled coal smoke into the rain.

I could see my car parked along the crooked sidewalk outside the churchyard gate. Then I realized that the blur behind it was a real shape, not a watery shadow. The same damn car! Together they waited, two brand-new MG Midgets, their greens almost black in the rain, both of their windshields marked with a registration sticker from the Base, and both of them tax-free. The wind blew coal smoke into the entryway, and I blew tax-free cigarette smoke back.

The door opened. As he came out, I almost panicked, absurdly feeling pursued by the Base, the United States; I was a tiny terrified creature cringing under the hovering talons of the American eagle. Nevertheless, I did look him over in the dank light. His American haircut was disconcertingly grizzled. I said, "Sorry I got the headdress one first."

"Sorry I barged in," he replied, lighting a Camel, lounging against the wall.

During my jaunts I'd secretly hoped to find love as well as thatched roofs and digestive biscuits, but I'd had in mind an English romance, my lover a version of—say, Albert Finney in *Tom Jones*.

This American, however, certainly wasn't someone I could dismiss. He moved gracefully. You didn't run across green-eyed men often, and what was my favorite color, what color had I chosen for my first new car? That he had also chosen green might mean he had no false modesty. Out of nowhere came my grandmother Dolly's startling comment I'd overheard as a child: "I'd let *him* put his shoes under my bed." She had been listening to her Rudy Vallee records. I glanced at this man's feet and saw he'd restored his sneakers.

He added, "The rector thought you'd be done by now."

"I'm very slow," I confessed, embarrassed. "I was one of those kids who couldn't stay inside the coloring-book lines." Maybe he too hoped for a foreign affair, a cheeky English bird, perhaps?

He said, "I've seen some brass-rubbing people who don't bother keeping the outlines clean, they cut out the figures and mount them to hide the mess they made. You're from the Base?"

"Unfortunately, I'm not much better at cutting. Are you? From the Base, that is?"

"I'm the librarian at the Base high school, it's my first year over here."

"Mine, too. I've got a dorm counseling job. What they call dorm counseling. It's babysitting, but it pays the rent."

"So you work afternoons and nights, that's why I haven't seen you."

Or heard me, I thought, realizing we both were listening intently to our voices and accents. Oh, Christ! Not only was he an American and from the Base high school, a colleague probably full of the Stateside camaraderie I was trying to avoid, but was he also—

He asked, "Had any trouble with your car?"

"Just learning how to get into it."

"I noticed you bought right-hand drive."

"I'm planning on staying here awhile. Did you?"

"I wasn't sure," he said. "I applied for overseas jobs in a fit of cabin fever last winter after almost five years of running a high-school library in Maine. I requested far-flung bases. I was offered England or Guam. Here I am, but I bought left-hand drive in case I move on. My kid brother, by the way, has an old MGA he and my father are devotedly fixing up, a great beauty. You're not from Maine. Vermont?"

"It's New Hampshire. Small world."

We stared at each other, fellow Granite-Staters, and then we quickly looked away, at the shops. A blue and yellow Wall's Ice Cream sign hung over the grocery store door, and I thought of the ice-cream signs at home. He would know Sealtest ice cream, and Durocher's and Hood's; he would know what Hoodsies were.

He asked, "Which town?"

"Bridgeford. Once a mill town, nowadays mostly a tourist trap."

"I've been to Bridgeford. In high school we used to drive up and go to the stock car races. I'm from Millsted."

"Millsted? Where's that?"

"Down near Exmouth. It's been bypassed so long hardly anyone driving past remembers there's a real town."

"Millsted. Millsted. Haven't I seen a sign for Millsted on that Route Whatever where everybody is always getting killed? The land is so flat down there I used to figure drivers had car crashes to break the monotony—oops."

But evidently he didn't feel I'd insulted his hometown, for instead of springing to its defense he laughed and said, "Our own informal stock car races? Suffolk is flat, too. I've heard that during the War all of East Anglia looked like an enormous airstrip. You must miss Bridgeford, then?"

"Not Bridgeford. I like it here very much, though I do get hungry for mountains."

"Do you also get hungry for food? I spotted a fish and chips shop near here, they should be open by the time we've finished and we could get a grease fix. I've become addicted. Have you been to one yet and tried vinegar on your chips?"

"No," I said. I added uncertainly, "Thank you. That would be fun."

"I'm Jacob Wetherbee."

"Isabel Pierce, Ib for short."

We went indoors, down the aisle to the brasses. I clambered back up on my tomb and, feeling my way ahead as if I were reading Braille, I found by touch the outline of the knight and picked up a crayon.

Once more we drove toward town along the boulevard of trailers, remembering how when we bought our place this had damn near been a cowpath, quiet, secret, its tree branches interlocking overhead. Now the widened road glittered in the headlights, ice crunching under our tires, the tree stumps rotting beneath snow.

We passed the cellarhole-family's estate, seemingly a construction site but one whose construction had stopped years ago, at the level of the first-floor platform roofed with tarpaper. A stovepipe and a board embossed with an electric meter rose out of the flat shoveled-off roof, and a TV antenna spread low wings. Through squinting cellar windows, a light shone wanly. There was a rusting yellow Fisher plow in the driveway snowbank. Beyond, a shoveled path led to a hapless outhouse.

"And," said Jacob, "there'll be another baby come spring."

Whenever we drove past I always tried to recall in what *Little House* book the Ingalls family had lived underground and I always resolved to research the question during my next trip to the Millsted Public Library. Library. I said, "I'm sure it was *On the Banks of Plum Creek.* Pretty sure."

At the front of other driveways, pickup trucks were parked with their noses to the road, as if to flaunt their quick-switch plows.

Jacob said, "Did Dorothy ask what I'm going to do? Gert did."

"A career. Last weekend I found myself looking it up in the dictionary, and besides the usual definitions there was 'A rapid course or swift progression, as of the sun through the heavens. Archaic.' Oh, see, our favorite mobile home is worshiping."

In the front yard of this burnt-out but restored trailer stood an upended old bathtub; its interior, painted a peeling blue, framed a floodlighted cement Virgin Mary who was serenely praying, unaware that two of the tub's feet protruded above her halo like horns.

"Christ," Jacob said, "I should have quit last June and never bothered starting another school year!"

Was he planning to tell his parents? I said, "It would have spared us the cost of a new pencil box."

On Crescent Street the Wetherbee house announced that guests were expected, both the frosted lamp over the unused front door and the yellow bug-light over the back door welcoming us. Like most houses in this particular downtown neighborhood, it clung grimly to respectability, a narrow prim house with only hints of frivolous gingerbread in the screened porch's scrollwork. Usually Jacob ignored the two-car garage behind the house, but tonight after he parked in the driveway he glanced at it before he opened the back door and we went into the kitchen.

Edna was stirring something in a saucepan on the stove—I sniffed and identified creamed cod; thank heavens, a meal easily stretched—and, smiling, bashful and pleased, she said slowly, "Hello there," loving the sight of Jacob. As she banged the spoon clean and came to kiss us, I sensed she was about to blurt out a secret, something she often did behind Phil's back. Childlike, her eyes beneath her demure gray coiffure and unlined brow were a clear artless brown. She had coped with Phil for forty-four years, a feat which I thought merited a sainthood or, at the very least, a bathtub shrine.

"That battery," she said. Jacob and I concentrated, because she almost always began everything in the middle. "I was going to phone you tonight if I got a chance alone, and that flat tire, I don't know what finally made me make up my mind—" Then Phil came into the kitchen, and she cut herself short with, "There's time for a drink. Isn't this a wonderful treat, Dad, on a Tuesday night!"

Jacob and I exchanged alarmed looks. She was obviously talking about a car. Did she mean the old MGA that had belonged to Timmy, Jacob's brother?

Phil lighted a cigarette. "I sure hope Moose caught those snowmobilers. Kids!"

Mixing drinks here was kitchenwork and thus Edna's chore; for a jigger she used a juice glass decorated with dancing peasants, her measurement mark the chin of a dirndled wench. Pouring these generous and innocently potent portions, she said, "Out the hall window I seen a robin when I went into the bathroom, but it was only the sunrise on one of them damn pigeons. I thought the robins had come back."

I said, "Such a reprieve, this weather."

Phil said, "We'll pay for it later."

Edna, more daring nowadays when choosing Phil's leisure wardrobe, had dressed him tonight in a bold after-work change from banker's gray: burgundy polyester pants and orchid cable-knit sweater. He looked like a psychedelic Humpty Dumpty. But he'd resisted her make-over efforts to change his plastic-rimmed glasses to fashionable aviator's; about that, resuming his role of lord and master, he had prevailed.

As for her own attire this evening, while adorning her azure polyester pantsuit Edna had exercised even less restraint than usual, decking herself out with a multitude of the gifts Jacob and I had given her over the years, bracelet, scarf, necklace, pin, and the silver earrings she kept touching uncertainly. A couple of months ago she'd had her ears pierced, and at Christmas the poor woman was inundated with little boxes of pierced earrings, from Phil, from Louise and Arthur and their children, from Jacob and me, all of us desperate for a new gift idea and overjoyed at this whim of hers that sent us rushing out to buy hoops and studs and bangles. When she touched the silver earrings again, for a moment I feared she was worrying about having put on a pair we hadn't given her, but then I remembered she never got presents confused, she kept an inventory list in her head; I realized she was just still unused to the security of pierced, after decades of clips. Apparently thinking about other presents, she said, "I don't know how people can be so mean. That frozen tomato soup you give us tasted specially good since we didn't have none of our own. Imagine, someone walking right into our backyard last summer and stealing all my nice ripe tomatoes!"

Jacob was watching her. "Have you decided whether or not to plant some again next summer? Tempt the Burpee Big Boy Bandit to strike again, and trap him?"

She said, "I don't know what the world is coming to," and added tap water to Scotch.

Carrying our drinks, we trooped through the dining room, which had been recently redone with mortar-and-pestle wallpaper, into the living room where the radiators were turned so high it smelled as densely of scorched steam as a dry cleaner's. Phil wasn't going to let any goddamn Arabs deprive him of his comfort, not while he could still pay the oil bills. On the Gay Nineties wallpaper and on every surface were more presents, Christmas, birthday, hallowed events, Louise and Arthur's lavish white wedding photograph, the strap of horsebrasses we'd sent from England, grandchildren's graduation photographs, great-grandchildren staring from the lacy depths of layettes, my novels clasped rather indecently between bronze bookends made from Jacob's baby shoes, fancy ashtrays and cute figurines and the subscription we'd given them to the stack of *Yankee* magazines on the coffee table and, above Phil's armchair, this year's Christmas present to him from Louise and Arthur, a banjo barometer. Phil tapped it and leaned back and peered through his bifocals before sitting down. A new ritual. "Falling," he said. "What did I tell you."

We sat. Bands of angels passed.

I said, "Well."

Phil's hand crept toward the *Manchester Union* on his

side table, then halted. He picked up his drink instead. "How's school?"

"Fine," Jacob said.

Knitting, Edna had lapsed into one of her reveries. Perhaps she was thinking about how codfish cost more nowadays than steak used to, or maybe she was worrying about Louise's working too hard doing clothing alterations for extra money because Arthur's welding business seemed to be going downhill; I suspected, however, she was plotting how to get Jacob aside to ask him about Timmy's car.

And, after the creamed cod, the bread pudding, the familiar discussion of TV programs and the comparison of their reception (downtown-snowy) to ours (country-clear), she managed this. Phil took his coffee into the living room, and we were helping her in the kitchen when beneath the sound of gushing hot water she whispered to Jacob, "You'll need to look it over, won't you, to know what it needs?"

He said, "Are you talking about what I think you are?"

She asked me mischievously, conspiratorially, "Want to come too?"

I didn't, but I also didn't want to continue scraping plates. Phil smoked during meals and put out his cigarettes in his food; I much preferred Dorothy's leftovers to the sight of these butts squashed in baked potato remains and Cool Whip. "Sure," I said.

Taking off her ruffled patchwork apron, Edna called, "Dad, we're going out to see if I got some old clay pots the right size for Ib."

The reply was a contented rustle of newspaper.

We grabbed jackets and went outdoors. Streetlights made the trim little backyard surrealistic, the snowbanks menacing. Not even an alley cat would skulk here.

Jacob hauled up the left-hand garage door, the only one used for years, and switched on the overhead light. We walked around the Wetherbees' Dodge into clutter. Beyond was an old white MGA splotched with rust-colored primer paint.

Resolutely, Edna began clearing a path to it, and then

Jacob joined her, moving aside a snow shovel, some lawn furniture, a barbecue grill, and I spotted the heap of clay flowerpots and chose two uncracked specimens, for an alibi.

"Spring-cleaning," Edna said. "Maybe this thaw is what made me decide."

We reached the car. Boxy, it was very handsome despite the primer birthmarks. Jacob's eyes went blanker than ever as he circled it.

He had been the baby of the family for thirteen years, until the arrival of Timmy. Telling me about this in England, he said that for months he'd refused to believe his mother was pregnant. "At her age? I was aghast. She must have been what? In her late thirties? Revolting! And my folks didn't say a word to me and Louise, we just watched Mom getting fatter and fatter, while we ourselves got more and more embarrassed, and then finally off she went to the hospital and that night Dad came into my room and woke me up and told me I had a baby brother. Then Dad sort of mumbled something, and I said huh?, and he said he guessed I knew how babies happened. I had a general idea and was doing my adolescent damnedest to find out details, but I just said yes as offhandedly as possible, man of the world." The gap in years, Jacob added, made Timmy seem more a nephew than a brother and therefore more fun.

Shivering, Jacob kicked a flat tire. "The thaw didn't penetrate in here. I don't suppose, Mom, you've told Dad you've taken this notion."

"Well, when everything's all done he can't stop me, can he?"

"A wrecker will have to haul it to a garage to be fixed. Dad will see that it's gone and what will you say? Blame a car theft on the Burpee Bandit?"

"Oh."

Timmy was seventeen when I met him upon our return from England, and he and Phil were still working on this car he'd bought two years earlier. It had been what Jacob called a junker, so the progress was slow. At the Sunday dinners we couldn't avoid, Timmy tried to ask us about England while Phil talked about a rebuilt engine, new brakes and brake lines, new fuel lines, a new fuel pump, and a rebuilt starter.

Then at last the bodywork was done, and Timmy and Phil tuned the car up and took it for a trial run to our house, too jubilant to worry about Moose's catching them without license plates. Jacob was permitted to take me for a spin.

Timmy had by then turned eighteen. While Phil talked Sundays about the car's future—new upholstery, a paint job, a new canvas top, frills—occasionally Timmy mentioned his own future, nervously joking about the draft. And one time Jacob remarked, "If I were you, I'd bolt to Canada." Phil nearly had a seizure in the mddle of carving the clove-studded baked ham. Edna emerged from a reverie to ask what on earth Jacob had said, and Jacob soothingly told her he'd just been teasing Timmy. Afterward, alone with Jacob and me, Timmy confided that Canada was exactly what he was considering.

Phil, alerted, wormed Timmy's plans out of him and immediately recruited Louise and Arthur to help with the "It's un-American and you'll break your mother's heart" campaign, ignoring frightened Edna who never got a chance to say, as we sensed she felt, that she'd much rather have a traitorous live son in Canada than a patriotic dead one in Vietnam.

The day after he graduated from high school, Timmy enlisted in the Navy and soon, a Seabee, joined a construction battalion headed for Vietnam. His "tour," he wrote, would be eight months. Reading his letters over and over, Edna murmured, "He'll be all right, Dad says he'll be all right," and she kept showing us the letters as if for confirmation. In Da Nang, Timmy wrote, "I live in a wooden frame camp—tin roof, screen and plywood walls, a plywood floor. My work day is about ten to twelve hours long. The recreation consists of movies, beer halls, and a fine beach for swimming. Most of the Vietnamese are friendly, the ones on our side, that is."

Jacob and I didn't show his parents Timmy's letters to us, in which he said, "My assignments are building wooden frame buildings, bunkers, fortification for the Marines, living and berthing spaces, etc., under slightly hazardous conditions. Except for the fact of getting shot at occasionally, I don't mind it too much. But I admit to moments of sheer terror of enemy attack (don't tell Mom and Dad) and do I ever look forward to being homeported! Thanks for the bundle of detective stories you sent. Sure am enjoying them and I'm passing them along."

After Timmy was killed, Phil had stored the MGA in the far side of the garage and removed the battery. He'd intended to put the car up on blocks but hadn't. Neither had he sold it.

Jacob said, "Let's go back indoors before we freeze. It's been sitting eight years, Mom, it'll need all new tires and a tuneup at the very least."

"Curly's," Edna said. "Can they fix it at Curly's Garage or do I have to go to Exmouth?"

I realized my teeth weren't chattering; my clay pots were rattling. As we went outside, Jacob turned off the light, pulled down the garage door, and said, "Okay. I'll call Curly for you tomorrow and have him send the wrecker over here while Dad's at work. If Dad blows his stack when he finds out—"

"He can't go bring the car home, can he? Not until it's fixed up?"

"I don't suppose so."

In the spooky streetlight, Edna smiled. "I didn't want to look at the car all these years, and I guess I finally made myself not see it at all, and that's wrong, like dusting his room as if it was really just a guest room. Will you teach me how to drive it? Dad never let me try that right-hand drive."

Jacob opened the back door. "Better not rush things."

While we quietly finished doing the dishes, I mentally finished a draft of Jacob's letter to the superintendent:

Dear Steve:

I resign my position of nearly ten years as Exmouth High School Librarian, in disgust.

The school's educational philosophy and the administration's operational policies are producing students who cannot read or write and who therefore cannot think.

With regret,

Carbons to the head of the school board and to the president of the Exmouth Teachers' Association. What was I forgetting? Back pay and retirement fund could be requested in a covering letter and, I brooded aloud, "Something should be stated about hiring Gert a substitute teacher to help her out until a new librarian is found."

Jacob said, "I told Steve that on the phone."

"Put it in writing," I said.

As I dried the last dish, Phil came into the kitchen to rummage in a drawer for matches.

"Before supper," Jacob said to his parents, folding his peppermint dishtowel stripe by stripe, "you asked about school. Truth is, the situation is so bad I've decided it's wisest to leave before my professional reputation goes down the drain along with Exmouth High's."

Professional! Jacob had said the magic word, and Phil replied, nodding, "I've heard that place isn't what it once was but I didn't want to tell you. Back in my day—"

Edna, lost in thought, observed absently, "You need a vacation, Jacob, you're white as a sheet tonight."

"—and," Phil continued, "the kids the Business Department is sending us nowadays, cashiers who can't even keep their minds on their counting—"

Jacob laughed. "The buzz bunch on an Exmouth High high."

"—disgraceful!" Phil lighted a cigarette. "Well, well, this is certainly big news. But there are plenty of other schools within commuting distance, one of them is bound to want a librarian next fall. Meantime, don't let Exmouth get to you, that's the way I'm winding down at the bank until my birthday. You can coast until June."

"I've already quit." And hanging up his dishtowel Jacob announced the untimely end of his career. "I'm not setting foot in that school or any other school ever again."

"Oh," Phil said. "Oh." I'd suspected Phil kept track of our bank balance; a computer-click look on his face now confirmed this. "Well, like Mom says, you need a vacation. It's not as if you have Louise and Arthur's responsibilities either, business and family. But what are you going to do in the long run?"

"I don't know."

"Come on."

"I don't."

"If you won't set foot in a school, you can always work in a public library."

"That's naive, Dad. I haven't got the proper degree for an equivalent position in a public library."

Anger flared. Phil threw his cigarette into the dishwater where it drowned hissing in soapsuds. "You'll think of something." Plumply wrathful, he rushed back to his newspaper.

Edna asked, "Could I have one of them bud vases I seen in fixed-up old cars?"

"Afraid not," Jacob said. "Not in an MGA."

"He was awful fond of lilies of the valley."

During our drive home, Jacob suddenly burst into song, as he used to when he was tired toward the end of sightseeing trips in England. With his Howard Keel voice he inquired about love, and I made wide-open eyes and bee-stung lips and, remembering my Kathryn Grayson trill, answered him.

At the house, the phone was ringing once again.

"Probably Dorothy," I said, clutching clay pots, reaching for the extension, "or maybe it's Batch, calling to congratulate you," but instead it was Louise, Jacob's sister, her voice low and fast in an apparent attempt to keep the lid tightly clamped down on hysteria.

"Ib? I've been calling and calling, trying to get Jacob, I hope I've done the right thing but if he's drunk and disorderly at the police station what would he be like here at home so I told Moose to keep him overnight. Why they considered letting him go in the first place—! I can't remember all the things Moose said they've booked him and his pal for, leaving the scene of an accident, resisting arrest, operating a vehicle to endanger, operating an O-R-V while intoxicated—"

"O-R-V?" I interrupted.

Jacob, putting in the refrigerator the pudding Edna had pressed on us, turned and looked at me.

Louise said, "Off-road vehicle, that's what they called his Christly snowmobile, he and Bob dented the fenders of the state trooper's car as well as Moose's before they got cornered, I don't know how I'm going to explain this to the kids, the grandchildren are too young to understand but someday they'll find out their grandfather was in jail, and *what do I tell Mom and Dad?* Dad has always thought Arthur was such a good provider, with a business all his own, but lately—is Jacob there?"

"Yes." I handed Jacob the receiver and watched him begin to listen, a grin twitching.

Mousy old Arthur, proprietor of the welding shop out on the main highway, a dark dirty Hades over which he and Louise lived in the large apartment that Louise, a spare and efficient woman, kept immaculate against all odds; drab old Arthur, father of four, grandfather of three; boring old Arthur had actually been one of the snowmobile carousers! Marveling, taking off my jacket, on my way to my office I flipped on the living-room television and saw Shirley MacLaine kicking up her heels. The special was titled *Gypsy in My Soul.*

How do you pack an eighteen-inch color television set? And the twelve-inch black-and-white set in the kitchen? We hadn't saved their cartons, had we?

After typing a draft of the resignation letter, I returned to the kitchen where I found Jacob concluding, "I'm sure that when he's himself again, Arthur will be glad you had him kept there. Uh-huh. With Mom and Dad, you'll just have to let the shit hit the fan. Okay, wait until tomorrow.

Cheer up, at least he didn't get hurt, he did use his helmet." I waited for Jacob to close with his disconcerting "Bye-bye," a farewell you'd expect to hear from a little old lady; indeed, he'd picked up the habit as a child, imitating his grandmother. "Sure, Louise," he said. "Bye-bye."

But he hadn't bothered to give the superintendent a polite bye-bye. I said, "Not the time to tell her you've quit."

"Hardly."

"Maybe you could ask Arthur for a job." I immediately regretted the joke. "Your beloved Shirley is on the tube."

"Good."

As he mixed drinks, I thought of what these kitchen cupboards contained, all the glasses, for instance, and I tried to imagine wrapping each glass in newspaper like fish and chips, fitting them into cartons, writing FRAGILE with a Magic Marker, all the wine glasses, tumblers, iced-tea glasses, Depression-pink champagne glasses we used for ice cream, dried-beef jars we used for juice; and then there were the lunchtime pottery and the dinnertime Limoges, not to mention other dining essentials such as the drop-leaf kitchen table here and the mahogany dining-room table at its end of the living room, and the woven place-mats and my grandmother's linen tablecloths and the heavy silver candlesticks one of which was already bent either by an ancestor's carelessness on, perhaps, a moving day, or by an ancestor's need for a blunt instrument—

"Jacob," I said, "what did we own when we got married? Almost nothing. We didn't even have a camera, we must be the only people in the world who both went to England without a camera and didn't even break down and buy one over there."

"The Afex camera prices did tempt me now and then. What did we own? We owned what we owned when we started shacking up. My Witney Point blanket I got irresistibly cheap at the Afex," he said, going into the living room, checking the stove, "and my Afex radio and my conversation-piece Charles de Gaulle nutcracker. Your London stuff, your Liberty scarves and the hiphuggers from Carnaby

Street which caught my eye atop a tomb, and all that food you used to buy in the village instead of at the Commissary." He readjusted the TV I had adjusted.

"Russian crabmeat," I said, following. "And the village supermarket had an ordinary American red-and-white wall of soup tins but there were the kinds you couldn't get at the Commissary, mulligatawny and oxtail and mock turtle."

"Those packets of curries and paella."

"I brought to our shacking-up some treacle and gooseberry jam." I sat down in a Queen Anne. "I wonder if Little Horace will make the eleven o'clock news. I wish you could have met Stella."

"Do you also wish we'd stayed over there?"

"Do you?"

Jacob collapsed into his wing chair. "If I had quit midyear over there like this, they wouldn't have paid our way home."

"Remember our pots of English ivy? Imagine, I didn't buy that ivy, I hacked it off the back doorway!"

The cottage I'd rented was in Clopton Park. A fairytale forest cleaved by fire roads, this estate had become a plantation of conifers and you could see far into the ranks of trees because underbrush wasn't permitted. Geese walked in the dooryard of the little stone storybook gatehouse. A gravel lane led to the manor house, which, along with the remodeled stables and laundry cottage, was rented by the U.S. Air Force Officers' Club who in turn rented its rooms and the apartments in the outbuildings to Air Force people seeking off-base housing or waiting for housing on the Base.

Ivy climbed the old pink walls of the laundry cottage, picturesque and enchanting. One of the two apartments in this cottage was empty, and, charmed, without considering such problems as heat, I hastily rented it for forty-eight dollars a month, collected some motley furniture from the meager selection offered by the Off-Base Housing Warehouse, and moved in.

The tiled floors of my five small rooms—scullery, kitchen, living room, bedroom, bathroom—were bare, the windows curtainless. Underneath the cracked formica top of the kitchen table and the torn plastic seats of the dinette chairs and on the slats of the bed and under the ragged living-room furniture, the words OFF-BASE HOUSING had been stamped, plus some numbers. Wooden orange crates were still available free back then; I used them for bookcases. At the Commissary, I bought a lot of Lestoil.

Soon it was necessary to keep three little squat kerosene heaters burning all day, and the wallpaper over the brick walls would blot with damp and the windows ran with wetness. Outdoors, the green forest became more stark. Scrubbing dishes in the playhouse scullery sink, or sitting at my portable Royal typewriter in my numbered dinette chair, I would look out the window at the trees and think: I am in England. When I left for work and stepped out of the soggy cottage into the pale mid-afternoon sun, I felt as if I were surfacing after a long swim, but my car was always filmed with moisture and the upholstery was slimy and as the MG scooted past the manor house it splashed through puddles which never dried, so there seemed to be no surface anywhere after all.

In the other laundry-cottage apartment lived the Morrisons, a black family. I'd only known one black in my whole life, a girl in the first grade of my Bridgeford grammar school who had quickly been shunted off into the "special" class for retarded kids. The Morrisons were an Air Force family as well as black, Ed a sergeant, and they had moved in just a week ahead of me.

I talked with Stella for the first time in our backyard where, appropriately enough, we were hanging up our laundry on the clotheslines which ran from our side-by-side back doorways. I had a lingerie handwash; she had a family-style wash and a tiny daughter, Amy, who solemnly gave me a clothespin; Stella and I both had bags of brand-new clothespins. Stella said, "This is probably futile, it looks like rain again," and I said, "The kitchen stove in your flat, has it got a square burner up front?"

"Yes, that's just a burner, but the little pan underneath it is a broiler."

"What's the metal sheet thing for?"

"I *think,*" she said fiercely, tall and slender, her long fingers busily pegging pajamas, "I think I've finally figured out that you keep the metal thing under the burner when you want to cook on top, and you take it out and slide the pan in its slot when you want it to be a broiler. It's been driving me nuts, and the stove is so damn small!"

"Well," I said, Pollyanna, "at least it's up top. The other stoves I've used at home, the broilers were always under the ovens and you had to cook your steaks on your hands and knees."

And it was an English stove; I am in England.

Stella said, "I've never seen such a small stove, I've ruined every single dinner so far. When our name comes up on the Base Housing List and we move onto the Base, I'll insist on a larger one, that's for sure. I sold mine to the couple moving into our apartment back in the States because they offered me such a good price, but I had no idea how old-fashioned these British appliances would be! The plumbing, too! We looked at your apartment before we chose ours—hate to tell you, but there's a fireplace in ours, that's why we picked it, filthy coal but better than heaters—so I know your toilet has an overhead tank and chain like ours, isn't it incredible?"

"I'm trying to think of it as a priceless antique." I considered the situation. I intended to avoid Americans, but this was different, yet would she want to be bothered with me, would she think I was presuming to apologize for slavery? Oh, what the hell, I told myself, stop dithering. "How about going for a walk, to get acquainted with Clopton?"

She hesitated, then agreed.

So Stella and Amy and I began to explore on foot, taking damp walks downtown into the village. We immediately learned we needed shopping bags if we didn't want to walk back juggling soup cans and tissue-wrapped heads of lettuce, so we invested in two large sensible straw shopping bags and soon, after some inconvenient forgetfulness, we always remembered to bring them with us.

The new little yellow brick bungalows on the outskirts of the village grew, as we neared the High Street, into tall old duplex houses of flint and brick, gray beneath chimney pots and mossy tiles except for their doors and drainpipes painted happy colors. I became very fond of a violet drainpipe. All the gardens behind the low walls and hedges were as neat as if each inch of earth were known and loved. When we reached the chilly stone shops, at the small supermarket we would buy cheese and marmalade and frozen steak-and-kidney pies, and at the greengrocer's we'd buy vegetables, fruit, flowers. We stopped at the stationer's for copies of *Woman's Realm* and *Woman's Own,* strange magazines that looked like Sunday supplements, and Amy dawdled before the glass cases of candy and dolls and toy double-decker buses and toy cash registers which counted in pence and shillings and pounds. Then, our shopping bags heavy, we headed home, and our walk back past the houses and the gardens to our forest seemed much longer than the walk down.

These shopping excursions weren't really necessary, since so many products were brought right to our doors. There was the milkman who arrived every morning to leave four pints for Stella and one for me, our amazement at learning that milk wasn't sold in quarts here equaled only by our astonishment at next realizing that refrigerators were not, to all British, as necessary as food itself. (And what, I wondered in horror, might happen to Dorothy's leftovers were she an English housewife?) Three times a week the breadwoman's van came honking through the forest and all of us Clopton Park womenfolk and children gathered under the trees to wait until she parked it and opened the doors in the back. Together, by trial and error, Stella and I discovered what to buy from those trays of cakes and crumpets and tarts and loaves unsliced or sliced. The butcher's car was a miniature station wagon, and his young helper carried to us in a big wicker basket the meat we had ordered. Kerosene was delivered once a week to my apartment by the man we called the Pink Man because kerosene was known as paraffin here and the brand was Pink Paraffin.

He arrived in a bus that combined a grocery store and a hardware store, and Stella and Amy would come out of their apartment and climb up into it with me and we would browse the shelves of saucepans and soap powders and teapots while he pumped paraffin into the barrel in the dooryard. The coalman came to Stella, and eventually, when I tired of going to the Base laundromat, the laundryman came to me. I felt that we had slipped backward in time. I kept thinking of Dolly, my grandmother, and how she would have been perfectly at home here. To my grandparents' Bridgeford house had come a meatman, a breadman, an eggman, a dry-cleaning man, and although these delivery services began dwindling away, Dolly still had a milkman and a fishman until the day she died. In contrast, Dorothy and supermarket-shopping were made for each other; one step into her first supermarket and Dorothy knew this was kismet.

Sometimes Stella and Amy visited me in my apartment but I sensed Stella found it depressingly bleak, dank with the inadequate heat from the toadstool heaters.

At the Morrisons', chunks of coal glowed red and snug in the fireplace grate. Stella had covered the sofa and armchairs with sheets to protect them from the coal smoke, so when I visited her I sat on three layers: white sheet, yellow slipcover, green upholstery. I wondered if she realized that the furniture seemed to have joined the Ku Klux Klan. This furniture was her own, painstakingly accumulated in newlywed days, unnumbered. But a rented television stood on top of the Morrisons' television; British TV wouldn't come in on an American set. She hadn't got her record player adapted, so it ran irritatingly slowly even though plugged into a transformer. These transformers, deceptively small gray boxes that weighed a ton, were necessary to convert electricity for appliances, yet despite the extra bother they caused, Stella refused to give up anything. If she was making a cake, instead of mixing it by hand she carried her electric beater and bowl of batter into the living room, plugged the beater into the record-player transformer because the transformer in the kitchen was already used for her refrigerator and toaster and blender and iron and coffeepot, and crouched on the rug she beat the batter right there amid Amy's panda, one-eyed elephant, blue fish, and Raggedy Ann.

Stella was the first person I knew who "fixed" food. "Before I fixed breakfast," she would say, or "Time to start fixing the stew." I myself "made" meals; I was used to hearing that. Long afterwards I always thought of Stella during women's chat or TV commercials, whenever somebody said, "As I was fixing lunch . . ."

One time when I got back from work at midnight, Stella invited me over for beer and pizza. She was homesick, she told me wryly, it was a homesickness party. The apartment seemed a different place so late at night, all of Amy's toys put away and Ed present, drinking a beer, leafing through a *Newsweek* from the Stars and Stripes bookstore. While Stella was in the kitchen convincing the stove it could handle a Chef Boyardee pizza, I tried to engage Ed in some guest-host smalltalk, jabbering relentlessly about brass-rubbing, describing my weekend jaunts, riding my hobby-horse until at last Ed's withdrawn look silenced me and I realized Stella and Ed never took sightseeing trips around the countryside, never even drove to London and joined the multicolored throngs of tourists there. To my embarrassed relief, Ed finished his beer, excused himself, went to bed.

As we were munching pizza, Stella suddenly said, "He must be asleep by now. I've got the funniest new record, it's a Moms Mabley," and she switched on the record player.

"What's a Moms Mabley?"

"He doesn't like it, you know. If anybody except us listens to these."

Although the slowness of the record player muffled Moms's voice, I soon learned that this wasn't Amos 'n' Andy. I wondered at the difference in attitude between Ed and Stella, husband and wife, man and woman.

Despite the increasing cold we continued to take walks to the village, past the yellow brick bungalows, the flint-

and-brick duplexes, the gardens. By this time we had got well-acquainted indeed with the High Street, with the sight of prams full of babies and shopping bags parked against the stone shops. I no longer shut my eyes to flesh and feathers when we passed the butcher-shop window where whole pigs and furry rabbits lay in repose and great haunches of meat hung naked. Gazing wistfully at the curtained windows of the pubs, the King's Head, the Swan, the Flintknappers, the Dog and Partridge, I wished I dared enter one; maybe sometime, feeling even more a native than I did now, I would suggest to Stella we stop and wet our whistles with some of England's famous warm beer—although room-temperature beer in this weather must be as chilled as American, mustn't it? An actual flintknapper worked in a small building beyond a low brick wall, and the piles of flint nodules in his dooryard looked like heaps of skulls.

One day at the greengrocer's, a woman customer turned and smiled down at Amy and said, "What a pretty little pickaninny."

I couldn't believe my ears.

Stella said evenly, "She is not a pickaninny," and took Amy's hand and we left without our Brussels sprouts (local) and grapefruit (Israeli). The walk home that day was very fast, but it felt just as long. We strode without speaking. Amy surprisingly didn't protest being yanked along at such a clip; had she understood? Worse than patronizing, the woman's voice had been truly *admiring*.

After this, Stella and Amy didn't shop in the village again. "The weather," said Stella, and she drove Ed to work so she could have the car to do her shopping at the Commissary and Afex.

Then I met Jacob amongst the tombs in that clammy church.

A few days later, the Morrisons' name came up on the Base Housing List. Packing cartons appeared in their living room, and before work one afternoon I sat for the last time on their sofa in front of their grate and listened to Frank Sinatra singing—singing slowly—from their record player. Tomorrow, however, it would be my grate, for I'd just got permission from my landlord, the Officers' Club, to switch apartments. A math teacher would be moving into my old apartment to cope with the paraffin heaters; he was white.

Stella said, "Come see our new place when you've got a spare moment."

I did, driving to the Base one murky day a week later, an hour before I was due at my dorm. The swift two-lane highway between Clopton and the Base was as unnerving as the butcher shop had been, always carpeted with run-over rabbits. Above the speeding cars, fighter jets screamed down across the open heath toward the airstrip, past the grassy Second World War bunkers and the Rod and Gun Club's rifle range. But in contrast to all these varieties of death represented, there was a warning, an admonishing finger, near the Base entrance: a huge wrecked Ford on display, its coral-pink fenders folded, its windshield splintered, an unnecessary sign on its crumpled hood saying DRIVE CAREFULLY.

Beyond, ducks cruised along the peaceful stream curving into American territory.

At the Class VI liquor store, I bought the Morrisons a housewarming bottle of champagne; it cost a dollar in this Big-Rock-Candy-Mountain paradise where a quart of bourbon cost a dollar thirty-five and the only serpents were Scotch and Drambuie, as expensive, because of satanic tax laws, as in the States. Then I set out to locate the Morrisons' new home.

I frequently still got lost on the Base, for the streets didn't seem to go anyplace and made no sense to me, and I found myself driving twice past the movie theater, which I had boycotted after learning that you had to time your arrival to miss standing through "The Star-Spangled Banner" while on the screen flocks of planes roared straight at you, tanks pounded, and soldiers waded swamps. The weather stopped fooling around; it began to rain, adding to my confusion.

Searching, driving the maze of streets which had humps

built into the pavement to keep you down to ten miles an hour, I passed encampments of brick duplexes and houses like little stucco cubes, and concentrating as though I were trying to bag a church for a rubbing, finally I discovered that the Morrisons' address was a number in the rows of silver trailers.

It was a cramped home, with all their overstuffed furniture pushing out from the living-room cell into the kitchen slot where stood a stove that was, if not the stove of Stella's dreams, at least large enough to obstruct completely what designers like to call a traffic pattern, but Stella seemed to be coping splendidly with the lack of elbowroom. In a relieved way she chattered about the merits of life here, the library so handy, the bowling alley, the movies, the grocery shopping with shopping carts and paper bags, not shopping bags, the playmates for Amy. The Base was sanctuary. Listening, at last I realized what courage our walks had taken. And I had thought *myself* an intrepid explorer!

"Great," I said, checking the Afex watch I'd bought to replace the one Gary had given me which I'd smashed while I was smashing things. "Oops, the time, and I've still got to pick up the mail and some cigarettes and stuff. Look, do come visit the old homestead if you miss your coal fire."

Then we laughed as I opened the trailer door into a yellowish gray fog that tasted of the coal smoke from the closest village, which had been almost obliterated by the Base but was fighting back with pollution.

On the humped streets again, I drove through a make-believe neighborhood of one-family houses whose picture windows all looked out at the street or into the picture windows of the houses next-door. Did Stella hope to move up to one of these someday?

I passed the American Express bank, prefab, gray, very small. Military paydays filled the place solid with queues which doubled back on themselves in such tightly packed convolutions that you couldn't figure out where your line went so you were apt to arrive, after an hour's wait, at the wrong window. On the gray walls, inducing both oblivion and wanderlust during your waiting, were big bright posters of springtime in Paris, a bullfight in Spain, gondolas and mountain goats and castles. There was a sign that told you always to carry travelers' checks when you traveled; another sign would tell you that on this day a pound was worth $2.81½.

I parked at the post office. The doorway was nearly blocked by two airmen steadying a ladder for a third who was nailing a red-white-and-blue emblem to the APO sign overhead. Indoors, I found the room empty but the cement floor tracked with mud, and I walked down the aisle between the metal wall and the wall of numbered boxes and peered through the window of mine. Nothing today. (Sometimes my mother sent a letter to my apartment because she liked addressing an envelope to Clopton Park, but that was more expensive.) Nothing from home, and no mash note, either, from the librarian who'd taken me to the Flintknappers last Saturday night for a beer and a packet of potato crisps before returning to the laundry cottage to neck on my swaybacked sofa in front of the coal grate.

En route to the Afex, I drove along the wide sandy verge where in the little cars parked beneath a row of trees the British car salesmen sat waiting for customers. Thinking of Jacob Wetherbee's almost identical car, I honked to the fellow I had bought mine from. The procedure had been so informal, sitting on the front fender of the salesman's car to discuss luggage racks and wire wheels, signing the papers on the hood, that I'd felt as if I were buying something extremely hot.

One lone airman waited by the PLEASE SHARE A RIDE sign at the corner.

A vacant lot lay like a muddy fairground at the outskirts of the Afex, and although no giant merry-go-round galloped in the rain, the American cars on sale here looked like big red and green and blue stallions. Beyond them were the somber old English cars used as taxis, the taxi drivers dozing behind steering wheels set on what I still thought of as the wrong side. In the Afex parking lot, a large sign bristling with stick figures warned me of the millions of accidents in the home as I parked my car and stepped forth to dodge other cars swerving splashily into parking spaces or shooting backwards out.

The Afex lobby featured a glass case whose contents seemed less a drugstore display of cosmetics than an invitation to a black market: amber flacons of perfume, gold tubes of lipstick, and pink bottles of nail polish a-gleam. I groped in my pocketbook for my identification card and shopping list.

"Thank you," said the elderly Englishman at the desk to my ID.

But, joining the shoppers and browsers, I hardly heard him, for the wares here could hypnotize you instantly; I knew my blinking rate was slowing as I forgot the cement floor, the walls and roof of galvanized metal. There were cuckoo clocks everywhere, and camel footstools and music boxes and embossed brass tables, and as I walked down the first aisle the shelves of glass vases and decanters chimed in my wake. Down the shining midway of the main aisle I moved, my list forgotten, the golf clubs and cameras and typewriters and jewelry a golden blur around me as though I had entered heaven.

In the women's clothing section, shoppers pawed in the racks of dresses crushed too tightly together to pry apart. Southern voices, a baby screaming. The counters were a tangle of mauve and rose and apricot nylon, lacy lingerie and nightgowns, ravished counters that spilled sweaters and blouses and jerseys all escaped from their plastic bags. Bra straps dangled like climbing ropes on mountains of padded bras.

Beyond, the men's section was a dry blue room, dark blue, light blue, highlighted with khaki; uniforms on racks, uniforms on men shopping.

My daze lifted slightly in the farthest room when I jerked a tiny pushcart out of its wire nest of mates and let my list guide me down the aisles of prosaic necessities. Tampax and shampoo. Lighter fluid. Two cartons of Kents, since of this month's ration there were only two squares left unpunched on my cigarette slip. (Jacob Wetherbee smoked

Camels, taking his cancer straight.) At the check-out counter, I came to. Never would I get used to such low totals!

Outdoors again in thickening fog, I drove past more metal buildings hooped over the flat land. After passing the bulk beer store twice, I took the right street to the Commissary and parked. One of the cashiers stood guarding the shopping carts inside the doorway; he nodded to my ID and whisked a cart to me, and I steered it past cellophaned vegetables. From the cash registers stretched lines of people waiting to check out, waiting, their hands resting on the bars of their overloaded carts. Deep into canned goods I went, where some of the labels were as familiar as friends and some were strangers I'd never seen at home, Mexican foods and scrapple. A housewife lurked near the mustards, smoking a forbidden cigarette. I grabbed some of the essentials I didn't buy in the shops on the High Street or have brought to my door, tuna fish and coffee and Ivory Liquid and toilet paper. In the white frozen-food cases the packages were a bright cold mosaic; I turned and glanced back at the bags of frozen shrimp, the cocktail tacos, before I reached the check-out lines. The things I could afford now which I couldn't on a typist's salary! I always liked to see what other people bought, and as my line inched nearer the row of cash registers I watched their purchases being sped backhanded by the cashiers down the countertops to the bagboys. Chicken breasts, dog biscuits, cake mixes, aluminum foil. The cash registers clicked and buzzed. Six little jars of baby food rolled downhill into a wall of chuck roast.

And so to work. I drove toward the high school that looked just like any new high school at home, as flat as the land, cinderblock sterile. Even an English fog couldn't make it mysterious. Its lights were on, the kids were still in there; I wasn't late. I parked in front of the dormitories and sat cradled in the bucket seat, staring at the empty tennis courts and baseball field, not wanting to go into my dorm, to my military job.

But I did. The dorm was quiet except for the gargle of

the drinking fountain in the lobby. The two other counselors were the ones who were going to be late. In our office I took off my raincoat, hung it up, and shook the electric kettle which stood on the filing cabinet. Water sloshed; I plugged the kettle in.

There was nothing to do now but to sit. Babysit. The lot of the dorm counselor. Because this was one of only two U.S. Air Force high schools in England, most of the kids going to school here came from other air bases, and these bases were too distant to return to every afternoon so the kids lived in the dorms all week. We were here to take care of them. We worked from three o'clock in the afternoon to eleven-thirty at night, Sundays through Thursdays, one counselor sleeping overnight in each dorm, and for the kids from bases so far away it was impossible to go home on weekends there was another shift of counselors who stayed in the dorms from Friday afternoon to Sunday afternoon. I gathered that nobody had ever been able to decide which was the better duty. Most of the counselors were American. The British were called UKs, and they were the ones who slept in the dorms; we were called DAFs, which meant, or so I understood, Dependent, Air Force.

On the office desk were demerit slips, a tin of shortbread, the base bulletins, some Clarkson Tours brochures, and a box of Savoury Tangs, bacon-flavored crackers—biscuits—made by an English branch of Nabisco. I'd bought the box of Savoury Tangs in Clopton and brought it to the dorm because reading the blurb on its back cheered me up, reminding me why I'd chosen to do this excruciatingly boring work. I am in England.

The central heat in the dorms was always turned up too high. I could smell my raincoat drying. The kettle spluttered steam, and I dropped an American tea bag in an Afex mug, poured, and while it steeped I read once again the Savoury Tangs box. *Elevenses: Savoury Tangs put extra flavour into your mid-morning break. After School-Time: Children love Savoury Tangs. Give them a handful when they come home. "They're smashing, Mum!" TV-Time: Your favourite programme. All the family together. Pass the Tangs packet round. Savoury Tangs are just the job when you feel peckish.*

I took my tea to the window and looked out at the quadrangle. School was over; clusters of kids stood on the paths in the fog, apparently talking. The dormitory door banged open. Girls calling, the slap of wet footsteps.

"Miss Pierce," said Bonnie damp in the doorway, "have you got change for the Coke machine?"

"Afraid not."

More girls came to the doorway, slowing down, loitering, not wanting to go to their rooms nor to the Day Room, any more than I had wanted to enter the dorm.

"Miss Pierce," Wendy said, "Lorna is going to get engaged this weekend."

"More power to her," I said, lifting my mug.

"She's getting her diamond Saturday."

One of the Lindas said, "Is there a dance tonight?"

Bonnie said, "You know what you ought to do is you ought to keep a box of Coke machine change in the lobby, it could be the honor system."

They stood there, they leaned against the doorjamb, against the pale blue cinderblock wall. Marilyn yawned. Carol adjusted the pearl buttons in her pierced ears. The smell of their raincoats merged with the smell of mine as I thought of best-friend Virginia and me in high school, dawdling homeward at close of day, our arms full of books, our talk full of boys. Did I dare write her yet about Jacob Wetherbee? Would saying his name out loud, even on paper, jinx this budding romance, wary though it was? How silly of my mended heart, anyway, to be pitter-pattering so tremulously, as though I were still the age of these girls instead of a jaded twenty-five!

I said, "I expect you've all got plenty of studying."

"Well," said the other Linda, "it'll be dinnertime pretty soon."

"Scram," I said, and they wandered off. Picking up the day's bulletin, I sat down at the desk and read that all personnel traveling on PCS or TDY on MAC aircraft were required to have a MAC Transportation Authorization,

DD Form 1482. I read that a 1960 Austin Mini was for sale, a 1962 Chevrolet, a 500-watt transformer, and three paraffin stoves. I read the Safety Slogan. I read the Sentence Sermon.

Then the two other counselors, Mrs. Elliott (UK) and Nancy Jordan (DAF), arrived. Out the window, a boy on a skateboard swooped along the path to Dorm Five, skidded in a puddle, and fell off. Beverly came in, asking, "Have you got change for the Coke machine?" In their little beige rooms banked with chipped blond bunks and bureaus, where no pictures were allowed on the walls and no reading was allowed after ten-thirty at night, the other girls settled down with their LP's of Barbra Streisand or their radios tuned to Radio Caroline, an offshore pirate. And from my pocketbook I took a Penguin with which to while away the hours.

As usual, Nancy and I left for supper together, bearing Mrs. Elliott's unvarying request for an untoasted tomato-and-cheese sandwich. (And when the sandwich was delivered by one of us, Mrs. Elliott would chew it sadly, saying, "After all these years, why can't I remember it will be American cheese?" I suggested, to no avail, "Think of it as delicious plastic.") Nancy was too plump to find the MG Midget comfortable, so we always took her Volkswagen; she drove with the steering wheel embedded in her stomach, and she didn't get lost, fog or no fog.

Beyond the school buildings we could see the headlights of the line of cars moving through the gates from the flight line. The slick streets were busy with other cars going home to the brick blocks of apartments, to the picture-window houses, to the silver trailers where Stella lived.

A recorded bugle began to bleat "Colors" through a loudspeaker. "Shit," Nancy said, and stepped on the brake. On the sidewalks the men stood and saluted in the rain, and all the cars stopped and waited until the last note ended.

We drove past the barracks and the gymnasium, then swung into the parking lot of the Officers' Club. Getting out of the car, I looked past the Club and the BOQ at the sparse line of trees above the flat horizon. On days like this, on most days, when you couldn't see the neighboring village beyond the trees, not even the square stone tower of the church, you felt as if you were standing on a plain—or a veldt. But I am in England.

The lobby of the Club was empty except for the portraits of Queen Elizabeth and President Johnson that contemplated each other across the expanse of blue sofas and green ashtrays. The corridor, however, was crowded; we had to squeeze past the people at the slot machines to reach the snack bar which was painted such a deep red that the moment you entered you felt as if you'd been swallowed by Jonah's whale. Nancy and I ordered Manhattans and plain hamburgers—"No roll, please, no chips"—and what passed for a salad. Lighting a cigarette, I eyed the eagle glaring at me from my paper place-mat.

"—the English," Nancy was saying. She'd worked in Wiesbaden for two years before coming here this fall. "Mostly the stores are closed, it's always an early-closing day, but if they do happen to be open they don't want to sell you anything! You have to practically *beg* them!"

The kitchen door swung back and forth, emitting steam, smells of grease, the voices of the waiters and cooks, Suffolk accents, southern accents, the rattle of plates, and out in the corridor there were coins clunking, the yank and spin of the slot machines. Someone in an orange flight suit leaned through the doorway, glanced around the room, and left. If my job was beginning to get to me by October, how long could I stand it, even for England?

Nancy usually balanced her complaints, and by the time we'd finished our gray hamburgers she was once again talking herself out of going home next spring. "They say," she told me, "you get on the plane and when you go in the bathroom and see those tissue-paper rings to put on the toilet seat you know you're already home."

"God shed his grace on thee," I said.

After we paid, in the corridor Nancy as usual dropped a nickel in a slot machine and, without halting, pulled the handle, not awaiting the result. Nearby, a woman was winning, yet the hill of dimes in the cup of her machine never grew, even as more jingled down over it, for she steadily fed them back into the slot, looking at nothing but the whirling fruit, her hand moving from cup to slot to handle, clunk pump spin, clunk pump spin. We paused to read the entertainment calendar's assorted announcements.

Tuesday: Lobster Newburg in Patty Shell $1.50

Bar Special: Old Fashioned 20¢

Officers' Wives Club Hi and Bye Coffee 10:30 A.M.

THE SPECIAL STEAKS LISTED ABOVE ARE NEWLY ARRIVED FROM THE STATES!

THE CLUB WILL PAY THE NURSERY ON ENTERTAINMENT NITES!

GO TO THE CHURCH OF YOUR CHOICE, THEN BRING THE FAMILY TO THE CLUB EVERY SUNDAY.

Through the doorway of the bar I could see some teachers standing about in the smoky darkness, talking, drinking. Was there a grizzled librarian in the crowd?

The rain had stopped, but the fog had become suffocating, white. We drove back to work and got out of the Volkswagen, Nancy taking the plastic sandwich in to Mrs. Elliott while I headed for study-hall duty at the high school. Now the school's quadrangle seemed a cloudy aquarium enclosed by the dormitories whose few lighted windows indicated quiet rooms where at their tables the honor students, back from supper, would be sitting curved over their books. Here outside, the kids who had to go to study hall swam slowly along the paths beneath the dripping trees toward the high school. Every night except dance nights, the girls went to study hall five minutes before the boys and, more importantly, left five minutes earlier to return to their dorms; hanky-panky in the bushes was supposedly scheduled out of existence.

I hadn't yet got accustomed to seeing the windows of the high school's upstairs corridor all wide awake each night as though a Parents' Night were continuing into eternity with its coffee, cookies, bullshit.

"Hi, Ib," said the study hall supervisor, sitting at his

desk in the corridor. He'd asked me to the Officers' Club for a drink a couple of times; mustering forgotten etiquette, I'd made excuses that probably bewildered him less than the real reason would have: He wasn't Albert Finney in *Tom Jones*. Not disheartened, he now asked, "How about next Saturday—" and then he suddenly scowled past me at the latest group of kids coming up the stairs. "Sullivan, just what the hell do you think you're doing?"

Sullivan hadn't bothered to wear any socks. I went down the corridor to my study, where for the next two hours I had to monitor a roomful of bowed heads lumpy with curlers, pajama tops hidden beneath sweaters. Taking my Penguin out, I changed my mind and hunted up some paper in the English teacher's desk at which I sat. I'd tell Virginia, after all.

Outdoors, study hall ended, we found the fog almost impenetrable, so the return to the dormitories was an adventure, albeit a chaste one. The dregs of the workday now. More cigarettes. More tea. Coffee, for Nancy. More reading, eyes grainy. A Savoury Tang.

At last Mrs. Elliott got up and switched on the loudspeaker. "Ten minutes to lights out," she said into the microphone, her voice echoing sepulchrally in the corridors, "ten minutes to lights out."

We tidied the office.

Mrs. Elliott reached again for the microphone. "Time for lights out. Lights out."

Bedcheck. Mrs. Elliott started down one corridor, Nancy another. I did the upstairs, opening doors, counting girls. In the bathroom there were bath-powder footprints on the tiled floor and the overheated atmosphere tingled with Jean Naté.

And then Nancy and I bade Mrs. Elliott goodnight and rushed out to our cars. The fog slowed us abruptly.

I tried to follow Nancy's car, but almost immediately I was alone and lost. The hanging fog broke in white drifts before my headlights and billowed back past the windows. I knew I'd reached the main road only when my headlights glinted off the cat's-eye reflectors in the center line. I'd left the Base, Stella's sanctuary. How nice it would be, I found myself singsonging, how very nice and warm it sure would be (pitter-patter) to drive home to the arms of Jacob Wetherbee (pitter-patter).

Soon a gap of night in the fog revealed the barbed-wire fence guarding the airstrip alongside the road. Then the fog began lightening to wisps like the angel's hair on a Christmas tree. A rabbit stood dead ahead, as hypnotized as I'd been in the Afex. I slowed and waited until it snapped conscious, leaping toward the fence.

When I drove down Clopton Park's lane to the laundry cottage, I discovered the twin car parked in my dooryard. Jacob got out. Casually he said, "This fucking fog had me kind of worried about you."

"They say it's not really bad until you have to leave your car and find the next cat's-eye by flashlight. You must be frozen."

"Have you got an extra key to your place? Maybe you could lend it to me."

"I'd have to have one made."

A few weeks later, continuing the pretense seemed ridiculous, so Jacob moved into my apartment, giving up the apartment he'd rented with a social studies teacher—male—in a village several miles farther from the Base. No more clandestine liaisons for me! Dividing my rent, we divided our days, waving at each other from our passing cars as I drove to work and he, his work done, drove back to the cottage to make his supper, read, listen to radio programs, sometimes waiting up for me but often not. I thought our living arrangement healthy and civilized, and I pictured it going on and on for years and years in England; this time I hadn't begun mentally filling a hope chest.

But evidently Stella's living arrangement wasn't so satisfactory, the differences between her and Ed too great. She and I inevitably fell out of touch, and when I did bring Jacob to the trailer to meet her, a neighbor told me Stella had suddenly left Ed and gone home to the States with Amy. I was stunned. I had never before known a woman who left her husband.

Jacob and I spent weekends brass-rubbing and sight-seeing, and soon we were regulars at the Flintknappers. Throughout the winter we went there almost every Saturday night. Jacob would throw himself against the pub's heavy lounge-bar door that always stuck and we entered into dark brown, dark red, and the smell of beer. Cigarette smoke burnt our eyes. We had learned we liked the smell and smoke; we liked pubs, we'd frequent pubs forever and I wouldn't think about the temperature of the water in which the glasses were washed. I am in England, in an English pub.

"Hello," we would say, and familiar voices would answer, while the Hinghams in their corner smiled and nodded, moving over to make room for us. I warmed my hands at the electric fire before I sat down on the bench. Jacob got our beers: a pint of mild for him, a half-pint for me. I would have preferred a whole pint, but the pub discriminated against women and only supplied a men's room which, Jacob reported, wasn't exactly luxurious, a wall in an outbuilding.

Mr. Hingham was round, made rounder by layers of plaid shirt, wool sweater, checked jacket, and tweed coat, all of different colors, all extremely thick. Mrs. Hingham sat solidly upright in her gray coat, in front of her gin-and-lime. They allowed themselves a weekday evening at the pub, and Saturday night, but they were worriedly thinking of cutting out the weekday treat in order to save that money to help their son and daughter-in-law buy a used car. (Mr. Hingham himself rode a bicycle to work at the village foundry.) We had progressed from polite greetings to smiles to cordial conversations between our neighboring tables, until on an especially crowded Saturday night they suggested we sit with them, and afterward they almost always extended a similar invitation.

While we talked, across the room the group of boys who played cards here would now and then laugh loudly and one of them would eventually stand up, adjust his tie, and carry to the bar for refills two dimpled-glass bunches of pint mugs strung on his fingers. The very very old man who crept in each Saturday night to smoke his pipe and nurse one half-pint of bitter would turn from his clouds of smoke and look at the boys and turn back.

So we drank our beers, talked with the Hinghams, and the electric fire glowed, as did, above us, the tubes in the fluorescent light on the four-hundred-year-old ceiling. Small pleasures, I mused occasionally, might really bloom into the secret of serenity; this might be how you made your truce with nonsense. From the public bar on the other side of the pub came the rattle of dominoes and the thud of darts.

It was springtime when, driving back from the Flint-knappers to the cottage, Jacob said, "The Hinghams have acted very broad-minded about our shacking-up, but I think we ought to get married to put their minds at ease."

Wondering what Jacob's father looked like, watching my hard-won sophistication smash into smithereens even faster than all the vases and bowls I'd hurled at bare-assed Gary, I said, "Get married for the Hinghams' sake? As good a reason as any."

When we announced our news, a beaming Mr. Hingham insisted on buying us brandies.

In the months following Jacob's resignation, there were spurts of travel but mostly spells of sitting.

Every noon when I emerged from my office I found him in his wing chair, brooding in cut velvet. Around him were the books and pamphlets he'd accumulated, self-help exhortations about how to grow greenhouse tomatoes commercially, how to build furniture, raise worms, grow mushrooms.

But despite all the instructions on building wooden push-pull toys and raising strawberries, despite *Up Your Own Organization!* and *You, Inc.*, Jacob couldn't concentrate enough to begin to make a decision. Luckily recognizing early that we were not parent material, we'd observed, amused and annoyed, how distracted our friends became after they had kids. Their attention was splintered; they couldn't complete one conversation, in person or on the phone, without hollering at least once, "Johnny, stop that this minute or I'll kill you!" We prided ourselves on our schedules, our lists, always keeping promises and doing what we'd said we'd do, efficient perfectionists, our lives uncluttered, our attention whole. (Not to mention our tidy refrigerator with its boxes of Arm & Hammer Baking Soda.) But now Jacob sat shattered.

He'd always liked to sleep late, so I rather expected him to spend this time in bed with the covers over his head. No. As stubborn as I am, he got up at six each morning with me, showered in the upstairs bathroom after I showered in the downstairs, ate a piece of toast, and took his coffee to the wing chair to face the question of his career. His chosen pursuit. His path or course. The progress of his sun. How can you get through a life that you know is all? Vainly he sought an answer during the black Maxwell House days.

But the first Friday night after he quit, I realized a wonderful thing was happening. We weren't fighting.

We certainly had had plenty of battles since we met, mostly (or so *I* claimed) whenever the dour side of Jacob's nature overwhelmed him. As I had remarked in the thick of one fight, "It isn't that you have bad moods once in a while, it's that once in a while you are happy. Like the BBC weather forecasts which seem backward, which instead of saying 'occasional showers' say 'sunny intervals.' "

Those fights, however, were lovers' quarrels in comparison to the fights that began as his job got worse. For the past year and a half, almost every Friday night he had ended up yelling at me, while I sobbed and wailed, "I'm not your fucking administration, don't take it out on me!" The searing agony of the Friday Night Fights, the feeling of being skinned alive. In the midst of my tears, the word "uxorious" kept occurring to me and on Saturdays I would open the dictionary and stare at: "Excessively or irrationally submissive or devoted to one's wife." Had a man or a woman written that definition? I bet I knew.

Now the fights had ended, at least for a time. And having Jacob underfoot was less a problem than I'd feared. I had always liked his company when he stayed home with a cold or the blues and when he puttered around on vacation; in our new routine I looked forward to it after my work. Yet as I set two places instead of one for lunch before I switched on *The Gong Show,* I felt that this was just a long summer vacation, in winter. Later, trying to fall asleep each night, I couldn't catch my breath, punched in the gut by the finality. Beside me, Jacob tossed and turned.

Inner resources, I kept thinking. My father had always taught me that having inner resources was more important than beauty and fame, though not necessarily more important than a balance sheet in the black. Inner resources and a *raison d'être*.

Colleagues reacted peculiarly to Jacob's quitting. Only the teachers he hardly knew phoned him to commiserate and congratulate. When he collected his Funk & Wagnalls coffee mug (which he no longer used; he took a plain pottery mug to his chair), Gert told him that his friends thought he had given up too easily and should have stuck it out. After he reported this to me, I quoted a sampler of Dorothy's:

> In prosperity friends are plenty.
> In adversity not one in twenty.

He replied, "Jacob Wetherbee is my name, America is my nation, Millsted is my dwelling place, and blank is my salvation," causing us both to wonder what his parents would say when they recovered from the shame of Arthur's snowmobile escapade and realized we were considering a move out of Millsted.

I said, "Maybe the MGA will keep Edna's mind off you."

"Doing racing changes on Crescent Street will not sidetrack her from the idea she is losing another son."

"But where can we move? Why are we moving? I don't know how to pack a birdbath!"

"Do you want to stay in Mangy Millsted?"

"No. We have overstayed."

He said, "Maybe we'll sell everything, birdbaths and all."

"Not my typewriter!"

"You've still got a couple of portables, you could tote one along the way you did in England."

"I'm spoiled by my electric, my wrist muscles are flaccid."

"Ah," he said, "if only I'd known you in your virginal youth. Think of the jerking-offs."

"I expect the plural is jerkings-off."

"Maybe we'll stay here and rot."

Eventually, just when I could actually see that while he sat and brooded his L.L. Bean Maine Guide shoes were starting to wear a hole in the oriental rug, he began daily to leave his chair for the outside world.

Grocery shopping always used to be a challenge for me, a game, but now, with no paycheck coming in, I was absolutely terrified of it. Jacob took over the supermarket chore; at the Exmouth Mall, he also did other errands, including the discount-drugstore shopping, and at my desk I imagined him clutching my list of toiletries, stepping sideways down the aisles in CVS hunting for Cover Girl Long 'N Lush Mascara (Lush Brown) the way he'd searched his library stacks for misshelved books.

He went to Brunelle's Lumberyard and bought wide boards for another woodworking experiment, three simple six-board blanket chests. Because the Millsted hardware store had folded, he had to go to Exmouth for tools and nails and things, and this killed more time. People asked him if he missed the high school. He told me, "I reply that I miss it like I miss banging my thumb with a hammer. Being a househusband," he added, perhaps too firmly, "is what I should've been doing all along."

Toward the end of each of his shopping expeditions he dropped in at Clem's Café, a beerjoint down a disreputable Millsted side-street opposite a garage that sold snowmobiles and chainsaws. Clem was not only the proprietor of the café but also the town Dog Officer to whom Jacob had made many complaints about the trailers and their loose dogs closing in on us. Clem had been in high school with Jacob;

he tried to be helpful, but not even the old school tie could make him do something really useful, such as secretly poisoning those barking automobile-and-people-chasing curs. Clem did, however, constantly refer to a poison. "DDT," he would say, "DDT, the three worst things about being a town officer: dogs, dumps, and taxes." He sold pizza too, and of course Jacob began gaining weight.

Spring came. We started jogging again. And Jacob stopped going to Clem's after he arrived one afternoon to find an excited crowd outside and learned that an irate chainsaw purchaser had come into the café and shot the garage owner dead on the pool table. I said to Jacob, "You're kidding!" Still in shock, Jacob said, "I almost didn't tell you."

He spent his fortieth birthday out in the barn, building an elaborate toolbox. Rushing into the house for the dozenth time to clean his contact lenses, he raged, "These goddamn things, I can't read the tape measure!" I suggested hesitantly, "You haven't had your eyes checked in over a year, so maybe you'd—?" He replied, "We can't afford it," but a few days later he was frustrated enough to agree. He returned from the Exmouth optometrist as pale as after the shooting. "Would you believe," he said, "that I have to wear bifocals?"

So now when he read or when he worked with his hands, he wore over his contacts a pair of half-glasses, peering down his nose. I told him they were darling; he glowered. When he didn't have his contacts in, he wore bifocal glasses that weren't darling, being far too reminiscent of Phil's although they were silver-rimmed.

"Maybe," he said, "I ought to trade in my wing chair for a wheelchair."

Throughout all this, I accompanied him on the longer trips. To look at workshops for sale, greenhouses, motels. In Maine, New Hampshire, Vermont. Nothing suited, but Jacob kept saying, "I'll try anything except applying at a school again," and off we would go to look at a gift shop for sale, a country store, a cabin colony.

"And to think," I said, "that I was the one who vowed never to set foot in a school again after I got through college."

"You worked for the Base high school."

"I only entered a classroom for study-hall duty."

After school was over in June 1965, we had been married at the Base chapel, instead of in an English civil ceremony, to avoid the complications of English legalities. (I remembered that according to family legend the first thing Dorothy had done the minute she and Sebastian were pronounced man and wife had been to ask the minister sternly, "Is it legal?") In a quonset hut with stained-glass windows, the Base chaplain joined us in holy matrimony.

But school wasn't really over, because Jacob earlier had inquired, "How would you like to spend some of our honeymoon summer in Oxford?"

Immediately suspicious, I asked, "What for?"

"To take some courses," he said, magically producing application forms. "They've got a summer school and we foreigners can go."

"Not this foreigner. When I graduated, I swore I would never take another course again as long as I lived." Then I reminded myself that he already had his master's degree, having stayed on a year at UNH after his undergraduate work before running for five years the high-school library in Stafford, Maine, a coastal town where the cannery and the canoe factory balanced the lobster-trap tourist traps. I said, "What do you want with more credits? Don't tell me you've been entertaining a secret desire for a doctorate! If so, no wedding bells will ring."

"I just thought it might be fun to stay awhile in Oxford."

I pondered, having imagined a honeymoon more romantic, perhaps touring the Riviera. "All right, but *I'm* not taking any courses. I won't even audit any."

"Fine."

What neither of us considered, when we rented by mail a bed-and-breakfast room for six weeks, was that this would be the first time we had really and truly lived together, not passing each other going to and coming from work, and we would be doing it not in a house or apartment but in one room.

Yet, looking back, the first thing I always remember about that summer isn't the room in the side-street guest-house, nor the bed, but the breakfast. Breakfasts and eggs.

Although the breakfasts there were enormous and greasy, Jacob and I couldn't resist them because we'd already paid for this meal when we rented the bed and we couldn't bear to let the money or the food go to waste. We had encountered such breakfasts in London and during our Christmas vacation exploring the south coast of England and our spring vacation when in *Shropshire Lad* territory we looked at the cherry hung with snow and checked to see if the Wenlock Edge wood were in trouble, but at the laundry cottage we were accustomed to nothing more than fruit and toast and coffee and cigarettes, so we found initially both the anticipation and the meal itself a stupefying delight. The breakfasts, never changing, grew routine, but the anticipation remained tantalizing; it was this that every morning led us, like the smell of bacon, hypnotized down the narrow carpeted stairs to the little dining room where we sat at the table which had become ours and doggedly ate and drank our way through canned grapefruit sections cut in half, bacon and fried egg, fried tomato, fried bread, fried mushrooms, slices of toast stiff in a silver rack, marmalade and butter, and a pot of coffee I poured with the pot of hot milk. As we ate, we looked out the window at the bright flowerbeds beneath a gray sky. I'd gathered that the sunny weather of the previous summer was a fluke, for there had been so much rain this summer you could drown like a turkey if you glanced up.

After breakfast we returned exhausted to our room. Declaiming diet resolutions, Jacob sank into the pink chintz armchair and opened a book. We used the rickety night-stand as a typing table, but because of the noise in this small space I didn't often write on the typewriter and mostly just typed up drafts of Jacob's papers on it. So while he studied, I unmade the top of the double bed I'd already made, dragged the pillows out from under the turquoise bedspread, took off my shoes, climbed onto the bed, and with the lumpy pillows crammed behind my back and a clipboard propped against my knees I wrote in longhand.

The bedroom wasn't exactly tiny, but the florid floral wallpaper shrank it, and the area around the bed was filled by a dark behemoth of a wardrobe, the nightstand, a straight-backed chair, a washbasin in the corner, an electric fire you had to put shillings in, and a bureau on which neat stacks of Jacob's books and papers flanked a china bowl of the fruit that, fearing scurvy, we bought at a fruitstand across the street from the nearby railroad station. Underneath the bed were tucked the supplies Jacob had brought from the Base, being practical, ignoring my theory that we should live off the land: American soap and razor blades and Kleenex, our rations of American cigarettes and booze, and rolls and rolls of American toilet paper. This last, as it happened, wasn't necessary, because the toilet paper in the bathroom down the hall was at least like crepe paper and not the usual waxed-paper variety we'd feared. I wondered what our landlady and her tweeny thought when they vacuumed under the bed.

Studying and writing meant staring out the window for great lengths of time. Geraniums bloomed pink in the window box. Over the geraniums we could see treetops and, across the street, the roofs of the lumberyard buildings against the sulky sky. No dreaming spires on this side of the tracks.

In the other rooms, washbasin drains slurped water. Footsteps sounded along the hall, and the front door opened and closed repeatedly as people went off to work, to school, to sightsee. And then the house fell quiet.

I kept expecting to feel caged. Instead it was so cozy here in this room with Jacob that I didn't want him to leave for his lectures. Certain clues assured me he felt the same—woo pitched, long clinches, and often when he left he sang Gilbert and Sullivan with broad gestures. " 'Farewell, my own,' " he sang, " 'light of my life, farewell! For crime unknown I go to a dungeon cell!' "

By now, thank heavens, the morning's housework had begun and the noise of the vacuum cleaner blotted out his serenade. After he'd gone, I waited until its roar reached the room next-door before I went downstairs to the Wilkinses' sitting room. Every morning I did this; every morning I felt guiltily lazy because it was not I but Mrs. Wilkins, our landlady, white-haired and chubby and wearing a shiny emerald nylon smock, who, aided by earnest but muddle-headed little Mary, was doing the housecleaning. I sat useless in a deep fuzzy armchair, my clipboard on my lap, and looked around me at the heavy old furniture crowding the stuffy room, at the shelves of memorial plates and glass horses, the *Mrs. Beeton's Cookery and Household Management* on the lamp table beside me, and the electric fake-coal fire cold in the fireplace. A thick green drape was hung on a curtain rod across the door into the hall, to keep out drafts. All the ashtrays here were so clean I never dared to smoke.

Jacob would have reached the Wimpy Bar downtown now and would be drinking coffee at one of the tiny tables sticky with other people's coffees. The place would be busy—tourists, students waiting between lectures, Americans and Germans and nuns and Englishmen and Swedes—and through the voices would come the sizzle of the cooking Wimpys which were supposedly hamburgers but seemed instead thin patties of fried meatloaf and mostly loaf, at that. Game to try nearly anything, I'd once ordered a curry Wimpy; it had chutney on it.

Over the banister Mrs. Wilkins called, "Mrs. Wetherbee!"

That was me, not Jacob's mother. I called back, "Thank you!" and returned to our vacuumed and dusted room. Nothing had been left for me to do. Even the toothbrushes and shaving cream on the shelf over the washbasin were put back exactly the way we'd arranged them. The geraniums were watered. Had Mrs. Wilkins polished the pale green grapes in the china bowl? I lighted a cigarette and sat down in Jacob's chintz chair. From here I could see the gilt-framed picture above the bed, a dull view of very English hills. I am in England.

And now Jacob would be at the lecture hall, listening to a lecture about Hardy or Auden or somebody, surrounded by Americans reading newspapers and writing letters and not paying attention because their subject most often wasn't literature but history yet they had to go to every lecture to get as many hours as possible stamped on their lecture cards so they would have enough for credit toward master's degrees at home. Jacob attended only the literature lectures. Occasionally I broke my vow and went along, paying two shillings to be with him; if the lecture bored, at least the accent entertained.

But usually I stayed in our room and worked until lunch as I did this particular day. When I realized it was time to meet Jacob at our pub, I put away the clipboard, straightened my white Levi's and the Villager shirt which had cost only four ninety-five at the Afex, and wondering how we were going to adjust back to our ships-that-pass routine this autumn, I went downstairs, smiled at the umbrellas in the entryway and the pamphlets about Oxford on the glove table, and strolled down the front walk between the neat flowerbeds to the gate. Automatically I glanced toward my car in which we'd driven here; we used mine for trips because its right-hand drive allowed us a fighting chance with the hair-raising breakneck speed of the English traffic that Jacob's left-hand drive mercifully but suicidally blinded us to. I blinked. Yellow was splashed across the rear of the MG, across the racing-green trunk and the silver luggage rack.

Not understanding, I opened the gate onto the sidewalk and hurried over to the car. It was so low I knelt as I gingerly touched the stuff. Eggs? Yes, the yolks hardening, the whites like the glaze I had painted on the French bread I used to make for arty suppers with Gary, playing peasant gourmet.

I ran toward the pub on the corner.

The Railway Arms was not listed in guidebooks. Its seedy lounge bar always smelled like the morning after a summer-cottage keg party, mildew and stale beer. Jacob, the only lunchtime customer so far, sat reading in his wicker chair at our table. He looked up and said, "I ordered a salad sandwich and a Scotch egg for us to split. Okay?"

"We've got egg on our car."

"Egg?"

"Raw."

Trembling, I sat down and lighted a cigarette. The ash-trays here were now as clean as Mrs. Wilkins's, but it was all right to use them, and by evening they would be brimming with butts and empty cigarette packets and crumpled cellophane bags which had once held potato crisps accompanied by the blue twists of salt that gave you a choice about the sodium in your diet and made you hate yourself as you sprinkled. In the evening, the room would be full of regulars like the old man with the spaniel and the teenage couple entangled on the window seat and the man who played the out-of-tune piano in the corner and the girl with long straight hair who wore sunglasses even at night and the husbands and wives who came from the narrow brick houses pressed against the sidewalks down the side-streets of this neighborhood, everyone talking, talking over the piano, talking over the jukebox which that summer was mostly playing "A World of Our Own," and Jacob and I, the only Americans, were regulars enough now so that last week the publican, who was the rosy-and-scrubbed type of Englishman, had bought us each a whisky to toast his win on the football pools and told us how he wanted someday to prospect for opals in Australia.

Jacob asked, "A bird's egg?"

"More like a half-dozen hen's."

"You're kidding."

"No."

He jumped up, and I followed him outdoors. The air was heavy with the smell of diesel fuel and factories and the inevitable rain. Alone, I had run, in a panic. Now I walked, trying to look dignified as I matched Jacob's rapid pace back past the other bed-and-breakfast guesthouses identical to the Wilkinses' except for the flowerbed arrangements. We stopped beside the MG.

"It *is* egg," Jacob said.

"Why?"

"Ours is the only car on the street with a U.S. Base registration sticker on the windshield."

"I've got to get something to clean it, but I don't want to ask Mrs. Wilkins for a pail."

He counted smashed yolks. "Wonder what'll happen to the finish."

I glanced behind us at the rows of curtained windows. "Maybe the fruit bowl would hold enough water. I could use our washcloths, they're due to go to the laundromat this afternoon anyway."

"We can give it a try," he said, opening the gate. Upstairs, he turned on the hot-water tap and lifted the grapes out of the bowl.

"I'll take care of this." I hunted under the bed for the detergent. "Your tutorial, you have to study."

"But—"

"I'm the one on vacation." Sloshing soapsuds, I carried the bowl down the stairs and out to the car. I scrubbed carefully, feeling eyes watching me from windows. In the lumberyard, boards thumped and men shouted.

Back upstairs I said, "I suppose I ought to rinse, but it's going to rain."

"That'll do the trick. Thanks."

I washed and dried the bowl. "Some kids, helling around?"

"Who knows."

"Yankee Go Home?"

"Would you blame them?"

"Well, that's certainly true Yankee, answering a question with a question."

Down the street came the peal of the ice-cream cart's calliope. On Thursdays, today, this meant it was time for Jacob to go to his tutorial and me to go to the laundromat. Our travel clock agreed. We again considered the weather and resignedly put on our Burberrys.

Jacob carried his books, a notebook, and the laundry bag; I carried a Penguin in my pocketbook and our furled umbrella. We went outdoors. Drying soap-froth made the MG look like a mad car.

We walked past the pub and on under the railroad overpass, enjoying the scents from the Indian restaurant where we sometimes had supper, scents so exotic and meals so delicious I almost managed not to imagine kitchen conditions worse than the Black Hole of Calcutta. Jane's Tuck Shop made us smile, as usual, and everything was familiar again, the theater where we'd seen the D'Oyly *Mikado* that had reawakened the Savoyard in Jacob, the movie theater where we'd seen *Von Ryan's Express* in which Sinatra had run much faster than he'd sung on Stella's record player. We always walked down Hythe Bridge Street to watch the family of ducks and ducklings who lived in this curve of the river. But today the family was gone. Along George Street we walked, and Cornmarket, our progress now a dancing maneuver of sidesteps and darts through the crowds, the way we had soon learned to walk on skinny English sidewalks. At Pembroke Street, Jacob gave me the laundry bag and entered the soot-blackened old house in which his tutorials were held, and I went on alone down the street to the laundromat.

The rain began while I was reading there. As the sky darkened, the grimy laundromat seemed to grow brighter and cleaner, a white world safe from the storm. It could be anywhere at all, I thought, except for the kind of money you put in the machines—and then I looked over at my red bottle of Wisk, my box of Snowy Bleach, aliens on the table beside me. My dryer stopped and I started pulling clothes out. The sweatshirts weren't dry yet.

The young woman at the next dryer said, "Those look nice and warm."

"They are." I returned them to the dryer. "But they take forever to dry. And they shrink."

Folding diapers, she said, "Everything shrinks in these machines."

"Still," I said, folding Jacob's undershorts, "it's better than hanging them out on rainy days."

"And in winter. Before I could afford coming here, I

used to suffer terribly with chilblains so I'd hang the clothes in the kitchen and they would smell of sausages."

I folded white shirts. Wifely hands folding Jacob's clothes, Afex wedding band gleaming. "Well, dryers have freed us from the clothesline, and if you just buy permanent press you can sooner or later stop ironing, so the next challenge for the manufacturers is how not to have us wash clothes to begin with."

"Permanent what? You don't have to iron?"

"Only some things nowadays."

"Those." She pointed at Jacob's shirts. "Those don't look as if they need it. You didn't get them over here?"

I confessed, "They've just come out. My husband had his mother send some because the Base we live near hasn't got any in yet."

"Oh."

"Before that, though," I added hastily, "he bought some of the nylon ones the Marks and Spencers carry. You don't have to iron those."

"Not at all?"

"Problem was, he didn't like nylon."

"I don't suppose my husband would either."

I said, "When I think of how I used to starch and iron about five blouses a week, I could go shoot myself. And how our mothers—our grandmothers, heating flatirons, slaving over ruffles. All those years."

"It makes you wonder, doesn't it."

My dryer had stopped. I opened the door, felt the sweatshirts, took them out. "They'll probably get soaked on the way home."

She asked, "Do you really think we won't have to wash clothes someday?"

I was being consulted about American ingenuity. Shoving the sweatshirts into the top of the laundry bag, I answered, "No. It would put too many people out of business—washing-machine companies, fabric-softener factories, maybe even soap operas. I hear there are paper dresses in the States now, but I doubt if it's more than a fad."

"Paper?"

"Instead of wash-and-wear, they're wear-and-toss." I unfurled my umbrella. "Here goes the plunge."

"Cheerio."

Outside, the rain pounded down on the umbrella as I ran toward Jacob's doorway. The sidewalk was so narrow it seemed only a cleft in the rock-face of dark wet houses rising above me. I was early, Jacob wasn't waiting, so I ran on to the bookshop at the corner, the laundry bag banging my knees, the umbrella yawing crazily back and forth over my head.

A church bookshop, its greeting cards were little reproductions of religious paintings, and the books were by clergymen and Lloyd C. Douglas and C. S. Lewis and mothers whose children had died of incurable diseases. Here, I was late; the coffee shop in the next room had closed. I stood dripping beside a display of cathedral guidebooks and looked out the window at the five o'clock traffic splashing along the street past the gates of Christ Church, headlights probing.

The gray-haired woman in a lavender cardigan jingled keys. I took the hint and left. Outside, I saw Jacob dashing toward me.

"It's closed," I said. "Do you want to wait out the downpour someplace else?"

"What the hell. We're drenched already."

The crowds on the sidewalks were now woven with bus queues, and umbrellas bumped umbrellas. Streets had become rivers of rain that demanded white-water navigation. Under the railroad overpass cars and motorcycles were stalled; we waded along the flooded walkway up out of the slimy cave to join a crowd at the railing, everyone watching the struggling vehicles below and urging on a double-decker bus that had decided to charge the waters. It stalled ignominiously, a helpless cute red giant, but then a helmeted girl on a motorscooter somehow churned her way across and we all cheered her instead. Beyond the overpass there were magnificent traffic jams in both directions.

When Jacob and I reached our bed-and-breakfast, we

saw that the rain had rinsed the car. Indoors, Mrs. Wilkins tsk-tsked over our drowned-rat state and bore our raincoats and the umbrella off to dry in the kitchen so that tomorrow, like the laundromat woman's past washes, they would smell of calories.

Up in our room we wrung out our clothes, poured out our shoes. Hanging the wet-again sweatshirts across the washbasin, I said, "I gather Mrs. W. didn't notice the car."

"Or," Jacob replied, stuffing our shoes with Sunday's *Observer,* "she isn't saying anything if we don't complain. Jesus, clammy! We need a hot toddy."

Making do, stripped, in our bathrobes we sat on the bed in front of the glowing electric fire and drank tooth glasses of Base bourbon and Oxford tap water. Sunlight, as pale green as the grapes in the china bowl, began seeping slowly into the room.

I asked, "How was the tutorial?"

"Same as usual. Phonies trying to impress each other and themselves. I think you took the right vow."

"I met a pleasant woman at the laundromat. She was doing diapers—nappies!—but she didn't have the baby with her, thank God. Probably her mum was babysitting."

"I wish you weren't going back to babysitting this fall. We could live on my pay, Ib."

"I'm the gravy. Travel money."

"We could travel on my pay, too, as well as live. Don't you realize I'm making a fortune here compared to a school back home, what with the higher pay scale and the housing allowance and everything?"

"So am I, compared to being a typist in a law office."

He sang, "When she was a lass she served a term as—" Then he said, "You should be writing full-time," planting that seed of temptation.

"Gravy!" I said. "I'm starved, let's go get some supper, we forgot our lunch!"

"Remind me to pay for it when we take a study break tonight. Foreign relations."

We put on dry clothes and sneakers and our bought-in-

Cambridge plastic jackets (his black, mine dark green), and when we went back outdoors the rain had stopped. Walking along the cleansed street in the opposite direction from downtown, we crossed the bridge over the Thames, astounded as always by the sight of the swans. Could you ever become blasé about swans? Twenty-odd swans a-drifting.

We reached the fish and chips shop. Its steamy window displayed in a little glass oven some Cornish pasties that made my stomach growl even though I had once adventurously eaten one and discovered it was a small football of concrete. For the first time I had understood why Jacob toted Tums.

Indoors, Jacob gave our order to the women at the vats. They wore long white smocks, their hair covered turban-fashion with white cloth. Grease hung in the air; grease lay like a skin on the tables, on the bottles of vinegar and jars of mussels. From its cage the mynah bird whistled its wolf whistle at me. It was a very greasy mynah bird, but undaunted.

Collecting the newspaper-wrapped bundles, Jacob asked, "Picnic?"

We avoided eating in this thick atmosphere whenever possible, so I replied, "Definitely."

As we walked down the green riverbank to the green river, one of the swans snarled at us. Jacob opened a bundle, selected a large vinegary chip, and tossed it to the swan. The chip buckled in midair; the two halves plopped into the water.

A civilized distance away from the lock keeper's cottage, near the towpath we spread our jackets on the wet grass littered with ice-cream sticks and soggy feathers, and while more and more swans cruised up we sat and threw them their ration of the chips and ate our pieces of plaice. In the drained sky the stars barely glimmered. I hoped a boat would come by and go through the lock.

The first swan to realize the food was gone swam away, climbed up on a sunken log near the bridge, and dug his bill into his feathers like a dog after a flea. Until this summer I hadn't known how big and ill-tempered such beautiful birds could be or how they managed the problem of their necks when they slept by curling the lengthiness back along their bodies. Sometimes we took night strolls here just to see the swans sleeping, floating white and headless on the inky river.

A boat was approaching, a punt shaded by a canopy, the kind of boat I liked best to watch. Taking a packet of Wipe 'n' Dry out of my pocketbook, I gave a little towel to Jacob, who was folding the greasy newspapers, and wiping our hands, we stood up. The man and woman in the punt waved at us.

"Lovely evening," the woman said.

"Isn't it," we said.

We followed along the towpath as the man poled toward the lock. The fleet of swans parted slowly.

Jacob asked, "Are you stopping here tonight?"

"I think not," the man said. "We want to try a bit farther on, away from the city."

The punt floated into the lock. We stood and waited, and the man and woman sat and waited. Two pairs of blue socks were drying on the canopy's line.

I asked Jacob, "A serious idea for next summer?"

Opening a food hamper, the woman glanced up. "Excuse me, you're Americans?"

"Yes," I said. "I've read a book by an American, Emily Kimbrough, about a vacation on the canals in the Midlands —partway with a converted barge and then a cabin cruiser —and we've been wondering."

As she took a heel of a loaf of bread from the hamper and tore it into hunks, she mused, "Would the pace suit Americans? The travel is quite slow, you know. Not lively."

Jacob said, "So we gather." I tried to fathom his blank eyes.

The woman threw a piece of bread to the swans. "But if you don't mind the slowness, it's a perfect peaceful holiday." She looked contentedly at her husband and threw more bread. The lock keeper came out of his cottage; she called to him, "Thank you," even before he'd done anything. The English and their thank-you's! Jacob had once counted five thank-you's he'd received while buying a pint of mild.

Suddenly two small boys rushed down the towpath and flung themselves at the bar of the lock gate. The lock keeper joined them and they all pushed mightily, and just when I'd reached the stage of concluding that the gate would never ever budge, it began to swing shut, forcing its way through the water, and the lock closed.

The sluice gates were opened. Lighting cigarettes, we watched the punt descend. I wondered if the man and woman felt at all foolish there in the punt, not doing anything, just sinking like upright bodies in a canopied coffin being lowered into a grave. The boys sat on the gate and swung their legs cockily over the emptying lock.

The woman asked us, "Maybe we'll meet you next summer on the canals?"

Jacob and I looked at each other. I thought of his aversion to Boy Scout hardships.

"Why not," said Jacob. "Yes, see you next summer."

The lock keeper began to push open the downstream gate, and the boys ran to help.

The woman waved. "Goodbye!"

"Goodbye!" We watched until the man had poled their punt past the bend in the river.

Then we went over to the little let's-play-store shop in the doorway of the lock keeper's cottage, where Jacob bought from the lock keeper's wife a Kit-Kat candy bar which he divided as we climbed the towpath to the bridge.

I said, "What size boat? Larger or smaller than our room?"

Two preening swans were standing on the sunken log, the water around them fluffy with feathers.

Jacob said, "We'll write for information and plan the route this winter."

Eating dessert, we walked past the Railway Arms, down the street toward our bed-and-breakfast. When we neared the guesthouse we saw that the trunk of our car had again been pelted yellow.

I said, "How about Dinsmere?"

"What?"

In my office, which was still cool this mid-July morning until the sun slid around the end of the house, I was paying bills before I started work, trying not to let my sweaty hands smear the Ultra Fine Flair ink. I'd put off writing these checks, a check-writer's block, and the sweat was caused by nerves, not by summer. Seven months since Jacob had quit, but inexorably the mortgage and electricity and telephone bills kept arriving, the car insurance fell due, our yearly dental exams came and we certainly couldn't skip those or our teeth would blacken and rot into gaps like poor people's did, like unemployed people's. "Dinsmere," I repeated. "Remember when we got back from England we were hunting all over northern New England for the right library job for you and we ran across Dinsmere and decided it was the best of the New Hampshire towns?"

From his wing chair in the living room, Jacob said, "But the high school nearest to it stunk."

"Well, we're not searching for a school now, are we. Dinsmere was beautiful and unspoiled. Maybe we could find an old house that would suit us there." For this was the latest idea: buy a wreck and fix it up and sell it, turning a profit and buying another. Jacob was clever at home repairs, and after ten years of coping with the idiosyncrasies of this professionally restored yellow house of ours, he figured he could handle such work himself.

Grumpily he replied, "Instead of mountains looming above Dinsmere, nowadays there are probably McDonald's Golden Arches."

"Let's drive up and take a look. Keep moving. Writing checks makes my blood pressure jump over the moon."

"Forgive me for freeloading."

Here we go again. Furious, I crammed the last check in

an envelope, tossed it at my Out basket, and stormed into the living room where I yanked the latest *New Hampshire Times* out of the magazine rack. Returning to my office, I flapped the newspaper's pages and lifted the telephone receiver.

Jacob abandoned his silence. "Who are you calling?"

"I saw a Dinsmere real-estate ad, that's what brought the town to mind. The ad's for a village house already fixed up, 'Authentic restoration—Indian shutters—Count Rumford fireplace—sixty-five thousand,' but maybe she has others. If you'd rather not drive to Dinsmere, I'll phone instead."

"Who's the realtor?"

"One Allegra Quigley. Classy ad, not flashy. Not humble, either. Do you want to phone her yourself?"

Brief brooding.

While I waited, listening to the dial tone, I thought of our money whispering farewell as it ever so stealthily tip-toed, toe by toe, out of our bank account, finger to lips. Tootle-oo.

Jacob said, "Okay, I'll call. You're awful on the phone, you babble."

A fatal flaw I trusted him to save me from. He came into the office, and handing him the receiver, remembering how I'd taken over for him on the phone when he told Dorothy he'd quit, I pointed to the ad.

He said, "She's probably not in, anyway. She's probably off showing condominiums to summer people."

"No doubt."

Leaving him, I went out through the kitchen to the porch and looked at the garden we had planted after all. Cooperating, it had produced the early peas in time for the traditional Fourth of July salmon-and-peas supper at Jacob's folks' house. During this bicentennial meal, the atmosphere was so tense I thought the mortars and pestles on the dining-room wallpaper would begin to rattle with jitters. The MGA had allowed Edna to say Timmy's name in front of Phil once again, but although Phil didn't squelch her, he himself still never mentioned Timmy or even the car which

Edna now used daily, shopping, basking in the honking applause from other cars and the admiration of crowds in parking lots.

After that Fourth of July supper, as Jacob chewed Tums while we drove home I thought over Phil's remarks about our house-hunting and wondered how he could want life imprisonment in Millsted for his remaining son. Was it just because Phil and Edna had themselves done time here all their lives? "You know, Ib," Edna had told me during dishes, "I'm going to get the sofa re-covered this summer even though it's not all worn out. Dad don't really mean you're making Jacob move away, but Jacob did come back here after England and—how can you leave that gorgeous house of yours!" Edna pronounced it "gaw-jis," in good New Hampshire style. She added, "Why don't you get *your* sofa re-covered, the house will seem all new again."

In the car I replied, "It's Naugahyde," and suddenly I realized the hot evening was pulsing with an electric beat too loud to comprehend. "Jesus!" Jacob said and stepped on the gas, yet then we saw that the road ahead was jammed with cars so we had to slow down and creep through the bottleneck, past the rock concert at the pink trailer on whose front door dangled an aluminum Christmas wreath decorated with aqua bells. The music's arrogant violence matched the fuck-you faces glimpsed in headlights. Even when we reached our house amid its protection of woods the noise still tortured, pounding and pounding, and we ran around indoors closing windows but their panes seemed about to burst inward from the blast. "Whoopee," Jacob said sardonically, reaching for the kitchen phone, "happy two-hundredth birthday, how far we have come from the fife and drum, what progress we have made!" He called the state trooper; I locked the doors. Throughout the night the noise did not abate, and eventually we gave up trying to sleep in our airless sweltering bedroom and came downstairs to the stifling living room where we watched on TV old movies that could have been silent for all we managed to hear of the dialogue. We recalled the evening we had gone to the NCO Club at the Base, to see what it was like, to compare a night-out there with Saturday night at our pub: In the American dark we drank sixty-cent doubles and let ourselves be bludgeoned senseless by the pandemonium of some pop group's amplified instruments, a young woman in a raucous dress and stupendously teased hairdo screaming into a microphone while blissful on the tiny crowded dance-floor the NCOs all jumped and twitched with their bouffant wives and girlfriends in pink and green dresses as electric as the guitars.

The morning after the Fourth, we discovered that out on the road our mailbox had been dynamited. We picked bits of it off trees, bicentennial fruit. The explosion had wrapped the little red metal flag into a tight curl, so it seemed to be hugging itself.

Besides peas, the garden now was producing lettuce and radishes and summer squash, but it had suffered from the neglect caused by our old-house searches, and weeds were shouldering aside the hay mulch. While we were away on a trip to Maine, a woodchuck ate the entire cole family. Helpless, exhausted, I drove into Exmouth and bought plants to replace those I had raised from seed, while Jacob lay in wait for the woodchuck who soon obligingly waddled into range, napkin tied around its neck, so to speak, its knife and fork at the ready. When I returned and found Jacob with a Hefty body bag, I said, "If I ever write a gardening book I'll have to call it *Blood on the Broccoli*. Why are we staying in New England, with goddamn gardens and gore, not to mention winters and blizzards? Why don't we move to the Sun Belt and maybe grow a few herbs on the windowsill?" Lugging the bag off toward the woodchuck graveyard in the woods, Jacob replied, "Because if you're going to live by your wits, you've got to know your territory, and we know northern New England."

When we had started searching for falling-down houses, we'd announced to realtors that we wanted a place where we would not be annoyed by snowmobiles and where we could jog without being hounded by neighbors' dogs. The realtors ignored such silliness and kept showing us impossible neighborhoods. After counting mutts in dooryards near one run-down Cape that we felt cried out to be saved, I said to the realtor, hearing fierce anger make my voice quiver, "Honest to God, the amount of money spent on pet food could feed the entire so-called Third World." "Not," said Jacob, his hand stroking my arm, calming, "that we would want the money spent on *food* for the Third World. If they and their children were still starving while they're being taught about birth control—and birth control is what we would spend the pet-food money on—then they might finally get the point." The scandalized realtor sped us back to his office in his white Mercedes.

Going into the house, I found Jacob emerging from my office, studying notes on the scrap-paper I made by recycling manuscript drafts. He looked reluctant.

I asked, "So Allegra Quigley was in?"

"She told me we could see the place anytime, she gave me directions. It's unlocked, and she's busy with appointments."

"What place?"

"Oh. A farmhouse she thinks might meet my description of what we want. She called it 'a modest dwelling.' "

"How modest?"

"Forty grand."

"Jesus Christ. How much land?"

"About three acres, which means two-and-a-half at the most. Hardly enough for a cornpatch."

I went into the bathroom and checked my makeup in the mirror. Giving my hair a quick brush, I said, "Let's go. I won't pack a lunch, we can stop at a country store and buy common crackers and some cheese for a picnic. Wasn't there a little grocery store in Dinsmere?"

"It's probably a mile-long supermarket now. Ib, I doubt if this is worth interrupting your schedule for. A house that expensive isn't what we had in mind, and I told her we'd think it over." He turned toward his chair.

"Are torn-off Levi's too informal for Dinsmere? I recall seeing linen skirts."

"Nowadays it's probably full of fat tourists in wet bathing suits playing miniature golf." He glanced at his notes. "Oh, hell. Okay, let's find out just how bad it has got."

Not taking the main highway, we drove out of Millsted past the Pot o' Gold, the smell of French fries wafting to us on the pond breeze, and then we continued along through scrubby woods inhabited by shacks and trailers.

Noodling, I asked, "Remember how, over there, whenever we drove through Thetford on our way to go shopping in Bury St. Edmunds we used to wave as we passed the statue of Thomas Paine?"

"And I would make my sound of vast crowds distantly cheering." Jacob demonstrated, breathing hurrahs. "Poor Tom, what an embarrassing statue, he looked like he'd just been goosed."

"What's the plural of goose?" I said as I used to say when we drove past Tom.

"A giggle of goose. And here we are on a wild-goose chase."

"Why did we come home? There was still extra money to travel with, to take a trip on the canals." For although we had certainly started out our second year there poorer because that seed of temptation did flower and I quit my job at the dorm, by spring I had sold a novel, actually being paid a thousand-dollar advance, a wonderful windfall.

"Why did we?" Jacob said. "Was there one reason?"

"I remember we were driving back to Clopton from the Lake District the second spring vacation and I suddenly got homesick for billboards, to my horror. Was that how it started?"

There had been lambs and daffodils along the way, but out of the blue I had exclaimed: "I miss billboards, I wonder what they're saying now at home!"

"Did you?" Jacob said.

"And you confessed you'd like to see some clapboard houses for a change instead of stone."

"No," he said. "What was happening in America began bothering us, remember? It'd begun itching at us. Vietnam—we kept thinking that something was happening at home and maybe we ought to go back and find out what was going on."

In the end, our decision must have come as swiftly as

Stella's had when she made up her mind to leave her husband and silver trailer in a foreign land. We finally just plain admitted to each other it was time for these two Yankees to go home.

So we didn't spend a lazy summer of canals and rivers and locks. At the close of the school year Jacob resigned, we sold my right-hand car, and we flew back to McGuire Air Force Base on a chartered jet on which only pineapple juice was available to ease expectations of crashes.

And then we were home, Jacob looking, I gathered, unchanged to his parents even though during our last trip to London he had been asked directions by a lost Englishman who mistook him for an Australian. And there was I, back in the States a bride, my skirt too short for American fashion just yet, my bangs too long.

After job-hunting all summer, Jacob had accepted the Exmouth High offer because its superintendent, rejoicing that an elderly set-in-her-ways librarian had retired, promised him sweeping improvements: increased budget, a secretary, enthusiasm.

I asked, "Would you want to go back to England now?"

"We couldn't live by our wits in England. Anyway, it's probably broken out with Wimpy Bars like measles."

"I suppose."

"How many years has it been since we drove the north shore of Winnipesaukee?"

We had reached the junction with the north shore road. I said, "Could it really be ten years?"

Taking this road, we held our breath, amazed. Surely the scenery must have changed in ten years! The southern route through Bridgeford, expanded to a three-lane highway, certainly had got worse and worse, gaudy with motels and restaurants, giddy with fun-and-game joints such as my mother's zoo and the Lollipop Village dwelt in by the likes of Red Riding Hood and the Three Little Pigs.

But up here, we could almost have been driving the lake road of our childhood. There were more houses, yes, and signs indicating private club developments, hidden condominiums; this *was* a resort region, offering tourists its Lake Breeze Lodges and Candlelight Cabins and even the Dutch Elm Golf Course which no longer had any elms. But unlike the other shore, it shone calmly with an old-fashioned dignity.

"Good God," Jacob said. "My camp is still in business!"

SACHEM CAMP, the sign announced. I peered down the road but saw only woods, the woods that were the background in the camp photograph on my office wall. Both Jacob and Louise had been sent to Y camps one summer, and in this photograph of small boys, Jacob, age six, sat amongst the youngest campers on the front row of bleachers, his arms folded over his sturdy chest, wearing regulation Sachem Camp shorts and sleeveless jersey and a puzzled but determined expression. Edna had shown me his treasured letters home, wrung out of him by camp counselors, and later I thought of them often when she began showing us Timmy's from Vietnam. Jacob had written:

> Dear Mom and Dad I like camp when are
> you coming over again.
>
> JACOB PHILIP WETHERBEE
>
> Dear Mom and Dad Yesterday we had movies.
> Tomorrow I am going on a hike.
>
> JACOB
>
> Dear Mom and Dad We are building a hut.
> I tried to pass my beginners swim test.
>
> MR. JACOB P. WETHERBEE

After reading that last letter, I had asked Jacob, " 'Tried' to pass the beginners' test? You're a water-baby now, weren't you then?" and Jacob explained, "I thought I was and I set off from one pier never doubting I'd reach the other. They had to fish me out midway. Another early lesson in humility —and humiliation."

As we drove on past the camp, I said, "I don't know how you stood whole weeks at camp." I'd hated my Girl Scout day-camp summers full of excruciatingly tiresome crafts and chores; the only part I had liked had been foraging for ferns and Indian paintbrush and daisies whenever I was assigned to centerpieces, decorating with my clumsy efforts the picnic tables at which we ate blackened hot dogs and too-sweet coleslaw, greedy little Brownies of Pine Cone Hollow.

Jacob said, "Anything was better than downtown Millsted in the summer. Living in downtown Bridgeford, you could walk to a beach."

"Decreed off limits by Dorothy. Polio scares."

"Oh. Yes."

We fell silent again, still fearing honky-tonk, but the suggestion remained of old slow summer lodging-places where you stayed a spell. Then as we left the lake and twisted up into the mountains the clean clarity reminded me of the way America had seemed to us when we returned from misty England; the bright sunlight had made us keep reaching for our sunglasses, even me who loathes sunglasses because I want to see things as is.

What our stunned eyes now saw was Dinsmere unchanged. A toy town, the white village posing under shade trees.

I fumbled in my pocketbook and found Jacob's notes. "A right here. Another right. How much of a down payment would we have to make on a forty-thousand-dollar house?"

"Ten or twelve thousand."

"God! A left here."

Along the country roads we drove. No killed-grass traces of snowmobiles. Dogs, of course. But might they perhaps be controlled dogs? Farmhouses restored by summer people. Lawns flowing up to flowers. A real farm, a cowbell gently tolling amongst the Guernseys in the pasture below the mountains. Mown fields, hay dropping square behind a baler. Sprawling old summer cottages with clay tennis courts. The woods looked taller here, and thicker.

I asked, "How do you pack an asparagus bed?"

As we came around a bend in the dirt road, we saw the sign and Jacob braked, startling a chipmunk couchant on a stone wall.

FOR SALE

ALLEGRA QUIGLEY PROPERTIES

The Cape and attached barn stood in a dip, the front yard a wild garden of black-eyed Susans. The house's white paint was peeling, and the gray barn was sinking to its knees like a dying elephant.

And over the front door we saw another sign, the flaking hand-lettered name of the farm:

SHELTERFIELD

Jacob said quietly, "Oh, shit," and drove down the driveway to the ell.

II

THE LAST ITEM loaded onto the moving van and the first off was the freezer, full of our organic vegetables and abstract cow.

"Well," Jacob said, helping with the dolly at the back of the van which had been driven across the front lawn around to Shelterfield's bulkhead, "we beat the snow."

"Don't speak too soon," said Curly, of Curly's Garage. His father had worked as a mover, so Curly did some moving on the side, for sentimental reasons. "You're tempting providence, my boy."

I thought both Curly and his helper were fooling with providence themselves by not wearing any red or orange except their hunting caps. It was early November now; time to kill deer. Although red is definitely not my color, I'd long ago realized I would have to wear unflattering clothes during deer season if I hoped to stay alive, and today above my Levi's I was wearing a red workshirt beneath my red nylon jacket, with the crowning touch an Edna-knitted scarlet cap. Our orange goosedown jackets were too expensive to use for grubby moving day, so Jacob had put on his orange fake-down workvest over his red-and-tan-checked flannel shirt. We were the colors that the autumn leaves had been as they fell from the deciduous trees in Shelterfield's yard, these oaks and maples a friendly foreground to the dark green pine forest. Now the leaves lay flattened, bronze and rust.

I watched the maneuvers with the freezer, feeling perilously exposed standing still, in the open, beside the heap of recently delivered cordwood; my red clothes were not bulletproof. There was a line of orange-garbed hunters stalking across the neighboring field toward the trail up the mountain behind the house, and I kept imagining in the woods around us a platoon crawling on its belly toward us, rifles cradled. I said, "I hope the stuff didn't have time to start thawing."

This wringing-of-hands was ignored. Planks laid on the bulkhead stairway to the cellar under the main house, the freezer poised, Curly said, "Here she goes."

All the freezer needed was Old Glory draped over it. Curly shoved, and it slid solemnly into the murky depths.

"Okay," Jacob said, clambering down, "I'll dolly her to the plug. We'll use the front door, Curly, not the ell door, for everything except the washer and dryer. The kitchen floor in the ell is so rotted that a contractor I had come look at it advised Ib not to do any jump-roping while she was cooking. I'm going to start tearing it up tomorrow. We'll put most of the furniture and cartons in the living room, only the bed and bureau in the bedroom, to keep the decks clear."

Curly said, "Got your work cut out for you, eh?"

I observed, "The ceilings in the ell are too low for anyone but a midget to jump-rope," and Curly and his helper climbed back into the van for the drive to the front door.

Like a soldier under crossfire, I raced around to the

driveway, and warily watching the string of hunters and also the yard of the posted but empty-until-next-summer big gray cottage and tennis court beyond, I began carrying from our car to the living room my pots of plants. This was, I thought as I hurried back and forth, an idiotic time of year to move, especially into a house whose new chimney had barely been tested and whose kitchen and bathroom had no running water except the toilet. In the lowery sky, snow continued to threaten, and although I knew a snowfall was more dangerous to the deer than to us, I felt it would display our telltale tracks too and betray our whereabouts, fate's prey that we were.

But if we wanted to accomplish our goal, fixing up the house, Jacob's fresh career, we had to face hardship and move now instead of waiting in Millsted, in our still unsold house, until sensible spring weather. Jacob simply couldn't get enough things done part-time, driving to and from almost daily as we had been since we bought Shelterfield in July, every curve of the lake road sickeningly known by heart now, a beaten path we wearily flogged. I had found myself writing on a clipboard again, during these rides and while sitting on a lawn chair in an unobtrusive corner of the downstairs room that would be our bedroom. The drives north; the eternal making of lunches for the Aladdin cooler, its slushy smell of ice cubes and the far too familiar arrangement of sandwiches, carrot sticks, pickles; at the house, the noise of drills and chainsaws if the workmen deigned to pay us a visit, the groans of the rotten cupboards Jacob attacked with his crowbar, the screams of the nails he pulled; but then, despite all this racket and activity, the frustration of not having much of anything to show for a day's work before we had to turn around and drive back to Millsted, where Jacob spent the evenings drawing electrical-wiring diagrams and plans for kitchen renovations and I froze and canned the garden and did some tentative packing. Eventually we hauled our fold-out sofa here and spent a few nights although the chimney wasn't finished, Shelterfield's furnace had died of old age, it was a cold autumn, and bundling no longer held much comfort come morning.

Surviving those nights, we decided to forge ahead and move.

"Ib," Curly pleaded as I took the last plant out of the car, "say it isn't so, you don't really mean you want this desk upstairs."

"I'm awfully sorry," I fluttered, clutching the Chinese evergreen, "but my office is going to have to be up there—"

Sweating in the chilly late-morning air, Curly yanked off his cap, produced from a pocket a red bandanna—some hidden red, a closet coward!—and wiped his bald head, turning to Jacob. "Can't you talk her out of it? A nice office downstairs, handy to the kitchen for a cup of coffee like her office in your other house?"

Two houses; two mortages. A grand total of nearly four hundred bucks paid out each month. I said, "Jacob will be working downstairs so I want to keep out from underfoot, there are those filing cabinets too, I'm terribly sorry—"

"Besides," Jacob said, harried, "she wants to starve in a garret for a change. Alley-oop."

Curly's helper emerged from the house, having deposited an armful of lamps, not looking for an honest man but gazing enviously at the field's latest band of hunters, whose jeeps and pickups had joined the others parked beyond our posted land, along the sides of the dirt road which were as crowded now as city curbs. Privately we called the sturdy little helper Goddamn because that word was a basic part of the rapid rhythm of his speech, besides being nearly the only word we could understand; his thick French-Canadian accent was unusual to hear nowadays and kept bringing back memories of how as a kid I'd enjoyed eavesdropping on black-coated mémères, dumpy and matronly, in Woolworth's admonishing their grandchildren, *"Touche pas!"* He said fervently, "Goddamn desk, goddamn!" and joined Curly and Jacob in carrying it across the ravaged front lawn.

The black-eyed Susans were deader than doornails. I doubted they would bloom next summer, victims of all the workmen's pickup trucks that had haphazardly parked on them. And the side lawns and backyard also showed no signs of recovery from the heavy equipment's version of a scorched-earth policy. Snow would, at least, swathe this with white.

Those vehicles had been here because we'd reluctantly realized we had to hire certain work done, and so Jacob had hunkered with contractors, getting estimates on a furnace, TV antenna, chimney, and an electrical panel to replace the old fuse box. We had expected, in our innocence, that after a deal was settled the workmen would show up promptly. We soon learned the harsh reality, and when a workman actually did appear we were so relieved to see him that we didn't dare complain about tire tracks, cigarette butts, candy wrappers; indeed, I felt we should offer him champagne and caviar and a choice of our nubile nieces.

I paused. Before me stood this strange place, this gamble. The price had appalled Jacob's father, a professional. Jacob's reaction: "He's thinking in terms of Millsted's property values, he can't comprehend Dinsmere." A wise investment? The gray-shingled barn had tragically been let go too long; Jacob feared he would have to tear it down. But the one-story ell was so crooked it could be deemed quaint, and the two-story main house, without dormers or shutters, was satisfyingly plain. Only our temporary residence however, hardly our home, even though I'd gone so far as to stake off on the battered ground a garden area which an obliging farmer who'd stopped by to inspect us had promised to plow up sometime before snow flew and who then had done a vanishing act. I thought of our yellow house abandoned again, hollow after ten years of Jacob and me. Shelterfield didn't have a porch. What were we doing, leaving our perfect yellow house and its porch we loved to sit on even in winter?

Going through the open front doorway, I added the Chinese evergreen to the patch of plants on the worn pine living-room floor. Jacob and Curly and Goddamn came groaning downstairs, went outdoors, and Jacob carried a birdbath's top and bottom to the barn while Curly and Goddamn returned with the first of the two filing cabinets and disappeared upstairs.

The long living room ran the length of the front of the house, not the normal arrangement in a Cape, and after being empty so long it was suddenly topsy-turvy with our possessions. I glimpsed the Boston rocker apparently anticipating news from the portable radio perched silent on the lap of a sheeted Queen Anne; under padding, the tall two-drawer blanket chest seemed anxious to start fooling guests again. Waiting in big cartons were the new bathtub, basin, kitchen sink, and hot-water tank, bought through Jacob's nephew Buddy who was the stock manager for a plumbing wholesaler. Such a jumble! And no feeling of hearthside order had yet been brought to the room by the Jøtul, installed yesterday on the hearthstone which was all that was left of the crumbling fireplace torn out when the new chimney was built. I tried to picture the white plaster walls and bisque woodwork we planned, but I saw far too clearly this frayed smelly wallpaper so old there wasn't even any faded pattern left, this shallow moulding instead of the deeply handmoulded woodwork of the yellow house, this vertical tongue-and-groove wainscoting dark with funereal varnish.

Complaining about hernias, downstairs a second time came Curly and Goddamn, and after they'd finished bringing in the other filing cabinet I hastily began lugging boxes of books to my office. The stairway went up one end of the living room, and Jacob, remarking that the people who'd built Shelterfield had been extraordinarily inept amateur carpenters, had wondered if the person who built the stairs had also been full of homebrew. The risers were too high, so that climbing them I felt like a child, like drawings of Christopher Robin going up to bed.

Nobody in Shelterfield's lifetime, over a century, had had either the inclination or the money to finish the upstairs, which remained one large room of unplastered laths under slanting eaves. In the middle a section of the new chimney rose through the rough board floor; it still startled me, a pillar of hideous cinderblocks that changed to aesthetic brick as it headed into the roof. Through motes of dust, my office equipment seemed creatures from outer space. When my parents came to view this house soon after Edna and Phil had made their disapproving tour of it, Dorothy had said, "You're going to go blind working up here, I suggest the first thing you do is install an enormous skylight," and Sebastian said mildly, "A fluorescent light wouldn't be quite so drastic," and Dorothy said, "Those things hum and give you headaches," and I herded them back downstairs to talk of less personal problems, such as plumbing.

Ever since I was six years old, I had put myself to sleep by imagining my dream office. In the morning room of a country estate, in a small-paned bay window, my desk would be a stretch of marble slab, gray-veined, cool and smooth, and working at it I would overlook flowerbeds, a long lawn, woods in the distance. I would have a green leather desk set and a jade inkstand. Other nights I chose Thoreau's cabin, but always I returned to that elegance which seemed as remote as Walden simplicity from what I had eventually settled on in the yellow house: Steelcase.

Jacob hollered, "Ib!"

Caught woolgathering, I ran down into the living room. Behind it to the left was the bedroom, and to the right the dining room.

I called, "Where are you?"

"The kitchen!"

So I dashed through the dining room—a table saw stood where the table should be, a utility light hung from where I envisioned a discreet chandelier, our Millsted refrigerator and stove were parked in corners—into the ell, from whence were coming grunts and goddamns.

"What's wrong?" I asked, hating chaos. In the kitchen the menfolk were wrestling with the washing machine, the bathroom door unhinged. "Isn't the floor going to hold?"

Jacob puffed, "Fatty-fatty-two-by-four, this won't fit

through the bathroom door. Are you absolutely positive you've got to have it there? Can't we put it and the dryer down in the main cellar?"

"Well, I hardly ever use a dryer anymore," I said, thinking of how the world had changed since in that Oxford laundromat I'd blithely assumed there would forever be cheap electricity for such happy-go-lucky labor-saving devices, "but it'd be much more convenient to have the washing machine up here."

"Admit the truth," Jacob said. "You're afraid of spiders and mice down there. 'Eek!' "

Out the crooked window under which the sink had been, chickadees were emptying the birdfeeder tube I'd hung this summer and most recently refilled this morning. I said, "We've got spiders and mice above as well as below stairs. And I agreed to the freezer down cellar, didn't I?"

"You had no choice. Okay," he told Curly and Goddamn, "take a break. If she wants this thing in the bathroom, she'll get it in the bathroom." He picked up his Wonder Bar and tore out a doorjamb, a stud, and a foot of the wall. Plaster drifted down.

Goddamn, hissing something that might have been *"Sacre bleu!"*, stared not at Jacob but at me, in terror, as if I might go berserk with a rolling pin. Curly said contentedly, "Always give the little lady what she asks for."

I looked at the wrecked doorway, at the entire room reeling with rubble, with spilled wood-shavings insulation, gummy generations of grease-spattered wallpaper, a mouse skeleton, motley paint, and I thought of my serene kitchen in the yellow house. Hot now, taking off my cap and cramming it in a jacket pocket, I said, "We must be nuts."

There was a knock on the ell door, and into the kitchen, bearing a gift assortment of Speedy Sadie mixes, stepped Batch.

He asked, "How much did you say you paid for this castle?"

Together Jacob and I replied, "Pound sand."

"Tut-tut," said Batch. "Mind your manners, I've come to whisk you two away for lunch." His cheerful jack-o'-

lantern face always seemed aglow with candlelight behind his triangular eyes. He liked to think of himself as a snappy dresser, but since his separation from Nicole his style had gradually changed; he still retained a leather car coat, yet under it today instead of a turtleneck and unfortunate plaid slacks he wore, of all things, a three-piece pinstripe suit. As he leaned down to kiss me, he said, "Brought you these, Ibby, but now I see you don't have any cupboards to put them in. Did a hurricane go through here?"

"Thank you." Awkwardly I held the box of mixes, wondering where on earth to set it. "Curly and Um, this is my brother, Batch Pierce."

"Good to meet you," Batch said, shaking hands in his genuinely enthusiastic manner. "Aren't you the genius who put the MGA back on the road? An honor."

Curly said, "The credit goes to Edna Wetherbee."

"Of course. Hey, look at that old stove! Planning to keep it? Some antique!"

Jacob cautioned, "Watch out for this floor, a petal could crash through. How did you find us?"

"Asked at the village store for the directions to the newcomers' place, the Wetherbees' house. The proprietor reprimanded, 'You mean Shelterfield.' " Batch tiptoed across to the big black iron wood range, the centerpiece of the hodgepodge of rooms that made up the ell. "Does it work?"

Eyeing this heavyset but helpless brother of mine, Curly and Goddamn deftly lifted the washing machine into the bathroom. The one and only bathroom. What were we doing, moving into a house that had just one bathroom and now had hardly any bathroom wall?

Jacob said, helping with the dryer, "Some damnfool converted the range to kerosene. But we'll use it to heat the ell."

"An MGA of stoves!" Batch surveyed the Beatrix-Potter proportions of the kitchen, the bathroom, and the pantry, which was Jacob's temporary toolroom. "I hate to point this out, but besides no cupboards you don't have some amenities like a sink and shower and it looks like the bathroom wall just fell down."

I said, "Come see the rest of the house, get out of their way, get off this floor."

"Where's your real stove? Oh," Batch said, following me into the dining room, "there it is. But why?"

I set the mixes on the table saw. "The electrician hooked up a new powerline for it in the kitchen, but Jacob has got to tear up the floor. Wonderful surprise to see you, Batch. I didn't know Dinsmere was on your route."

"You haven't got a *working stove?* How are you going to cook?"

Curly and Goddamn lugged the bureau into the bedroom and Jacob the box spring. "Finials," Curly said. "I thought I put them in this drawer."

I said, "I've baked potatoes in the Jøtul before, I've heated soup on it during power failures. And we'll eat sandwiches and such, indoor picnics. Have you ever noticed how the electricity company has expunged 'failures' from its language and calls them 'power outages'?"

Undiverted, prowling on, Batch said, "Me and my Diners Club arrived in the nick of time. Hey, at least you do have the Jøtul installed. But is there a back-up furnace?"

"Christ," Curly said, "I always put the bureau finials away in a bureau drawer, I learned that at my father's knee!"

I looked at the hole in the wall where the fireplace had been, at the raw cinderblock bulk of this new chimney. "The furnace is another antique, coal converted to oil. With the price of oil these days, we wouldn't have used it anyway, even if it wasn't worn out. We decided not to buy a new furnace, at least not yet. Don't worry. We'll manage. The new chimney is safe, and so's the old one in the ell, Jacob had it fixed, and he's sure the Jøtul will heat the main house, the floor space is nearly the same as our house —our other house, I mean—"

"However," Batch said, striding up the staircase, "I bet the insulation isn't the same. What's the matter with these stairs, how come you need pitons to climb them? Wow, so this is your office?"

"The whole top floor to myself," I said behind him, now

fretting about the finials. Vintage early Jordan Marsh, our bureau had cost us fourteen dollars at a secondhand store ten years ago, and if it was cumbersome and its mahogany veneer ugly, its big mirror was as clear as the day it was born, and I liked it. Something must always get lost or broken during a move, but who could be philosophical about such mishaps? When our crate of belongings arrived in Millsted from England, we found that the Base movers had packed my Royal typewriter upside down. It never recovered. But I didn't trade it in; I kept it and the subsequent Olivetti, and here they were with my Olympia electric, hoarded like those old cars saved for spare parts by certain men who gradually transform the yards of their houses into junkyards. I added reassuringly, "This office might not be so neat and trim as my other, but it's larger, and ever since the chimney guys finished I've been busy vacuuming and Windexing. Someday there'll be walls and less dust. See, my desk, everything's all set up, ready to plug in the typewriter."

Batch said, "So you really do have electricity?"

"The electrician did the minimum. Jacob's got to replace the old wiring, he says the insulation in it is cracking and drying, inadequate, dangerous."

"He ever done any wiring?"

"Some. He's not all thumbs, Batch, like you, you know that. He'll do the plumbing, he's already put in the new toilet."

"To think I assumed Dorothy was exaggerating about your plans. She didn't even mention tearing up the kitchen floor and—"

"It's going to be a great kitchen. I'd show you the diagrams but you couldn't make head or tail of them."

"Can you?"

"This house is Jacob's job, not mine."

"Ib!" Curly yelled. "I didn't by any chance put those finials in one of the boxes of books, did I?"

I said softly, "God almighty." Then I yelled back, "I'll look!"

Batch said, "Let me help."

"Thanks, but you never can find anything."

"Neither can you."

I had arranged the cartons up here by the Magic Marker labels I'd written on them; it wasn't the Library of Congress system or even the Dewey Decimal, but it made sense to me and I'd planned to be able to find any book I wanted. Yet now as the cartons were unpacked in our hasty search, gardening books soon mingled with high-school yearbooks, with cookbooks and college textbooks and bird books, and fiction was strewn everywhere. What was Jane Austen doing with *Who the Hell* is *William Loeb?*

Batch said, "It just dawned on me. You don't have any bookcases in this office!"

"Jacob will build some, someday. The bookshelves at the other house had to stay, they're built-in."

"I gather there's also a reason why you don't have cupboards or cabinets in the kitchen?"

"They had to come out if the floor was coming up. Besides, they and the other stuff like the sink were incredibly foul and disgusting, the bathroom wasn't much less primitive than the two-holer in the barn."

"If you heat with wood, why don't you love privies?"

"So Jacob pretty much gutted the ell. You know how fastidious he is: Out goes everything! We drove back and forth to the Dinsmere dump—we got a dump sticker before we got a library card—and if the Dinsmere dump was closed we'd fill up the trailer anyway and lug everything home to the Millsted dump. How are Nicole and the kids?"

"Any luck?" Jacob asked, coming upstairs, a heap of garment bags over his shoulder. He hung the bags on convenient nails. "Curly and Goddamn will be leaving in a few minutes, we're almost done and it's starting to snow."

I went to the window beside my typing table and looked down at the pile of cordwood, the devastated side lawn, the brook bordered with thin black poplars. The first snowfall on a moving day did not seem a good omen. "I suppose the finials will turn up eventually."

Batch said, "Are those nails your closet?" He studied us,

his candle flame flickering. "You two aren't the type to live in a mess."

I said, "It's an organized mess."

Batch said, "Next thing I know, you'll be saving left-overs."

"Unlikely," I said. Trying to divert Batch again as we all started down the off-balance stairs, I continued, "Remember how Dorothy would keep a slice of salami until you could patch a tire with it and then one day she'd notice it, but would she throw it in the garbage?"

Batch said, "She'd make a sandwich. Still does."

" 'Tis amazing," I said, "that our father is not in heaven."

Jacob rubbed a shoulder. "He's built up a resistance."

I asked, "Have you popped your shoulders again?"

"Couldn't avoid it. I'll be right with you, some last things for the barn."

Batch said, "Where's that well I heard about?" and as Jacob went out the front door, Batch opened the back door in the dining room. It was barricaded by a lilac bush gone wild; I'd mentally scrapped it for a French door through which we could gaze at the lilac blossoms while we dined. Pushing past the bare branches, Batch loped over to the cast-iron well cap in the backyard.

I suddenly realized he wasn't wearing any red, not even a thread in his pinstripe. "Jesus, Batch, come back indoors, no red and you're wearing *leather!*"

"They'll provide the red." He pointed.

Amid the light snow flurry, onto the lawn, a robin migration was descending. They began searching for food, their faded breasts the russet shade of the fallen leaves they were flinging aside; the entire yard seemed in motion.

"They're late," I said, clutching the door. "Batch, get your ass back in here!"

"How deep did you say this well is?"

The well had been the biggest project. There were two old dug wells here, in the backyard and behind the barn, the latter gone dry and filled in with rocks. So Jacob hired, to check out the backyard well, a plumber and helper who at long last hove over the horizon in their truck which they drove like a Sherman tank across the lawn, and after they had a consultation they languidly removed the decaying wooden well house, lighted cigarettes, and contemplated the weather. Rested up, the helper inserted a ladder into the well, and the plumber, as the expert, started climbing down. No sooner had his head disappeared from view than it reappeared, saying to Jacob, "Nosiree. Ain't ten men could make me go down there. She's ready to cave in."

If you're going to do something, we thought, you should do it right. Besides, a dependable artesian well would help us sell the restored house. There were hunkerings again, and estimates, and then a well-drilling rig rumbled into the yard, and days and days of piercing artesian whining ensued. I would occasionally leave my clipboard, go to the window, and look at the green-uniformed crew lounging around or wandering off into the woods to take a leak. What must it be like to get up every morning to drive to work to watch this rig, this monstrous green grasshopper, feeding it a section of drill-pipe periodically? Was the job worse than babysitting in a dormitory? They didn't seem exactly thrilled by the suspense. Did they have any eardrums left? At lunchtime they picnicked on a stone wall: desultory chat beneath the noise and the pines, an occasional laugh, a Twinkie.

When they reached six hundred feet, they stopped. Not for the day, apparently, but for good. No water. The contractor, summoned from his Bridgeford office by radio, arrived in his swanky green Chevy El Camino pickup which looked like what Cadillac would produce if they made trucks; its door panel boasted the Bridgeford Well Company's slogan: WE'LL DO WELL FOR YOU. Dexter Warren was a nervous man—who wouldn't be, in that business?—and he scattered chainsmoked filtertips around the yard as he paced, pondering the situation. Finally he announced his decision. "Let's wait and see," he said.

After two tense weeks of continuing drought down the well, while everyone in Millsted told us his own well tale and suggested a dowser, again into Shelterfield's yard glided

Dexter (he and Jacob were on a first-name basis by now). This time Dexter had decided to try dry ice. "Pressurize the veins," he informed Jacob. "Sure," Jacob said, "*any*thing!" Gripping my clipboard, I offered prayers to Neptune.

And we got water. Ah, the lovely phallic sight when at last the crew, after unrolling across the yard and up the road the six hundred feet of black plastic pipe, began to shove it in!

"Batch," I said, "do come back. Jacob slapped up those quick no-trespassing signs, but even before deer season began we were blasted out of our boots by a couple of duck hunters who'd come wading along the brook with their shotguns. They thought the place was still empty, and they were none too pleased to learn it had been bought."

"Dare I ask who you bought it from?"

Giving up, I left the doorway, went over to the trash can of sunflower seeds, and filled the birdfeeder. "One Elizabeth Briggs, via a realtor, Allegra Quigley. The property was left to all three Briggs children, who'd moved elsewhere. They agreed to sell most of the land to a lumber baron who wanted access to some other land up the mountain, but apparently that was the first and last thing they ever agreed on in their lives. They certainly couldn't agree on this place. To sell or not to sell the old homestead? And at what price? Elizabeth was the most obstinate. She outlived her two brothers, and after she buried the second one she reached for the phone and called Allegra. Forty grand, no dickering."

"I guess I can understand the price, now I've seen the town. Dinsmere isn't on my route, too far north. Wish it were!"

"Why are you up this way, then? Just paying a housewarming call?"

"Chasing a waitress, actually. So that's the pond you said you'd bought."

What was particularly infuriating about the expensive depth of the well was the nearness of very visible water. Ever since we had done that act disconcertingly known as "passing papers," I had wondered how we, two supposedly intelligent people, had managed to buy an overpriced farmhouse with just a smidgen of land left—and most of that land under water. For during the years the house had stood empty, beavers had arrived, occupying the stretch of brook behind it. The long dam they built had swelled this stream to a big swampy pond which overflowed just enough to let the brook continue wending its diminished way into the woods. A trapper was requested by phone to come rid us of the beavers (and, Jacob had hesitantly reported to me, he wouldn't use Havaharts) and afterwards a Fish and Game man would dynamite the dam, but the trapper of course hadn't put in an appearance and I envisioned us next spring during flood season standing on the roof of the house while the water rose higher and higher.

I said, "Waitress?"

"Kind of nice to have a pond in your backyard, even if it has killed all those trees. A pond and a petrified forest!" Batch swung his left arm in circles and then pirouetted. He was winding his self-winding watch. It dated from his early-salesman days and he stubbornly, superstitiously, refused to replace it with a digital or battery-operated.

I asked, "Is my stomach right, we're overdue for lunch?"

"Indeed, two-thirty. I suppose this place does suit Jacob better than running some business full of dealing-with-the-public hassles, doesn't it? The Murmuring Pines Motel, with guests complaining?"

"Especially after years and years of dealing with hordes of teenagers. Our pines here don't murmur, incidentally, they sough and sigh."

"I wouldn't mind running a business, if it didn't mean you were tied down."

The moving van rumbled into a roar, and the robins soared off, getting on with their own moving day, smarter than we, heading south.

"That's that, then," I said. "We're here. We're moved."

Jacob came wearily out the back door through the lilac. "Curly only charged a hundred and twenty-five dollars, less than his estimate, probably because of the finials fuck-up.

I paid him with the first check in our new checkbook. Seemed appropriate."

"Yes," I agreed, embarrassed. Paying two mortgages had finally wrecked my check-writing nerves completely, destroying my ability to sign my name, so this fall Jacob had taken over the management of our money, a responsibility both of us hated but one that, like cleaning the toilet, I had assumed at the outset of our marriage.

Batch asked, "You ever been to a restaurant called the Sidelines? She claimed she was getting a job there."

"Who?" Jacob said, rubbing his other shoulder. "It's off the main road to Meader Intervale, we've been meaning to try it because it looks like a greasy spoon, you wouldn't believe the prices at the tourist-trap restaurants on the main drag—yes, *you* would. Talk about highway robbery! Who?"

I said, "His waitress." I pulled my knitted cap out of my pocket and inquired naively, "Which car do we take?"

We took both cars, because Batch hinted in his galumphing way that he might need his for dalliance. Starting back toward the village, leading the Chrysler station wagon, Jacob and I drove around the curve to the Thibodeaus' unposted land where more hunters' vehicles were parked, and as usual we tried to assess our nearest year-round neighbors: the farmhouse once painted white, the ceramic cat spreadeagled on the roof, the aged mongrel snoozing through the snow on the porch steps, the SAW SHARPENING sign on the door of the weathered barn. The Thibodeaus were obviously not retired from city life; they must be natives.

I said, "Thank heavens our other neighbors post their land," and the road became clear along the stretch of woods belonging to another farmhouse, this one agleam with fresh white paint and lived in by the elderly Dr. and Mrs. Lord and their toy poodle. Farther down the road we passed the red one-room schoolhouse which had been remodeled into a winsome bungalow for an elderly Mrs. Sisson and her Irish setter. I added, "Now that we're officially moved in, will the neighbors pay us calls instead of just waving as they drive past?"

"God forbid."

"It's a wonder they even wave. The well-drilling noise should have ostracized us."

Living in a neighborhood, in a house right on a road, after ten years of comparative isolation down our lane, was going to be one hell of a shock. I felt stark naked without our thirty-five acres around us. But before we bought Shelterfield we had discussed the problem over and over, we had sat outdoors and listened for barking dogs and demented stereos yet heard only birds, pines, brook, and we'd reassured ourselves that this time we knew what we were buying: Although Dinsmere had hardly any zoning, its citizens either lacking foresight or consumed by a self-destructive urge nearly equal to that of Millsted's citizens who in their wisdom consistently voted down all zoning, the cost of property would keep the town from becoming a rural slum. And we *did* have acres of woods around us. A forest! The only differences were that someone else was paying the taxes and the land wasn't flat. Here, they had a tendency to call hills what in Millsted were called mountains.

Jacob said, "So we're going to meet one of Batch's inamoratas at long last."

I often wondered if Jacob envied Batch. "Wait'll I tell Dorothy. She suspected waitresses, Batch's job being what it is."

"Does our meeting her mean it's serious? I feel like a father whose son is bringing his girl to dinner for our inspection."

"Do you suppose he still goes for Nicole's type? Vaguely resembling Dorothy? Freudian!"

"A little brown wren?"

I said, "The quickest guess would be the opposite extreme, so I predict a golden goddess."

"I predict a JV cheerleader."

"We'll get used to living in a neighborhood, we'll get used to it. Remind me not to run out to the garden in a towel to pick our breakfast."

"Just put on a bathrobe," Jacob said. "This seems a bathrobe town. People sitting around in bathrobes all morning reading *The Wall Street Journal*."

"If we ever do have a garden. That fraudulent Farmer Hayseed!"

"Haven't you yet learned? He'll appear when he gets good and ready."

"He promised before snow flew. Snow is flying at this very moment."

And it had powdered the village, now a miniature village in the Christmas-decorated window of an expensive shop. Church steeple; old white houses; hitching posts along the common. There was even a pocket-mirror pond, but, as yet unfrozen, it held no tiny Currier and Ives skaters, woolen scarves flying.

I glanced over my shoulder and saw Batch laughing at the scene. "Lucky Batch," I said. "Happy as a lark in his bachelor pad. We should stop for bread on our way back."

"And for the mail."

We drove past the grocery store and the Town Hall and the Historical Society museum.

Jacob said, "There's Allegra, and she—"

Stepping out of her cream Audi in the driveway of her residence and office, an old brick house veiled with the lacy traceries of delicate dead vines, Allegra Quigley imperiously signaled us to stop. Jacob obeyed, Batch braking behind us.

"So," she said, unbelting her wraparound polo coat as Jacob rolled down his window. "It's moving day, isn't it? I trust you've got your woodstove installed by now?"

Hard to believe that she was probably only seven or eight years older than I, for somehow she always made me feel like a toddler. Her brunette chocolate-box beauty masked cutthroat efficiency. She used terms such as "square one" and "the bottom line" and she called the future "down the road," but we had stopped wincing after she, learning of our fruitless search for an available mason, found one for us who agreed to build our chimney before the millennium and actually did.

Jacob replied, "Yes, the stove has begun taking the chill off." Batch had also opened his window—but effortlessly, it was automatic—so Jacob made introductions through the snowflakes. "Allegra, my doubting brother-in-law, Sebastian Pierce. Batch, Allegra Quigley, who has faith in houses."

"A devout believer," she said, sweeping her gloved hand in a gesture that seemed to encompass the entire town, as if she had sold every house in Dinsmere at least once. And perhaps she dreamed she had. "You're keeping warm, then? Welcome to Dinsmere!"

"Thank you," we said.

"Have a nice day." She nodded dismissal.

Jacob rolled up his window and we drove on.

The fairly new elementary school matched the town's basic color, white, if not the town's architecture, and in the schoolyard beside the one-story building some teachers were getting into their cars, going home after work. Nowadays this was Dinsmere's only school. Fifteen years ago the town had stupidly let itself be talked out of its small quiet high school; back then, the New Hampshire Department of Education had been browbeating little schools with threats of dropping their accreditation if they didn't join regional high schools which provided such dubious benefits as language labs, post-Sputnik science programs, and a greater variety of athletic facilities and intramural sports. The result was busing as extensive as any you saw on the evening news, although there were no rocks thrown, no bombs or riots. The Dinsmere high-school kids daily made the twenty-mile bus trek to and from the Meader Intervale Regional High School of aqua and chrome, while the old brick high school in the village did business as a clinic.

I sneaked a peek at Jacob. The elementary teachers' car doors slammed, and he said, "The poor sonsofbitches," his reaction all summer to the sight of any school. This war horse was not, apparently, hearing phantom bugles. He added, "I hope Allegra is right."

"Don't let Batch bother you, you know his taste in houses. Anyone who would buy a split-level mansion in a Bridgeford housing development—"

"I thought he and Nicole figured the house would make up for his being away on the road all week."

But in this luxurious nest Nicole had started neglecting the little-brown-wren duties she'd really seemed to love, until eventually, after hatching her third egg, she stopped doing the housework altogether and instead began attending endless classes in music appreciation, yoga, calligraphy; she even took the pottery classes that my ex-lover, Gary Bates, offered to desperate housewives. (I'd speculated about what else he, now twice divorced, offered them.) Dorothy, on a mission of mercy after Batch moved out, had learned, aghast, while helping one of their daughters with some laundry, that Nicole no longer even ironed Batch's handkerchiefs.

My nieces and nephew. Kate was a sophomore at Connecticut College and according to Dorothy would avoid Bridgeford on Thanksgiving and Christmas this year by going to her roommate's house. At home with Nicole were Melissa, a disdainful sixteen, and five-year-old Davy. These nieces, this nephew, were as close to having kids of my own as I'd ever get. Indeed, Melissa actually looked like me. Jacob's attitude toward his nieces and nephews, none of whom resembled him, was totally detached; their welfare and upbringing were completely Louise and Arthur's business, for people who were foolish enough to have children deserved them. My attitude toward Batch's children could best be described by comparing it to a form of English housing: semidetached.

I said to Jacob, "I think Dorothy is truly convinced that Batch left because Nicole didn't iron his handkerchiefs anymore. She keeps inquiring occasionally if I still iron yours."

"Mmm."

"And I keep saying they're the only things of yours I do iron."

"Imbecile."

"Perhaps you'll start using red bandannas now."

We were driving past some shabbier village houses where natives lived, and then we swung down along Dinsmere's lake road of splendid Victorian cottages and boathouses hogging Lake Pequawket's shoreline.

Jacob said, "I've got it. Dinsmere is Town and Gown."

The snow flurries were letting up now, but instead of taking heart from this I felt myself suddenly sagging with exhaustion. November was such a sad time of year; nobody should ever move in November.

"But maybe," I said, sitting up straighter, "moving is the remedy."

"For what?"

"I don't know. Depression."

As if we'd lived here always, Jacob chose a series of short-cuts through the woods over to the main route south toward Meader Intervale, a two-lane highway driven with daredevil recklessness by everyone even after the frantic tourist season ended. Its pace reminded us of the rabbit-carpeted road to the Base, but it was right-handed so we called it the Indy. Jacob jumped into the traffic and, speeding out of necessity, we tore around curves past farms on whose pastures a motel or gift shop grazed here and there, until we reached a corner by a defunct gas station where, Batch tailgating, we screeched off onto the Second Neck Road and slowed to a halt in the parking lot of the Sidelines. I expected pit-stop mechanics to rush up and change our tires. The snowfall had melted on the asphalt.

"Well," said Batch, stepping out of his station wagon, "if she did take a job here, she must have been serious about a change of atmosphere."

A blotchy pink stucco chalet, the Sidelines combined the Mediterranean and the Alps; surrounded by gravel pits, it seemed distant from Dinsmere in more than just miles.

Yet not entirely far removed, for in Dinsmere we'd seen the same bumper-stickers as the one, commenting on the

1976 Presidential offerings, which was still stuck to the Toyota parked on the other side of us: HONK WHEN THE ELECTION'S OVER. And on our workmen's pickups we had seen the likes of this nearby Blazer's:

GOD, GUNS AND GUTS
MADE AMERICA FREE.

I asked, "Does 'she' have a name?"

"Miriam Holt," Batch replied. "She quit her job at the Lighthouse—you've heard of it, down on the coast, swanky seafood—to come up to the mountains. Claimed she wanted an informal place for a change, but Jesus, I think she overdid it. Is there a Mr. Allegra Quigley?"

Jacob said, "Haven't seen hide nor hair of one."

I said, "Batch!"

"Just wondering." Unhesitatingly dismissing the door marked RESTAURANT, Batch opened the door marked LOUNGE. Like us, he mostly ate in restaurant bars to avoid families with children.

But I myself paused, nervous about hazards other than food since the killing at Clem's Café.

Batch said, "Coming?"

We entered into midnight. Then, as we groped forward from the vestibule, I spied light ahead, a silver glow, moonrise, and we followed its path to a cavern where men in muted red and orange sat talking while, on a television screen nearly the size of a drive-in movie's, soap-opera seduction was going on, smooching faces huge, pores as deep as craters. I realized our feet had been crunching.

"Hey," Batch said, "peanuts in the shell!" Choosing a table without consultation, he pulled out a chair for me and scooped up a handful of peanuts from the plastic basket beside the catsup bottle. "Maybe that's really the reason, maybe instead of wall-to-wall she prefers to tread on peanut shells!" Munching, he tossed his peanut shells into the air and like magic who should appear but—"Miriam!" he rejoiced, leaping up.

Embarrassed, thinking of Nicole, Jacob and I averted

our gaze and considered the Sidelines's decor, a basketball hoop over the bar, crossed skis and tennis rackets over doorways, and on all the walls giant pinups of football players, basketball players, baseball, hockey, intermingled with inspiring posters of boxing, golf, horse racing, snowmobiling, wrestling. The average patron, a hard-core sports fan, seemed also to be the sort of entrepreneur we'd become familiar with, the owner of a pickup truck with a plow, his name in magnetic letters on the door, a broom sticking up out of the back. We overheard one of these at the bar, wearing a salty hammer holster, ask another, "What job you doing tomorrow?" To which his friend replied, "Oh, I'll have to wait to see who hollers the loudest. You know how it is."

Jacob and I exchanged exasperated glances and reached for the peanuts.

"Well, now!" Reunited, Batch remembered our presence, so Jacob stood up. Batch said, "Miriam, this is the baby sister I've told you all about, and here's my brother-in-law, the lapsed librarian."

Jacob flinched. "How do you do."

Both our predictions were wrong, but Jacob's came the closest because Miriam was wearing an athletic outfit. It wasn't, however, a cheerleading uniform; it was a modified football referee's uniform. Brunette like Nicole, I would report to Dorothy, but taller, more a starling than a wren. And my age if she was a day; Batch had surprisingly turned out not to be a cradle-robber. "Hello," I said. "Er—has Batch mentioned how our mother became a great football fan when Batch played in high school and she still is?"

"Are you?" Miriam asked.

Batch said, "Ib's sport is the sport of kings. Miriam, what the hell are you doing up here?"

"If you want pizza," she said, "we haven't got any. The entire north country is out of pizza cheese."

"What?" Batch was immediately off baying down this sidetrack. "Why? The foliage freaks, the leafers? No, the foliage must have peaked up here a month ago and—"

Miriam asked me, "Would you like a tour of the kitchen?"

She'd heard about my phobia. I blushed, and Jacob said, "Thanks, but we'll just wash up instead, it's moving day and we've got ingrained grime." He led me off toward a sign that said LOCKER ROOM; in a cramped hallway we discovered two doors, BALLS and STRIKES. We parted, correctly deducing the appropriate bathrooms, and when we emerged he remarked, "I bet she once *was* a JV cheerleader."

"I hope the kitchen isn't like the bathroom. Funny, I thought I'd be too fascinated to mind about Nicole. Why on earth doesn't Nicole take matters into her own hands and go ahead and get a divorce!"

"Batch was gone so much anyway, maybe she hasn't noticed the change. Can you imagine what this place must be like when there's a big game or a fight on TV?"

At our table, sipping his drink, the basket of peanuts replenished, Batch said, "She claims nobody knows why the supplier ran out of mozzarella. Incredible. *I* have never ever let down a restaurant. Ordered us pastrami on rye—and onion rings, hard to get good onion rings these days but she recommends them and she should know."

I said, "Speaking of rings, Miriam isn't wearing any. Is there a Mr. Miriam Holt?"

"She went back to her maiden name. There's an ex and one kid, a daughter, Lesley. Come to find out, you're fellow citizens, Miriam has rented a house in East Dinsmere."

"That's nice."

"Don't panic, I won't be barging in on you every day. Or on her. I've got my route to do. And finesse to practice. How come your other house still hasn't sold?"

Trying to change that subject, I said, "I wonder if they tune in to *The Gong Show* here. We could come see the Unknown Comic, Jacob, on this giant silver screen!"

"Price," Jacob said. "We're not ready to drop it from forty-eight, not after what that well is costing us."

Batch agreed, "Yes, the well must have really thrown your plans out of whack."

"Four thousand two hundred dollars," Jacob said. "Had to adjust our calculations."

"Ouch!" Batch said.

Jacob said, "We haven't actually paid yet, not until we get the water-test results. It's undrinkable now. There's still too much sediment from the drilling, but I've only got the new plumbing as far as the toilet, anyway."

I said, my appetite lost, "Where is Miriam from?" and then through the flickering gloom I glimpsed her approaching with food.

"Here you go," she said. Confused, Jacob and Batch sprang to their feet, remembered they were customers, sat down. Lowering her round tray, Miriam now seemed determined not to lower her guard also, setting out our plates as impersonally as any anonymous waitress, while Batch clumsily tried to assist, pretending it was a family meal.

Once again Jacob and I exchanged glances, this time prurient. We were attempting to picture Batch and Miriam in bed, pinstripe suit and referee's uniform discarded in wild abandon.

"Crotch," Jacob said, and I said, *"What?"* and he said hastily, "All these football posters just reminded me of what my old coach used to tell us: If you keep your eye on their crotches, they're not going to have much luck trying to fake you out. The crotch is a center of gravity."

"Indeed," I said.

Miriam became a family member again. "Then is your sport football, like Batch's?"

Jacob said, "I am allowed to watch two football games a year, on Thanksgiving and New Year's. Ib allows herself *three* races."

I said defensively, "The Triple Crown, and horse races only take a split-second, they don't go on for eons like your games."

Jacob said, "You've read every Dick Francis."

I said, "You've read *Semi-Tough*."

"You watched the movie."

"So did you."

"In England," Jacob said, "you dragged me to the races at Newmarket."

"You bet on them."

"Only because it was a change from the slot machines at the Officers' Club. But you bet, too."

"Once. On a horse named Clarity because I liked the name, and I won more that once than you ever did."

"Next year may I watch the Super Bowl?"

Christ, we were playing squabbling-old-married-couple to these young lovers!

"Ah." Batch bit into an onion ring and pronounced, "Perfect. They change their fat here more often than appearances would suggest. But Miriam, I implore you, leave your peanut shells and come back down to civilization!"

Miriam said, "I've got a half-hour break before dinner," and disappeared.

I asked, "Did she have to start waitressing to support herself after the divorce?"

"The dinner shift also." Batch consulted his self-winding watch. "She worked in school systems downstate before and after she kicked her husband out. She was something called an In-Service Training Specialist complete with a doctorate in Special Education, but one day she walked out of a school and into the Lighthouse and applied for a job. Are you going to rent the Millsted house this winter?"

"Huh?" Jacob said, his mind apparently now on Miriam's exit from school as he inspected the rye bread for the caraway seeds that Batch didn't know he hated. "No, we decided we didn't want the bother. My folks are keeping an eye on the place so we don't need people living there to protect it. Gives my father something to do, now he's retired."

"Is the riffraff why it hasn't sold? Buyers put off by all those trailers?"

"At first," Jacob said slowly, "we thought so, but then we realized that most people up from the city don't seem to see them."

I said, "Thank God for that," but I was sure the house

would never sell and we would go on paying two mortgages until our money ran out and we went bankrupt; I could vividly envision us left without even a clipboard or a Wonder Bar. If only Jacob hadn't quit, if only we were safe instead of in this crazy predicament!

Yet we were here, moved. We had a new address and a new telephone number. It *was* done, I told myself as I watched two entrepreneurs indulge in a fast-draw contest with their cigarette lighters, whipping them against their pantlegs, slashing the Zippos aflame.

And we had a new grocery store, to which, after we said goodbye to Batch and left him keeping a vigil by the peanuts until Miriam's break, we headed, driving back to Dinsmere in the late afternoon dusk that seemed high noon in comparison to the Sidelines's ambiance.

If Jacob hadn't quit, I thought, he would be arriving home from work right now and I would be awaiting him in the Millsted house, my private chunk of the afternoon over, the walk in the woods, the reading; I would be switching gears to conversation and cooking. I would not be wondering where our next meal was coming from and I would not expect to see a wolf whenever I opened a door.

"Bread," I said as we reached the village. "What about supper later? Will you be feeling peckish?"

"Will you?"

Lengths of early lamplight hung yellow between straight white curtains in the windows of the white houses. I said, "I just want to dig out some sheets and your Witney Point blanket and make up the bed before I collapse. When I reorganized for moving, did I pack them in the new blanket chests or the old one? We've got an embarrassment of blanket chests."

"Maybe a few nibblies." Jacob parked in front of the grocery store which we'd come to call simply the store because it was, after all, the only store in the village. "Do we need milk too?"

"Is the refrigerator plugged in, even though it's in the dining room? I don't have to use the damn cooler anymore?"

"Yes, but it's slanting a bit, I haven't yet leveled the the feet."

"Okay, milk."

Getting out of the car, we paused to admire the store's old-fashioned gas pump; instead of a flashy jukebox pump, it was the tall skinny type with a small window and, on top, a black-and-white globe which despite its sober colors spun as merrily as a barber pole when gasoline was dispensed. We crossed the sagging porch and stopped to glance at the items thumbtacked to the wall near the door: a woodsplitter for rent, church notices and sales, a calico cat lost. And then we entered this old white high-peaked building and confronted the grill of the post office, the tier of gleaming brass boxes. Our experience with a dynamited rural mailbox had made us decide to rent a post-office box here, and Jacob bent and checked it.

"Nothing. We're not even an 'Occupant' yet. Nibblies, nibblies." Rubbing a shoulder, he went on into the store proper, which was empty of customers, Mr. Dobbins, the scrawny owner, reading a *Manchester Union* behind the ancient cash register.

I followed, scolding myself for not having made a list. But there were only two rows of shelves, a meat case, a produce counter, and a freezer to choose from, so I could be reminded almost at once of what I needed. The straightforward store had refrained from returning to a potbellied stove, a cracker barrel, old men playing checkers, yet it did have a wheel of rattrap cheese on the meat case and Jacob asked for half a pound.

Mr. Dobbins folded his newspaper. "Your company find you?"

"What?" Jacob said. "Oh, yes, thanks for giving him our directions."

"Guess he wasn't up here hunting."

"What? No, just hunting for us. He's Ib's brother, my wife's brother, my brother-in-law—"

In his next breath, I thought, Jacob would be reporting into the interested silence Batch's pursuit of a Miriam Holt who'd recently rented a house in East Dinsmere, so I said,

"And may we have three hot dogs, please? Natural casing." If in college I had grilled illicit hot dogs smack on the radiator in my room, I could steam or sauté hot dogs on the Jøtul, more elegantly in a pot or pan, couldn't I? And baked beans and salad, I decided, walking down the only aisle, the challenge beginning to revive me. That would be tomorrow's supper, and we'd have soup for tomorrow's lunch; Batch's misgivings notwithstanding, we would manage very well. I was a pioneer woman with a can of Friend's Brick Oven Baked Beans! Toast for tomorrow's breakfast. I'd been relieved to learn the store carried Pepperidge Farm bread, a stack of solid loaves for the Gown element, I assumed, beside the softer array of squishy bread for the Town. When the kitchen had cupboards, when the kitchen had a floor and countertops, I would resume making my own bread and continue my unsuccessful campaign to convert Jacob to whole-wheat. And when the kitchen had cupboards and cabinets, I thought as I chose the head of iceberg lettuce that seemed the least rusty and rejected the oranges because of the price, when the kitchen was finished I would unpack our emergency larder from its carton and feel deceptively secure again. "Yikes," I said to Jacob, "what have you got there?"

He was clutching cans of smoked oysters, anchovies, Vienna sausages. "Celebration. It's not every day we move. I found these in the gourmet section, beside the cans of antifreeze."

"Moving once every ten years is more than I can bear." But if all went according to plan, Jacob would have the house fixed up within the year and we'd be moving on to another. We were celebrating a new career, too; I reached for a sack of oranges.

The quaintest thing about the store was its lack of an adding machine. With a ballpoint Mr. Dobbins totted up our purchases on the half-pound of cheese he'd wrapped in white paper. He was performing. He was a math whiz.

As we drove away past the village spring-fed trough, I said, "We forgot to bring our water jugs. Batch's visit disorganized me—and moving day in general—the finials!"

"There's enough water from home for tonight."

"Home? Shouldn't this be home now? Have we got as many homes as we've got blanket chests?"

"Millsted is my hometown."

"Is there also enough water to wash up in tomorrow morning, enough for you to shave? What about using the brook water?"

"I'm thinking of growing a beard."

"But you haven't wanted a white beard."

"Maybe it suits the mountains."

When we neared Shelterfield, we found the dirt road entirely clear of hunters' pickups and jeeps, for the woods were nocturnal now and illegal. Despite the exhalation of smoke from the new chimney, the house still seemed uninhabited, cold.

"Snow flurries," I said, "and dark by five o'clock. Winter is here."

"Look! Hayward came while we were gone and plowed up a garden."

Tired though we were, our sleep was jumpy the first night in this downstairs bedroom more unfamiliar than a Holiday Inn. Before daybreak I gave up rearranging my dream office and soon realized I was counting not sheep but the telephones in the places I'd lived, trying to remember their exact locations: the phone on the end table beside the sofa in the apartment where we'd lived until I was ten, the soft red roses of the sofa's old chintz slipcover, my grown-up feeling as I'd lift the receiver to call Virginia and then the humiliation of the number-please operator's commanding me, "Speak up, dear!"; the phone in my grandparents' home that was shifted from the front hall into my father's front-room CPA office when Dorothy inherited the place, with a kitchen extension on which I had spent entire evenings doing homework with Virginia and gossiping; the college phone booth that was my first stand-up wallphone endurance test; the domestic phone respectably occupying its portion of the love-seat telephone bench in my Bridgeford furnished apartment; no phone at all in the laundry cottage so when we needed one—rarely—we used the manor house's or the High Street booth; the efficient office and kitchen phones in Millsted; and now, installed this summer, a wallphone in Shelterfield's kitchen but none in my office because if I was going to work in a garret I should be remote. Besides, an extension cost extra.

"Good God," I said, forgetting Jacob's no-conversation-until-first-cup-of-coffee rule laid down to discourage my Merry Sunshine chattiness. "When we decided to have just the kitchen phone, we hadn't learned the kitchen floor was going to have to be torn up. How can we talk on the phone without a floor under us?"

Jacob threw back the covers, which didn't yet include my grandmother's ecru bedspread packed safely away from carpentry; he fumbled under the bed for the flashlight. As he plodded through the dining room and into the ell and tiptoed across that kitchen floor into the bathroom, I decided a pioneer woman would accept wakefulness and get up and start the day. Hell, she would already be up and doing.

Belting my bathrobe, by the distant light from the jagged bathroom doorway I went into the dining room, where I switched on the utility light over the table saw and considered our drop-leaf pine table, which I planned to use in here as a makeshift kitchen counter, all the leaves up. The sight caused absolute panic to surge from my toes to my temples. How could I cope? No cupboards, no sink, no *drainpipe!* Then my nerves were rallied by the prospect of organizing this, and I recalled that in my Girl Scout days what had for me brought order to the confusion of camping out had been the satisfying way in which the pieces of my mess kit fitted together.

In the dim living room I located a couple of appropriate cartons and lugged them into the dining room. APPLIANCES said my Magic Marker on one, out of which I took the Corning Ware electric coffeepot that all at once looked very suburbanly out-of-place and the General Electric toaster that was so infuriatingly erratic I would have consigned it to either the Millsted or the Dinsmere dump if I could have afforded a new one of a different brand. From our last half-full plastic jug I poured into the coffeepot enough water for four cups, and I was unpacking the IMMEDIATE KITCHEN SUPPLIES carton when Jacob began tiptoeing back. Snapping the lid off the can of Maxwell House, I called out a Milton quote from a sampler of Dorothy's:

> The childhood shows the man,
> As morning shows the day.

I added, "And this first morning of your new career—"

Jacob said, "I don't know how to tell you but the toilet won't flush I can't figure out what's wrong."

Beside the APPLIANCES carton was a paper bag we had used last night for a wastebasket because the kitchen wastebasket was packed with annoying under-the-sink spillables such as Formula 409 and Lysol. Contemplating our little collection of the celebration's containers which smelled of fishy oil and nitrites, I thought of the English factory-girl's dream of a wastebasket.

Then with a steady pioneer hand I measured coffee. "You can fix the toilet, you can fix anything."

"I'll get you an extension cord, you'll need some extension cords in here."

"How nostalgic. It will look like Stella's network of cords and transformers without the slow record player."

"No, it won't. Too dangerous."

"What are we going to do?"

"Priorities." Jacob went into the ell to his toolroom and returned with a couple of extension cords dangling. "Organization. The most important thing is to get some heat in the ell. So. First I'll dismantle the oil range and move it out of the kitchen, then I'll rip up and replace the floor, then I'll reassemble the stove and get it going, and then I'll tackle the toilet."

"Easy as apple pie."

"Sure. Meantime . . ."

"I'm already ahead of you."

As he went into the living room and raked the coals in the Jøtul, I fetched the roll of toilet paper from the bathroom and clicked on the flashlight and followed its beam through the bedroom doorway into the intact but arctic end of the collapsing barn.

Here, in a cunning closet, was the two-holer. It emptied, the same way the mucking-out slots for the cow stalls had, into the barn cellar twenty feet below. The draft created under there tried to lift me off the wooden seat.

In England, the first time Jacob had begun reminiscing about his mother's apple pies and hinting I make one, I had ignored him; the second time I had passionately demanded, "Have you ever noticed the amount of work that goes into making an apple pie? Have *you* ever made one? I hate making pies, particularly *apple!*" He asked, "What's the big deal? Don't you just roll out some crust and slice up some apples?" I said, "Hah!" "Okay," he said, "I'll make one. There must be a reason for 'easy as pie.' " "Wonderful," I said, leaving the kitchen. I kept a discreet distance, reading in the living room, until the swearing drew me back to find Jacob in the midst of a slapstick routine with recalcitrant dough, flour everywhere, impatient apple slices turning brown. He said, "Don't say it." I didn't at that moment, but afterwards anything complicated became in our language "as easy as apple pie." And nothing, I thought, is ever easy.

When I sprinted back to the bedroom, I discovered naked Jacob rummaging in the finials-barren bureau. He asked, "Do you remember where you packed our long underwear?"

"A blanket chest."

I reached the Jøtul and had a shivering fit before I opened the nearest blanket chest, the dark red one whose interior was papered with a Williamsburg pattern. Around me, the sheet-covered living-room furniture resembled Stella's KKK decor and I suddenly longed to be back in the Suffolk-pink laundry cottage, at the very beginning, before I had met Jacob. What if we hadn't both happened to decide to rub the brasses in that particular church on that wet autumn Saturday? But surely sooner or later we would have encountered each other at the Officers' Club or a faculty-staff party, wouldn't we? I said, *"Voilà,* long underwear." We possessed three pairs each; we were, I realized, going to need them all.

Jacob came in. "Of course. Packed with the mittens and wool socks."

"Jesus, Jacob! Get back in the bedroom, we're living on a road now, someone might drive past and see you!"

"And go blind?" But he pulled on his shorts.

"Packing our long underwear with the winter things makes sense."

"I'll never trust anyone who files her spice jars alphabetically but won't use a bookmark because she wants to refresh her memory."

"One of those has no relation to the other."

"They do to me," said Jacob, unfolding his Duofold.

"It's getting light. Let's hope the weather report was true and we'll have some solar energy today." I yanked the TV's knob. "I don't understand why that gigantic antenna cost us a fortune but doesn't get anything."

Jacob went back to the bedroom. "You don't understand mountains?"

"Blurry Maine channels. PBS from Lewiston or Augusta or wherever. CBS from Burlington, Vermont, in an electronic snowstorm. I now sympathize with your folks' reception." I switched off TV static and turned the radio on to the National Public Broadcasting Network's *Morning Magazine* program from Orono, Maine, which daringly played jazz at breakfasttime. A clarinet was meandering. I said, "I wish we'd had enough water to heat up on the Jøtul overnight."

"Well, we didn't."

But I had steeled myself for this. Going into the dining room, I turned the makeshift kitchen into a makeshift bathroom by tipping a puddle of water from the jug into a tooth glass, and a pool into the Rubbermaid dishpan. Brushing my teeth, opening the back door to spit and shiver, I fortified myself with images of basins and ewers on commodes, women in flannel nightdresses cracking the ice to pour out the water for their bracing ablutions. Good for the complexion! Invigorating!

Jacob came in from the bedroom, bulky with layers, fake-down vest, sweatshirt, Levi's, long underwear. He checked the growling coffeepot. "How's your filth phobia?"

"Under control," I said, rinsing off nightcream. "The mugs are in that carton, the oranges in the fridge, and there's your vitamin pill." I tossed the water out the back door into the lilac and added the last from the jug. "I'm through," I said, applying moisturizer, "it's all yours."

He doused his white stubble. "I'll get some more later this morning."

In the bedroom, while I hauled on underpants and my blue long underwear with white snowflakes and a plaid flannel shirt and my threadbare overalls, I cursed my childhood deprived of daily baths. Dorothy saved hot water as well as leftovers. Only one real bath a week was permitted; the rest of the time you had to make do with sponge baths. At college, what a gusher of hot water I struck! Such steam and suds! I spent those four years in the shower, and naturally I vowed that I would never economize on hot water in my own household, I would starve in order to pay the hot-water bills. Another phobia. How long, I wondered, would it be until Jacob got the hot-water tank out of its carton in the living room and into the ell cellar, hooked up? How long until the bathtub resided in the bathroom, a shower wall built? How many mornings like this? The Great Unwashed, I tied my bootlaces, returned to the dining room, plugged the temperamental toaster's cord into an extension cord, located a second outlet, and listened to Jacob clanging around with the kitchen range.

He called, "The sun is coming up."

"Have you decided yet if you trust the brook water?" Out the dining-room window the sky was an effervescent pink like a bubbly strawberry soda. "I could start heating a kettle to wash the lunch dishes."

"Oh, why not, I guess it must be safe for washing. There's

nothing nowadays above us except forest. Any drainoffs from barnyards happened long ago."

Carrying toast to him on a paper plate, I discovered a minstrel man. "Heavens," I said. "Who would have thought the old range to have had so much blacking on it! Need help? More coffee?"

He'd taken the range apart and was dragging heavy pieces into the toolroom. "Stay. Off. The floor."

I located the canning kettle in the living room and removed its neatly packed innards of rack and funnel and tongs. Would red be necessary this early in the morning? Yes. I put on my red jacket and went out the back door, kettle on hip.

Yesterday's snow flurries were cemented by a frost that lay like another snowfall on the trees, the neighboring field, the newly turned earth of the garden. Underfoot, the hard ground crackled with the same brittleness as the Sidelines's peanut-shell carpet, and I wondered if Batch had spent the night in East Dinsmere. The sunrise had begun paling now to become the inside of a huge seashell, pearly pink.

The petrified forest caused by the beavers was a stand of dead pine ankle-deep in water between the backyard and the spreading bowl of the beaver pond. Chickadees darted from its branches to the lilac to the kitchen birdfeeder and returned; they were so quick I couldn't really see their wings moving. But the morning was whispery with the motion of those wings. "Birdbrain," I said to a chickadee who, perched on a sere twig, kept bam-bam-bamming a sunflower seed.

Across the pond, the beaver lodge seemed as uninhabited as our house. But they were in there, ignorant of their fate. Their probable fate. (Would we ever trap the trapper? If we did, then after he'd done his terrible deed we next might get fast dynamite results by seeking out the rock-concert patrons who'd blasted our Millsted mailbox.) This lodge looked like a fragile version of that heap of cordwood beside the bulkhead down which I'd have to start throwing our winter's supply this afternoon. The cordwood had been heaved haphazardly off a pickup, load after load; the arrangement of the beaver lodge also appeared to be without design, just gray sticks accidentally spilled, and only when I studied it carefully could I remind myself it was a construction. Beyond, the dark green forest climbed the mountain.

In a little waterfall the pond overflowed into the brook's resumed course, and I crashed through frosty bushes to the brink. Dunking the kettle, holding it against the flow, I silently recited:

> I come from haunts of coot and hern,
> I make a sudden sally,
> And sparkle out among the fern
> To bicker down a valley.

Then, feeling swiftly bereft, I realized that of course I could no longer accept the refrain's assumption as I had when I learned the poem in my childhood.

> For men may come and men may go
> But I go on forever.

Wings flitted. A hairy woodpecker tapped a drumroll on a dead treetop. Chickadees continued beating their brains out. I knew these noises from the other house, but they seemed wilder here. I looked up and met a deer whose own heart seemed to have stopped, as mine did.

A doe, she stood in the pines on the other side of the brook, ears alert, large eyes blanker than Jacob's. Had she heard me, not seen me? Or had she smelled the Unwashed? My hands were freezing onto the icy kettle. Her ears twitched, and I too heard a car halting down around the curve at the Thibodeaus'.

Trembling, I said ridiculously, "Shoo."

Querying look.

"Scram. Skedaddle. Shake a leg." At last I remembered to move. Lifting the kettle out of the brook, I straightened up. "Run for your life." The motion made her do just that, white tail up.

And, sloshing, I ran to the house, where the telephone

began ringing. Probably it was Dorothy, even though she'd already given us a housewarming phone call last night at the very moment we had collapsed into our sheeted chairs after doing some exhausted unpacking. Probably she wanted to continue interrogating me about Miriam Holt.

Jacob said into the receiver, "I'll be damned!"

"Who is it?" The range was gone from the kitchen now, and one floorboard was ripped up.

"Yes," he said, "yesterday. The new life commences. Here's Ib, and if she starts shouting it's because I'm in the throes of tearing up the kitchen floor around her." Letting the receiver swing, he took the kettle from me and mouthed, "Virginia."

I grabbed the phone. "For God's sake!" I'd sent best-friend Virginia a change-of-address notice, even though she was one of the world's worst correspondents. "First I see a deer closer than I ever have before, and now a call from you! What a Welcome Wagon!"

"—so early, before classes," Virginia said, referring to, I supposed, the private-school dance classes she taught down in Massachusetts. "A trip to New Hampshire doesn't necessarily mean I *have* to see my folks, my car won't automatically pull in at their door, I'm thirty-seven years old and entitled to a private life—"

Suddenly terrorstricken, I remembered that Virginia was like the Richter scale; a calm person, she measured only earthquakes. What had happened since I saw her last Christmas in Bridgeford? I cried, "Oh, God, what's wrong, Max or Willie or—"

"—I'll bypass Bridgeford heavily disguised," she said, and Jacob returned from taking the kettle to the Jøtul and picked up his Wonder Bar and a small sledgehammer, made an apologetic gesture followed by a John Henry flexing of muscles, and set to work again, and through the racket Virginia went on about facing another Thanksgiving and getting away from it all and something-or-other until I finally had the bright idea of opening the kitchen door beside the wallphone, slipping outside onto the granite doorstep and closing the door on the cord, a maneuver that removed the telephone receiver from the pounding hammer and squawking boards, and then I heard her say in a clear wail, "And you must have known how I *loathed* Max's nicknaming me Ginger!"

I replied distractedly, "He couldn't very well call you Virgin, could he? I figured he was thinking of Ginger Rogers."

"And I'm so sick of listening to him drone on about his computer print-outs of students' grades, and—I never told you this, but you know how when you go to a drive-in restaurant there are two types of couples in the other cars, the type with the husband who gets out and gives the order and carries the ice-cream cones or whatever back, and the type with the wife who does, beast of burden? I'm the wife type. Unwillingly."

"You are?" I said, trying to adjust my assessment of seemingly mild-mannered Max, a curriculum coordinator (i.e., guidance counselor) at a public high school down there.

"Are you?" Virginia asked. "The wife type?"

I confessed, "Jacob does the ordering. But it's mainly because he takes forever to make up his mind, to choose between chocolate or an experiment—"

"My pencil is poised, give me directions. I don't think I've ever been to Dinsmere."

"Directions?"

"I know you've just moved, but Thanksgiving is two whole weeks away, you'll have settled in by then, except maybe for rearranging some furniture. You still have your fold-out sofa, don't you? I could sleep on that if your guest room isn't ready."

"Virginia! Didn't you hear Jacob about the floor? We're camping out! The toilet broke down! We're *primitive!*"

"I wish I could leave this very minute, but my job—I'll arrive the Wednesday afternoon before Thanksgiving and please make sure you don't tell Dorothy so she won't tell my mother so I won't have to explain, okay? Now, directions!"

I rattled off the directions. "Virginia—"

"Fine, that seems clear enough but let's hope I don't end

up in Canada by mistake. Thank you, Ib. Now I have something to look forward to, something to live for, love to Jacob, goodbye, goodbye!"

As Virginia hung up, around the curve in the dirt road an Irish setter bounded, wearing a big red bow on its collar; catching sight of me, it streaked down the driveway at this delightful new target while I, too distraught to think to leap back indoors, prepared to defend myself with the telephone receiver.

"Abigail! Sit!"

I'd only seen Mrs. Sisson at the helm of her wine-colored Mercedes, chubby face peering through its steering wheel. In Dinsmere, we had soon realized, you learned to recognize people by their cars and didn't rely on physiognomy. Now she was scurrying along the driveway in anxious pursuit of well-trained Abigail, who'd promptly sat down, and when she neared me I saw that my windshield-impression of this schoolhouse neighbor was right after all, for Mrs. Sisson did resemble a chipmunk, cheek pouches full. She was wearing an elegant city coat of red wool whose cost I could only guess at; I could, however, quote the L.L. Bean prices of her Icelandic toque and her mukluks. She carried a dainty flared wicker basket cuddling something in a red napkin.

"Good morning," I said. The sky was sliding now from gold to silver, too dramatic, like a panoramic vision of the world's birth. "Good doggie."

Mrs. Sisson said, "That's why I hardly ever take Abigail walking up this way, don't you know."

From indoors came the insane screaming of a mother partridge doing her hysterical broken-wing act to draw attention away from her babies, a noise which had scared the daylights out of me in our Millsted woods more than once. "I'm sorry," I said. "Floorboards. How do you do, I'm Isabel Wetherbee."

"Abigail gets so overexcited by going past the Thibodeaus' Sarge—she can't understand why the lame old fellow won't jump off his porch and come play—that she forgets her manners. And of course today there was the extra excitement of two hunters. If only it wasn't against Caca

Thibodeau's principles to post his land!" She gave the telephone receiver a puzzled glance. "I'm Flossie Sisson, how do you do, I can't begin to tell you how wonderful it will be to see lights on in Shelterfield at long last."

I had been admiring her bravery in walking this deer-season road to pay us a call when from her fastidious little lips had come rollicking that French slang for shit. Amazed, I said, "I'll fetch Jacob, I'd ask you to come in but our floor is disappearing," and pushing open the door, I hung up the receiver and tried to signal Jacob, who was wrenching free another obstinate board. Joists were visible above stone cellar walls.

"Heavens to Betsy!" Flossie Sisson pounced past me onto the threshold and into the house. "No, Abigail, stay. Look at this! Oh, you poor things!"

I stepped indoors. "Jacob, a guest. Jacob!"

Sooty, unshaven, he could have been one of the pickup entrepreneurs. Until he started talking. Suddenly noticing us, he said, "I've learned once again that wrecking things isn't so much fun as it's cracked up to be, not when you know you've got to rebuild. How do you do?"

As I made introductions, I simultaneously wondered where to buy him a hammer holster for Christmas and how Flossie would go about inquiring what he did for a living.

She said, staring at the pile of rotted boards, "I walked Abigail this way this morning to see if there was anything you needed, don't you know, but I hadn't realized you aren't really moved in yet. Though didn't I see a moving van when I drove past yesterday?"

What would she say if I told her I desperately needed a shower? I said, "We *are* moved in, actually. Very kind of you, but we seem to be coping, aren't we, Jacob?"

He laughed and began pounding at another board. "All I need is a dump truck. But thank you. Excuse me, excuse the commotion."

Flossie remembered her adorable basket. "Not in time for breakfast, I gather, but perhaps for brunch?"

"Thank you, how nice." Here I was again, standing in the kitchen holding a present without a place to set it down.

"Bran muffins, a package, not from scratch." Flossie eyed the makeshift-kitchen arrangement through the doorway and seemed to try to reconcile it with the notion of brunch. "You do have butter? I never thought."

"Oh, yes. Er—won't you come in?"

Eagerly she followed me into the dining room. "I've never been inside, don't you know. It was already empty when we bought our place, and we didn't come snooping because Harold, my husband, feared the floors would be unsafe. Harold always considered those things. My, my, such a crying shame it was left so long!"

Putting the basket on the table saw, I unwrapped the muffins and placed them on a paper plate. Maybe I could begin to think of the table saw as a butcherblock island. "Of course all this is only temporary while the kitchen is being fixed up."

"Are those water jugs? You don't have any water? But the drilling went on and on—" Flossie turned as pink as the sunrise.

"And on and on. We're awfully sorry about the noise, it must have driven the neighborhood nuts."

"I didn't mean—I meant the frightening expense—don't bother sending back the basket, I'll pick it up some other time—thank you." She tucked the basket securely over her arm. "You did strike water, didn't you? It was mentioned in the store."

"We did, thank goodness. It's just not hooked up, not until the floor is finished and the new plumbing is done, but luckily there's that village spring we'll use for drinking water."

"No, no, no," Flossie said, tweaking the red napkin I'd refolded in the basket, "you can't stand out in the cold filling those jugs, you must stop by my house, I insist. My well can scarcely contain itself. A hundred and fifty feet, fifty gallons a minute."

In the kitchen, Jacob groaned louder than the floorboard he was extracting.

Flossie said, "I agree, perfectly indecent, and we were only using the place as a summer cottage when we had the well drilled, we'd only begun making the change from schoolhouse to real house, it wasn't year-round yet. How Harold did brag at parties about that well! Wasn't it silly of me to use a Christmas napkin, as if a hunter might mistake my basket for a deer?"

"Extremely sensible," I said, raising my voice, trying to catch Jacob's attention again. "I'm surprised some hunter hasn't shot the ceramic cat off the roof of—what did you say their first names were?"

"The Thibodeaus? Theresa and Caca? Naturally I worry more about live pets than ceramic ones, and—"

Work stopped in the kitchen. Jacob leaned around the doorway. "We haven't formally met the Thibodeaus yet, but he waves."

"Theresa's eggs are fresh and reasonable, and I'll put in a word for you if you want a chicken. You'll have dealings soon enough with Caca, he's the road agent—oh, dear me, that's his nickname, don't you know, I gather it stuck since childhood, I haven't the faintest idea what his given name is although I must have seen it on a ballot. Theresa keeps herself to herself, but Caca keeps tabs on all the goings-on. An odd man. He acted as if I didn't exist while my husband was alive and in charge. And I can never tell if he's joking. For instance, when I met him in the store after I got back from a jaunt to Spain last spring, I happened to say what a relief it was to be back where people speak English, and he asked me, 'Where have you been, Connecticut?' Now, how would you take that?"

Jacob said, "Caca is a card."

Abigail barked, and Flossie scuttled to the ell door. "Shame on me, she can sit still only so long. Home we go, Abigail, and mind your manners when you see Sarge. Going past the Lords' hardly ever presents a problem, I'm happy to say, because the Lords keep Charlemagne indoors except for walks. Percy Lord was an ears-nose-and-throat, don't you know, in Boston. Stop by for water, I really do insist."

"Thank you," I said, thinking of my frozen hands in the brook and the woman in the Oxford laundromat mentioning her chilblains. "Perhaps just today, while we're getting organized, but we can't impose."

"I'll be home this morning. This afternoon I'm gallivanting off with the girls to Bridgeford. Shopping and dinner, to chase away the November grays."

I attempted to picture Bridgeford as bright lights and glitter, but it was my hometown. "I'm from Bridgeford, I grew up there."

This confused her. "Did you? And did you, Mr. Wetherbee—Jacob?"

"I'm from Millsted."

"Is that in New Hampshire?"

"Yes, down near Exmouth."

I added, "We've been living in Millsted the past ten years, that's where we've moved from."

"Oh," Flossie said, looking more bewildered. We were natives, yet not quite; we were neither fish nor flesh nor good red herring, we were neither Town nor Gown. She glanced at Jacob's hair and mine. "But you have decided to—retire—in Dinsmere?"

I realized that all at once Jacob had become tongue-tied. Shockingly tongue-tied. He was in agony, literally unable to speak, to say out loud what his work had been and now would be.

In a rush I filled the silence with, "Sort of retired, one more fed-up teacher, what they call 'teacher burn-out,' except Jacob was a high-school librarian, and now he's going to rescue Shelterfield. Thank you again for the water offer, we'll take you up on it just this once, thank you so much for the muffins, so thoughtful, watch out for the damn hunters."

When she left with beribboned Abigail lively at her side, I turned to Jacob.

He asked, "What's the theater term for forgetting your lines?"

"Go dry? Dry up?"

"You didn't have to babble."

" 'I come from haunts of coot and hern.' Your hair! It dawned on me that Flossie Sisson thinks I'm your second wife, your poppet. I've never imagined myself a second wife before. Let's hop in the sack."

Not funny. He muttered, "Retired," and attacked another floorboard.

I began, "But you used to want to be retired," and then I thought: Oh, drop it.

The trapdoor into the ell cellar had been, inexplicably, under the old sink. I had declined Jacob's invitation to climb down the busted ladder after him to investigate. Now the cellar was revealing itself as a slimy rocky pit in which alligators might lurk.

Jacob asked, "Why did Virginia call?"

"She's gone crazy, she wants to come here for Thanksgiving, her Richter scale wouldn't register that we're in chaos. She sounded awfully upset."

"Thanksgiving?" Jacob paused, sledgehammer raised. "We've wiggled out of going to my folks' for Thanksgiving this year because of the work here. Nothing could be as bad as those sessions. What's she upset about?"

"Max, I guess. Domestic crisis? She didn't even say whether or not she was coming all alone or bringing Willie, but I hardly think a ten-year-old would want to be dragged away from his friends during a vacation. How on earth can I make a Thanksgiving dinner here?"

"We'll take her to the Sidelines for a turkey sandwich. 'Over the river and through the wood,' " Jacob sang, the sunny interval in his mood returning as the predicted sunshine began warming the house, " 'to Grandmother's house we'll go,' " and more sledgehammering ensued.

Jacob pounding. Chickadees pounding. I went into the living room and checked the kettle; the icy brook water had warmed to a tepid broth with a few shreds of weeds and twigs afloat like crumbled herbs.

Assembling a muffin break, I thought of the things Jacob's head was full of under his white locks, information I'd always taken for granted and relied upon or not understood at all: Dewey Decimal, Library of Congress, *Sears Guide to Subject Headings, Books in Print, Subject Guide to Books in Print, Booklist, Library Journal, Bartlett's, Acronyms and Initialisms, Who's Who, Who Was Who,* ISBN, card-catalog tracings, the idiosyncrasies of encyclopedia sets, bibliographies, reference books about reference books, Baker and Taylor, Bro-Dart, Demco, spine labels, vertical files, film projectors, cassettes, microphones, amplifiers, the replacement projector lamp code, projection and reverse projection screens, microfilm, microfiche, readers and printers, copying machines, shelf lists, card filing, sorting trays, book repair, Mylar dust-jacket covers, bookends, shelf labels, book carts, drop boxes, circulation pockets and cards, magazine covers, newspaper sticks, and tapes and glues and scissors and erasing knives and electric erasers. Upon entering the Dinsmere library for the first time, he'd instantly picked up the scent and found all the books we wanted without consulting the card catalog.

I said, pouring coffee dregs, "Flossie mentioned being glad there'll be lights on in Shelterfield. It hadn't occurred to me that the neighbors must have felt uneasy about this dark house, dying. Ghosts?"

"I didn't know bran muffins came in a packaged mix."

"Remember how you used to divide the world into people who were good book-returners and those who were bad book-returners? Which kind is Flossie Sisson? Batch sells muffin mixes, Jacob, and haven't you noticed TV commercials? You're spoiled by homemade."

"Ironed handkerchiefs, too." He sat down on the edge of what was left of the floor and picnicked, his legs dangling over the cellar the way the little boys' had over the Oxford lock. "Despite her concern for us, she's self-consumed. Therefore, a bad book-returner. Her butter question reminded me that I don't think I ever thought to tell you how I used to steal butter from the hot-lunch program at my first job. Did I? Have you seen the butter that's stored in school-cafeteria freezers? Looks like the stacks of the surplus stuff they sold at the Base Commissary, remember?"

"One-pound blocks in messy wrappers, thirty-three cents a pound. You stole butter?"

"I hung around the kitchen and made friends with the school cook, and then when everyone's backs were turned

I'd sneak open the freezer and chuck a pound into my briefcase."

"I'm horrified."

"Well, I got so damn sick of seeing them throw whole pounds of it into vats of peas just to use it up, and there I was on my salary eating margarine. Is the dump open today?"

I said absently, "Winter hours, Thursday, nine to two," wondering if he'd shared his butter booty with my Maine predecessors about whom I'd been unable to worm out of him any more information than that one had been the girls' gym coach (!) and another the town librarian.

"I'll load up the trailer," he said. "Have to do at least two dump runs before I'm done with this floor."

"I'll tag along."

"Junkyard junkie."

With many dire warnings about nails, Jacob let me help him lug the floorboards to the trailer. Then we carried empty water jugs to the car and set off, heading away from the village. Hunters again were crossing the field, intent upon turning my doe into venison. We squeezed between their pickups and drove past Mrs. Crandall's gray summer cottage and took a series of hunter-invaded dirt roads up toward the Dinsmere dump.

The final approach was littered with trash; this was the main way in which the Dinsmere dump resembled Millsted's. In Millsted, we used to drive through a gate up a zigzag course around beer cans and automobile tires and bedsprings to reach a scene from hell. For, although Millsted pretended to go along with the state's burning ban, the dump regularly and mysteriously caught on fire. Smelly smoke would roll into the sky, and on the gravel plateau the "accidental" fires burned in the garbage piled at the brink of a cliff. Disturbed momentarily by our arrival, sea gulls would soar up and circle, mewing. Aerosol cans exploded. Choking, eyes streaming, we would fling our own offerings onto the flames, while the sea gulls alighted and walked around digging with their bills into ripped plastic garbage bags. We became acquainted with a one-legged sea gull whose missing leg, we assumed, had been amputated by an aerosol explosion. This sea gull would balance on its one leg and then fly up and come down and balance again, doing a hornpipe without a peg leg.

The Dinsmere dump was a true landfill, its garbage buried beneath the sandy soil, its dunes kept ever-changing by bulldozers. It had a million-dollar view of the mountains enjoyed year-round by Jonathan Ferguson, an old man who lived here with his pet rat. Their winter residence was a tarpaper shack set precariously on a knoll surrounded by a collection of broken chairs, discarded lawnmowers, doorless refrigerators, and scrap metal. In the summer, we had learned when we introduced ourselves to him during our first dump run, they moved to the airy chambers of their vacation home, an old station wagon lacy with rust, where the rat roomed in the upholstery. At any time of year the rat accompanied Jonathan Ferguson whenever he drove the station wagon to the village to seek supplies; the rat was fond of going for rides.

As Jacob did complicated backing-up maneuvers with the trailer, I chided myself for being so distressed about our finances. Jacob could always return to pinching surplus butter. When our money ran out and we couldn't pay our two mortgages, we could throw ourselves on the mercy of the town and perhaps be allowed to live at the dump, neighbors of Jonathan Ferguson. And not only did the Dinsmere dump have its mountains' majesty to offer, but it also had recycling bins that were themselves very beautiful, a joy not experienced at the Millsted dump because Millsted, disdaining such environmental foolishness, refused to recycle.

Jacob ogled those bins as we unloaded the floorboards. Another of his clever-with-his-hands talents was a knack for using palette and brush, but he'd got discouraged after one winter of Sunday painting during which he mostly produced still lifes of Mason jars. The first sight of the recycling bins, however, had made his fingers itch: all the green glass bottles heaped together, the clear bottles sparkling separate, brown bottles glowing, the tin cans' interiors shining, the colorful labels cheerfully prevaricating. We could live here at the dump, I thought, and he would paint recycling pictures and we would hold tailgate showings. The Garbage Gallery! "Hello," I said to Jonathan Ferguson who was trudging over from his shack to see what we had to contribute today.

"Morning," said Jonathan Ferguson. He was so incredibly dirty that I supposed my Spartan wash in the dishpan would seem to him like wallowing in a bubble-bath. "Clearing now."

Jacob said, "Your view is certainly showing off."

Jonathan Ferguson smiled, lacking teeth, filled with pride. "So she is."

I said, "I'm always startled by the clarity of November weather, when most of the leaves are down and you can see what was hidden by foliage. An unexpected pond, a bird's nest."

"So you can."

Jacob said, "A veil lifted? Cataracts removed?"

I said, "Or a return from England, I suppose."

Dismissing as useless our spongy boards, Jonathan Ferguson launched into a listing of his mountains, pointing out each peak. We interrupted his chant to say goodbye, and then we drove down along different roads—more pickups, jeeps, guns carried swaggeringly by red and orange men and boys—into the village to the store.

"Hunters!" I said, getting out of the car. "It's like living in an armed camp."

"If we can survive a few more days the season will be over."

"For this year. What *is* that weird look in their eyes when we drive by? We're wearing red and orange, we could be hunters too, even though we don't have a gun hanging in the rear window. Is it a look of plain hostility? Belligerence? Defensiveness? Self-righteousness, like born-again Christians? All of the above?"

"Bloodthirstiness."

"Not that alone, either. It's beginning to remind me of somebody. But who?"

The post-office section of the store was busy. People, most of them seemingly Gown, nodded to us or said, "Good morning," and continued their conversations, bending to boxes, twisting dials, sorting through their mail and tossing much of it straight into the big waist-high wastebasket. They were talking, I overheard, about Veterans Day, complaining about the confusion between the federal holiday and the state holiday. This was a New Hampshire muddle, for the entire country hadn't yet returned to November eleventh, New Hampshire being at the forefront of the zealous patriotic fight by the American Legion to change back the date.

"Oh, damn," I murmured to Jacob. "We forgot."

"Is today the real Veterans Day, not the make-believe?"

"It must be, the post office is open. The make-believe was last month."

"Mom will be bound to call when Dad isn't within earshot."

"If you've got the floor all up by then, you won't be able to answer."

"You've figured out a doorstep system."

In our mailbox was a large envelope. We were truly Dinsmere residents now! The envelope contained *Supermarket Strategy,* a Consumer Survival Kit booklet I'd sent for so long ago I'd now almost lost even the memory of the impetus and desire for the mail-order purchase, the way I used to forget as a child whenever a once avidly awaited item advertised in a magazine or comic book or on a favorite radio program would finally arrive; somebody else, not me, must have sent for this Straight Arrow ring bejeweled with my locket-size photograph set into a miniature version of the famous gold-vaulted cave.

The Millsted post office had forwarded the booklet, an ordinary procedure but one that felt eerie. I said, "It's for you. I sent for it for you. Half in jest."

"Wow! But I bet I already have learned by myself all its helpful hints, I get out my spectacles and study the unit-pricing—"

"Hi there!" Miriam Holt hurriedly emerged from the store doorway carrying a loaf of, surprisingly, squishy bread. No, not surprising; she had a kid. But the daughter must be in school, for Miriam was alone as she dodged through the chatting and reading post-office crowd, ran across the porch, and jumped into a beat-up oft-repainted Volkswagen. Batch the Dandy apparently hadn't been attracted to her for her taste in clothes, either; instead of her referee's uniform, she was wearing a peculiar assortment of shirt-tails and sweatshirt and sagging skirt, in hues as varied as her Volkswagen's but none of them red although I'd've guessed red would be her color.

Jacob said, "Wasn't that Miriam? My God, she dresses like someone who broke out of prison and grabbed some clothes off a clothesline. What's for lunch, do we need anything in the store?"

"We need water."

As he drove back toward our part of town, I realized I should have taken the wheel, to learn this route. If I'd set out for the mail alone, I might not have found my way home and perhaps I'd have got as lost as I used to on the Base.

At Flossie Sisson's, Abigail greeted us barking, running along on her leash hooked to a traverse wire strung from a window casing to the front-yard maple. Abigail was still wearing her festive bow; Flossie obviously didn't trust hunters not to blast her to bits as she wagged at them in the supposed safety of her posted yard.

"At least," Jacob said, looking at the one-room schoolhouse, "they never had a library in the goddamn place."

"Lucky to have a slate, I guess."

We walked up the front path, carrying cartons of water jugs.

A dillar, a dollar,
A ten o'clock scholar,
What makes you come so soon?
You used to come at ten o'clock,
But now you come at noon.

The frost had melted, leaving blades of lawn brown above the remaining snow. This gussied-up schoolhouse was a more restrained shade of red than hunters' red, and it had a perky white trim that it probably hadn't sported back when it was a working school. Neither had it had the aluminum storm door upon which I knocked, reaching around my carton.

"Abigail!" Flossie scolded. "Quiet! Do come in, I'm so glad you'll partake of my bountiful well. The kitchen is at the back, we made it out of the woodshed, don't you know, the woodshed and the outhouses. Jacob, if you'd like to fill the jugs there—yes, take Isabel's, too—I'll meanwhile show Isabel my little treasures."

"Fine," Jacob said, keeping a straight face as he crossed the room to the kitchen doorway.

I said weakly, "I'm Ib for short." I gazed thunderstruck.

Into the tiny schoolhouse had been crammed the spoils of Poynton.

"Harold, my husband," said Flossie, her chipmunk pouches comfy, "Harold was in plastics. He would always say, 'Plastics are made to be sold, not to be used.' And so he devoted himself to collecting these."

Flossie and I started off with a silver-inlaid piecrust table and continued on through a blur of side chairs with mother-of-pearl marquetry, Chinese vases and lamps and trays, gold leaf here, cloisonné there, a marble bust of Socrates upon a marble pedestal. We finished in the boxed-off bedroom which, more crowded than our Oxford bed-and-breakfast, featured Louis XV furniture. On the dressing table stood a photograph of a tour group seated on camels in front of the Pyramids; I spotted diminutive Flossie Sisson and noted that she was the only one except the guides and the camels who didn't look extremely apprehensive.

As Jacob and I departed, I sang out to her, "Give my regards to Bridgeford," and then in the car I said to Jacob, "I haven't got an ooh or aah left in me."

"It's a wonder she hasn't been murdered in her bed."

"You ought to've seen the bed. What a way to go!"

Driving past the Lords' white farmhouse, rounding a

curve, we encountered a horse and rider approaching. The stout rider was wearing jodhpurs and a formal black jacket but, instead of a black cap, the headgear was a scarlet balaclava out of which an elderly female face smiled benignly at us. The horse wore red ribbons braided into its mane and tail.

I said, "Isn't this Mrs. Lord?" I had seen her at the wheel of her Subaru and walking her toy poodle and interrupting Dr. Lord whose patients now were flowerbeds, a vegetable plot. "Do the Lords have a horse?"

"I've never noticed one," Jacob said, "and how can you not notice a horse?"

"Maybe they just bought it."

"Or borrowed it."

"Like a cup of sugar?"

We waved sedately, and Mrs. Lord saluted us with her riding crop. We had thought we were getting the hang of the Dinsmere wave, done from car to car or car to pedestrian, but from car to equestrian was a first for us. I'd made copying the wave of Allegra Quigley in her real-estate Audi my goal; she waved like Queen Elizabeth, only more so.

Jacob asked, "The hardy older folk, the ones who stay here all winter and don't flee to warmer climes except maybe for a short vacation, is that the way we'll be?"

Wondering if and how Flossie had waved from her camel, I replied, "You told me we have to stay in northern New England because we know it."

"You're assuming we're still living by our wits in our old age."

And, I thought as we drove the gauntlet of hunters' vehicles along the Thibodeaus' property, I'm assuming we're still living together. I said, "Maybe we'll be gaga in Arizona."

Nearing the bend to Shelterfield, I realized I had become adjusted enough to this house as home to feel a thrill of fear that it wouldn't be here. When we'd installed the Jøtul in the Millsted house during the first so-called energy crisis, we had learned that we'd lost an oil bill but gained a new fear, a woodstove worry, a new question mark always in our heads: Driving up the lane, we always wondered if we would find the house burned flat.

Shelterfield stood. Indoors, the brook water was simmering on the back of the Jøtul. While Jacob returned to his noisy work, a discordant contrast to library work, I started making lunch, digging the electric can-opener out of the APPLIANCES carton and placing it on the floor by an outlet, and as I roared open a can of Campbell's Vegetarian Vegetable Soup, I pictured Stella crouching in her living room mixing cake batter. Where was a saucepan—a stirring spoon—Flossie's water? Setting the soup on the Jøtul to heat up, I saw that every meal ahead was going to be a project, every chore a double effort, for a long long time. This was not a roughing-it lark. I searched for bowls and peanut butter and wished I had the guts to call Virginia back and tell her rudely that she simply could not come here. What were best friends for if you couldn't tell them no?

During lunch at the dining-room table in the living room, Jacob watched a hazy *Gong Show* and remarked, "The bust of Socrates did suit the schoolhouse, though it was too fancy," and I remembered that he'd had a plaster-of-Paris bust of Daniel Webster in his Exmouth library.

Washing the lunch dishes seemed to take half the afternoon, what with hauling water from the canning kettle to the dishpan first for scrubbing and then for rinsing, and the result was not a dish-detergent commercial with squeaky-clean surfaces you could see your reflection in. At the brook, I refilled the kettle; I didn't serenade the brook with a poem and I didn't meet a deer. I thought of my built-in dishwasher sitting unused in the yellow house.

Then I set to work on the heap of cordwood. I'm not good at this sort of job, but stubbornness can balance impatience, and we'd long ago agreed that I should do most of the coolie labor because I was incapable of doing the more complicated chores which Jacob understood. So I threw wood down the bulkhead, managing to miss and not dent the freezer, and when the bulkhead stairwell was full I went indoors by the back door and toted the portable radio down the main cellar's stairway. Opera, I'd learned, was best for stacking wood, and I found one on the radio and let it surge over me as I carried armloads of wood from the foot of the bulkhead stairs to a nearby wall and started building the woodpile. Back and forth, back and forth, back and forth. Eventually I reached a logjam on the stairwell and had to lean in and grab a key log and leap away as the heap unlocked and tumbled free. For a clumsy person, I was agile enough to avoid crushed toes. Above the open bulkhead doors came the sound of a blue jay shrieking along with a soprano.

In England, I recalled, the first time I'd ever heard a cuckoo I had been hanging up a handwash in the backyard, and I had assumed it was a clock at the manor house until I began counting; it cuckooed to twelve and kept right on, like military time.

This bulkhead load stacked, I turned off the radio and went up the bulkhead stairs to start throwing down another.

"Good afternoon!"

A toy poodle wearing a red jacket, straining on a red leash, came prancing around the corner of the house, Dr. Lord on the other end of the leash, Mrs. Lord following.

Mrs. Lord said, "We knocked and we peeked in the window but your husband was in the cellar and we didn't catch his attention."

"*In* the cellar?" I asked. "He hadn't fallen in?"

Dr. Lord said, "The floor is gone, but he was fine. He seemed to be contemplating things. Charlemagne, sit!"

"Goodness," Mrs. Lord said, "we've seen you so often, driving past, that it seems we've already met, but introductions are in order. I'm Hannah Lord, this is Percy, and we live in the white house near the schoolhouse. As you saw this morning, we have a recent addition to our household—"

Up close, the Lords reminded me of the Hinghams in England, our pub friends for whose sake we had respectably tied the knot. Rosy, looking fresh from afternoon naps, Percy Lord was softly round and Hannah was solidly stalwart. They were not, of course, working-class; I thought of how the Hinghams had agonized over their decision to stop coming to the Flintknappers on their weekday evening in order to save money toward a used car for Peter and Susan, their son and daughter-in-law. We hadn't received a Christmas card from the Hinghams in two years. Mrs. Hingham was the one who had always sent us the cards, so this cessation must mean she had died, but how could I write Mr. Hingham with such a ghoulish inquiry? What delight Mrs. Hingham had taken in Christmas! Over her glass of gin-and-lime, in her gray coat, she would tell us of the Christmas clubs she belonged to at the village supermarket and greengrocer's, where she saved up all year for the Hinghams' Christmas feast.

"—moving into a retirement home," Hannah was saying, "and knowing my love for horses, they asked me if I would like to take Gay Blade."

Percy snorted happily. "Retirement home! I warned them, I told them you'll have drinks at four-thirty and dinner at five! Barbarous! But when did your brother ever listen to me?"

I suddenly saw Dinsmere's Gown population dining at eight on Stouffer's Chicken à la King.

"Thus providing," Hannah continued, "a retirement home here in Dinsmere for Gay Blade. Well, what could I say? If I didn't take him, I could never look *All Creatures Great and Small* in the eye again, could I? And it's not as though we didn't already have a barn full of stalls standing empty."

"The glue factory!" said Percy. "The knacker's!"

"And it's also not as though we go away during the winter and would have to board him, unlike Flossie Sisson who has a very restless foot, Isabel, and puts poor sweet Abigail in a *kennel* whenever she goes dashing off to the Costa Brava or to Anchorage, Alaska."

Percy was now dreamily gazing at the beaver pond. He recited, " 'One white foot, try him; two white feet, buy him; three white feet and a white nose, rip off his skin and throw him to the crows!' "

"Hush, Percy," Hannah said. "You know you'll love the manure for your gardens next spring. So, Isabel, I got my riding togs out of mothballs. The red ribbon in Gay Blade's tail, by the way, is protection against hunters, it isn't a warning that he kicks. Gay Blade is gentle. Do you ride?"

"Not since I fell off as a kid. I admire horses from afar."

"You should have got right back on, weren't you taught that rule? Oh, is your phone ringing?"

I said, "Excuse me."

Percy said, "Charlemagne, stay!"

I raced around the house to the ell door, and Jacob shouted, scrambling up an aluminum ladder from the cellar, "Look out, the floor is gone!"

"I can see that. It's probably your mother, do I answer?"

"I'll go out the main door."

On the threshold, I reached across emptiness and snatched the receiver.

Edna said, "We was over to your place this morning and I looked at your dead tomato vines and I thought of that damn bugger who stole my tomatoes again last summer, and I can't make up my mind what to do next summer, do I give up? I been going through some things, Ib, and in a shoebox I found Jacob's kindergarten report card, it's so cute, are you sure you can't come here for Thanksgiving? He got VS—that's Very Satisfactory, the highest mark—in Originality and in Correct Use of Paste, Scissors, Crayons, and let's see, in Politeness, Ability to Express Ideas, Identify Things to Be Done, and Care of Toys. But he only got FS—Fairly Satisfactory, the lowest mark—in Plays Harmoniously with a Group, I don't know, he and Louise, they didn't have no fights, not to speak of, and he was just wonderful with Timmy—"

The Lords were walking back toward the road, Charlemagne yapping, his pompoms quivering. Jacob had clambered out of the cellar onto the dining-room threshold and run through the living room, out the front door, and as he tore across the front lawn he shot the Lords a surprised glance and greeting and then he took the phone, took over.

Joining the Lords, I asked, "Mrs. Sisson goes to Alaska in the *winter?*"

"She did one year," Hannah replied. "A restless foot,

indeed! She's talking about Japan now, so if you want a kimono, put in your order. Charlemagne, hush! We'll be on our way, we just wanted to offer you the use of our phone if yours hadn't been installed yet. It didn't occur to us that we should instead be offering a kitchen floor. You do have cooking facilities elsewhere in the house?"

Percy said, "Sills, I suppose. Nothing worse than punky sills."

"The sills aren't too bad," I said, "but the floor joists were rotten. Yes, we're managing quite well, thank you."

Hannah said, "If we can be of any help—"

"Judas Priest!" Percy said. "It's starting to snow! We're in for a very long winter."

The weather was our fault, I thought; Jacob and I were to blame for a hard winter ahead because we had moved in November into a decaying skeleton of a house, just asking for trouble. I said, "Thanks so much for stopping by, I'm sorry Jacob's been too busy to get a chance to meet you properly."

Hannah said, "There'll be plenty of time. Come along, Percy. Come along, Charlemagne. The sun is setting, and the eyesight of hunters is notoriously bad in broad daylight, to say nothing of dusk."

Led by Charlemagne, they started walking back. Jacob, sitting on the granite doorstep, gave them another version of the Dinsmere wave, a doorstep wave, and kept listening to Edna.

No more wood-throwing or wood-stacking today. I closed the bulkhead doors. Time to start the supper project. I went through the back door into the makeshift kitchen, but then, just as Jacob hung up, while I was searching out two civilized china plates for supper, more company arrived, this time in a royal-blue pickup.

It was Caca Thibodeau, a short dark paunchy man probably about sixty, wearing olive-green workclothes. He talked at the top of his lungs; ignoring me, he hollered at Jacob in the ell dooryard, "Thought I'd let you have a chance to get settled before I dropped in—and by God, I'd've really dropped in if I wasn't looking where I was going, wouldn't

I! All the years I've lived next-door, I never knew there was a cellar under this ell. How's about a beer? If you ain't got any I got some in the truck."

Jacob offered, "We're out of beer but we have Scotch. Sherry? Chablis?"

"Never touch the stuff." Caca went to the pickup, hoisted a six-pack of Schlitz from its bed, came into the house via the main door, and halted at the sight of the Jøtul. Obviously acquainted only with woodstoves of the potbellied or Franklin ilk, he slowly inspected this green enamel creature in the wary manner of the blind men examining the elephant.

Then, not commenting, he continued into the ell and walked, facing frontwards, without using his hands, down the ladder into the ell cellar, where he looked around and said, "I would've sworn there was just a crawl-space. Learn something new every day, don't you. Planning on doing some replumbing down here?"

Jacob explained, "It's a crawl-space except under the kitchen." Giving me a sheepish glance, he proceeded to descend the ladder the same way. A beer party commenced in the alligator pit.

I poured myself a pre-prandial and postponed supper. Upstairs, I reorganized our scattered books, transforming the cartons, on their sides, into bookcases along the walls. Stacking wood, stacking books. Then I unpacked the camp photograph of little Jacob and hung it on a nail. By the bare overhead light-bulb, sipping Chablis, I studied that puzzled but determined expression on his six-year-old face.

When I went back downstairs I found Caca and Jacob in the living room, Caca holding his depleted six-pack and telling Jacob all about culverts. "Water," he expounded. "Water is a road agent's main job. If you take care of the water, the roads will take care of themselves."

I interrupted timidly, "Did I understand from Mrs. Sisson that you sell eggs? I've noticed your saw-sharpening sign but not an eggs sign. Could we buy maybe a half-dozen a week?"

How strange to be invisible. Caca stared straight through me and said, "That's the wife's department, you'll have to stop in and see her about that. But it looks to me, Jake, like you'll be needing some saws sharpened, so just leave them off at my barn."

I said, testing, "Have I got this right? You can rip with a crosscut saw but you can't cross with a ripsaw?"

Sure enough, Caca headed for the door, his subject now frost heaves.

After escorting Caca to his pickup, Jacob returned and said, "Mom kept harping about Thanksgiving, and I kept saying we haven't time for it, we're fighting the elements. She's been in the attic, going through things."

"She read me your kindergarten report card. Had she gone to the cemetery?"

"Yes. And she polished the MGA."

"How's your father?"

"Who knows. Caca, I learned, was in the Army Corps of Engineers during the War. The Second World War. Then he came back here and worked construction."

"Uh—I suppose Caca inquired what you do?"

"I told him I don't do anything."

As I washed lettuce with Flossie's water, as I started the baked beans and hot dogs heating on the Jøtul, I thought about how, back when Veterans Day was Armistice Day, I in my childhood had collected First World War poems, copying them into a notebook anthology, shedding an enjoyable tear now and then. Rupert Brooke. Siegfried Sassoon. Alan Seeger having his rendezvous with Death. Imagine, I had found "In Flanders Field" exquisitely romantic!

Heeding Caca's comment about dropping in, Jacob drove nails into the ell's front-door casing and into the dining-room entry to the ell and strung warning ropes as barricades. Of course he then had to bow like a maitre d' whenever he opened with a flourish the dining-room's rope before disappearing into the cellar.

I said, "This just occurred to me. What if the toilet hadn't broken down? How did you plan to have us get across that pit to the bathroom after the floor was torn up?"

"I was going to give you a choice of walking across planks or using the outhouse."

"Walking the plank?"

Late into the night Jacob worked in the cellar, sweeping the rocky walls, shoveling debris into boxes, drawing plumbing diagrams on my clipboard. He hummed; he even whistled. And as I did my chores, I marveled at the mystery of his skills but mostly I held my breath. He wasn't sitting in his wing chair, wearing a hole in the rug. He wasn't sucking a Tums.

Easy as apple pie.

Jacob installed new joists on metal hangers, and slowly the cellar pit was covered as he laid a plywood subfloor; and lo and behold the trapper at last came to set his traps for the beavers—death underwater, struggling, drowning, what would Cleveland Amory say?—and new firm floorboards began to march across the subfloor, while occasionally Miriam Holt ran in and out of the makeshift kitchen, sometimes wearing her escaped-prisoner outfits and sometimes her referee's uniform, pausing only to call, "Hi there!" and drop off a Sidelines doggie-bag; and finally the combination storm windows were delivered but because Jacob had his hands full with the floor and putting them on was certainly beyond my coolie capabilities the rampaging cold wind known in the north country with affectionate respect as the Montreal Express continued howling through the house.

How cold was it? It was so cold that we wore long underwear every day and every night instead of, as in the past, just for outdoor play. It was so cold and I got so accustomed to this layer that when we did have one day mild enough to risk leaving them off, I found myself out in the two-holer automatically reaching to pull up, after my underpants, my Duofold. We wore two pairs each of wool socks during the day and one each to bed, and up in my garret at the typewriter I was so fat with sweater layers I could hardly bend my arms to touch the keys with stiff hands in knit gloves whose fingertips I'd cut off.

Now that Jacob had begun working again, I resumed the household errands. My stint upstairs done, I would go to the village for mail and bread and milk and spring water; I would read the store's wall of notices and bring Jacob news of a rummage sale, free kittens, a chimney sweep. I browsed in the library and discovered that *Gourmet* magazine was taken out more often than *Time*. I went to the laundromat in Meader Intervale, and while my wash, which mainly seemed to consist of long underwear, was sloshing away in one of the chipped machines, I learned the layout and prices of the supermarket in the mini-mall. Small is beautiful, but of course it can be more expensive, and the groceries here cost more, as they did in the village store, than those in the vast Exmouth Mall supermarket; although it was Jacob's job now to watch over our budget, paying at the check-out made me tremble with sick worry.

Eggs I bought from Theresa Thibodeau. After the first purchase, I wished I hadn't started this tradition, but she was a neighbor and I didn't know how not to return a second time. Flossie Sisson hadn't warned me about carnage. The first visit, I had unsuspectingly climbed the Thibodeaus' porch steps past aged Sarge, who only flopped his tail at me, and when my knock was answered with an uninflected "Come in," I had stepped into a scrubbed old kitchen and had seen a sinkful of plucked chickens standing on where their heads used to be, all their yellow legs sticking straight up. Somehow I hadn't passed out; somehow I hadn't puked all over Theresa's worn but highly waxed linoleum. The second visit, I gathered all my courage, reminding myself of how I'd got used to the High Street butcher shop, and when I entered I tried to look only at Theresa's tired closed face which contrasted with the determinedly titian hair above her small body which was mostly bosom. But out of the corner of my eye I couldn't help glimpsing an awkward hunk of bloody carcass on a cutting board. The Welcome-Wagon doe? What would it be next week? Sarge? Exchanging with her my empty egg box and fifty cents for the egg box she took off the aqua-oilcloth tabletop, I said, "Still colder than Greenland." "Yes," she replied in her flat tone. I fled with my half-dozen, remembering how the village supermarket in Clopton had splurged on paper bags for, of all things, eggs; the clerk would count out my half-dozen into a little white paper bag which I'd balance on top of my straw shopping bag during the walk home, hoping to get to the laundry cottage without scrambling.

Jacob's beard was lengthening from stubble to an itchy white crewcut.

When he wasn't working, he mostly seemed to be contemplating things, as Percy Lord had put it. Standing in the kitchen, hammer in one hand, drinking coffee so slowly that it cooled to a bitter puddle, with the black-and-white television on the floor tuned low to a *Password* or the radio murmuring symphonies, he would study his work. He did this outdoors, too. Once as he stood too near the bird-feeder, an exasperated chickadee alighted on the T-square he was holding.

In the evenings we huddled around the warmth of the Jøtul and the color TV. Jacob's tendency had always been to read and watch at the same time, usually combining diverse subjects; years ago, when I had come across him reading *Atlantic* while watching *Hee-Haw,* I made some wisecrack and he explained, "It kind of takes the edge off each." Now, during programs like *Masterpiece Theatre* he was apt to be reading *The Do-It-Yourself Plumbing Handbook* and *Easi-Bild Simplifies Electrical Repairs.*

The trapper returned. I stayed away from windows while he checked the traps. He reported to Jacob that he'd caught five. Later that afternoon I made myself go out to the pond, tramping through the petrified forest. Had the beavers, as I'd read other animals caught in traps sometimes did, tried to chew their legs free? In the pond's ice-skimmed surface a few brown leaves lay as if suspended in jellied consommé, and around me dried goldenrod and crumpled ferns were shades of beige, the setting sun a-glitter on the glossy brook. The situation had reversed itself. Shelterfield was occupied; the beaver lodge was empty.

And then Jacob got the floor finished, and I cautiously jumped up and down on it beneath the quaint low ceiling. He reassembled the oil range, brooding over wicks. Kerosene was delivered, and while it was being pumped into the oil barrel behind the ell I thought of the Pink Man in Clopton and compared his fascinating bus full of wares with this dull oil truck. Later that afternoon Jacob's reeking attempts at lighting the burners drove me gasping out of the house, but when I ventured back I discovered he'd been successful.

At last we had heat in the ell!

Sidling up to the range, getting acquainted, I put a teakettle of spring water on a front burner. It boiled. Becoming braver, I made an omelet for supper. By the time the next day Jacob got the electric stove moved into the kitchen from the dining room and hooked up, I was merrily busy at the range, smoothly sliding pots and pans from hottest burner to coolest, I was in love with this squat black nickel-plated New Leader.

I exclaimed, "I'll use the range all winter, except for broiling and the things its oven won't get hot enough for. Think of the electricity we'll save!"

Jacob said, "Think of the price of kerosene."

"You can't win. But look, I'm heating the dinnerplates on the warming shelf. Now, isn't that a gracious-living touch?"

When Caca brought Jacob's sharpened saws, he inspected the way the range was installed and leveled, grudgingly admitted Jacob had done this correctly, and thundered at him, "You better keep an eye out for the census taker! One of them stopped at a farmer's I know and asked if his place was a ranch, and the farmer told the fellow, 'Sure it is, there's a range in the kitchen!' "

The Fish and Game man arrived in his official car, as tickled as a kid with a new cap pistol (or as I was with my range), although he attempted to maintain an air of great solemnity while he told Jacob about the prowess necessary to blow up a beaver dam. After placing the dynamite he retreated to his car, no longer trying to conceal his delight.

Jacob and I watched from the back door. There was a sound like a sonic boom, and then a spray of black earth flew as high as the treetops. Impressed, we hurried outdoors to congratulate the Fish and Game man who said proudly, "I used four sticks of forty percent nitrogen, buried deep."

Next, the toilet. Jacob, I noticed, was developing a new habit: thinking out loud. The toilet monologue I kept overhearing went something like this: "Nothing goes down, okay, it's probably clogged up, all that sediment, I'll check the soil pipe. Better go to the Intervale and buy a soil-pipe snake even though the hardware store will want at least twenty bucks for one." Returning from the hardware store with a contraption that resembled a tricycle wheel, he yanked up the new trapdoor, descended the new ladder, and as I was musing on the term "soil-pipe snake," I heard him begin to use it, the noise teaching me that a soil-pipe snake was a rattlesnake. He reappeared and continued mumbling, "Well, if snaking out the system didn't work, what else could be wrong? Better rip the toilet out, take it outdoors, flush it with the hose, where the hell is the hose?"

I looked at the white toilet sitting in the backyard on the snow and asked, "Instead of Mason jars and recycling bins, why don't you paint this?"

"I'm about ready to dynamite the fucking thing."

One night in our pub, I suddenly recalled, when I'd complained about our ancient toilet chain, the Hinghams told us they had an outdoor toilet behind their old flint house, but it was a flush. They didn't have a bathroom, however, so they had used all those years a tin tub in the kitchen; they informed us helpfully, "You can get one at the ironmonger's, but it'll probably cost you two pound nowadays."

Back in the bathroom, the toilet still wouldn't flush. Jacob phoned the Intervale plumber who'd declined to climb down our collapsing well; he came over and concluded, mystified, "Pitch of the soil pipe's okay. It just don't make sense."

That evening, Jacob didn't join me in the living room. Sitting beside the range, he rocked in the Boston rocker and stared through the jagged bathroom doorway at the toilet.

Finally I went into the kitchen and announced, "Bedtime. For me, anyway."

"Eureka!" He leaped to his feet. "That dry ice they used, remember?"

" 'Pressurize the veins'?"

"It must have blown the well water full of bubbles—hold on, my very elementary physics are coming back to me—the water doesn't weigh enough to flush!"

If this, I thought, were a movie about the life of a famous inventer, we would now join hands and dance ring-around-a-rosy with joy. Instead, I hugged him.

And the next day Jacob phoned Dexter, our well-company contractor, who, apparently taken aback, said he'd never heard of dry ice's causing this problem. That day and the following day, Jacob drained the pressurized water out of the well, letting the outdoor faucet run and creating a gully down the backyard like a miniature Grand Canyon. While this was going on, he unpacked the new stainless steel kitchen sink, set it onto a frame braced under the crooked window, and hooked it up.

Then he said, acting casual, "The system is drained. When the well has recovered, we'll try a flush. You do the honors."

"No, you. You had the brainstorm."

Oh, the awful suspense of that flush.

"Hooray!" I shouted. "By God, we may not have a bathroom or even an entire bathroom wall, we may not have drinking water or hot water or a shower, but we've got a kitchen floor and an oil range and a kitchen sink with cold running water—and we've got a toilet! What luxury! Your new career is launched!"

I was in the dining room, changing the drop-leaf table into a makeshift pantry because the dishpan was no longer needed here, when Jacob emerged through the trapdoor opening to wash up for his coffee break.

"Funny," I said. "I've been thinking about my tendency to panic when I'm cooking. I've been trying to figure out why the oil range makes me more serene than any electric or gas stove I've ever used."

Jacob came to the dining-room doorway. "I don't know how to tell you but we've run out of water."

It was the Saturday before Thanksgiving, before Virginia's arrival.

Jacob had been working in the trench he'd dug in the crawl-space under the bathroom. An hour or so ago I'd climbed down the trapdoor ladder into the alligator pit to view the project and had found him flat on his back in that claustrophobic furrow, hooking up plumbing for the bathtub, and I'd immediately been reminded of our excursion to the Grime's Graves flintmines outside Clopton. One misty day we'd driven from our forest out through another plantation of conifers where in the midst of the trees there was a picnic area, open boots of parked cars held picnic baskets, steam rose from teakettles, and families ate. Driving on past this damp domestic scene, we came to a strange chalky landscape, its trees sparse. At the Grime's Graves information booth we bought a pamphlet from an old man, paid the admission, and read of neolithic man who'd mined this earth. Nobody else was visiting the site. The empty land seemed a great thick crust over the shafts and galleries whose entrances looked like craters. The largest craters had been capped with cement. Jacob took a flashlight from my glove compartment—an alcove in the dashboard, the compartment was so embarrassingly neat, the flashlight lying beside the frost-scraper beside the Royal Automobile Club handbook under the block of Base gas ration coupons, that it didn't resemble a glove compartment at all—and we walked across to the brink of an expanse of cement. In a round hatch a ladder descended into darkness. Jacob switched on the flashlight and started down, and telling myself that with Jacob I could feel free to chicken-out instead of feeling I must put up a false front of courage, I followed. Thirty feet, that's how deep this shaft was according to the pamphlet, and my hands were sweaty and I could get no real grip on the metal ladder; I would fall to my death in an ancient flintmine. Jacob said, "The next one's ground," and I stepped off the last rung. We were in a bowl of chalk. Jacob shone the flashlight over chalk floor, chalk walls, a terribly cramped space, and when the flashlight beam sank into the chalk I saw the tunnel entrances to galleries that radiated out from the shaft like spokes. I had not expected the holes to be so small. Goose-bumps suddenly tingled the back of my neck. Jacob asked, "You all right?" and crouched and crawled into the nearest tunnel. Before I could change my mind, I again followed. The smell of chalk was suffocating. The tunnel tightened around us as we crept forward on our hands and knees, and I couldn't see anything, not even the flashlight beam. I gulped, "Jacob." Men had worked here by the light of chalk cups filled with grease, their tools the antlers of red deer. Lying prone right here, they'd extracted flint for axes with which to chop down the now replanted forest. "Jacob!" I repeated, grabbing the heel of his sneaker ahead of me. He said, "Okay." There wasn't room to turn around, so we had to back out. In the chalk bowl, rejoicing at standing straight again, I swarmed up the ladder and lighted a soggy cigarette. The mist had become rain. We walked around from crater to crater across this barren land, the only sound the rain rattling on our plastic jackets.

In the cellar, looking at Jacob buried alive in the crawl-space trench, I had said, "I don't know why you don't go stark raving mad, neolithic man." Now, looking at him in the doorway, I said, "You can fix it, you can fix anything." He was covered with dirt, cobwebs, and probably mouse-shit.

"Sure," he said.

"What happened? You turned on the kitchen faucet and no water came out? Could it be the work you're doing in the crawl-space?"

"Nope."

On the makeshift-pantry table, I lined up a Grape-Nuts box beside Uncle Ben's Brown Rice. "The toilet—if we've no water, the toilet won't flush? The outhouse again?"

"Yes."

I added a box of Prince Egg Noodles (Broad, #95) and lined it also up carefully. Then I reached for my jacket. "I'm not running away, I'm going to the village for mail." I went out to the car and returned. "I don't know how to tell you but the car won't start."

"Jesus fucking Christ."

While he worked on the car, I did a chore I'd assumed we'd put behind us, going to the brook for washing water. At lunch, he thought out loud about fuel pumps, and in the afternoon he managed to fix the car. He began a monologue about another pump, the well pump. I threw cordwood savagely and stacked it.

The next day, I came down from my office and found him sitting in the rocker with his clipboard diagrams, watching one of the Sunday-morning programs on which a panel of reporters supposedly grills a politician. We called these shows, collectively, *Lying Time,* borrowing from a country song about crying time. Jacob sputtered at the screen, "Listen to that goddamn liar, that bland two-faced—what's the matter?"

"My typewriter broke down."

We looked at each other. The television talked suave gibberish.

Jacob asked, "Do you want to say the hell with this? We could give up and go back to the Millsted house until spring. Things are easier to handle in warm weather."

"Nothing is ever easy."

"Or you could go there and I'll keep on working here."

"And send for me when you've earned the passage money? Got the sod house built? The crops planted?"

"Creature comforts, Ib. I can turn the water back on in the Millsted house. You could take showers to your heart's content."

"For a person with dry skin, I take too many showers anyway."

He heaved himself out of the rocker. "I'll see if I can fix the typewriter."

He couldn't, and the next day when I went out to cart

it off to the office-supplies store in Bridgeford, the car again wouldn't start. I returned to the house, where Jacob was talking on the phone to Dexter of the Bridgeford Well Company; after that conversation ended, Jacob went outdoors and dived under the car's hood, came indoors, consulted the yellow pages, and phoned a garage in the Intervale. Dexter arrived and paced around the backyard, dotting the snow with filtertips. I dug my old Olivetti out of my typewriter junkyard. When Dexter left and Jacob came into the kitchen, I forced myself to go downstairs and ask, "What's the verdict?"

"He's pretty sure the pump is okay, but it isn't pumping water. The well has gone dry."

"Oh, God. My worst fear."

"Got to drill a new well."

"Are you insane, Jacob Wetherbee, we can't afford another well!"

"It's on the house, so to speak. Dexter has to get us water. His reputation. Thank God we haven't yet paid him or he might not be so honorable."

"But the noise! All that *noise* again! The neighbors!"

"Here's the wrecker from the garage, sooner than I expected."

Le Car was towed off, dangling pathetically.

I asked, "And what's the verdict about the car? How long will we be stranded?"

"Can't say. Do you want to phone Dorothy and ask to borrow her car?"

"She needs it for her job. Your mother's?"

The MGA. Eyes blank, Jacob said, "I'd rather not."

My brain was being engorged with blood. I was going to explode like the dam.

Jacob went into the dining room to the pantry table. "We got any Tums?"

"How the hell should I know, you're the one who buys them. I wish we could jog. Why can't this town appropriate enough sand so we could do some running on that icy road, work off some steam, without slipping and breaking our necks? Bastards, the same as Millsted!"

"Caca is hoarding his sand for the long winter."

"So we're trapped until spring? Let's go for a walk at least, let's get out of here."

"I've got to start on the storm windows. You go."

I changed to my heaviest grippiest boots, in which I had to walk like Frankenstein, and as I strode down the treacherous road past the closed summer cottage, I thought of how I'd exulted the other day about luxuries. I remembered the luxury of two cars, two racing-green MG Midgets that had sat in our Clopton Park dooryard side by side, their opposite steering wheels sometimes close together or, depending on how we'd happened to park, sometimes a touch-me-not distance apart, as if they'd had a spat.

Nowadays what we possessed two of was houses. Two mortgages.

Then I realized that I was thinking how, for all Gary Bates's faults, he had made up his mind what he wanted to do, and evidently still satisfied by his work if not his lovelife, he had stuck to it, to his making those bowls and vases, platters, flowerpots, mugs, pitchers, those clickety-clackety pottery earrings.

And I suddenly wanted to go someplace warm and sleep on a beach for days. Looking up from the road's rippled ice, I saw that above the mountains there were long white clouds lying like ocean liners on the blue sky.

Since such a vacation was impossible, I could instead just keep walking forever, keep stomping along. I would imitate Little Horace; I would escape from the zoo.

But Little Horace had been caught, hadn't he, and eventually I turned back toward Shelterfield, recalling a newspaper article about a fiftieth-wedding-anniversary party. When the wife was asked how her marriage had been over those many years, she'd replied, "Well, the sun didn't shine all the time."

One night recently, as Jacob and I were clambering into bed, pulling up the bedclothes, snuggling, I had commented, "Going to sleep together is so trusting," and he'd said, "No, it isn't, it's so atavistic, a throwback, huddling together against the darkness." Falling asleep, I had wondered about my impatience with people who emphasized love over work. Could I, alone, without Jacob, make even a stab at a truce with nonsense?

The immediate nonsense, I saw as I rounded a bend, was Batch's big station wagon approaching, driven not by Batch but by Jacob. I hastened toward it as fast as my monster gait allowed.

"Jacob?"

He motioned for me to get in. "Batch just dropped by and I stole his car to come find you. I thought you and he could visit and I'd go into the village and pick up the mail and water plus more supplies for the duration, but what do we need?"

"Will the car be back by Thanksgiving?"

"Probably not."

"I've decided I've *got* to get rude and phone Virginia and tell her about the well and the car, tell her not to come."

"She would arrive on four wheels. She'd be transportation."

"I couldn't stand it, Jacob, company and no water."

We came to a branch in the road, and laboriously Jacob turned the station wagon around. As we started back, I took scrap-paper and a ballpoint out of my jacket pocket.

Jacobs said, "There are those fresh turkeys at the store you mentioned."

I had been amazed to realize that I'd never cooked a fresh turkey. "Are you hinting you want a holiday meal?"

"Never mind."

But I was scribbling "Ocean Spray Cranberry Sauce, Whole Berry." Thanksgiving at Shelterfield might augur well for Jacob's new career. And it would be our first Thanksgiving by ourselves since we returned from England where our holidays had been private and fun; there wouldn't be the strain of his parents' presence. Trying not to think about scrubbing a crusty roasting pan in heated brook-water, I said, "A challenge! I'll cook the turkey in our wonderful range."

"I sort of thought you'd like that."

We reached our house. I gave him the list of supplies and jumped out of the station wagon and ran indoors. There was a pizza box on the table saw.

Batch, wearing another three-piece suit, gray flannel, stood warming his hands at the range and watching the noon news on the kitchen TV. "I've been out to view your blasted dam, sorry I missed the event!" As he bent down to peck my cheek, he added, "They just had a newsflash about trouble at some airport somewhere, and an authority announced on camera it was because 'the structural integrity of the pavement is impaired.' Took me three beats to realize he meant that the goddamn runway isn't safe. I told Jacob that you two have got to come stay at my apartment until you have water again, you know I'm hardly ever there."

Batch's Concord condominium. "Thank you, but we'll hang on here."

"Stubborn duo, aren't you. Don't throw a fit, I'm not hoping for lunch, have to make up time. Oh, I brought you a mushroom pizza from that Godforsaken restaurant of Miriam's, she said you could heat it back up but I told her that cold pizza is one of your peculiarities." Batch bounced on the new floor. "Jacob must be working like a bat out of hell."

"Thank you." I put the pizza box in the refrigerator and took out a half-gallon of Chablis. "If the Sidelines has pizza again, I gather the mystery of the missing mozzarella is solved? Miriam has been awfully thoughtful, she understood that cooking here was difficult until the range was hooked up, but she hardly ever said anything, she would run in with her goodies and dash off. Who was that masked woman?"

This startled Batch. "She brought food a lot? I wonder how come the boss is so generous to her." Then he said, "Has Dorothy heard yet about drilling another well? You realize she'll offer you your old bedroom, and turkey that's left over from last year, and maybe even a bath."

"Unlike Jacob's folks, Dorothy doesn't have to be browbeaten to take no for an answer." I poured wine into the two good glasses I'd unpacked and thought of shaving my legs in a bath, in a shower, instead of in the dishpan.

Sipping, Batch wandered into the dining room and gazed upon his Speedy Sadie gift assortment arranged on the pantry table. The happy flame in his triangular eyes had died.

I said awkwardly, "If my memory is right, this will be your first Thanksgiving since the separation."

"I guess I've joined your club of holiday-haters. I took Melissa and Davy to one of my best restaurants last weekend. Typical, of course. Davy whined for McDonald's, and Melissa conned me into buying her a gold chain in the gift shop."

Unlacing my boots, fetching my moccasins from the bedroom, I considered this, more than he'd ever volunteered yet about the situation.

Batch roamed on into the living room to study our little island of order surrounded by cartons. He asked, "What's that sampler of Dorothy's say about duty?"

"Dorothy has many samplers on the subject of duty."

"Duty and beauty."

"Oh, that one." Surprised, I recited:

> Straight is the line of Duty.
> Curved is the line of Beauty.

Batch said, "I hear the car, I'll be on my way. Are you sure you won't change your mind, Ibby? I understand why Jacob wants to be here during the drilling, but do you? I can drive you down to my place right now, I'm heading through Concord."

I'd been thinking how I would even like to hitch a ride with him along his route of restaurants in order to stay at motels with their mock-sterile bathrooms, their silly little soapcakes, *showers!* However, as we returned to the ell, I said, "No. Thank you again, though. If the second well doesn't produce any water, I may then take you up on it. Or commit suicide."

"Jesus, you two! What next? The chimney will fall down?"

"Bite your tongue." I handed him his leather car coat.

But it wasn't Jacob who'd pulled into the driveway. Allegra Quigley leaned out her Audi window and exclaimed, looking like a winter chocolate-box cover girl in her fur-trimmed snow-white hood, "I met Jacob at the store! How incredible, back to square one with the well, but hopefully the second well will come in at a hundred feet! Hello, Mr. Pierce. Have you changed your mind about houses in general and Dinsmere houses in particular? If so, here's my card."

Instantly perking up, Batch leaped off the granite doorstep and accepted the card with a flourish. "Do you deal in businesses too?"

"Of course! My motto is: Everything is for sale, and I can sell everything!"

Jacob arrived then, parking the station wagon along the road, and he and I lugged into the house the filled water jugs and a carton on whose side Mr. Dobbins had added up the price of the groceries it contained (including, I noticed, Tums), while Batch leaned against Allegra's car and Allegra continued to lean out her window and I began to wonder if the jargon of real estate could serve as the language of courtship.

Jacob said to me, "Did Batch offer you his place? I got the turkey anyway, figuring what your answer would be, but if you've had enough of this mess go down there with him or go to your folks'. Thanksgiving here is ridiculous."

I put the turkey in the refrigerator. "Oh, shut up, you ass."

Allegra departed with a wave. Batch returned to the kitchen to say, "If you want to take Miriam to work and pick her up, I'm sure she wouldn't mind lending you her hunk of junk."

I said, "Maybe in an emergency. Why were you inquiring about a business? You once remarked that a business tied a person down."

"I'm forty-two now," Batch replied, "and who knows? After all these years I might be getting ready to hang up my steel-belted radials."

When he'd left, and the cold-pizza lunch and my chores were over and Jacob was back outdoors installing storm windows, I forced myself to set aside etiquette and phone Virginia, who'd just got home from her dance classes. But I could not make her register me on her Richter scale.

"Don't worry," she said. "You always fret so. Camping out is exactly the breath of fresh air I need. And you and Jacob need a car. See you day after tomorrow!"

Virginia's calmness had often irritated me. Now, I was so furious I shook wildly as I hung up the receiver. How could I entertain a guest here? How could I cope under these circumstances, I whose house always had to be immaculate perfection when company was expected, whose guest towels had always hung ready with fringes precise? This was too much to bear! Just washing my hair in the dishpan with a Pyrex measuring cup was too much, too much!

Carrying the canning kettle out to the brook for the supper-dishes water, I looked at the way the pond was draining, becoming a brook again and leaving behind upright dead trees whose peeled trunks felt to my touch like bone.

And then I was boohooing, bawling my head off, while the bird noises around me played counterpoint to the zipping spurts of Jacob's electric drill busy at the front of the house.

"Okay," I sobbed, searching my pockets for Kleenex and finding only scrap-paper. If he could keep going, keep on crawling through this Grime's Graves tunnel, so could I. No chickening-out. Crimson hands cold in the brook, I filled the kettle.

Hoping I didn't sound astonished, I said, "Thanks, but if I ever tried one of those I'd be back to chainsmoking Kents in two seconds flat."

"That's erroneous," said Virginia, toking up. "What a lovely village, like an American version of an Agatha

Christie village. Little Chippendale-Under-Glass." She rolled down her window.

Poor Virginia! After her long trip, here she was back again in her buttercup Honda, but with me driving. Upon arrival, she had complimented Jacob's beard, presented him with a bottle of wine and me with a dozen #1 Ticonderoga pencils, and then I had rushed her through the tour of the house, a tour that was in its way new to me too, because I'd been working so madly through yesterday and this morning, attempting to make Shelterfield more civilized (such as extra lime down the outhouse), that I hadn't until the tour stood back to see the result. The old farmhouse looked as though summer people had packed up to leave but, foolhardy, had changed their minds, decided to stay, to remodel the ell, and, partly unpacked, were braving the winter.

We had been accompanied during the tour by the constant keening of the artesian rig. Finally I'd said, "That's it, that's the house. Would you mind if I borrowed your car? I'm going crazy cooped up listening to the drilling, and I need to get the mail and water."

Virginia had reached for her blue down jacket. "I'll come with you. I concentrated on the directions so much I didn't see the sights."

Gray-eyed Virginia was still a blonde, as she had been when I met her in kindergarten. She maintained a subtle shade that reminded me of our pale yellow house, and she ignored changing styles, keeping her straight Alice-in-Wonderland hair very long; she used to call her hair her fifth limb and choreograph it. Today it was piled into one of those cloudy topknots she'd never been able to teach me to manage, and she was wearing faded Levi's and a black leotard which had a rip in one armpit.

So at the village spring I'd filled the water jugs, and then I'd picked up the mail, bought more groceries, introduced Virginia to Mr. Dobbins, learned that he didn't carry whole nutmegs, and now we were on the Indy, heading toward the General Store where Mr. Dobbins had a notion I might be able to find some—"I'll bet you," he'd added, "they even got those grating gadgets, but I guess you must already have one?"

I said to Virginia as we sped along, "An example of my stupid logic. When I used up the last nutmeg in Millsted I didn't buy a replacement because it'd be one more thing to pack."

"Max wants me to sleep with a friend of his."

Jesus God in heaven, don't tell me something like that at fifty-five miles an hour on a lake-road's twists and turns!

"With his friend," Virginia said, "and himself, together."

After a considerable pause, during which I thought of that airport's jargon, "structural integrity is impaired," and applied it to marriage, I asked, "Is this a new form of counseling in the guidance world?"

"Max is called a curriculum coordinator."

"Yes."

"Stanley, his friend, runs a Peer Instruction program in some school system out in western Mass. They—"

"Peer Instruction?"

"I don't know. I think it's supposed to teach kids to teach each other."

"Oh." This sounded similar to what had gone on, untitled, in one-room schoolhouses like Flossie Sisson's.

"He and Max met at a convention this fall and got talking. Stanley was just divorced and feeling low, so Max invited him to come visit us, change of scenery, that sort of thing, home-cooked meals made by my fair hands. And so Stanley has stayed with us a few weekends. We've all gone into Boston together, Cambridge, walked around, tried to get some history into Willie by osmosis. And Max and Stanley play chess."

Because we hated turnpike-driving, Jacob and I had only once visited Virginia and Max in Massachusetts, four years ago, and instead of thinking of her as dwelling in their white Victorian house in a town that had become another Boston bedroom, I had a tendency to place her back in her grubby old New York loft apartment with its freight elevator and its dizzy sleeping platforms. I'd always been sad that she'd given up her performing ambitions—the swift progression of her sun through the heavens—to move to suburbia with a guidance counselor and take a job teaching dance. Yet, as one of Dorothy's samplers commented, the heart has its reasons which reason knows nothing of. Or had Virginia, under the guise of romance, just plain opted for the easy way out? But that was a question you couldn't ask even a best friend.

"You mentioned logic," Virginia was saying. "I cannot argue with men. Their pile-driver self-righteous logic always stops me cold. I knew if I kept having to listen to Max's list of reasons why these kinky high jinks would be healthy for our marriage besides being great fun—you see, I *had* to get out of there as soon as my job allowed. If I'm away all vacation, if he's not talking about it, maybe he'll come to his senses."

I pulled into the parking lot of the General Store and looked at her.

Eyes brimming silver, she said, "What's the word I want? Cherish? He can't cherish me anymore, Ib, can he, if such an idea entered his head?"

"And to think he came right out and asked you!" I was trying to remember Max exactly. A child's drawing of a man, a father, security. Max even wore a hat, I recalled, but it was an alpine hat, with a little feather, not a fedora. "He seems such a nice kind man."

"Well-meaning," Virginia said. "People consider him a well-meaning man. Concerned with students' schedules. What would you do if it were Jacob asking you?"

"He wouldn't. And anyway, he doesn't have any real friends. Except me."

"Don't sidestep, and don't be too sure he wouldn't. The way Max approached it, I thought he was going to suggest we go ahead and buy a snow-thrower, for Christ's sake! I've been wanting us to get one now that we're pushing forty and heart-attack age, it'd be simpler than fighting with Willie over doing the shoveling. A snow-thrower!" She dashed the tears from her eyes and unbuckled her seatbelt. "Do I smell too much of the forbidden weed? My, my, a very charming store."

The dim low-ceilinged General Store had done what Mr. Dobbins had balked at, gone rustic for the summer folk; it immediately reminded me of the Milkpail Parlor, a coy little restaurant in Bridgeford I'd worked at part of one high-school summer, where we waitresses wore discreet milkmaid frocks instead of uniforms, all the ice-cream flavors were prefixed "Old-Fashioned," and there was a player piano instead of a jukebox. The player piano played "I'll Be Happy" a lot, but this did not describe my mood. The slavedriver owner of the restaurant was too miserly to hire enough waitresses to handle the business, and night after night I found myself working alone with only the useless short-order cook, a college kid who spent his time lounging around trying to impress me with his fraternity tales while I busted my ass waiting on the tables and concocting the sundaes and frappes the customers ordered. One night, the restaurant empty at last, as I was getting ready to close, doing the straightening-up and cleanup, scrubbing the soda fountain bright with soda water, there came the final straw: A party of eight men and women entered, pushed together two white ice-cream-parlor tables, sat down in the white ice-cream-parlor chairs, and ordered eight Old-Fashioned Banana Splits. The short-order cook laughed at my plight. I kicked him in the shins, amazing myself more than him. I made those eight banana splits, and after the customers left I straightened the tables and chairs and cleaned the fountain again, but what did I do the next day? I phoned the owner and quit. By God, I had done a Jacob, way back then! Yet that next day I'd also gone out and found another waitressing job.

Like the Milkpail Parlor, the General Store was decorated with brown reproductions of posters and handbills advertising everything from Lydia Pinkham's elixirs to stove polish, tobacco, sarsaparilla. Virginia and I searched the crowded shelves and finally, after penny candy and sunbonnets, lavender soap and hand-dipped candles, maple syrup and bolts of calico, we came to the herbs and spices, and I bought from the ex-hippy owner a horribly expensive jar of nutmegs while Virginia continued on past duck decoys, a cracker barrel, bouquets of wooden kitchen utensils, a pickle barrel, and returned with a Lake Winnipesaukee T-shirt.

"For Willie," she said. As we were leaving, she looked back at the store and remarked, "The good old days. I'd've probably died in childbirth. But would a husband in those days have wanted to share his property?"

The Honda darted onto the Indy. Driving, I dithered, "I'll have to tell Mr. Dobbins he was right about nutmeg graters. Is Willie interested in stamp-collecting or skateboards or what? I don't know how you do it, coping with a kid. I still haven't recovered from having Melissa stay with us one week back when she was—about Willie's age, ten? The shock of waking up each morning and realizing there was a third person in the house." Oops, that's what you get for babbling; I had just reminded Virginia she was a third person, an outsider if best friend, in our house. "I mean, we're simply not used to a *kid*—"

"Think of the shock of a third person in your bed."

I fell silent.

She said, "Willie is bewildered by my going away during Thanksgiving, but Max has been explaining at great length how sometimes mothers have to have vacations alone. A well-meaning man."

"Mmm," I said, hoping she would not repeat again any phrase that included a well, artesian or otherwise.

"If only the vacation could be longer. And—don't take this personally—if only it could be much farther away. From Max. I keep thinking about those three weeks in England before I met him. Twelve years ago, unbelievable! Remember Anne Hathaway's cottage with the outdoors Ladies' and Gents' they don't show in pictures? Remember how we walked to Buckingham Palace and stood outside the fence and for the first time in our lives we felt as if we were a class? Remember how I got sick on all the food and drink at the Elizabethan Room? On wine and mead and pheasant."

"And syllabub. The floor strewn with rushes. Madrigals."

"And," said Virginia, "the hangovers the next day at the Tate."

We drove past the Thibodeaus', where the driveway was full of cars apparently belonging to offspring returning to their harvest home and Sarge was in a tizzy with grandchildren. We neared Shelterfield.

I said, "Thanks for the use of the car. I didn't expect Jacob to buy a frozen pumpkin pie, we've never had one before. I figure I can jazz it up with some nutmeg—"

"Ib, I know you tell Jacob everything. Could this be an exception?"

"But Jacob is a man. Whenever I have to consult him about some peculiar male behavior that I don't understand, I call him my penis-in-residence. Maybe he could give us an idea of why Max—"

"Please?"

"Okay."

"Nutmeg. Just think, for four days I won't be hearing Max call me Ginger."

The drilling rig still sat like a huge science-fiction grasshopper in our yard, yet the crew and their trucks were gone. Jacob was in the bathroom working on plumbing.

"For the washing machine?" I asked. "Does this mean we've struck water? Easy as pumpkin pie?"

"It doesn't," he said tensely, rubbing a shoulder. "I've got to keep going anyway, haven't I? They've reached two hundred and fifty feet. Nothing."

"Are they taking tomorrow off?"

"Tomorrow and right through the weekend. They'll be back Monday."

I screamed, "Not until *Monday?* That goddamn Dexter! Doesn't he have any feelings, how can he leave us like this?"

Virginia said, "Give me a lesson in hauling water."

A very odd holiday. I had only made informal turkey dinners for two before, but now I was struggling to assemble a traditional Thanksgiving feast in a kitchen which looked as though a bomb had hit it. All of Shelterfield, for that matter, began to seem like a farmhouse in a war-torn countryside, or a Red Cross field hospital or M.A.S.H. unit catering to the variously wounded, the walking and talking wounded.

First there was Virginia, unusually loquacious, a chatty traveler down Memory Lane who never mentioned her husband again. "Remember," she would ask, sitting cross-legged on the dining room's old pine floor or the kitchen's new pine floor, balancing an ashtray on a knee, her spine extremely straight, "remember the little printing press you had back in our grammar-school days? On a card table in your bedroom, the type arranged in egg cartons? Remember how you had to rewrite your poems when we printed them because we always ran out of *e*'s?" To this one I replied, seeking sage in a carton, "And we did the programs for the dance recitals you gave in your garage." "I've kept those programs," she said, "those programs and all my scrapbooks, from my *Nutcracker* debut and tap, right through Martha Graham. Up in my attic."

Then there was the arrival, once again unannounced, of Batch, who tried to talk Jacob into going with him to the Sidelines to watch Thanksgiving football on its enormous screen. "Oh, come on, Jacob," he said, "you can't spend Thanksgiving in a crawl-space when you could be yelling for a touchdown!" Jacob snapped, "Sorry." Virginia said, "Ib, remember how in junior high we'd go to the varsity games and try to keep track of Batch's number?" and I told Batch, tacitly apologizing for Jacob's brusqueness, "You're present at a historic event! For once I've got enough food on hand to offer unexpected company! Let me lay an extra place." But Batch, after hesitation and a glass of sherry, declined and left, looking confused, at loose ends. Wondering if Nicole might be giving thanks that he wasn't around, I checked the turkey roasting in the range. A fresh turkey, I had learned, did seem much more fresh from the chopping block than a frozen bird in its plastic shroud; while I was stuffing it I'd had to fight to blank out the image of Theresa Thibodeau's sinkful of headless chickens, thinking instead of how one night in the Flintknappers I'd asked Mrs. Hingham if she draped her Christmas turkey with a necklace of sausages, as I'd seen pictures of in English women's magazines, and she'd replied, "No, I don't like the taste of sausages with turkey," and Mr. Hingham had remarked, "The sausages would get cold, wouldn't they, while everyone concentrated on the turkey," and she'd told him, "Bert, *some* people take only a slice of white and a slice of dark and maybe two sausages, they don't dig in the way you do!" On the High Street at Christmastime, the butcher shop was festooned with birds whose heads were feathery but whose bodies were bald.

Dorothy phoned that evening and complained, "I tried to call Batch to wish him happy Thanksgiving but all I got was his answering service. It was almost as bad as his birthday, when I had to wish a happy birthday to my son's answering service! Do you know where he is? Dare I hope he's with Nicole?" Dorothy managed to catch my attention as usual, diverting me from Virginia's frantic signals not to let slip she was visiting, and I found myself thinking of Allegra Quigley and speculating, "He stopped by here, but perhaps Miriam wasn't expecting him; he seemed to want Jacob as an excuse to go to her restaurant." Dorothy said, "I plan to try to talk your father into dropping in for a drink there sometime." I said, "Dorothy, don't!"

Come Saturday, who should appear in our driveway but the Wetherbee contingent in the Wetherbee Dodge, Phil and Edna with a back seat of Louise and Arthur and Jacob's niece Cindy's two toddling daughters, all out for a supposedly aimless drive. The sight of the children made Virginia exclaim, "I'd forgotten Jacob is a great-uncle," an observation that did nothing to alleviate Jacob's enraged reaction to the family reunion. Phil's bearing as he re-examined the house clearly implied that he still thought Jacob was out of his mind. But Edna ignored Shelterfield during this visit. She noticed only Jacob's beard and even that came in at least third to our absence from their Thanksgiving dinner and her recent purchase of new driving gloves (she'd begun creating a wardrobe for antique car shows); while she unpacked a CARE package of Thanksgiving pie samples she'd brought to keep Jacob from wasting away to nothing, she admired her gloves and whispered to me, "Don't Louise look dreadful? She's working too hard at them damn alterations, I almost couldn't get her and Arthur to go for an outing." Behind me Jacob muttered, "Outing, shmouting." I agreed, "Louise does seem tired, Edna." Glancing at Louise, reminded of Theresa Thibodeau although Louise was tall, thin, and sandy, I suddenly did a double take at Arthur, mousy old Arthur, drab old Arthur, boring old Arthur, and I realized that his eyes were those I'd been reminded of by the look in hunters' eyes. I had always supposed what bothered me about him was his Adam's apple. Just one of those slow men with a quick wife, that's the way I'd considered him even after his snowmobile adventure.

When Virginia was leaving Sunday afternoon, I myself reminded me of someone.

"I'll write," Virginia said in her Honda, while Jacob and I stood in the driveway, Jacob trying to hide his impatience, disliking farewells as much as I.

I said, "You know you won't write. But best of luck with the snow-thrower."

"I will write," she said. "When I get back, everything will be a fresh start, after all this fresh air and fresh turkey. Goodbye, goodbye!"

We waved as she drove off, and Jacob said to me, "I'm going to work on hooking up the washbasin now, is there anything on TV to fill my void? Any Sunday-afternoon terrible movies?"

"I think there's a good one, a Darren McGavin."

Darren McGavin was his favorite actor, and Jacob went indoors and hastily located the movie on the kitchen TV. "Have they bought a snow-thrower? If we could afford one, I suppose we should, although living next-door to the road agent means our driveway ought to get plowed faster than in Millsted. Did you find out why Virginia insisted on visiting?"

The urge to tell him, under shaky control these past days,

nearly overpowered me. Nothing could be real until shared with Jacob. "Oh," I said, "marital blahs, that's all."

"Are you okay? Go collapse with a book."

"I wish I could soak in a tub. No running water, and it seems as if I did nothing but wash dishes throughout the holiday."

The wrong comment to make to a Jacob who was getting more and more sensitive about the situation. He snarled, "Sorry the conditions are so primitive."

"What the hell," I said lightly. "It was a pilgrim Thanksgiving. A pioneer Thanksgiving."

This eased him, and in unison we added, "Complete with a fresh-killed turkey," and then I went on into the living room and checked the Jøtul, feeling like Edna keeping secrets from Phil, whispering conspiratorially behind his back. Were Virginia and I in cahoots?

"Good Christ," I said when I stepped outdoors Monday morning. "Jacob, come here!"

The stink was like that from a pulp mill, a burnt-cabbage stench which fiercely stung my eyes and made me gag. Yet I wasn't looking at a river-valley town whose mills pumped brown smoke over tiers of wooden houses on the hillsides; I was looking at a white winter scene, a light snow falling, a brook below a forest.

Jacob joined me. "Virginia spoke too soon about fresh air."

"Pollution! But where's it coming from?"

"Could be from anywhere, I guess, depending on the atmosphere and winds. Pollution drifting through the weekend into pristine Dinsmere."

"We've already got acid rain—acid snow—here. There's no escape."

But soon after the well crew arrived, so did our car, repaired, and I escaped at least the drilling noise, driving the Indy through Meader Intervale to Bridgeford, to my hometown pollution of ruined lakeshore and a downtown with a split personality because its urban renewal had abruptly ended when the money ran out, leaving a disorienting combination of dowdy old Main Street stores and the hideous homogeneity of the new mall. The snowfall, weakening, died.

Thinking about how childhoods were disfigured by progress, I tried to negotiate the one-way streets that kept banging their heads against the mall's promenade. At last I reached the office-supplies store, but I couldn't find a parking space near it, for although one of the benefits of the new downtown was supposed to have been an abundance of parking spaces, the parking problem was worse than ever. Finally I did find a space, and I lugged the ton of typewriter several furlongs to the office-supplies store, gave it into the care of the repairman, wished it a speedy recovery, and then I went on to the hardware store next-door where my distress about the downtown was lost in fascination as I learned about hammer holsters. It seemed there were many sorts, from simple to elaborate, from all-leather to leather with metal rings. After examining them and being tempted by frills, I chose the plainest. Jacob was a purist.

While I fought my way out of the urban destroyal, debating the pros and cons of stopping at Dorothy and Sebastian's, I made a detour past Virginia's house in which I had so often heard Virginia's mother's tale about the emergency larder that had kept them fed during a layoff at the textile mill. Since those days, Mr. Lyford had become management, but the Lyfords had stayed on in this house because Mrs. Lyford couldn't bear to abandon the flowerbeds she'd nurtured, overcoming city soil, dogs, cats, schoolchildren. Around the brown-shingled mill-house there was an English garden, now in hibernation. "Watch me," Virginia would say, twirling among rosebushes, "I'm dancing 'The Waltz of the Flowers.' "

Was taking a shower worth facing more memories?

I approached my folks' house by a side-street slanting upward, so I could get the angle that made it look like a sketch of an eccentric townhouse in *The New Yorker*. Mansard roof sloping down to narrow shoulders; dainty iron balconies here and there for no good reason; gray second-floor clapboards and maroon first-floor clapboards all seeming to blend into brownstone. Built with my grandfather's legal fees, it had been inherited by Dorothy when Batch and I were, respectively, fifteen and ten. My grandfather was a quiet shadowy man who had lived only six months after Dolly had died of a heart attack as unexpected as it was characteristically decisive, and six more months the house had stood empty except for a feeling of dumbfounded grief until Dorothy recovered and Sebastian decided they were able to afford the upkeep.

Sebastian's CPA office occupied part of the front of the house. I drove around to the backyard of snowy hedges and a closed-for-winter granite fountain.

Hoisting my shoulderbag off the passenger seat, I got out of the car, knocked on the back door, and went into the kitchen, where Thimble, Dorothy's latest Siamese, was lying on the open oven door near the pilot light, warming himself, and Dorothy was doing her double-chin exercises in the mirror beside the coat-hooks. My entry startled her; could she be going deaf? Mid-exercise, she jerked her tongue up at her nose too quickly and almost choked.

Then, recovering, she hugged me and began her brown-wren twitter. "Ib, what a wonderful surprise, is everything all right—oh, my God, you haven't left Jacob, have you?"

"Huh?" As always, the moment I came into this house I started reading. Alphabets, numbers, verses. Dorothy even hung her samplers in the kitchen, glass protecting them, and over the deacon's bench there was one in particular that was guaranteed to take your appetite away:

When I am dead and worms me eat,
Here you shall see my name complete.

"Goodness," Dorothy said, "I shouldn't have asked, it popped out, but ever since Batch—I never know what to expect—"

"I'm not carrying a suitcase, see? Yet I just happen to have a change of underwear and a razor in my pocketbook. I'll *pay* you for a shower."

"Don't be ridiculous, of course you may take a shower here whenever you want, I've never denied you a shower, I don't know why you and Batch delight in teasing me about hot water."

"You're rewriting history. Thanks. I remember where the towels are."

When I passed my room upstairs and glanced into it, now a guest room for summer visitors, I concluded that I must have conquered my filth phobia if I was wishing I'd skipped this visit, avoided these ghosts of a little printing press and poems without *e*'s. In the shower, however, I changed my mind. For cleanliness I would confront any spectral shade!

Downstairs, Dorothy had started a pot of coffee, had rousted Sebastian out of his office, and was rummaging in the crammed refrigerator, a sight that made me quail.

"Well, well," Sebastian said, kissing me somewhere past my ear. "To what do we owe this unexpected pleasure?"

"Don't say 'well,' " I implored, warming myself at the floor register over which I used to stand before bedtime to let the heat inflate my nightgown like a hot-air balloon, my version of Thimble's pilot light. "Please don't say 'well' to me. I'm here because my typewriter broke down and I brought it to the Bridgeford store to be repaired."

From Sebastian, Batch had inherited his jack-o'-lantern eyes but not his build or manner. Sebastian was slight, rumpled, muted; yet as he stood near the cupboard on the side of which hung the plaster-of-Paris cast of my right hand I'd made in kindergarten, he glanced from the tiny white hand to grown-up me and back with a baffled look reminiscent of the way Batch sometimes stared in amazement at Kate and Melissa. "Your typewriter? Nothing too serious, I hope?"

"I don't know," I said, warily watching Dorothy select what seemed to be a leftover turnover. "It just wheezed and stopped, but don't worry, I have a couple of manuals.

Dorothy, thank you, I'm really not hungry and I've got to get back."

"That brother of yours!" Suddenly forgetting food, Dorothy slammed the refrigerator door on the teeming shelves. "I called Nicole this morning to see how she'd weathered Thanksgiving, and she told me she and a friend, Pris Patterson's daughter, are planning to open a thrift shop. See what your brother has driven her to? Other people's castoffs!"

"But," I said, "isn't Batch still paying all the bills? She doesn't need the money, does she? Maybe she wants the work. What about her courses, though? Wasn't the last one a course in making stained glass—or was it jewelry?"

Sebastian poured himself some coffee. "I thought it was the Civil War."

"No, no," Dorothy said, "her latest course is called 'Facing Life's Challenges.' See what he's driven her to?"

Sebastian said soothingly, "The immediate problem would seem to be finding a way to inquire about Ib and Jacob's water supply without mentioning the painful subject directly."

I put on my jacket. "They'd just started drilling again when I left. How's the zoo?"

"This afternoon," Dorothy said, straightening my folded-down hood, "I'm babysitting primates."

"You are? Sounds like my job at the dormitory!"

"Some vandals broke in yesterday after we were closed and threw all the smaller turtles into the monkey cage. Pris discovered the break-in this morning when she opened up, and she phoned me after she phoned the police. The poor monkeys were still distraught—and they were still playing catch with the turtles and they didn't want to relinquish their new toys but Pris charged right into the cage to the rescue."

I asked, "Was she risking life and limb again because she has to give another pep talk to the Chamber of Commerce? How did the turtles react?"

"Pris says the monkeys are furious, they want their turtles back, and I'm to try to restore order. I suppose it's difficult, of course, to tell any subtle details of how the turtles reacted, Pris didn't mention that. Is your hair dry enough to go outdoors? Promise you'll call if you strike water. Collect."

"Thank you for the shower."

Driving out of Bridgeford along the rimy lakeshore, I dawdled, not wanting to arrive home to more bad news about the well, and I thought of Nicole's thrift-shop plans, wondering if she would take things on consignment. If she did, what could we sell to earn some pin money? Old clothes? Living mainly in Levi's and overalls, I'd already given away most of my dresses and skirts to nieces. Aha! Jacob's suits, his schoolclothes! Getting rid of those would prove absolutely his commitment to his new career.

Schoolclothes. I was considering his neckties when I drove under the footbridge (CLEARANCE 15 FT. said its sign) that linked the Echo Cove Cottages to a beach, I was selling his overcoats and dress shoes, when, surprised, I saw ahead a bright new sign: GARY BATES, POTTER. No whimsical names for Gary's studio; just his own name and his occupation, loud and clear, in lake-blue letters on white. So he'd recently changed locations, had he? From his renovated ice-cream-stand studio near the Lollipop Village farther down the lake, the studio in which I'd discovered him in the arms of another, he had moved to this handsome old boathouse stretching its dark-green length out over the partially frozen lake, a boathouse I'd always admired. It used to belong to a big cottage across the road, but the cottage had burned last summer, leaving only the boathouse to remind the passerby of days when cabin cruisers were built like good furniture and, packed with picnic hampers, carried their comfortable owners and merry guests out to islands as yet uninhabited.

Was it buying the hammer holster for a Christmas present that now suggested this little shopping spree? Was it my mentioning Nicole's jewelry course and recalling she'd also taken pottery? Did I really hate returning to Shelterfield so intensely I'd find any excuse for postponement? Did the devil make me do it?

I pulled into the boathouse dooryard and parked beside a red Volkswagen Rabbit whose GB vanity license plates struck me the same way as the GB travel-abroad stickers some people in Great Britain put on their cars, whether or not they actually did travel abroad. The Volkswagen must be Gary's latest car; I was the only customer.

Before I opened my car door, I couldn't help giving myself a once-over in the rearview mirror. At least I felt cleaner than I had in almost a month, no matter how I looked. The Unwashed would not have stopped at this studio.

"Hi," I said as I entered talking fast. "My mother-in-law has had her ears pierced, so I'm in the market for some earrings for Christmas, do you still make them?"

He was in the midst of unpacking his wares; I could not escape from cartons and crates.

"Jesus, Ib!" At a display table, he nearly dropped the tureen he was unwrapping. If he hadn't done a nimble quarterback maneuver and caught it, my reappearance in his life would have been accompanied by the same sound effects as my departure twelve years ago, smashed shards flying. Quicksilver, a lean man now thickening, his hair still dark but receding, Gary hadn't really aged. Alas, I was unable to make the gleeful discovery that he'd let himself go, that those two ex-wives and X number of children and their alimony and child-support payments had worn him to a frazzle.

While he set the tureen down and stared, I surveyed the interior of the studio, trying to look nonchalant and politely curious. The boathouse had been, as had the ice-cream stand, remodeled into two rooms, this showroom of new shelves and stark tables, and, beyond, the workshop with its wheel and kiln. In macramé hangers, his flowerpots dripped ivy. There were the smells of sawdust, paint, clay, and there was a feeling of walking on water.

I said, "So you put a floor down across the boat-slip. We've been coping with a floor too, our kitchen floor had to be replaced. Oh—a picture window for the lake view, very wise, that'll transfix the tourists."

Regaining his composure, Gary started laughing. He was one of the few men I'd ever known who laughed out loud a lot, delighted laughter, not he-man, and he was fully aware of how infectious it could be.

So hilarity reigned briefly in the boathouse, contrasting with our last words when he'd come to my apartment and banged on my locked door, attempting an explanation and apology clumsy with clichés that dug him in deeper and deeper: "I'm sorry, it's over, I've told her it's over, all my cheating is over, it didn't mean anything, let me come in and talk!" I hadn't wanted him to learn from my voice how much I'd been crying, but finally I spoke: "Go fuck yourself—and anybody else you want, but never me again." Whatever my tone was, it made him cease and desist. He left, and after a terrible night I moved out of that apartment in which I would be susceptible not only to any further pleas from him but also to memories of his presence. I went home, where, to her everlasting credit, Dorothy strangled herself with discretion. Three years of loving Gary were finished and done. As I told Virginia when I could dare to try phoning her New York apartment without bursting into sobs, "You might say the affair petered out. Unfortunately, that's only correct in one sense, Gary enthusiastically poking the other woman on the floor of his workshop, all covered with clay dust. The truth is, things didn't taper off—oh, Christ, another pun! Was I the last to know? The ending felt like getting killed by a falling sky." Virginia said, "When's your summer vacation from that office, how much money have you got? You always wanted to go to England. Let's beg, borrow, and steal enough money and go!"

Out the new picture window, the thin ice led to open water as blue and cold as the mountains above. Beyond that mountain range was Jacob, listening to an artesian rig, stubbornly working on plumbing that might never be put to use if the drilling proved a failure.

"Sure," Gary said, "I'm still doing earrings, but the question is, where are they packed? Though why am I asking you, you couldn't ever find anything."

Suddenly speechless, wishing I'd stepped on the gas instead of the brakes, I began searching the cartons, reading labels. Gary too had used a Magic Marker, but because he was an artisan his lettering was far more decorative than my scribble. And then I realized that his handwriting resembled Jacob's.

He asked, "Your folks okay? You're not in Bridgeford to visit sick relatives? I used to see Batch once in a while downtown and Nicole took one of my courses a year or so ago, but didn't I hear they're divorced and he's living in Manchester?"

"Separated. In Concord."

"And didn't I hear you married a guy from Exmouth and are living down there?"

"Millsted. A town that's bypassed, you've probably never driven through. Only we're not living there anymore, we've just moved up to Dinsmere."

"You have? Where's he teaching—didn't I hear he's a teacher?"

"A librarian, a high-school librarian. Only he isn't anymore, he's working on fixing up our house, a wreck of a farmhouse."

"He's *retired?*"

Because Gary was now obviously trying to fit a Sugar Daddy into his image of a librarian, I explained, "No, he quit. He's forty and ready for a change. What do you mean I can't find anything, this label says EARRINGS plain as day. Perhaps sometime I'll find the bureau finials we lost in our move. May I go shopping through this carton? I'm sure you haven't added anything cutesy like antique cars, but an old MGA is my mother-in-law's hobby—I know, a flower. She wants a bud vase in the car but it's not suitable—"

"I suppose you've heard of my trips to the altar."

I looked up from the carton at him. His turn to affect nonchalance. Hands in Levi's hip pockets, he was gazing out the picture window at the lake. I thought: I have actually slept with this man. Slept sexually and slept huddled against the night.

"Yes," I said, deciding to try frankness and objectivity.

"I'm amazed you made the second trip. You're not the marrying kind."

"Guess what? I am."

"You are?"

He laughed. "I started late, but I seem to have got into the habit. I'm about to make a third trip, next month."

Thanking my lucky stars for the late start that saved me from becoming his first wife, I began spreading out cotton-swathed earrings on a display table, and seeking conversational refuge in a topic Jacob and I occasionally discussed, I remarked, "Sometimes I can understand why women still get married nowadays but I can't understand at all why men do, except to have a slave and is that worth it?" And as I said this, I remembered with a shocked chill one of Jacob's replies: To a wife-beater, it probably is.

Gary said, "What does Winnipesaukee mean? Tourists ask and I always forget."

Idiotic suspicion; Gary had never threatened, had never even kidded about hitting me. I replied, "It means 'Beautiful Water in a High Place.' "

"That's nice, isn't it. Here I am at last now, working right over it. I should be able to remember the meaning."

"Write it down," I said, the way Jacob would say, Look it up.

But Gary wasn't one for either writing things down or looking them up. He turned from the window and came over to me. "See, I'm still doing the daisy earrings. How about tulips? I've read your books, by the way. And you know I don't read fiction."

"Thank you for reading them. But did you *buy* them?"

He laughed. "Got me there."

Together we reached into the carton and lifted out the cotton bundles. It still seemed extraordinary that his hands could do such fragile work, geometric and abstract designs, beads, petals, enameled pistils and stamens. The boathouse fell quiet.

If this were summer, the beautiful water would be lapping under the floorboards, providing romantic music in case

Gary was still limber enough for passion on his workshop floor, the kiln an indulgent chaperon.

I said, "Do you have lilies of the valley?"

"Afraid not. Sorry."

"That's okay." Timmy's favorite flower might be appropriate for a bud vase but, on second thought, not for Edna herself. "Here, rosebuds, perfect." Virginia dancing in her mother's garden; Virginia saying after school one day, "I shouldn't tell you because you'll hate me for telling you, but Gary made a pass at me during lunch. I know you're not going steady, but he can't be trusted, Ib."

Gary asked, "Do you still make French bread?"

"What? Yes, I started bread-baking again when we came back from England." Was that how he remembered me, as a baker of French bread? "Don't bother hunting up your packaging stuff. And don't get for-old-times'-sake about the price. How much?"

"If you say so. You may regret it. Twenty dollars, please."

Good God. "Ah, inflation," I said, taking out my wallet and searching for the emergency twenty-dollar bill hidden away in its pocket larder.

He accepted the twenty and I wondered if earrings could be classified as an emergency; the boathouse began creaking in a gust of wind; heaven help me, we were kissing so frenziedly it was a wonder we didn't steam up the picture window the way we had the windows of his parked car! Old times' sake? He used to call the kind of blouse you don't tuck in an "easy-access blouse," but that was twelve and more years ago, and now his hand sliding up the front of my untucked-in chambray shirt could not be allowed access, it was an invasion, an attempted Norman Conquest, and Gary was on the brink of marrying again so that made *me* at this moment the other woman—or one of his bevy of other women! Feeling more disoriented than I had downtown, I pushed the scoundrel away.

"Well," he said, smiling.

I smoothed mussed hair, wrinkled jacket. "Don't mention wells. Do you want all the other earrings put back in the carton or left unpacked?"

"Unpacked." He watched me fumble the rosebud earrings into their cotton. He said, "Have a happy Chester Greenwood Day next month. I'll be off in Bermuda on my honeymoon or I'd invite you out to dinner to celebrate it."

He actually remembered that we used to celebrate the birth, on December twenty-first, of Chester Greenwood of Farmington, Maine, the man who had invented earmuffs!

Earrings; earmuffs. I was so confused I came right out and asked, "I gather your first two wives were summer people, but is number three from Bridgeford, anyone I'd know?"

Resembling the cat who'd gulped down the canary, he replied, "You might know her mother, Barbara Rouleau, she was in the class ahead of us," and waited for me to do math.

"Christ, a child-bride!"

Much laughter from Gary.

I headed for the door.

He said, "I'll be open until December fifteenth and I'll reopen after New Year's. Stop by anytime. Maybe your mother-in-law might like a new set of dinnerware?"

As I stepped outdoors, I began praying that the car would start, would not have broken down again. Gary followed me out into the cold air which should be polluted but instead was clear and as bracing as a basin and ewer bath. Looking amused, he watched me start the car, nervously stall, start again. I did think to give him my Allegra Quigley wave as I drove off.

I'd gone and done it, hadn't I; I'd added a second item to the list of things I couldn't tell Jacob.

The lake road curved in and out and in and out and soon accelerated to become the Indy. Maybe today would be the day I hit the headwall.

How could I explain the earrings to Jacob? We'd joked about Edna's receiving too many pairs last Christmas, and implied in that was the plan to buy her something else this year. *Pottery* earrings! Jacob wasn't so supposedly indifferent to my previous lovelife that he'd have forgotten I had a potter in my past, a man who had been the reason for my going to England with a broken heart as luggage. But Gary did sell his wares at, besides his studio, the Granite State Craftsmen Cooperative shops, and the Bridgeford branch of the Coop was open year-round and I could say I had stopped in there to look for Christmas presents and had been reminded by the rosebuds of Edna's desire for a bud vase; that might touch off a malediction from Jacob about what the Exmouth branch had done to his two-drawer blanket chest and he would forget the earrings. Or should I simply hide them, throw them away, twenty bucks wasted on—on what?

Then, when I reached Meader Intervale and did some shopping at the supermarket while two washing machines caught up on our long underwear and other laundry, I began to wonder if all such subterfuge might be unnecessary. Maybe Jacob wouldn't make the Gary connection. There were plenty of potters in this area. Returning to the laundromat, shifting the wash into dryers, I reflected: If Jacob did know I'd seen Gary, would he give a damn? Would learning of my little interlude in a boathouse heat up his sangfroid?

And how sidesplittingly uproarious, anyway, for me to be berating myself over a fleeting kiss, an attempt to cop a feel, when everybody else nowadays seemed more carefree than bunnies!

But as I loaded the wicker laundry basket into the car I was ambushed by a thought so unexpected I nearly dropped in my tracks. Had I stopped at the studio to make Jacob jealous, because I was jealous of the other woman in his life? Had I begun to consider Shelterfield my rival?

Leaving the Indy the first chance I could, I drove along Dinsmere's Lake Pequawket, a relief from Winnipesaukee and as much a wilderness lake as you were still able to find around here. The old cottages, closed and shuttered, became part of the trees.

I had been so clean from that wonderful shower.

At the village store, I read every word of the notices. Cordwood for sale, a Christmas bazaar at the church, a stableboy wanted by the Lords. Then I picked up the mail, filled our water jugs, and slowly continued home. As I approached Shelterfield I could hear the whine of the drilling.

The kitchen's trapdoor was open, and I went on to the bedroom and hid the earrings and hammer holster in my underwear drawer—which Jacob of course called my drawers drawer—before I returned and yelled down into the alligator pit, "I'm back!" Then I began putting the groceries away, in the refrigerator, on the makeshift pantry table.

Jacob climbed wearily up the ladder, dirty, disheveled. "The car run all right?"

"Yes. How deep have they got, have they hit China yet?"

"Four hundred feet, the last time I could bring myself to inquire."

I glanced out a window at the crew bundled up in lined green twill jackets instead of sweating in the green shirtsleeves of last summer. "They look frozen," I said. "Should I offer coffee? It'd be an awful chore, unpacking extra cups, washing up." More than coffee, what they could use was Chester Greenwood's invention. "Did you make yourself any lunch?"

"They have their thermoses. I didn't get around to lunch. Did you go to your folks' for a shower, did you eat there?"

"Lunch at Dorothy's, are you crazy? After I put the laundry away I'll make us a sandwich—no, I'm starving, I'll feed us first." Then, still reading walls, still in the thrall of Dorothy's samplers, I happened to spot a note written on the crumbling plaster beside the telephone, above the important numbers Jacob had inscribed on the wall in his Jacob-Gary handwriting: the Bridgeford Well Company; the mason; the Meader Intervale hardware store. " 'Call V.' Did Virginia phone?"

"Oh, I forgot. Exmouth Realty phoned immediately afterward but don't get your hopes up, they showed the place again over the weekend but no bites yet."

"Damn." Two mortgages, the car-repair bill, the typewriter repair, everything was piling up to a towering height and I'd just wasted twenty bucks!

Jacob said, "Virginia called not five minutes after you'd

left. She sounded so urgent I told her she might be able to catch you at your folks', but she said no and asked you to call when you got back. I told her around lunchtime, I didn't expect you'd be gone this long."

"You know how Dorothy starts me wandering down byways, and her latest news is a break-in at the zoo and Nicole's plans to open a thrift shop." I hurried off, going upstairs to look up Virginia's telephone number in my address book, and when I came back downstairs Jacob had disappeared into the cellar where I could hear him thinking aloud about a sump pump.

I dialed. No answer. I hung up and went to the pantry table in the dining room to make a belated lunch of salad sandwiches, a bit of a project, a penance, shredding lettuce, slicing tomatoes, chopping an onion, grating cheese. Jacob came up out of the cellar and I presented him with this lunch from our Oxford summer, the Railway Arms, our honeymoon.

Before I lugged hot water to the sink to do dishes, I tried Virginia's number again. Virginia, despite her aversion to letter-writing, had been brought up by Mrs. Lyford to drop bread-and-butter notes when necessary, yet even though she'd said she would write I hadn't expected one; was her call a bread-and-butter phone call? Urgent? Simple etiquette wouldn't register on her Richter scale.

As I hung up again without an answer, there came a knock on the back door. I opened the door to see a vision. Amid the wild lilac bush, hand raised to knock once more, stood the head of the well crew, an angel wearing a slogan above the visor of his green cap: WE'LL DO WELL FOR YOU. He was beaming; I realized the rig was silent.

I gasped, "Have you—"

"Mr. Wetherbee around?"

I raced into the kitchen and screamed down the cellar, "*Jacob! The well!*" Then at the back door I invited, "Do come in and get warm," but the angel only shook his head and waited.

Jacob burst through the trapdoor opening as though shot from a cannon. "Water? How deep?"

The angel said, "Five hundred and fifty feet."

"Jesus."

"Three gallons a minute, should get better. We'll be back tomorrow to switch wells."

"Thank you for your perseverance."

"No trouble."

Jacob closed the door and looked at me, and we both said, *"Whew!"*

While we were hugging, bumping into the table saw which I'd actually begun to use as a butcherblock worktable, the telephone rang.

I said, "I'll get it, you break out the champagne."

"Probably Virginia?"

"Maybe it's Exmouth Realty, maybe our luck has changed."

"My God, Ib, don't say that, don't tempt fate."

I lifted the receiver. "Hello?"

"Funny," Virginia said, "it's really funny how the information you didn't know you'd picked up from magazines and TV comes to the surface when you need it. I've done what they tell you. I arranged to have Willie go to a friend's house after school and spend the night. I called in sick and canceled my classes for a couple of days so I'd have time for everything. I packed Max's clothes and put the suitcases in the garage. I looked up a female lawyer in the yellow pages and made an appointment for tomorrow. I've had a locksmith do a rush job changing locks. I've gone to the bank and got my paws on our savings. Have you been phoning here? Can you think of anything I've forgotten? I've locked the doors. Max should be home from school any minute. He'll find a *fait accompli*."

Her voice was the artesian rig still drilling. But the drilling had stopped and the noises outside were now the slamming of truck doors and revving of engines as the crew prepared to depart.

Virginia said, "When I got home yesterday, our friend Stanley was just leaving. He'd spent his vacation here."

"I think I've missed a beat."

"So did I, Ib, so did I. I was kind of surprised, but okay,

two bachelors whiling away a lonely vacation playing chess. I unpacked and started a wash to get stuff ready for school, and I noticed there were no guest-room sheets so I went upstairs to change the guest-room bed and I saw it hadn't been slept in. Poor dears, such novices!"

Jacob had taken a couple of Miller High Lifes out of the refrigerator, the seven-ounce type of bottles which I liked and which he called sissy beers. Opening them, humming an old commercial, " 'The Champagne of Bottled Beers,' " he started to hand me one. Then he set it down on the windowsill. "What's the matter?"

Virginia was saying, "I went into our bedroom—I thought I was dreaming *Goldilocks*—who's been sleeping in *my* bed? I couldn't believe it. I went back downstairs and looked at Max playing Ping-Pong with Willie. Max was radiant. Remember how when we fell in love with someone we'd be just dying to tell the world? That's how Max looked. So I retreated into the upstairs bathroom and threw up."

The flatbed truck bearing the giant grasshopper rolled down the driveway to the road and, shaking the house, made its ponderous exit.

"All became clear," Virginia said. "The threesome idea had just been an excuse. They wanted to frolic with each other, not with me."

"Are you sure? It's impossible!"

"I feel as if I've got malaria, shivers and sweats, and I keep throwing up even though there's nothing left to throw. I spent last night in the bathroom, heaving. Afraid I used your turkey as the reason. Finally I got some sleep on the bathmat, and when I woke up this morning I'd remembered the procedure you're supposed to follow when you throw your husband out. Max was still radiant, down in the kitchen eating cornflakes with Willie. I waved merrily as they left for school. Another funny thing, Ib, is how *outraged* I am that Max did this while Willie was under the same roof. I am *incensed!* My innocent son! Why the hell should I be so sanctimonious about *that,* when everything else is falling to pieces—goodbye, goodbye, Max just drove in and I'm going to throw up again."

Replacing the receiver, I in a way also threw up, emptying myself of Virginia's secret and its subsequence. Jacob, listening, walked around the empty kitchen, stretching his metal tape measure wide, measuring imaginary cabinets, snapping the tape measure shut.

He said, "Hadn't you better call her back, to see if she's all right?"

Caca's pickup bounced into the driveway, its plow clanging, and Caca stepped out. As Jacob opened the ell door, Caca inquired loudly enough to be heard in Meader Intervale, "Saw the rig go past, you finally struck water—or oil?"

Jacob went outdoors, and I shakily dialed.

Max said, "Hello?"

I almost hung up, but then I asked, "Is Virginia there?"

Pause. Sounding put-upon, he said, "We're in the midst of—Ginger, it's for you."

Virginia said, "Hello?"

"How come he's indoors?"

"Logic," she said. "I'll be in touch. Goodbye."

I turned on the kitchen TV and stared at Merv Griffin interrupting a guest. Virginia's Victorian house in her Boston suburb had two bathrooms and she'd done up the upstairs bathroom in Alice-in-Wonderland blues and yellows. The bathmat, I recalled, was pale blue sculptured plush, and, knowing her, I suspected she hadn't bought a new one since our visit four years ago, so upon that very mat she had spent last night with her malaria.

Looking at the jagged doorless wall between our bombed-out kitchen and our one-and-only bathroom where new fixtures stood awaiting water, I clicked the TV off and found myself thinking of how sophisticated Virginia and I had considered ourselves when in high school we'd tittered over the development of her dancer's diaphragm.

And while I put folded long underwear into a blanket chest, I remembered the way that, in her Bridgeford bedroom, tossed aside after dance classes her leotard and tights would lie curled humanly on the floor.

Jacob came indoors, crossing to the range to warm his hands. "Caca sure does keep tabs on things. Wanted to know if my brother-in-law was planning to move up here. Then after appropriate circumlocution he mentioned seeing Batch with Allegra, in her car, driving along the lake road yesterday afternoon. So Batch *is* pursuing either real estate or realtor. Did you get Virginia?"

"She must've unlocked the door. Max answered the phone."

"Counseling-time?"

"To think I drove past the Lyford house just this morning. Though I don't know why that should seem so odd."

"Will Virginia want to go-home-to-mother? Should you invite her back here, what should we do?"

"Her job. She'll have to stay and stick with her job, if she's going to get a divorce. And there's Willie's school. Maybe she won't get a divorce, maybe all the years with Max will—" I started to cry.

Jacob put his arms around me. This was different from our jubilant hugging about the well; his familiar embrace felt as strange now compared with Gary's as it had when that initial fish and chips date stretched into an evening of getting further acquainted in his apartment.

I blubbered, "Does the new well look like the first well did before they put the pipe down it?"

"Come see."

Yanking my jacket on, I went with him out the back door into the gray dusk, past the first well's question-mark vent poking above the snow. Where the monster and its attendants had labored the second time, out of the trampled ground rose two feet of well casing, the tip of the iceberg. I said, "I won't believe we're really going to have water again until I turn on a faucet and something happens."

"If we had a couple of pistols, we could unwind with a water fight."

"I thought you once told me kids don't bother with namby-pamby water pistols anymore, that instead of concealed weapons in school they carry big industrial-size spray bottles."

"At Exmouth, yes. Besides each other, the assistant principal was their favorite target, and he cowered and put up with it, one of the boys." Jacob removed the wooden cork from the well-casing top and pretended to peer down five hundred and fifty feet. "A telescope in reverse! If only I could get that far from Exmouth High."

"Give it time."

"Did I ever tell you about how back in my Maine days I used to accumulate an arsenal of water pistols from kids in the library, and so did the teachers in their classrooms, and the night after the last day of school each year all of us, the so-called faculty, would go down to the beach with our confiscated weapons and have a shoot-out to work off the end-of-school crazies? It was ferocious, and Debbie was especially feared because when she aimed you were certain to get a soaked crotch, and she could reload like a bandit—"

"Debbie?"

"One of the teachers."

"She sounds athletic. Perhaps that girls' gym coach of yours? Soaking your center of gravity?"

Jacob grinned, resembling Gary and the canary-digesting cat; fairly licking his white whiskers, he said, "What girls' gym coach of whose? Since we don't have any water pistols, let's unwind with a snowball fight," and he leaned down to scoop snow, but I'd anticipated this and I drew faster, smashing a snowball between his shoulderblades. He yelled, "Shoot me in the back, will you, you lily-livered coward?"

As we pelted each other, as he chased me around the house and caught me and stuffed snow down my collar, I thought how wholesome we would look to anybody driving by, how healthy and high-spirited, Shelterfield's new occupants gamboling together. Or, if everyone shared Flossie Sisson's assumption that I was Jacob's second wife, the observers might smile wryly.

After a supper late enough to qualify us as Dinsmere Gown, like a good obedient daughter I phoned Dorothy to tell her we'd hit water, though I didn't tell her about Batch's real-estate explorations, and when I hung up I stood looking at the telephone, wishing I could call Virginia and suggest we beg, borrow, steal some money so we could again flee.

"Embarrassed," I said to Jacob. "I bet that Virginia in this first shock wave is embarrassed as well as angry."

"Embarrassed about what people will say?"

"No, about finding out she doesn't know the person you're supposed to know better than anyone else in the whole world. And guilty, too. She must be thinking it's her fault."

"Seems peculiar that she never had an inkling."

"For God's sake, Jacob, hear yourself! Who'd expect an affair with another man instead of another woman?"

"When I get the water hooked up, I'll start in on the shower wall. And there's the weatherstripping to do next, and the wiring . . . "

Trying to fall asleep that night, I couldn't make my dream-office schemes obscure Virginia's waking nightmare, but eventually I was traveling along the White Cliffs with Jacob, our first Christmas-vacation trip together, unmarried though nervously braced to masquerade as hitched when we entered inns, and my telescope was turned right-way-around so I could see closely the rainy cobblestone streets of Rye where we found a room at the Mermaid. An ancient town. Having coffee in the lounge after dinner, I rhapsodized over Rye and this half-timbered inn with its famous giant fireplace, its linen-fold paneling, its 1420 date, and Jacob was remarking, "Hard to grasp that we're sitting in an inn that was built seventy-two years before Columbus discovered America," when at a nearby table two New Zealand women, whom Jacob earlier had helped park their rented car in a quaint but cramped space behind the inn, looked up from their Scrabble board, smiled at us, and one of them said, "We've just come from Italy. Visiting Rome makes a fourteen-twenty inn seem a newborn."

Things somewhat in perspective, we'd continued on the next day to contemplate Stonehenge.

We got a room for the night at another half-timbered inn, the King's Arms in Salisbury, and our enlightening encounter on this occasion occurred in the bar of beams and paneling, brass, coal fire, where we fell into conversation with an English couple who were about our age. We learned we had all played musical countries; they were living and working in America. But they had come back here for the Christmas holiday, and their main topic was the appalling way the English drove. "We didn't *realize,*" they said again and again, "we didn't realize how perfectly *mad* it is until we left and returned!" Jacob and I nodded sympathetically but didn't comment aloud, because although I wanted to lean forward and pat their hands and say, "We know, we know, my God, we know," we sensed we should leave it for the English to bewail the English.

Despite demented English drivers, however, onward down the coast we went the next day, through Devon, past little signs mentioning Devon cream as casually as farmhouses at home advertised maple syrup. Reaching Cornwall, we crossed Bodmin Moor in a Daphne du Maurier spell cast by the sight of Jamaica Inn. And then we got lost in Penzance when Jacob's rendition of "Poor Wandering One" distracted me from my duties as bucket-seat navigator, but eventually, driving along the sea wall, we found we were on the road to Mousehole, pronounced Mouzel, a village the English couple had recommended.

The road continued along the sea wall, and it got narrower. We squeezed into the little fishing port.

In my childhood I had collected travel brochures that I sent away for with mail-order blanks I cut from the back pages of *National Geographic*. I used the photographs in the brochures to suggest backgrounds for and to illustrate my stories, and once upon a time there had been a photograph of an English fishing village just like this, the inspiration for an ocean yarn in which my pirate battles on the high seas were less full of derring-do than the spine-tingling adventures of my smuggler heroine in hidden coastal caves. I had lived an imaginary life here years ago; now, when we reached the harbor and parked on the quay, I, enchanted, decided that I wanted to spend the rest of my life in Mousehole.

Jacob said, "I bet it's mobbed with tourists in the summer."

"I'm from Bridgeford, I'm used to that. We could rent

our picturesque cottage to them and tour the Continent. We'd prefer the village in the off-seasons. Okay, okay, one night here will have to do me."

Overlooking the harbor was the Ship Inn which, according to the guidebook, had five bedrooms. Indoors, the smell of fresh paint greeted us, and the woman in charge told us the inn wasn't really open because the bedrooms and lounge were being painted. So there wouldn't even be one night.

Perhaps my woebegone expression made her reconsider, perhaps it was America's reputation for informality, or perhaps a certain Christmas tale about lack of room at an inn was what made her hesitate and then say, "One room is dry, though it still smells of paint. If you don't mind the paint smell, and if you don't mind chicken-in-the-rough instead of a proper dinner—"

After unpacking upstairs in a shipshape room warmed by a small electric fire, we went down to the bar, which was filling up with locals. Real mistletoe and paper Christmas decorations were everywhere. Sitting amid sea charts, lobster traps, an old ship's compass with an oil lamp, and collection boxes for present-day shipwreck survivors, we drank beer and dined on chicken and chips, wondering why a seacoast inn didn't have *fish* and chips always on hand. Once again we were enlightened; a patron in a rakish beret began complaining over his beer about all the damned crayfish and clams and fish he had to eat while he was at sea.

But fish was apparently appreciated here in emergencies, at least, because our beer coasters commemorated Tom Bowcock's Eve, December twenty-third, a few days hence, the celebration of a brave deed done more than two centuries ago when Tom had put out to sea in a gale and landed a large catch of fish to feed the starving villagers:

> A merry plaace, you may believe
> Was Mouzel 'pon Tom Bowcock's Eve.
> To be there then who wudn' wesh,
> To sup o' sibm soorts o' fesh!
> When morgy brath had cleared the path,

Comed lances for a fry,
And then us had a bit o' scad,
An starry gazy pie.

We lingered as long as another beer before leaving the bar to the villagers and retiring upstairs to the dropcloth-draped lounge, where on a big sofa we sat and watched some television, getting up often to go to the bay window. Down by the water Christmas lights had been switched on, outlining the quay in red and yellow and green and blue. Soon from the bar came the sound of voices raised in song.

Land's End, with its touristy shops and gas stations named the First and the Last, had a familiar feel to this Bridgeford native when we drove there the next day. Then up the west coast we went, on roads gouged out of barren rocky hills, through rocky villages which blurred into the landscape, across land so open that it made a horseman riding up the side of a hill a mile away seem much larger than he should have at that distance. Eventually we detoured onto a little road to Tintagel, to take a gander at what was billed as the legendary site of King Arthur's castle. The legendary weather provided an idyllic dreamy green mist.

" 'Live pure,' " I recited from my childhood, " 'speak true, right wrong, follow the King—Else, wherefore born?' "

The guidebook had lied about the inn in Ilfracombe for which we'd been aiming; it wasn't open year-round. Night had fallen. Jacob always maintained that if we got stranded we could become contortionists and sleep in the MG Midget, but we'd never yet had to attempt that feat, and he kept driving. The narrow road convoluted into hairpin turns, dropping away to a dark abyss I glimpsed with a shudder whenever we leaned out our windows to try to read by flashlight the hedge-hidden signposts. And then we found ourselves at the top of a hill above a village named Porlock. "Oh, God," I moaned, "it's got gradient signs." These signs started out with a gradient of one in seven and, as we crept nose downward, Jacob in lowest gear and standing on the brake, the gradient increased to one in four before other ominous signs began advising cyclists to walk, the warnings culminating in a sign that announced what was apparently an escape route, a little road which seemed to plunge over a cliff into the sea.

At the foot of the hill stood another Ship Inn, dimly white in our headlights and thatched. The guidebook, consulted, told us it was early thirteenth-century. Sitting limp, trying to make our hearts stop pounding, we thought of all the travelers over the centuries who'd collapsed like this in the inn's dooryard after descending that hill. We had joined their ranks.

Although the oldest we'd stayed at during the trip, the inn obviously wasn't inclined to capitalize on its age, at least not until summertime. A simple place to lay your weary head. Walking past the bar off the entrance hall, we heard villagers conversing in yet another incomprehensible accent. Mine hostess didn't bat an eye at our late and unexpected and somewhat hysterical arrival, but her equable manner seemed a bit jarred when, after she escorted us up to our room, we asked uncertainly about supper at this hour. Why, of course guests would be fed! Plain fare, we gathered, and as we sat alone in the bleak dining room we were prepared for bread and drippings when an enormous meal began being presented matter-of-factly to us: cream of mushroom soup, roast lamb and potatoes, Brussels sprouts, trifle, cheese and biscuits. I tried to picture the invisible kitchen in which such sustenance was kept in warming ovens for demoralized guests. Were there collection boxes placed around, too, for survivors of the hill? Stuffed and sleepy, we took our coffee into the lounge and discovered that the other overnight guests were an elderly couple watching television, their toothless spaniel drooling on the worn carpet. I assumed the spaniel's dental problem to be caused by age, but the moment we introduced ourselves the couple launched into a sad yet resigned explanation of how on a beach recently the dog had run off to chase sticks with some boys who, they later learned, had instead played a cruel game of tossing stones to the dog to catch.

Ever since I'd seen Porlock on a signpost, its name had been nagging at me. I almost clutched the elusive reference when we went upstairs, but distractions interfered, Jacob's putting a shilling in the bedroom electric fire, our doing exhausting chores like brushing our teeth. So it wasn't until the middle of the night that I got the answer, awakening in a flash, sitting up straight and exulting, " 'The person from Porlock'! That's who interrupted Coleridge at his farmhouse when he was writing down 'Kubla Khan' as fast as he could remember his opium dream!" From under his pillow Jacob groaned, "Jesus Christ, you interrupted me and my dream to tell me that?" Then he too suddenly sat bolt upright, saying, " 'The person from Porlock'! You're right! My God, he *really* must've wanted to see Coleridge if he climbed that hill to visit him!" I said, "Maybe he was an ardent fan." "No," Jacob said, reflecting, "probably Coleridge owed him money."

Now, the next morning at Shelterfield, thinking wistfully of the inn's porridge and bacon and eggs and potato cakes all made by somebody else, the dishes washed by somebody else, I buttered English muffins on the table saw and considered unpacking our carefully rolled brass rubbings and hanging them up, ignoring the problems of putrefying wallpaper and lumpy wainscoting.

Jacob sipped coffee. "During the wee hours I figured out why guys like Caca always holler. It's because they've got into the habit from yelling over the racket of trucks and machines."

"And the women holler over the children, and the children holler on general principle. I don't suppose we can unpack the brass rubbings yet."

"We aren't unpacking anything unnecessary until each room is finished. When the kitchen is done, we unpack the kitchen stuff, et cetera."

In the cold sunrise, metallic trees were splayed against the pink silk sky like a brooch on a frigid gown. Earrings, anyone?

The well crew arrived just as I'd begun chasing the little Olivetti across the slick surface of my desk; from my office windows I looked down at the flatbed truck parked below, bearing a backhoe, and I thought how most people were deprived of the character-building experience of two wells drilled in their yard in less than five months. What a wondrous opportunity now to observe once more this phase of the operation! A ramp was attached to the rear of the flatbed, the crew boss climbed into the backhoe seat and, a mortal again, started the engine, apparently never yet having realized how silly he looked there, and then the backhoe, after much jerking and snorting, gathered itself together and descended the ramp as slowly as we had crept down Porlock's hill. Crunching snow, it rolled across the yard toward the new well site where Jacob joined the crew to watch its crablike shovel make the first slicing incision in the ground, cutting a new trench to the house.

Through the earth-moving noises came the peremptory command of the telephone. I ran downstairs.

"Counseling," Virginia said. "Max's plan for us is counseling. The blind leading the blind, I call it."

"Is he still in the house?"

"He went to work. He's going to make us an appointment with a marriage counselor and we'll discuss how to deal with the situation. That's a term Max uses a lot, 'deal with.' "

"What does it mean? More positive than 'cope with'?"

" 'Nurturing' and 'caring,' those are a couple of his other favorites."

"What about the money, have you still got the savings?" Out the sink window I saw one of the crew standing atop the first well, balancing on the rim of a contraption made of three plump little wheels through which the well's black pipe was emerging like a noodle from a pasta machine. Another crew member began guiding the pipe across the snow to the new well.

"I guessed right," Virginia said, "he was dying to talk, and after he talked his way indoors he sat me down as if he intended to go over my SAT scores but instead away he went about loving me as much as ever and this will rejuvenate our marriage, all very logical, not exactly a ménage à trois, me during the week, Stanley on weekends, that's his initial suggestion but he's open to what he calls 'options' which we'll consider during counseling, although I got the distinct feeling I should be glad it isn't the other way around, me relegated to weekends."

Now the crew, having installed a new pump on the end of the pipe, started lowering it into the second well as the pipe continued coming up from the first, forming a black arch.

Virginia said, "Infatuation, obsessed! He kept talking about his rediscovered zest for life, he didn't notice my state at all, and soon I stopped thinking I should strangle myself with my fifth limb, die like Isadora Duncan, instead I began thinking things like we had to stay together for the kid's sake but in the nick of time just before he began to make sense to me something jolted in my head and I came to, and there I was out in the garage jumping over Max's suitcases to get to my car. I did one of those stints we used to do when we first got our licenses, remember, driving and driving, and then I stopped at a Dunkin' Donuts and started eating my way down the list of varieties to keep from looking as if I was loitering—a good sign, I told myself, I was eating, not puking—and then I was just plain bone-deep tired and I drove home. After midnight, but Max was on the phone in the midst of what I assumed to be a long intimate session of billing and cooing. I didn't spend last night on the bathmat, I spent it locked in the guest room where Stanley should have slept during vacation."

"What are you going to do?"

"I'm not insane, am I, to keep trying to picture them together? I'd try to if Max had fallen for a woman, but I'd have better luck at succeeding. I can't—I can't!"

As Virginia hung up in a paroxysm of sobs, Jacob came storming into the house and grabbed the coffeepot. "Dexter!" he said, pouring. "That goddamn fool! Jesus Christ, when the crew gets back to the office and tells him, he ought to go drown himself in his nearest well! They just got all the pipe up out of the first well and down into the second, and what do we see but within two feet of the old pump there's a burst blister. We didn't run out of water at all."

"Huh?"

"It'd be like trying to suck through a straw with a hole in it. That dumb bastard, that chainsmoking cretin, he simply assumed too much. He should've pulled up the pipe and checked it before he wasted all our time and his money to drill a second well."

"Does this mean we won't have any water? I knew it, I knew it."

Jacob gulped coffee. "No, of course not. Everything is transferred, the new pump is in the second well and now they're going to connect it up to the house."

"I think I'm having a heart attack. The first well isn't dry? There was no need to drill another? We could have been spared all this?"

"Come see that pipe."

I followed him outdoors to the stone wall where the blown-out section of pipe lay on display, the green-clad crew gazing down upon it, shaking their heads. The crew boss said over and over, "Wait'll they see this at the office, just wait."

The backhoe had finished the trench to the cellar. Last summer the final stages of the well project had made me rejoice; now I only wanted to weep. Chickadees bounced through the air from the pines to the birdfeeder like small stones being skipped across a lake.

I asked Jacob, "You'll hook things up this afternoon?"

"You can take a bath tonight."

"Remember when we went on to Bath from Porlock and I hoped the Roman baths would make me as blasé about the age of English inns as those New Zealand women were, but still I was just as agog in the Pump Room as in the baths, if not more so?"

"I'm not promising a Roman bath. You'll have to be content with American Standard."

"I will."

By lunchtime they had all left. The crew, their thermoses, their trucks, their Twinkies. I felt as though an encampment had been broken up, its fires doused. Shelterfield was quiet again except for the clanking noises of Jacob's wrench in the cellar.

Heating tomato soup from our Millsted garden, I called, "Lunch is almost ready!" Oh, why not. I took the hammer holster out of my drawers drawer and put it beside Jacob's place-mat on the dining table.

Soon he came up through the trapdoor opening and into the living room, saying, "I heard the phone earlier. Virginia?"

"Max wants both her and Stanley." I tried to adjust the color TV. "I've got an awful feeling I'm going to say he wants to have his cake and eat it too."

"He wants what—hey, what's this?"

"It was a Christmas present, but I couldn't wait. Instead, now it's to celebrate the well."

"You chose it yourself?"

"With a little help from a clerk. Is it okay? For a hammer, if not for a water pistol?"

He threaded the holster onto his belt. "There's always a debate over whether to wear it on your right or your left, nobody can decide, but since I'm so thoroughly right-handed I guess probably my left would be better—"

I said, "I don't know how to tell you this but I think there's something wrong with the picture tube."

III

Most of the women were wearing long evening skirts of tartan, brocade, patchwork, so it was impossible to distinguish by sight female Town from female Gown. Could this kind woman offering us Brie be one of the help hired for the Lords' New Year's Eve party or was she a guest pressed into service?

"Thank you," I said, and when she moved on I murmured to Jacob, "I've concluded we really are the youngest here. Incredible."

"The Wetherbees!" Percy Lord was making a roly-poly progress toward us through the crowd. "I didn't see you come in, has Hannah introduced you around?"

"Yes," I said, forbearing to explain that we'd arrived at least an hour ago but five minutes later had become separated from Hannah and her introductions by the entrance of a throng of Meader Intervale widowed socialites. "We're doing fine."

Percy said, "Good, good. Are your drinks all right? And are you all shoveled out from that snowstorm? Are you keeping warm in that house? Charlemagne, if you don't behave yourself I'll chop you up and serve you on a cracker. Oh, Freddy, have you met the Wetherbees? They're the brave souls who bought Shelterfield. Excuse me, another log for the fire."

"How do you do," said Freddy. It took me a moment to recognize him without his parka hood; he was the octogenarian I often passed in our car as he skied cross-country to the village and along Main Street to the store where he collected his mail, trimly fitting into his backpack his *New York Times*. "Shelterfield, eh? I don't know what could have been going on in old Mr. Briggs's head, except sheer deviltry, to leave that property to those three children who could never even agree on whether or not the sun set in the west—"

Beneath the low-beamed ceilings of the Lords' farmhouse, the living room and dining room were absorbing firelight into all the textures and patinas, upholstery, braided rugs, tabletops; men's faces looked pinkly shaved above tweed jackets and sedate ties; and the fat Christmas tree glowed at its wavery reflection distorted on the little hand-blown windowpanes, its colored lights on the dark glass a nighttime substitute for the mountain view.

Jacob said to Freddy, "Yes, a shame about the barn."

"Oops," a woman in paisley drapery said to another woman near us, trying to squeeze past her in the crush. "I'm sorry, did I spill your drink? I seem to be taking up more room these days."

Much amused, the other replied, "Now that I've caught you, I must tell you my terrible problem. Your meadow is blowing snow all over my place."

"Oh, dear! I suppose I ought to keep my snow where it belongs."

"You see, that's what I wanted to speak to you about."

Jacob and I had put aside our long underwear for this

occasion and I'd rooted around in garment bags and suitcases to come up with our most classic Edna-knitted sweaters, my pair of dark brown corduroys which were so old they had hardly any cord left but which were at least nondenim, and a pair of Jacob's khakis unsullied by the labors of his new career. As I expected, we were underdressed, yet that, as Dorothy always said, was better than over. I thought it miraculous we could manage to emerge from Shelterfield resembling at all remotely a species of the human race closer to the twentieth century than those miners seeking flint in Grime's Graves.

"—before tackling Shelterfield," Freddy was saying, "I suppose you practiced on a house elsewhere that hadn't been let go to such rack and ruin?"

Jacob looked at me, suddenly tongue-tied again, tortured. So, as I had when other people here with whom we'd chatted began inquiring obliquely about what Jacob had done and was doing, I attempted an explanation; this time I said, "Our last house had already been fixed up, which was just as well because Jacob was too busy running a library then to work on it. But now he can concentrate on Shelterfield."

"I wish you luck," Freddy said, and pushed off. "Jim, whatever happened about that variance request?"

At the settle bench folded down into a table draped with a holly-embroidered cloth, a woman in a velour pantsuit dipped a ladleful from the cut-glass punchbowl and exclaimed, "My God, I just remembered that New Year's Eve means February is coming soon and we'll have to listen to its being mispronounced for an entire month for yet another year!"

I asked Jacob, "Did you get Freddy's last name?"

"I haven't got anybody's, as usual."

"Neither have I."

"If these people were only in their cars, I could keep them straight. They ought to have name tags telling the makes of their cars."

I said, "I thought I saw Caca's car here, not his truck. Did you? Does that mean the Thibodeaus are guests or is Theresa helping? When I picked up our eggs the other day,

I started thinking about the mysterious Oxford egg-thrower and why he stopped after two pitching sessions—"

"Ah, Ib and Jacob." To reach us, Allegra Quigley adroitly avoided underfoot-Charlemagne, who kept disappearing beneath billows of long skirts and yelping for help. Allegra's white blouse was frothy, her raspberry taffeta skirt's wide black grosgrain cummerbund gave the impression of a corset hoping to be loosened, and her chocolate-box pulchritude tonight definitely suggested soft-centeredness beneath its shell. Why should I, comparatively tailored, still feel like a toddler in her presence? She said, "Isn't it wonderful nowadays at parties not to have to worry about getting cigarette burns on your clothes because most people have quit smoking? *Most* people," she repeated, smiling sweetly at a retired executive lurking in the shadow of a pumpkin-pine hutch, covert cigarette cupped. He began to look hunted.

Jacob said, "There are always other hazards," and ducked somebody's hand gesturing dangerously with a small speared meatball. "Good evening, Allegra. Do you know where I might find a tinker? I need a flange braised."

"Let me think." Drawing us nearer the living-room fireplace, Allegra indicated the gatherings of guests here and beside the dining-room fireplace. "Hopefully you've changed your mind and will put restoring your fireplace at the top of your list. Look at these people enjoying these! A fireplace, not a woodstove, sells houses. How *is* your house coming along? I hear you're doing the rewiring now?"

"Learning as I go," Jacob said. "My general knowledge of wiring didn't include three-way switches."

We hadn't seen Allegra to talk to since the rewiring project began, so she must have heard about this from Batch and was letting us know she had. Such subtleties! Flustered, I said, "I'm playing electrician's assistant because I can reach through electrical-box openings into spaces too small for Jacob's hands. Some snowstorm the other day, wasn't it?"

"Are you really?" Allegra said. "I've knocked down walls, but I wouldn't ever want to reach in where I couldn't see."

"Well, I got less scared about touching mouse skeletons in the walls when they started falling out of the ceilings on me. Our first month here, Jacob kept disappearing into the ell cellar. This past month, he's been disappearing through ceilings."

Behind us a man said to his male companions, "I don't know why, but ever since we moved here year-round I can't seem to get anything done," and a wool-skirted woman making her way past with a depleted tray of canapés commented, "Of course you can't, dear, not if you start work at eleven and stop at noon."

Allegra asked us, "Your icicles are very picturesque, but I suppose indoors you've got waterstains from ice dams? Have you decided yet to install electric heat-tapes? They're a good selling point."

"Expensive," Jacob said. "I've shoveled off the edges of the roofs out back, I'll get the front shoveled tomorrow. Tried to convince Ib she should be doing this chore, since she's the one who began complaining when the ice started dripping in and sizzling on the oil range."

"Ice dams?" Hannah Lord, looking rosy and as solid as a bolster in her hostess outfit of quilted calico, stopped to offer us a platter of finger rolls. "Percy thought you'd have ice-dam troubles at Shelterfield, just as we did when this place was being restored, before we had the heat-tapes put on. Charlemagne, sit! I never saw such a sight, water invading our ceilings without so much as a by-your-leave. Chicken salad on this side, tuna there."

"Thank you," I said. "How is Gay Blade?"

"Percy says horses aren't smart enough to be bored, but I'm sure the poor darling hates being cooped up by these blizzards—"

Allegra said, "Hannah, I think Theresa wants you."

"Does she? Heavens, I hope we haven't run out of anything, I'd hate to have to ask Mr. Dobbins to open up the store on New Year's Eve."

As Hannah steered her platter across the living room and dining room toward the wedge of Theresa Thibodeau's titian perm peeking out from behind the kitchen door, I sampled a roll in which chicken salad didn't taste like the Pot o' Gold's kindergarten paste, and struck again by the Lords' resemblance to our Hingham friends in England, I thought of Mrs. Hingham's note on the last Christmas card we'd received from her. It'd been three years ago, now.

Dear Ib and Jacob,

Hello once again. Trust you are both quite well. Bert is enjoying his retirement, he keeps busy on our garden, weather permitting, and we have plenty of vegetables all the year and a nice garden of roses in the summer. He is in great demand in the spring and summer to attend people's gardens, it's his favorite pastime. This time of the year he goes out with the pheasant shoot. Keeps him fit and happy. Peter and Susan have moved from their caravan to a nice bungalow with electric central heating, quite a warm and very pretty little place. Now for an extra news item. At last we will be grandparents, we are quite thrilled about it (hope it's a boy). Next Christmas I will be able to send you a picture of Baby. A very happy Christmas and prosperous New Year to you both.

"—the mortgage rates," Allegra was saying to Jacob.

"If they keep climbing," he said, rubbing a shoulder popped during one of his acrobatic swings up off a step-stool into the gaping hole in the ell ceiling out of which cascaded snakeskins and wood-shavings insulation as well as mouse skeletons and through which you could see smaller holes in the roof itself where the winter sky was spying down on our struggles. "Where will it end?"

"But," Allegra said, "at this point in time the rates are—"

I observed, "There's huggermugger going on. Excuse me, Allegra, you're being summoned now to the kitchen."

"I was born in this house." Allegra, heeding Hannah's dishtowel-signal over the heads of guests, handed Jacob her empty glass and waved back. "Hannah and Percy think I miss it, and they like to say I should always consider it home and myself one of the family. Coming!"

"The Wetherbees." Flossie Sisson popped up as Allegra

sallied forth. "I've found you, I've been looking all over for you." Wearing beige velvet, Flossie sipped at her punch cup as delicately as a chipmunk lapping at the saucer of water I put out in summer, its tiny claws poised on the brim. "The arrangements are made, Abigail's kennel is awaiting her, and one of the Hayward boys will be living in my house, babysitting it, don't you know, the usual arrangements, but I'd appreciate your keeping an eye out whenever you're driving past. If you see a moving van in the dooryard, be assured I didn't authorize it!"

Overhearing, a man of military mien contributed, "My sister's place in Vermont, the neighbors who were supposed to be the caretakers watched from their windows while a moving van was loaded up and driven off, and later, when questioned, they told the police they thought it was just those summer people taking a notion to have some things moved."

"Whales," continued Flossie, who'd obviously heard that tale before. "Hannah Lord is anxious enough for me to bring her back a kimono from Japan, but she insists on giving me Save-the-Whales buttons and bumper-stickers to take over there and I hardly think that's the sort of exchange which encourages international goodwill. Hannah is naive about diplomacy. Not that I condone their slaughter of our fellow mammals, but, don't you know, being a guest in their country—"

I said, "Excuse me, now *we're* being signaled, or is it just for you, Jacob?"

"Better find out, excuse us."

As we sidled through the crowd, Jacob left our glasses and Allegra's on the tavern table which had appropriately become a bar, and I compared our route through these pages of *Antiques* magazine to that we used to follow at early-Exmouth teachers' parties when we set off toward a kitchen or bathroom; there had been battered wallboard then, and incomplete furnishings, the handmade bobbly café curtains hanging skinny from rusty rods, the cheap living-room set already disemboweled by children. And the beer and potato chips and onion dip then, the teachers'-

room jokes lost upon spouses, while underfoot you had to watch out not only for a canine but also for a choo-choo train. Later had come lined drapes, hors d'oeuvres, the same jokes, liquor, and slipcovers.

"What's wrong?" Jacob asked Allegra as we gained the alcove, the gateway to workaday life, the back door opening off it, the back staircase going up, the kitchen door ajar.

Allegra said, "Jacob, I realize you're an electrician right now, but—"

At that moment Miriam Holt stepped out of a room that was apparently the downstairs bathroom, for I glimpsed tiled walls where I might have expected stenciling. What I hadn't expected was to see Miriam here. This evening she had stolen from a clothesline a short dark blue shirt-dress, floral-sprigged and rickrack-trimmed, a pilly gray cardigan, and a pair of striped tube socks that added a Sidelines sporty accent to the ensemble. She said, "The toilet won't flush."

"—but hopefully," Allegra finished, "you're still in the plumbing trade. They've run out of water in the kitchen. My educated guess is the pump has blown its fuse, don't you agree?"

Jacob glanced at me. Tonight was supposed to be party-time, a reprieve.

I said, "You're overdressed for plumbing."

He asked Allegra, "Is that the cellar door?" and she led him into the kitchen, a place of old pine where long-skirted women were reassembling provender beneath beams from which bunches of dried herbs depended.

"In another life," Miriam said to me, "back when I gave parties, I always ran out of booze, not water. Would this kitchen pass your inspection?"

We jumped out of the way of an advancing chafing-dish.

I said, "It looks like one of those vanishing kitchens, doesn't it? I bet that when they're not being used, the sink and stove and dishwasher are all hidden."

"They are? Murphy beds?"

"Pine cabinets."

"I'm not moonlighting tonight, but Lesley is. My daughter. She's the kid over there by the fridge refilling that heirloom ice-bucket. Should ice cubes be rationed if we've run out of water? Her regular job is Gay Blade, he's her after-school job."

"Oh," I said, comprehension dawning as through the kitchen activity I spotted a small red-headed girl, frizzy and flushed, whose long pink gingham dress was enough too long to make her resemble Popeye's Sweetpea creeping in a trailing baby gown. This Lesley, then, must be the youngest here. "Did she answer the stableboy ad the Lords put up at the store? I mean, stable-person."

"She and Gay Blade fell in love during the interview—Lesley doesn't find Gay Blade's name funny, as I gather other candidates did, to Hannah's annoyance—but transportation seemed a problem because she's only fourteen and hasn't got her license, much less a car, as if we could afford another car. Then Hannah spoke to the schoolbus driver, and the problem was solved, with Lesley dropped off here after school and Percy taking her home after the chores. Hannah, what about ice cubes, should you hoard them?"

Hannah left her post at the top of the cellar stairs. "Jacob is *sloshing* down there, we must have burst a pipe, not blown a fuse. I've got to tell the guests, to keep them from using the bathrooms, but should I tell Percy? He'll go to pieces, he always does in an emergency."

"Pearl Harbor!" came Percy's voice from the dining room, and we turned and saw him reprimanding Flossie Sisson at the edge of the crowd. "What will you say about Pearl Harbor?"

Flossie replied, "I simply won't mention it. They could always throw Hiroshima up at me."

"Their fault, they started it!"

Flossie shook a shrimp at him. "Do stop being so ridiculous, Percy. You're the one who owns a Subaru."

"Aha, but yours is a German car! Don't try to sidetrack me. Now, these shrimp here, they're cooked, but what are you going to find in Japan? Raw fish! And what about those baths?"

I said, "Japanese baths, Roman baths, and we still don't have a door on our bathroom or even half a bathroom wall." I was about to add that the outhouse afforded more privacy than the bathroom, when first Allegra and then Jacob appeared in the cellar doorway, Allegra holding knee-high her skirt and aloft her black slingback pumps which reminded me that crippling shoes were inexplicably once again becoming fashionable even in daytime, perhaps precursors of bound feet.

Hannah demanded, "Are we flooded?"

"Some," Jacob said, his squelchy moccasins agreeing. "I shut the water off so the cellar wouldn't get any wetter. There's a pretty good-sized split in the main line near the cellar window."

"Merciful heavens," Hannah said. "A party with no running water, quite impossible. Unless—can the pipe be mended?"

While Jacob hesitated, I thought of a Thanksgiving holiday with no running water, and Allegra said, slipping her pumps on, "Houses never cease to amaze me, they'll always surprise you. If he was alive, my grandfather would tell us that the old pipes in his day were predictable and never broke unless it was sixty below. Of course, he'd be lying through his dentures, as my grandmother would've been quick to point out. Endlessly fascinating, houses are."

Jacob said to Hannah, "You won't get a plumber tonight."

In the dining room Flossie cried triumphantly, "I know what's bothering you! Geisha girls!" and Percy, looking pleased but routed, fled toward our powwow in the alcove where Hannah broke the news to him none too gently, "Percy, buck up and don't go to pieces, we must tell our guests that our pipes have burst and the johns won't work so everyone will just have to go home and see in the New Year by themselves."

"What?" Percy asked. "I can't make my toast? I always make my Dickens toast, every year!"

Green eyes blank, Jacob said, "Uh, I've got enough pipe

to fix you up but it'll take a little while to go get my stuff and do it."

Hannah said swiftly, "How long?"

Percy said, "Oh, no, Jacob, that's kind of you but we should hire a plumber. You might cause damage, unintentionally but—"

"Percy," Hannah said, "shut up and keep out of his way. Thank you, Jacob. How long?"

"I'll have it fixed within an hour."

There were whisking rustles as Allegra lifted her taffeta skirt, took off her pumps again, and reached for the tall leather boots keeled over beneath a long black cloak hanging on a peg by the back door. "And I'm sure, Ib, that you'll want to supply some water for the interim. Do you still have all those water bottles I used to see you with in the village? Miriam, would you like to come help? Lesley? Hannah, could we borrow Lesley? We'll take my car, so Jacob can hurry back in his."

The headlights of Allegra's cream Audi behind us, Jacob and I found ourselves driving home in a state of coitus interruptus, the party not over, the old year unfinished. Snowbanks were snowplow-packed high and flat and silvery sharp on either side of the slippery white road.

Jacob said, "What if the Lords offer to pay me? Awkward."

"Say you'll take it out in wassail. Startling to learn that Allegra is a Dinsmere native, I'd've guessed she was a flatlander."

"Is Batch hoping the natives are restless? I'll need a couple of couplings plus the propane torch, and copper tubing and—oh, what the hell, I'd better bring my toolbox."

"And you'd better change into your rubber boots."

Caca Thibodeau's plowing technique was to shove our driveway snow smack up against the ell so he'd have room for succeeding snowstorms. Such foresight suffocated the ell with a huge pillow of snow over its face. Only the old wooden storm door and the new outside light managed to breathe. Spreading up above the ell roof, this snowpile had broken off the icicles here, but icicles thicker and longer than my arms hung all along the front eaves of the main house in a deep North-Pole frieze that perhaps was what, as much as Jacob's appropriate hirsuteness, had inspired the principal of the village elementary school to phone him and make a request, politely declined, that he play Santa Claus at the younger children's Christmas party. ("Holy shit," Jacob had said, replacing the receiver aghast, "ho-ho-hoing to a horde of keyed-up little fuckers. Not to mention just plain entering a school again.")

In the kitchen, which felt like an igloo because of the frosty ceiling and the snow blocking out the windows, I said to Allegra, Miriam, Lesley, "Don't bother about your boots. Really."

Allegra cried, "Oh, God, you're not going to paint the floors instead of finishing them, are you?"

The kitchen floor now looked as though it had cut itself shaving and had stanched the nicks with bits of toilet paper, for Jacob had daubed spots of white primer on the innumerable knots.

"Yes," he said firmly, going into his toolroom.

Lesley, teenage inscrutable, glanced from the hole in the bathroom wall to Jacob's entrance hole in the ceiling.

"You can't!" Allegra unclasped her cloak. "Jacob, you mustn't! If you value at all my input into your work here—"

Durance vile, I thought as I went into the dining room and crawled under the pantry table to reach the water jugs I'd stored away after we'd had the second well's water tested and learned it was clear of poison and plague. Why didn't the luxury of hot and cold drinkable water transform Shelterfield? Why was it still so cheerless? The raw emptiness of the gutted ell and the decay of the main house were the obvious answers, yet lately I'd sensed something else. The Briggs ghosts, the families who'd built this place and farmed it and then left it for better prospects either above or below ground, had seemed to be returning to see what was happening now to the homestead they'd abandoned to the forest and to beavers. But these interested presences didn't warm the house with a sense of comforting tradition, hardships overcome, chestnuts roasting. The ghosts were watching Jacob sardonically; they chilled my marrow.

In her betoggled car coat, Miriam squatted down beside the table. "Here, pass me that carton."

"What does 'In-Service Training Specialist' mean?"

After a moment she said, "So Batch squealed."

"And 'Special Education,' your doctorate in Special Education." Fearing Miriam would be as sensitive about the job she'd quit as Jacob was, I impulsively dared to ask such personal questions only because I was hidden, barricaded by this sub-table assortment of paraphernalia. "Batch just happened to say in passing that before you came up here you'd worked at a seacoast restaurant, and before that you'd—well, Jacob tried to interpret your title for me, but he's been away from schools a while and he's probably getting rusty."

"And you're probably being polite," Miriam said. "Teachers despise what I did."

Keeping low behind a double boiler and a Dutch oven, groping for the last carton, remembering our American supplies stored under our Oxford bed, I demurred, "Jacob wasn't actually a teacher."

"I suppose he mentioned 'mainstreaming.' "

"But I got it confused with 'mainlining.' "

Jacob leaned into the dining room and asked, "It was the teachers, then, not the administration or the kids, that made you quit?"

Miriam said, "Lesley, come get these and start filling them."

"Let there be light!" Jacob dropped the subject and switched the outside light off and on. "Allegra, forget the floors and instead admire the new wiring and congratulate me on still being alive. As whatshisname, the electrician, told me when he put in the panel, 'Electricity will bite anybody, it don't care who you are.' See you back at the party. Ib, could you give the stove a stir before you leave?"

"Yes." I straightened up and looked at him. "We'll be right along."

The moment the door closed behind Jacob and his toolbox, Allegra said, "Ib, you must make Jacob stop planning to paint the floors, and, anyway, the interior decorating should be your business, not his."

Miriam went into the living room.

I said, "The house is Jacob's job. The whole house."

"Then," Allegra said, *"I'll* have to keep working on him." Scanning all the wires sticking out of little square holes in the plaster, she proceeded to inspect the other rooms, and I pictured her showing Shelterfield to customers while Jacob and I, embarrassed, made ourselves scarce, as we had when the Exmouth Realty people showed the yellow house while we were in it. "Granted," she called back, "granted the floors are poor quality, and granted the old Briggses would have painted them if they'd had two dimes to rub together, but buyers love refinished floors, pine or not, so Jacob must sacrifice his taste to theirs if he wants a quick turnover. How many electrical outlets is he planning upstairs? You never can have too many outlets."

Lesley had taken off her parka and hitched up her Sweetpea dress. Carrying a carton of water jugs, she approached the sink the way I'd approach a horse, trepidation and resolution vying.

"I'm sorry," I said, recollecting that a sink perched on two-by-fours took some getting used to, "I'll fill." So this was the child whom Batch perhaps saw more of than he did his own children. "You and your mother are renting a house in East Dinsmere? I hope it's in better shape than this."

"It's okay."

I wished Jacob hadn't volunteered his services to the Lords; I wished the party had ended precipitately and we were now climbing into bed between the blue-striped flannel sheets Dorothy and Sebastian had given us for Christmas. As I pushed the sink faucet on, the thought of Gary in Bermuda enjoying his third honeymoon floated into my mind. Gary always worked with a mirror hung behind his potter's wheel so he could see the far side of what he was doing; he had longed for a mirror on the bedroom ceiling although he knew full well that it would have elicited from me not erotic panting but gales of incapacitating giggles.

I said to Lesley, "That bathroom wall is missing because of moving-day ferocity. Lately I've been putting myself to sleep by imagining a dream bathroom, a green-and-white bathroom all decked out with such frills as an apothecary jar of soap balls but equipped with a wall and a door, too. The apartment we lived in in England, it had a toilet chain. Over there, they called our type of mechanism a low-down flush."

Handing me the next jug, Lesley smiled uncertainly.

Encouraged, I continued, "I expect you've heard of Newmarket? A racing town made fashionable by Charles the Second? We lived nearby, and we used to go there shopping. Instead of Beware of Dog signs, there were signs saying 'Beware Race Horses.' "

"Really?"

"And they meant it. Horses everywhere. Splendid sight, to come into the town past horses being exercised on vast expanses of green. Market days were a madhouse, though, with stalls along the street instead of in a square. Their main street became Filene's Basement."

"Is that a birdfeeder out this window? Your brother said you'd hung a birdfeeder even before you moved in. He was trying to hang one of ours, but he got kind of tangled up in it so I did."

"He what? Yes, yes, we're getting mostly chickadees nowadays, aren't you? They're my favorite, I'm a chickadee groupie."

"I like evening grosbeaks best of winter birds."

Virginia was erratic about Christmas cards, but a National Wildlife postcard of chickadees had arrived two weeks ago on which she'd scrawled, "Willie spending vacation in Bridgeford with Mother and Daddy. Max and I are supposed to play newlyweds." Under its postmark, the postcard instructed: USE THIS HOLIDAY POSTCARD TO PROMOTE CONSERVATION OF AMERICA'S PRICELESS WILD HERITAGE.

Miriam came into the kitchen, Allegra behind her saying, "I take it Paul gave you the choice of working either tonight or the football crowd tomorrow? The bottom line is tips and—"

I had never realized until Shelterfield how hard it is to wash dishes at a nearly free-standing sink, without a counter at one's elbow. But now, filling these jugs, I suddenly had a bucket brigade, Lesley passing me the empties, Allegra taking the filled and handing them to Miriam who set them into cartons on the floor. Yet why the hell, it belatedly occurred to me, was I, not Batch, spending New Year's Eve in the company of Miriam and Lesley—and Allegra? And, come to think of it, were Miriam and Allegra, perhaps, prospective sisters-in-law, good or bad book-returners? Nicole was a bad. Batch had been as a kid a surprisingly good, but on the road he bought and forgot paperbacks. If Miriam married Batch, what would I be to Lesley? A step-aunt? Had Miriam and Allegra preferred the Lords' party to ringing in the new year with Batch? Had romance withered?

"My grandchildren," said Allegra, almost causing me to spurt the ceiling with our hard-won water. "Dick and Mike both put their children on the phone when they called at Christmas, and I gather that the NFL bedspreads I sent the grandsons were acceptable but even the two-year-old would have preferred a Dallas Cowboys helmet. Is that the last? Then we can be on our way."

"The stove." I dried my hands, went into the living room, and as I added a log I heard Allegra telling Miriam, "When I sold Paul the Sidelines I kept my misgivings to myself but I was afraid it wasn't viable and he'd be wanting to sell within the year and go back to the classroom. I'm happy for once to be proved wrong."

"Well," Miriam said vaguely.

"And if you too decide to settle up here for good and you don't like wasting rent money, stop in anytime and look at the listings."

"Thank you."

At the Audi, Miriam and I did an after-you-my-dear-

Alphonse until Miriam, becoming a member of our family again, said, "Don't you get carsick in back?"

"Centuries ago!"

"You always had to be fed Canada Mints."

That defeated me; I got into the front seat. Miriam and Lesley and I held on our laps the cartons, and I looked across at Allegra driving the white road and ventured, "You have children who live long-distance?"

"Dick in Atlanta, Mike in Los Angeles, both of them in the computer game and neither of them complaining about heating bills although they won't tell me the cost of their air-conditioning."

"Oh."

"Richard, my husband, was a Crandall on his mother's side. I'm sure you've heard all about how he drowned in Lake Pequawket in nineteen-fifty-one."

"No. No, I haven't."

"We were living in the Crandall cottage beyond your place, we were their caretakers that fall, and Richard was working at the Meader Intervale Appliance Center, learning TV repair. He foresaw the possibilities for TV repair."

"That must be where we took our TV to be fixed last month?"

"They made house calls back then. Dick was a year old, and I was eight months pregnant with Mike. At last, it's come to me, there's a little man in the Intervale who might be the tinker Jacob wants, he works for the boatyard but he has a fix-it shop at home, he did the Lords' barn-door hinges."

"I'll tell Jacob. Thanks."

"His name will come to me next. He played the blacksmith in the Intervale's bicentennial pageant. It's an apple, his name."

"McIntosh?" Miriam suggested from the back seat. "Baldwin?"

"Not quite," Allegra said, "and not Delicious, either. The Crandalls helped me until the boys were in school and I could go to work, they were good about keeping me on as a caretaker until then, and whether or not it was conscience money makes no difference, it put food on the table. Cortland."

I pulled scrap-paper and pen out of my pocket.

"Joe Cortland." Allegra turned up the dashboard light while I scribbled. "For me, this was less a bicentennial year than the twenty-fifth anniversary of Richard's death."

Miriam asked, "Conscience money?"

"You hadn't heard, either? But then, you and Ib haven't joined the Grange or a sewing circle or anything, have you. Richard was with a woman. Sailing, at night, in late fall. She drowned too, which at first made me glad. Hello there, Lesley, I forgot you were with us, but I suppose you're old enough. I wasn't much older when I married Richard, seventeen and starry-eyed. Let that be a lesson."

The road now became congested with the parked cars not of hunters or rock-concert patrons but of the Lords' guests, all the bumper-to-bumper steel and chrome seeming to have failed in attempts to muscle the snowbanks for space. Along the eaves of the farmhouse, the Lords' heat-tapes zigzagged like the rickrack adorning Miriam's dress.

Allegra located the parking gap she'd left, maneuvered her car into it, and led us with our cartons down the heavily sanded path to the back door. "That used to be my bedroom up there, that window. You could always hear the pines. Well, by God, look at this, I might have predicted Jacob would draw a crowd!"

And so as 1976 came to a close, I helped Miriam and Lesley replenish carafes and ice-cube trays while the kitchen audience offered advice and libations down the cellar stairs to Jacob who soon climbed up to accept congratulations from these enthusiastic spectators and a hug from Hannah, his rubber boots glistening, his khakis sullied.

"My toast!" Percy shouted from the living room. "Charlemagne, sit!"

Everyone moved out toward where Percy stood beside the fireplace. Jacob and I reached the tavern table and poured Scotch. Before chiming, the grandfather clock made a preliminary whirring rattle, copying Percy by clearing its throat.

" 'My best of wishes,' " said Percy, " 'for your merry Christmases and your happy New Years, your long lives and your true prosperities. Here's a final prescription added. "To be taken for life." ' "

Snowshoeing on the frozen beaver swamp produced a peculiarly tropical sensation which at last on this early afternoon I identified as Floridian, pinning it down to movies and TV shows I'd seen about the Everglades; like an airboat skimming water thick with saw grass, my snowshoes were parting the tangles of dead bushes ahead and crushing underfoot dry stalks and papery brown reeds. Swish, snap.

A year ago today, I thought as eventually I returned to the banking and crossed along our packed path under the pines to the backyard raised ever higher by more snowstorms, a year ago right now Jacob and I were sitting in shock in the Pot o' Gold Restaurant. There had been a January thaw then. No such brilliant warmth today, except in my Everglades imagination, for this was the very dullest of winter weather, closed in, gray, cold.

"One year," I said to the chickadees tapping away on the bare lilac branches, "we have survived one year without a paycheck—or a royalty check." But although Jacob continued to handle the bills because the sight of a checkbook still made me shake so much I couldn't sign my name, I had not lost the ability to do mental math and I knew quite well that all that remained in our savings account was about five thousand dollars.

While I unbuckled my snowshoes and clapped them as if I were cleaning blackboard erasers, shedding snow instead of chalk, I remembered with wistful sadness the battle I'd fought in vain years ago with the Millsted bank, trying to get my name added to Jacob's on the checkbook folder. It was the bank's policy to print the husband's name alone on the folder, only permitting the two joint-account names on the checks themselves and there the husband's name always came first, not alphabetically. Since time immemorial; case closed. Jacob's father never even bothered to help us, much less to understand my outrage at his bank, for this was just one of Ib's quirks which Jacob humored. When we were given at the People's National, our new bank in Meader Intervale, a joint-checking-account checkbook folder stamped with Jacob's name in solitary gilt splendor, I had made no protest.

As I went into the barn to hang up the snowshoes, I heard the phone begin to ring. After lunch Jacob had gone back to work on the clothesdryer wiring, a task that involved, instead of ceilings, the crawl-space under the bathroom once again. Could he hear the telephone down deep in the trench?

Jacob usually liked our various anniversaries, excuses for revelry, but he seemed to be trying to sneak through this day without attracting its attention, and if I hadn't mentioned it yesterday, saying, "How should we celebrate tomorrow? We've got one last Porterhouse steak in the freezer I could start thawing," I doubted he would have acknowledged the occasion at all. He'd replied, "Don't they claim that only the British celebrate defeats?" And so, constrained, I hadn't decorated a cake with independence colors and lettered it RAISON D'ÊTRE, or made funny though clumsy posters showing the progress of his sun through the heavens, or planned more than a kale casserole for supper.

The phone kept ringing. I dashed indoors into the igloo kitchen and found Jacob grabbing the receiver, dusting ineffectually at his overalls stiff with frozen cellar slime. "Hello? Oh. Hello, Dad."

His parents' careful calendar of official and family events like Mother's Day and great-grandchildren's birthdays—and those dates never spoken of, Timmy's birth and death and whatever other milestones, such as his first tooth, his first word, his first two-wheel bike, Edna marked in her reveries—did not include, I would have bet my snowshoes, the first anniversary of Jacob's quitting; Phil couldn't be calling to reaffirm disapprobation and inquire when Jacob was going to resume his true career.

"Sonofabitch," Jacob said. "Okay, we'll be right down. Bye-bye." He hung up. "The house has been broken into."

"Our house? Our other house?"

"Dad phoned Moose. We've got to go down there, see if anything's missing."

"Standing empty. Asking for it."

"They smashed the bathroom window to get in. Looks like snow, what was the forecast?"

"Just cloudy."

"Cock the faucets open, will you, in case we're gone too long, and I'll stoke the stove."

"Change your clothes."

We left Shelterfield fast. A year ago today we had fled the feelings in the house we were now rushing to succor.

"A risk," Jacob said as he drove past the Thibodeaus' where Sarge gazed at us from the porch step, "but I'd hoped any prospective burglars would be put off by Dad's patrols. Lucky he didn't surprise them and get himself killed. Fucking bastards!"

"Did they come from afar or from the trailers? The plowed driveway must've looked very inviting."

"An unplowed drive wouldn't have stopped them, only slowed them up, they could've used snowmobiles, and it would have signaled that the house wasn't lived in."

We glanced out the window at Flossie Sisson's red schoolhouse. No moving van in the yard.

I said, "It's not like Flossie's treasure-trove. We didn't leave anything for them to steal."

"The telephones. They probably stole the phones."

"Your father wasn't calling from there?"

"Of course not, Ib, he was calling from home."

"Oh. Yes."

"He didn't mention our phones, I gather he was too shook up to check more than the busted window. Who knows what else besides the phones they found to steal. Christ, probably they yanked out all the copper tubing."

The village pond, circled by trampled snowbanks, was empty of skaters; under the gloomy sky an unattended Labrador retriever was taking a crap on the ice.

I said, "Everyone is going to say we were 'ripped off.' Why is it easier for everyone to call it that? Because it sounds like a prank, not a crime, less terrifying, is that why?"

"Maybe we should have rented the place until it sold."

"Another risk. No matter how tidy the people might appear, they could be slobs. Most people are slobs."

"I know."

We both were thinking that this wouldn't have happened if we'd stayed there through the winter instead of moving to Shelterfield to camp out. It wouldn't have happened if Jacob hadn't quit. It wouldn't have happened if—

I said, "Drag such thoughts back far enough and it wouldn't have happened if we hadn't been born, so let's drop that nonsense."

"I wish to God the house had sold."

Leaving Dinsmere behind, emerging from mountains decapitated by clouds, we tried to settle down for the drive we had done so often last summer and autumn, back and forth, back and forth, my clipboard on my lap then, the utility trailer looping each curve behind us, Jacob silently confronting his new career, back and forth as the leaves of the trees turned and fell. Now in Winnipesaukee's coves there were shantytowns of bobhouses painted leftover colors bright enough to melt the ice and sink the surrounding pickups and snowmobiles.

Abstracted, I made the mistake of saying, "What are those men doing out there fishing and hunkering on a Thursday?"

"Retired," Jacob replied. "Laid off. Goofing off."

He didn't speak again for nearly an hour, until, after we'd left the north shore, entered the sparse woods of shacks and trailers, passed Rainbow Lake (née Skinner Pond) with the Pot o' Gold's deep-fat smell oozing through our closed windows, and reached Millsted's Main Street, he suddenly asked, "When we bought our house here, why did we think it was for good?"

"We liked it." I did not add: And you liked your job.

"Always hard to remember how one's head worked."

"There were the woods, *our* woods. Complete with underbrush, unlike Clopton Park's plantation. A whole house to ourselves, after half a laundry cottage. Mangy Millsted had its drawbacks, such as Sunday dinners at your folks', but our place was fine then."

Main Street seemed as deserted as usual; tumbleweed still waited off-camera.

Parking alongside the wooden Victorian police station painted a municipal gray, Jacob said, "What was the dispatcher's name? Peggy?" and went inside, while I looked at this station and recalled the cozy flowerbeds outside the Clopton police station, too modern a building, however, a small yellow-brick nonentity, to figure in a proper English murder mystery. Beyond that station had lain the alternate route from the High Street to Clopton Park that we had discovered come spring when I introduced Jacob to walking. A quiet footpath sheltered in an avenue of trees whose lumpy branches looked like cavemen's clubs, it was lined with the backs of old flint-and-brick houses and on either side were glimpses of privacy, back gardens, dooryards, little curtained windows. The bowling green astounded us each time, a sudden meadow. Soon came the vicarage, and we would take a shortcut through the churchyard, past the crooked headstones sunk lower than the grass growing tall around them, out through the gate and down an ancient street where the almshouse too was sinking, crumbling into weeds and flowers gone wild. And then we were in the newest yellow-brick housing development, where some of the bungalows' meticulous yards were so neat they didn't have any lawns at all, just clean smooth pebbles. Beyond were shells of even newer bungalows, their cement mixers and stacks of new bricks and tiles encroaching on the last of a neighborhood of flint houses that stood empty, windows broken. Crossing a dirt road between this development and the sugar-beet fields, we would study the sky, and once in a while we saw a skylark up there, playing like a surfboarder on the waves of the wind.

Jacob got back into the car. "Peggy radioed Moose, he'll meet us at the house."

The Millsted Shopping Center's parking lot was vacant except for a Coca-Cola truck at the A&P. In the window of the hardware store the FOR SALE sign still was propped, somewhat more faded and curled.

"Hardware," Jacob said. "I'll need glass to fix the window —no, maybe it'd be easier to ask Dad to do it. Why didn't we consider buying this hardware store?"

"We wanted to escape Millsted. And you told me it had never exactly been a thriving business even before the hardware chains in Exmouth dealt it a death blow."

"Maybe I should've tried."

The dreary afternoon kept darkening. Now we were amid the trailers that had invaded our country road: new trailers, old trailers, burnt-out trailers; the capped cellarhole; rusty plows and drooping clotheslines; the aluminum wreath with aqua bells still hanging on the door of the pink trailer, having served through yet another Christmas and reminding me as always of the real holly wreaths we had bought for the laundry-cottage door each Christmas at the greengrocer's, eight shillings and sixpence.

"How come," Jacob said, "that within just three months everything has shrunk?"

For, like childhood scenes returned to, these had constricted, so the long driveway twisting through the woods seemed narrower between its snowbanks than we'd ever seen it, the trees were puny, and the pale yellow house and barn when we came to them could not possibly have contained ten years of our lives.

Jacob parked in front of the barn and took a flashlight from the glove compartment.

He said, "Feels as if we're a cross between guests paying a call and the Mounties to the rescue, doesn't it. At least the barn is still here, they didn't dismantle it for beams."

"I'd forgotten how flat the land is," I said and without warning burst into tears that were too hot to freeze.

"Shit," he said.

"I'm crying for two, I'll shed your tears, you get my ulcer." I hauled a wad of Kleenex out of my jacket pocket. "Do those tracks belong to the burglars?"

"Looks like one burglar."

"The Lone Robber?"

The intruder had scrambled up the snowbank above the driveway and plunged across the deep snow around the side of the barn.

I said, "There aren't any birds, your father forgot to fill the feeder."

"Might he be forgiven, under the circumstances?"

Taking a jangle of keys from his pocket, with gloved fingers Jacob deftly selected a barn key. Phil had kept the barn doorway shoveled out, disregarding our requests that he hire a kid to do the chore; Edna hadn't joined us in trying to dissuade him, whispering to us behind his back, "It don't bother him none if he goes slow, it gives him something to do—and it gets him out of my house!" Jacob unlocked the small door to the left of the big barn doors and we stepped into a great contained cold that seemed more penetrating than a northeast gale.

I said, "I always used to be suspicious of the burglary victims, especially men, who compared it to being raped. Exaggerating, I used to think. I ought to think so still, of course it isn't that devastating—"

"A violation, though." Jacob scanned the barn he'd completely cleaned of his years of puttering, leaving nary a woodshaving tendril; who else at the last hectic minute on moving day would sweep a barn floor? "The troughs and stanchion rails weren't stolen for the wrought iron, I thought for sure they'd be gone." He unlocked the door onto the porch. "Well. Good thing we told Dad not to bother hooking the screen door, it didn't get kicked in. Should've left the whole house unlocked."

The burglar had come around the barn, struggling in the snow, floundering, almost playing an unintentional game of "angels" here and there, his trail a wide splashy wake past the garden where only a few beige cornstalks poked through the drifts. He had entered the porch by the screen door, which, like the porch screens themselves, was covered with winter plastic. On the porch floor were ridges of hard snow-spatters stomped off his boots. He had actually paused to wipe his feet! Beside the back door to the kitchen, above the trash can of sunflower seeds, the bathroom window gaped.

"Bastard," Jacob said, striding over to inspect it. "He could care less what a combination storm window costs. Oh, Jesus."

I followed him and looked in through the sash at the downstairs bathroom. Glass lay on the wideboard floor, shards and sprinkles. Its hinges twisted, the toilet seat was skidded across the bowl, revealing the pool of purple anti-freeze Jacob had poured in when he turned off the water.

Jacob said, "Climbed from the birdseed can through the window onto the toilet."

This reminded me, and I brought in the birdfeeder tube from its hook by the screen door. "Okay to open the can, will Moose want to check it for fingerprints?"

"Are you serious?"

"How did the burglar figure out how to break in a combination storm? I never know how to open them at all, what part slides up, what part slides down."

Re-enacting the entry gave Jacob brief objectivity. "Simple, because the screens were off. He broke the bottom storm, raised it, broke a pane in the window, and reached up and unlatched the lock."

"Daytime or night?" I hung up the birdfeeder.

"Whichever, he wouldn't be seen from the road." Jacob went to the back door and took out his keys again, then stopped. "What the hell am I doing, the door is unlocked. He went in through the window, came out through the door."

In the kitchen I unslung my pocketbook and automatically flipped on the light-switch. But, like the phones, the electricity had been shut off. A year ago we had returned from the Pot o' Gold to find our saucepan of tomato soup abandoned on the kitchen stove. Now there was an empty slot in the cabinets where that stove had been before we moved it to Shelterfield. We too had robbed this house.

Jacob said, "The wallphone is still here."

"So's the dishwasher."

"Christ, it's as cold indoors as a tomb."

Unwillingly, we continued our investigation. The echoing living room. My office, its mute telephone sitting on the floor. Early dusk made everything hazy, like the dust motes we stirred up.

In the downstairs bathroom Jacob said, "Honest to God, lately my life seems to consist of nothing but toilets. At least this creep did break just the seat hinges, not the tank or bowl."

"If we hadn't left the lid down, he wouldn't have stepped onto it. We must be the only people who religiously put the lid as well as the seat down every time, and what reward do we get?"

"If we had left the lid up, we might've got rewarded with a mouse pickled in antifreeze." Jacob went back into the living room. "Why should the rooms have shrunk as well? They ought to look larger, without furniture."

"There must be some principle about that."

Down cellar we next went, by flashlight. I felt like an illustration in a *Nancy Drew*. Or was I remembering our descending a ladder into Grime's Graves? Jacob, however, was moved to song.

" 'With cat-like tread, upon our prey we steal; in silence dread, our cautious way we feel.' "

The granite-block walls looked positively civilized compared to Shelterfield's two rough cellars.

Jacob said, "I'll be goddamned. The water pump is still here. Copper tubing. Everything."

"A vandal, not a thief?"

"I don't know."

We retreated up to the living room.

"Save batteries," Jacob said, switching off the flashlight. "Upstairs, next."

We climbed the steep staircase to the hallway. The upstairs bathroom was intact, yet, like the downstairs bathroom, it seemed as naked as ghosts of us bathing, for it had been denuded on moving day of its green shower curtain. Newer than the downstairs curtain, this was the one Jacob had chosen to hang across Shelterfield's tub and shower last month while I suggested to no avail that we hang the other across the doorless doorway and the missing section of bathroom wall.

Our boots thumping over hollow rooms below, we checked the guest rooms and our bedroom and found only chill dust clouding the floors I'd dry-mopped after Curly and Goddamn had removed the furniture and rugs.

Back in the hallway, Jacob switched on the flashlight again. We climbed steeper stairs to the attic and peered along the flashlight beam at blank space, tidy corners. This had never been, for us, a grandmother's attic jam-packed with dress-up trunks, love letters, age-pocked photographs; empty before our move of anything but our suitcases and my typewriter junkyard, it now still held no secrets. We returned to the hallway and looked at each other.

I said, "Nothing at all has been stolen?"

"Vandalism."

"And the turtles weren't even thrown into the monkey cage."

"No."

"It's awfully cold."

In the driveway a car door slammed.

"Moose," Jacob said.

As Jacob dived down the stairs, I looked around our dim bedroom once more. Because of the turmoil of moving day, it hadn't occurred to me when I bade the house farewell that during our ten years here we had made love in every single room, not to mention on the porch and in the barn and harum-scarum amongst the thirty-five acres. Well, we wouldn't be staying at Shelterfield long enough to repeat unplanned such a moveable romance.

"Insurance?" Jacob was saying to Moose in the living room when I reached them. "We've got a hundred dollars deductible. What are the chances of catching this bastard?"

Moose wasn't a reverse joke; he loomed as large as his nickname. A few years older than Jacob, he had for a time dated Jacob's sister in high school, and the inroads he'd made on the Wetherbee refrigerator after escorting Louise to a double feature had consternated Edna, used though she was to Jacob's raids. "Don't get your hopes up," he told Jacob, clanking with equipment as he hauled out a notebook which became lilliputian when he gripped it against his straining blue uniform. "Hi, Ib. Let's see, Jacob, your dad said you have a set of keys, he has a set, and they have a set at Exmouth Reality, right? When did he last check this place?"

"Sunday, shoveling out after that storm."

Moose had been the first policeman I'd seen when we returned from England; spared the sight of American cops for two years, it had taken me at least a full minute to register what he was, this apparition walking along Main Street with weaponry. If not the village idiot, I'd thought, then at least the town eccentric, an overgrown baby still playing cowboys and Indians.

"False alarm, then," Moose said. "Too bad you had to drive all the way down, but no way of telling."

I sensed Jacob's instant exasperated fury, though he replied mildly enough, "Not exactly a false alarm. Those trailers look like a good place to start, don't they, and of course we'll want the damage paid for."

"I'll see what we can do, but I can't promise anything. What's your estimate?"

"Two hundred bucks."

"That's kind of high, isn't it? You can buy a toilet seat for five bucks. Be glad he didn't use the toilet, they usually do—if they don't use the floor or anyplace else that strikes them."

"Two hundred dollars. The toilet seat, the window, our gasoline getting here, and the assault on our nervous systems."

Moose whacked shut his notebook and headed toward the back door. "Had any offers for this house yet?"

"Nothing definite."

"I hear you're asking forty-eight? Well, you can always drop the price."

Outside, Moose's radio crackled with discourse as he opened the car door and eased himself into the seat, causing the cruiser to sink on its springs.

The birdfeeder was clustered with chickadees. From the porch we waved our Dinsmere wave.

Then after Moose's taillights had disappeared down the driveway, Jacob said, "Let's get the hell out of here. Come on."

How wearisome this road again! Our headlights stroked each trailer. No kids were playing in the snow, so they must instead be indoors in front of the TV glimmer while outdoors packs of dogs were hanging around much like the ice-fishing men. Next time when I tried to fall asleep, I thought, I shouldn't rearrange dream offices, dream bathrooms, or count telephones; I should map these trailers in my memory, getting their sequence correct, to town and from. Yet that way lay madness, not repose. As we passed the shrine, its floodlight came on, illuminating the cement Virgin Mary and her devilish bathtub horns.

I said, "We weren't 'ripped off' and we weren't 'trashed.' Why?"

"Maybe something scared him. The house creaking, an owl."

Downtown, we turned onto the Wetherbee side-street. Although the houses here were still hanging on for dear life, even their snowbanks trying to look like pillars of society, they seemed to await the fate of those Clopton flint houses. The Wetherbees' front light beamed, in honor of us.

I asked, "What about supper? Your mother will have made extra."

"I've got the excuse all ready, we have to get home before the Jøtul goes out."

"They heard Jøtul excuses at Christmastime and didn't think much of them." Phil and Edna had, in the end, however, grudgingly accepted both our need to keep the stove stoked and our invitation to Boxing Day eggnog at Shelterfield, so their Christmas Day was bereft of us but full of Louise-Arthur-grandchildren-great-grandchildren, which seemed to us enough festive commotion for anybody, and the next day they came to Dinsmere and looked at the holes in our ceilings and walls.

"Before the pipes freeze," Jacob said, parking in the

driveway. "The stove and the pipes. No need to feel guilty."

But as we entered the kitchen we smelled chicken fricassee, a Jacob favorite never made by me. Pouring Scotch into her juice-glass jigger, Edna was wearing fruit and flowers, a plum-colored pantsuit and Gary's rosebud earrings that Jacob hadn't blinked a blank eye at when I produced them along with some Granite State Coop camouflage—leather bookmark for Phil, a needlepoint needlecase for Dorothy (coals to Newcastle), and silkscreened memo pads for Sebastian—which I'd bought when I picked up my repaired typewriter in Bridgeford before Christmas.

"Just like my tomatoes," Edna said, hurrying to kiss us. "After what they did to that gorgeous house of yours, I seen you drive in and thought you'd want a drink right away."

"I'm sorry," Jacob said, "we can't stay even for a drink—"

"Of course you can. Dad thinks maybe it was someone the real-estate people showed it to. That saying about an ill wind, at least it brought you here, didn't it, Dad?"

Trailing cigarette smoke, Phil came into the kitchen, today's retirement outfit of jaunty tangerine cardigan and blue stretchknit pants more outlandish than ever because of his thunderstruck pallor. But he attempted everyday exasperation (acting casual, I thought; for once, like father, like son) as he corrected, "Your mother has gotten it all wrong, the way she always does. What I said was, maybe some of the realtors have teenage children who know which houses are empty. Anything missing?"

"No," Jacob said, momentarily distracted. I realized that, accustomed by now to an oil range as well as a woodstove, he'd taken off his gloves and was looking for a place to warm his hands, but he couldn't even warm them over the radiators here because Phil had finally capitulated to the Arabs and had lowered the thermostat so drastically that Edna at last had knitted some thick sweaters for herself instead of for everyone else in the family. "The window, though," Jacob continued, shoving his hands into his jacket pockets, "would you mind fixing it, and the toilet seat got broken, could you buy a new one and let me know how much for everything? No, Mom, please, don't pour any for us, really, we have to dash back and tend the stove before the house seizes up."

"Cute as a button," Edna said, "Buddy's baby and Cindy's girls, we got the pictures from Christmas in them red snowsuits we give them, you can stay long enough to look at the pictures."

Jacob said, "We really—"

Sucking his teeth, Phil began his story. "You could have knocked me over with a feather when I got out of the car and saw those tracks. Something you *expect*, that's why I'm checking the house, but still when you see the real thing you don't believe it. By Jesus, I told myself, this is the real thing. Then I saw the broken window. Wellsir, the question was, were they still in there? I wasn't about to find out the answer, that's for sure!"

"Really, please," Jacob said. "We just stopped by to tell you nothing's missing and thanks for spotting the break-in. Yes, Dad, the better part of valor. We'll be in touch. Moose will be in touch."

"Thank you," I said. "Wish we could stay. Ah, the responsibilities of heating with wood!"

Out in the car, our self-loathing was as dense as the kitchen's smell of chicken gravy. Jacob said, "I guess we might as well take the zoomer just in case the stove actually has gone out," so instead of turning off toward the road to the Pot o' Gold he drove across downtown, closed now except for the 6 Bits Diner, to the main highway.

I said, "We'll never be reimbursed, will we. The culprit will go scot-free."

"Are there any Tums in the glove compartment?"

Along the highway, straight, flat, and unabashedly ugly, were shallow woods; our headlights glimpsed billboards still advertising PRIME BUILDING SITES on hardscrabble fields smoothed by snow. I found the stub of a tube of Tums in the far corner of the glove compartment. Beside the state highway plow-sheds and their bright yellow plows were two heights of land, the salt pile and the sand pile, covered with black plastic.

This was the highway that bypassed Millsted so thoroughly the town was forgotten, only the highway known. It catered to tourists and natives alike, offering in intervals, between gravel pits and cars abandoned off the shoulders, its seedy assortment of services: a body shop, Hal's Junqtiques & Old Bottles, a log-cabin model home, the Curious Kitten Gift Shoppe, a used-car lot, trailerparks, a bowling alley, the Country Bumpkin Flea Market, assorted real estate offices, a Lions Club clubhouse, a mobile-home saleslot, Betty's Snack Bar and Beauty Salon, and a discount furniture emporium.

Jacob said, "I wonder which is worse, having parents or being parents. At least we'll never sin on the latter side. Oh, for Christ's sake, why didn't I think of Arthur?" He braked, flicking directionals. "I'll drop the flange off here instead of at whatshisname's, Joe Apple."

"Will Arthur do it cheaper? He's an apple too, an Adam's apple."

"We'll work it out."

For a wedding present twenty-four years ago, Phil had arranged and cosigned the mortgage loan so Louise and Arthur could buy this building into whose parking lot Jacob was making a U-turn. It had been a debilitated garage then; it still was shingled with that rust-colored asphalt siding everyone had slapped on everything during the Depression, but when I'd first seen the place ten years ago it had had a spruce air of proudly grimy prosperity and Jacob had remarked that instead of saying SMITH'S WELDING, the sign should say FILTHY LUCRE. Now the building had slid into a depression again, and on the wall near the outside staircase was a more recent sign, smaller, shyer, CLOTHING ALTERATIONS, with an arrow pointing to the second-floor apartment in which Louise and Arthur had lived and raised their family all these years.

Parking beside Arthur's pickup, we got out of the car. Jacob produced from the trunk a round metal cup that I took to be the flange, and passing a nightlight in the double-door windows which showed shadows of an anvil and acetylene tanks, we climbed the staircase to the landing above the snowbanks.

"Jacob!" Louise opened the door and hugged us. Nearly Jacob's height, eyes not green but Edna's brown, her sandy hair somehow more aging than Jacob's white, she was a thin woman, shoulderblades, hipbones, and quick. As authoritative as Jacob with inanimate objects, in high school she had been a drum majorette, exercising authority over batons; this evening she was wearing brown wool slacks she'd made years ago and an Edna-knitted brown crewneck sweater, but when she moved they transformed themselves into the short white satin uniform with frogged bodice of red braid I'd seen in her photograph albums and yearbook, and you expected her to start strutting, twirling.

Jacob said, "You've heard the news?"

"Mom called, what a hell of a note! I don't suppose Moose was any help. What was stolen? Come in, come in, can you stay to supper, how about a drink? Eric, your Uncle Jacob is here, say hello, where's your father gone to—oh, the bathroom."

Louise kept this big apartment pristine and as distant from the business below as a penthouse. She defied dirt with pale-patterned wallpaper; the windows were veiled with loops of sheer priscilla curtains. Across the gold wall-to-wall carpet lay a path of plastic leading from this door and the inside-staircase door to the nubbly oatmeal-colored sofa which had been very modern twenty-four years ago, its gauntness matching Louise's.

And cantilevered upon the sofa, watching an *All-in-the-Family* rerun at pitched-battle pitch, sprawled Eric. Long-legged, sixteen years old, their youngest child, the spitting image of boring Arthur, he was the only kid still at home. Nineteen-year-old Lynne, in management training at the Exmouth McDonald's, shared an Exmouth apartment with girlfriends; twenty-two-year-old Buddy (Arthur Philip), the plumbing-wholesaler stock manager who'd got us our fixtures at cost, lived in an Exmouth trailerpark with his wife, Sharon, who, in addition to taking care of their baby, Jason, worked part-time at a Zayre's Department Store; and also in Exmouth lived twenty-three-year-old Cindy, in a development of little pastel houses on a stripped hillside, with her daughters, Kim and Michelle, and her husband, Don Vachon, who drove a Wise Potato Chip truck.

"No," Jacob was answering Louise, crossing to the TV to turn the volume down, "nothing had been stolen, strangely enough—yes, thank you, we could use a quick belt, but don't tell the folks, we begged off there. Hello, Eric, are you going deaf like the rest of your generation? How're things at school?"

"All right," Eric replied. His Adam's apple seemed to be his only personality.

Setting my pocketbook in a bentwood rocker, I unzipped my jacket and followed Louise into the kitchen. On the chopping block was a mound of meatloaf of which she assumed control, scooping it up, plopping it into the waiting loafpan. Sliding the pan into the oven, she asked, "Have you been able to hang your brass rubbings yet? I always loved to look at them and think of you and Jacob doing them."

"I did fewer and fewer. Instead, while Jacob was rubbing I would wander around the church and read things like how Lady Somebody left an income of so many pounds to be used for buying waistcoats and loaves of bread for the poor."

Louise washed her hands, snaked an ice-cube tray from the refrigerator, set out two smoked-glass tumblers, poured Scotch. "Even if nothing was stolen, Ib, you and Jacob must still be pissed off. When she called me, Mom kept going on and on about her stolen tomatoes, and that was an example to me not to tell you again about how my pocketbook was ripped off at the supermarket last summer but I'd already bought my groceries so all I lost was my precious time wasted filing a police report and a dollar seventy-seven cents and my compact and lipstick and a damn good pair of nail scissors."

The sewing room off the kitchen had once been Cindy and Lynne's bedroom; through the doorway I could see an open closet in which the clothes now hanging weren't the girls' but were pinned with customers' names. Insisting she charge me her official rate, I had brought my occasional trade here when Louise went into the alterations business, and, until Jacob quit, as I paid her the two dollars now and then for shortening a pair of jeans I'd just bought, I had thought how I would prefer starving or the introduction of bamboo slivers under my fingernails to sitting down at a sewing machine for extra money.

"How are the kids?" I asked.

"Oh, fine." Louise gave me a glass and carried the other into the living room to Jacob. "Can't you stay to supper?"

Jacob said, "Thanks very much, but we've got woodstove responsibilities—hi, Arthur."

Arthur came out of the bathroom, balding, spindly, wearing dark green workclothes. Unlike Phil's specialized outfits, these workclothes were apparently all-occasion attire, for I couldn't remember seeing Arthur ever wear anything else, be he in his shop, or watching television, or even sitting down to one of Edna's holiday feasts; I'd never dared ask Louise if he also wore them to bed. But the workclothes were always crisp, and when he shook hands with Jacob there was a smell of Lava soap.

"How's it going?" Jacob asked. "I was wondering if you might braise this for me. No hurry, I just want to have the sump pump ready for the spring thaw."

Louise's face had closed when Arthur appeared, reminding me, as during their Thanksgiving visit, of Theresa Thibodeau's shuttered look, but now she laughed affectionately. "Jacob, you and your foresight."

"Fuck that," said Arthur, Adam's apple bobbing. "What you been doing lately, Jacob? Nothing? No, that's right, you had to leave off doing nothing and come down here because you got yourself a break-in."

Arthur might have punched Jacob instead of shaken hands. Flaring crimson, Jacob set his glass on an end table beside a miniature lobster trap bought at Old Orchard Beach. "Sorry," he gasped, "shouldn't have dropped in unannounced, I'll get the flange done elsewhere, we'll be on our way."

"Good idea," Arthur agreed. Slow on the uptake, I'd immediately assumed he must be drunk; but he wasn't. "First, though," he said, "aren't you going to thank me for not busting the place up more? I could have set it on fire, you know, and who would pay forty-eight thousand for a cellarhole?"

Louise's efficient hands flailed air.

"Don't believe me?" Arthur asked. "Well, I took your thermostat, I bet you didn't even notice. The one in my shop was broken, and I figured yours would work just fine. It does. Two houses, and one of them left empty like that."

Without spilling, I put my glass down on the other side of the lobster trap. I slung my pocketbook over my shoulder. Civilities must be maintained at all cost. "Jacob, the stove, aren't we leaving?"

But Jacob had gone strange too. Very still; deadly; oblivious of Louise and me. Men *are* foreign creatures, I thought wildly, you have to stop and remember this every once in a while as you wend your way through life pretending they're natives like you.

Louise said, "Eric, go do your homework in your room," but Eric, seemingly deaf indeed, at least to grownups' talk, stayed glued to a Kentucky Fried Chicken commercial.

"Moose," I reassured her, beginning to babble, "Moose won't pursue it, don't worry, you know what we say about Moose, change one letter in his name and he's Mouse— unless, do you want him to?"

"Yes," Louise said.

Arthur said, "Who are you to turn up your nose at a paycheck and walk away, huh? Bet I scared the shit out of your old man, didn't I? I was still in there when he came poking around."

Jacob reached for him.

Dodging, Arthur slipped on the plastic path and fell. "Get out of here. All of you." He scrambled up, ran across the room, and opened the door to the inside staircase that led to the shop. "Get out of here. I mean it." He tried to slam the door behind him as he plunged down the stairs, but it gave up midway, only slinking shut.

Jacob's spirit rejoined us. "What the hell do I do about Dad, Louise? If he finds out Arthur was the one who—"

"I think," she said, "that maybe Arthur means it this time. Usually when he says I should get out because he's going to blow the place up, usually he's drunk, but he's not now."

I said, "Blow it up?"

Jacob said, "You're kidding."

Louise looked around the room. "He means it this time. If he did that to your house."

I said, "Let's go."

"Wait," Jacob said, "does he have that much gas down there?"

"A half-dozen tanks," Louise said. "Maybe more. I always wondered what I'd grab as I left—for God's sake, don't waste time going down there and doing something stupid like trying to talk him out of it—"

The door to the inside staircase opened. Arthur leaned into the room. "I told you. I'm going to blow this fucking place up, so get out of here." Now when he closed the door on himself he made sure it shut; a bolt slid softly.

Louise yanked Eric off the sofa, pushed us all toward the outside door, switched on the outside light. "Eric, where's your jacket?"

"Don't know."

"Doesn't matter, come on, got to get as far away as possible."

Jacob said, "Jesus Christ," and pellmell we were at the bottom of the staircase where through the black-and-white striped darkness shone the shop's windows full of the fluorescent lighting of a laboratory. Arthur was in there, I could see him busy in there. Jacob said, "I should—"

"No time." Louise shoved Eric into the back of our car. "No time, Jacob, all he's got to do is strike a spark."

"What about your Maverick?"

"Repossessed." She stepped neatly in after Eric.

As Jacob and I jumped into the front seat, I thought: The car won't start, or it will stall. He turned on the ignition; it started up. I realized I'd hooked my seatbelt but for the first time that I could remember Jacob hadn't fastened his. He forgot the headlights, too, until we'd bucked out of the parking lot and were tearing along the highway the way we'd come, toward Millsted to find Moose. When I turned and looked back at the building's lights beyond a snowy field, I saw that Eric was also looking back but Louise, like Jacob, was staring straight ahead.

A sound like a thousand beaver dams exploding. Our car leapt. Off the ground rose Smith's Welding, its walls peeling away. A great bright cloud of dust showered the sky before the flames began.

"Hello?" I said, snatching the impatient phone as we came indoors from the trip home after the funeral in Millsted.

"Is it incest?" Virginia asked. "I called in sick yesterday and did one of those driving and driving stints, thinking and thinking, and I found myself over the border—"

"Mexican? Canadian?"

"No, Ib, into New Hampshire—"

"Aha," I exclaimed, post-funeral giddy, so dolled-up I was actually wearing a dress, "those border towns where Massachusetts people hide from taxes!"

"—and when I finally made up my mind to go ahead with that divorce I'd wanted at the beginning, because 'dealing with' the problems hasn't got us anywhere, I was dying of hunger so I made another decision and pulled into a wayside restaurant, not a chain, deciding I would like to have a hamburger once again without some corporation's special repulsive sauce on it, and who should I meet coming out of the restaurant kitchen but Batch and he looked even better than a good old-fashioned hamburger, so when he said that instead of crying in public maybe I ought to follow him up to Concord and cry in the privacy of his apartment, I went, have you ever been there?"

Although the days were now getting longer, at this time of year afternoon seemed always to be drawing in. I switched on Jacob's newly wired overhead light, but the low ceiling allowed the shadows only to be nudged. "Batch's apartment?" I said. "No, I've never been there."

Jacob put into the refrigerator the Tupperware boxes of mostly noodle casseroles that Edna had packed for us and insisted we take. "Dorothy?" he silently asked me, going back out to the car to fetch—or so I assumed, unable to see him there because the front windows were still blanked out by snowbanks—the packages of ham, roast beef, cookies, and an entire applesauce cake.

Virginia was saying, "God knows I had a crush on him when I was in junior high, but after all he's five years older than us, he wasn't even in high school when we were, so I knew it was doomed to be unrequited—oh, Jesus, I just remembered, wasn't today the funeral, isn't this awful, I can't remember Jacob's brother-in-law's name but I did only meet him that once, last Thanksgiving. Batch told me what he did. Why didn't you phone me? Thank God he warned you in time—Arthur?"

"Yes, Arthur made a point of not taking us with him, a good deed that wasn't mentioned in the understandably brief service. Where are you now? In Concord—at Batch's?"

Coming laden indoors, Jacob raised his eyebrows.

"I'm home, making lists and lists of lists. I'm going to move out, not kick Max out, I came back from Batch's this morning and found an apartment to rent here just like his, anonymous, I love it. But Ib, I know this will sound gross, as Willie would say, but how could they have a real funeral? Was there anything left to bury?"

I thought of our mailbox flag, red metal curled tightly. "You don't want to hear—Moose told Jacob, figuring it was unsuitable for my ears but of course Jacob told me. Not smithereens. After they got the fire out, they found him in a corner. Missing a leg. Jacob says he must've gone flying and it was torn off on something."

Jacob shucked his overcoat, his suit jacket. Unknotting his tie, he mouthed, "Virginia?" I nodded.

"Louise," Virginia was saying, "the poor poor woman. Is

she staying with your in-laws? Batch guessed her kids wouldn't have room."

"Phil has been helping her organize what's to be done. Last week, right after it happened, he was the one who acted like a zombie, not Louise. I swear Louise hasn't taken even one Valium, and she was zonked on tranquilizers for a couple of months after Timmy. But now Phil is suddenly rallying, right in his element, settling the mortgage insurance, making sure the home-owner's insurance will cover Arthur's business debts, looking into bankruptcy possibilities. Louise will have the land, not worth much but it's still got a cellarhole, a septic system, there's the well. The place is on that ghastly highway, the one where I used to think people had car crashes to break the monotony, she can sell it sooner or later to some business. Arthur left ten grand in life insurance."

"Can she collect? If he committed suicide?"

"Arthur bought the insurance ages ago when they had their first kid, he didn't buy it the day before he killed himself."

"You know that I want to go back to New York."

Jacob was in the living room now, adding logs to the stove.

Virginia said, "But I'm too old."

"Are you really going to stay in the same town as Max?"

"It's a city."

"Okay, city."

"There's the matter of Willie's school. And the easy commute to my school, and I do have to keep my job, don't I, though I wish I could quit like Jacob. Private school or public school, kids *smell*. And so does my teaching, after all these years. Did Jacob begin to see himself as the Mr. Chips of the library? I'm Ms. Chips, the creaky Terpsichore."

"When are you moving?" I found a very cold pencil on the windowsill. "Your address, your phone number."

"It's one of those make-believe addresses, like Batch's. We still can't get over, Ib, how we saw each other at your house at Thanksgiving but we were so immersed in our own messes that we didn't—it was the wrong situation, same as seeing each other at your folks' house. Ten Blueberry Court, Apartment Twenty-Two. I haven't got a phone yet. The complex, as they call the place, looks like a Holiday Inn, and I'm on the second floor. My lists are what to take, weeding out, what to leave here for Max. Peculiar how little I want. Willie's things. My clothes, that jet hatpin of my grandmother's, remember, that egg cup of my grandfather's my mother painted the flowers on when she was a girl, enough dishes and pots and pans to play house the way you wrote me you set up your laundry cottage, and I guess I'll lug my scrapbooks down from the attic and take them too. I've got two bedrooms at Blueberry Court, the kitchen is a closet but it has a dishwasher and a garbage disposal, and my outdoors is a little balcony I can maybe just barely wedge a chaise longue onto come spring."

I traced over the address I'd written on the wall under Jacob's important numbers. "And moving day is—?"

"Next Tuesday, first of February, not quite Groundhog Day. Batch is going to come down and help."

"Oh? Don't bother asking him to hang a birdfeeder on your balcony."

"Good God, I know he's more unmechanical than you are. But he'll be moral support. I'm off now, to pick up Willie at his violin lesson, I've got to hype the idea of the apartment and explain to him where I was last night. Uh, Ib, did I do okay explaining to you?"

I started laughing.

Long-distance relief loud and clear, Virginia said, "What will Dorothy say! Goodbye, goodbye!"

Jacob asked, "Virginia? Batch?"

"She sounds radiant."

Outside, a car door shut solidly. Jacob opened our doors, inside and storm, and we saw parked behind our car Flossie Sisson's Mercedes, with a reddish blur that must be Abigail lunging around the interior. Flossie came tripping carefully along the snow-smooth driveway to the doorstep.

"Such a bitter cold," she said, handing Jacob a Japanese

doll. "No, I can't come in, Abigail gets so keyed-up after a stay in the kennel she hates to let me out of her sight. This is just to thank you for keeping an eye on my schoolhouse."

"Why, thank you," we chimed, taken aback. "How was your trip?"

"A delight," she said, peering past us, "a delight. Heavens to Betsy, you still don't have any kitchen cabinets?"

"They're ordered," Jacob said shortly.

I said, "Should be arriving any day. Did you try raw fish?"

"I've tried it before, don't you know, at parties, but it always tasted like lime juice. In Japan, raw fish tastes like raw fat."

I asked, "Did you dine sitting on the floor? I'd be in agonies."

"Oh, they provided us round-eyes with seat-backs to lean against. I can't wait to tell Percy Lord all about the vegetables and flowers, when what he really wants to hear about, don't you know, is the geisha girls. The cabbages are frilled like lacy nosegays! Which reminds me; after seeing Percy driving that little girl home just now, the one who looks after Gay Blade, it occurred to me that maybe Percy isn't daydreaming about geishas anymore. Yes, the trip was a delight, despite the raw fish."

"Great," we said.

"I'm thinking of China next, if that's possible, but for now I'm glad to be back in this dreadful New Hampshire weather—and to find all my things not stolen, intact and unbroken. Young Hayward, don't you know, is so terrified of breaking something while he babysits my place that I believe he hardly moves or breathes. Well, I mustn't keep you. The taxicabs there have antimacassars on the drivers' seats!"

"Really?" I said. "Thank you again. Welcome home."

We waved as she drove off, and then Jacob shut the doors on the cold and looked at the doll. "What did she tell us her husband did?"

" 'Harold was in plastics.' " I took the demure kimono-wrapped geisha. "Thoughtful of Flossie. Maybe she's a good book-returner after all. These goddamned pantyhose, I've got to get out of them and into long underwear."

Remembering Timmy's ceremonial funeral, Jacob had had no appetite at the small WASP wake at the Wetherbees' house, but now while I undressed by the kitchen range he began raiding the funeral baked meats he'd put in the refrigerator. He asked again, "Virginia and Batch?"

"Perhaps a passing fancy."

"A return to the haven of childhood?"

"This food, all the food the friends and neighbors bring to wakes, potluck parties, church suppers, food sales, who knows what the kitchens are like where the grub is made? Odds are they're unhygienic, to say the least. Jacob, should you be eating that stuff?"

Suddenly there was less bathroom wall than ever. Jacob had put his fist through it. "Listen, cunt!" he shouted. "You and your fucking phobias, I lived my life perfectly fine until I met you and I can do the same again! If I want to eat this fucking tuna casserole, I'll eat this fucking tuna casserole, understand?"

"Gotcha." Clutching clothes, I fled into the bedroom. The Friday Night Fights, I thought as I sobbed and shivered, those Friday Night Fights, Jacob's version of wife-beating, here we go again. In the kitchen, Tupperware popped and burped.

We'd never obeyed the dictum that you shouldn't go to bed mad, but at least in the past we had always gone to bed together, seething with fury though we were. That evening, in the living room I watched *Roots* puffy-eyed; whenever I lowered the volume during commercials, I could hear the kitchen TV echoing. Finally I changed out of Levi's and sweatshirt into my nightgown, bathrobe, slippers, and went into the ell. He was sitting in the rocker beside the range, Scotch in hand, staring grimly at the little television on the primer-daubed floor. He didn't leave to give me privacy in the bathroom, so after I brushed my teeth and washed my face and anointed it with nightcream, I used the outhouse instead before climbing dog-tired into bed. Awakening during the night, I reached out to find half a bed empty. The clock radio glowed 2:19. I listened; the house was snapping as it chilled, and in the living room he was snoring. If he'd been snoring beside me, I would as usual have heaved him over onto his stomach in affectionate exasperation. Now I got out of bed, groped my way to the living-room sofa but discovered it also empty, then realized he was sleeping in his wing chair, having moved in here to watch the color TV. I turned off the test pattern. Oh, Christ, had he fallen asleep with his contacts in and blinded himself? I fumbled, learned he'd switched to his glasses, and unhooking them from over his ears I placed them beside his glass on the candlestand at his chair's elbow. He hadn't loaded the Jøtul for the night. I did that, expecting the thud of logs to wake him. He slept on. Like a mother in a movie, I took a blanket out of a blanket chest and spread it across him. I stood back and looked at him asleep on this island of furniture and plants surrounded by stacks of cartons topped with lampshades. My chum, my boon companion. Back in bed, I cried and cried.

When he came into the dining room the next morning as I was making coffee on the table saw, I said, "I'm sorry."

"You're always sorry." He went into the bathroom, emerged, walked past me into the bedroom where he took off his clothes and got into bed and fell asleep again.

So began what I'd expected to happen a year ago. Morning after morning Jacob stayed in bed with the covers over his head, sleeping until noon.

In my office I found myself often checking "succubus" in the dictionary. " 'A female demon,' " I read over and over, " 'supposed to descend upon and have sexual intercourse with a man while he sleeps. Compare incubus.' " Did I hear the Briggs ghosts chortling?

Afternoons, Jacob took to his wing chair with a book I'd asked the village library to order for him from the state library, as a joke. But he was reading it so earnestly he might have been studying it for a final exam, this *"Shake-*

speare" Identified in Edward de Vere, 17th Earl of Oxford, Volume I, by J. Thomas Looney. Through the sharp sunny afternoons he read, the gloomy afternoons, the snow, and into the evenings with television.

Dorothy phoned me and said, "I know you won't approve, dear, but your father and I stopped in at the Sidelines yesterday. Why didn't you warn me it would be slumming? I spotted Miriam right away from your description, but I don't see that she bears any resemblance to Nicole. The only reaction I could get from your father was that she seemed too solemn for Batch. Have you heard from Batch lately? Seen him?" Bracing myself, I replied, "Surprise! He's courting Virginia." *"Virginia,"* she exclaimed, a-thrill with news, "our Virginia? But she's married!" I said, "Not for long." "Oh, my God, what is the world coming to, what next, do her parents know? Isabel," Dorothy commanded, catching her breath, "tell all." Scratching at the frost on the ceiling above me, I began to edit.

The cupboards and cabinets and light-green formica counters were brought by a Meader Intervale Lumber Company truck. Jacob got out of his chair to help the driver carry the big cartons into the kitchen, but then he rejoined the Earl of Oxford. Looking at the cartons blocking my path to the sink and range, I remembered how in towns near and far we'd searched the kitchen sections of building-supply companies, all of which seemed to feature Spanish Mediterranean styles of dead dark wood with pulls like brass medallions, until we'd come back to our first choice, pine and particle board, the plainest and the cheapest. In the Meader Intervale Lumber Company's model-kitchen area, where on false walls the sample cupboards hung top-heavy over sample cabinets on a rucked-up patch of shag carpet and the counters displayed acoustical-ceiling tiles and chips of countertop colors and pamphlets about washerless faucets, I had listened to Jacob discussing measurements with the salesman and thought that soon the kitchen walls would be painted, the kitchen floor would be painted, the cabinets and cupboards would be installed and painted, and I would be wrestling with shelving paper and unpacking our kitchen at last. There would once again be fripperies like our demitasse cups! Now, however, after a few days of squeezing past the cartons to wash dishes and cook while envying Virginia her ready-made midget kitchen of gadgets, I pushed the cartons against the stripped walls out of my way and tried to forget their contents.

But after my shower one morning I asked, "Although putting up towel racks isn't coolie labor, couldn't I do it? Even though the bathroom isn't painted yet? That Christly flimsy drying rack, it won't stop collapsing under wet towels, and no matter how often that old floor is scrubbed it's still filthy, so the towels get filthy—" I was stopped by those nearsighted eyes of his, which, instead of hinting they saw more than other people's did, were at this moment totally impenetrable. He went into the bathroom, then back to bed.

On my makeshift pantry counter in the dining room, I continued readying meals. Skipping breakfast, Jacob duly ate the rest. In the Flintknappers, I recalled, one evening we had suddenly heard above the click of dominoes in the other side of the bar some fellow concluding some argument with, "Well, eating's a dirty habit too, of course it is, you do it breakfast, dinner, tea, and bloody supper!"

I missed pubs. Once, I had thought we'd go to pubs forever.

For my thirty-eighth birthday, Edna knitted me a shawl. Wearing it, I felt like a ball of wool.

Yet the long winter began melting into mud season, we could see out the ell's windows again, and on the first of April, when red-winged blackbirds arrived at sunrise in the lilac, like an April Fool I unpacked my running shorts and shoes, pulled on a sweatshirt, and before my breakfast I ran up the washboard road past the empty Crandall cottage where a huge old weeping willow, budded yellow, was fluttering unfettered. How embarrassing, I thought as I slogged along, to have taken up a form of exercise that became a national craze, how conventional!—a term Virginia and I had used so disparagingly in high school and I had used mock-lightly about Jacob's midlife crisis the weekend before he quit. Usually when I ran I sang Pete Seeger songs silently to myself to keep my mind free from other words (such as apoplectic letters to my congressman, which increased the hypertension I was supposed to be running off together with calories), but that didn't work today on the first run of the year. By the time I'd gone a modest mile and turned back, I'd rewritten Jacob's letter of resignation endlessly, quite drowning out "If I Had a Hammer," so I tried poems instead, remembering one time in the Flintknappers when Mrs. Hingham said out of the blue, "We had to learn Longfellow in school, did you?" and began reciting *Hiawatha* to us right there, under the four-hundred-year-old ceiling, over her gin-and-lime. Pete Seeger; his uncle Alan Seeger and a rendezvous with Death. My mind snarled into one question repeating in rhythm as I ran: How do you get through a life you know is all? That old familiar favorite. Fragments of serenity? But should there be no truce with nonsense? Or had we had the answer at the beginning: brass rubbings, to give our travels a reason cluttered with paraphernalia? Did some of the English have the right idea: think small, think eccentric? "The pheasant shoot," Mrs. Hingham had written us, "keeps Bert fit and happy." Frozen red and sweating, I reached Shelterfield and saw that a migration of grackles had alighted in the trees; the racket they were making as they announced their presence sounded like the creaking clatter of primitive machinery, a winged factory. Time's wingèd chariot?

And soon the early mornings were earsplitting with birdsong. In the swamp out back, spring peepers gave themselves up to paroxysms of hiccups. Jacob slept through it all; his stubbornness had disappeared like the snowbanks.

"The ell cellar," I told him one afternoon, interrupting his reading of Volume II, "it's flooded. What about the sump pump? Will you go see Cortland about the—you know, the flange?" Jacob didn't reply, but a few minutes later he hauled himself out of his chair, went outdoors to the car, and drove off. I wondered if he'd ever come back. He did, disappearing into the cellar. Soon there was the constant chug of the sump pump, as though every day we were plowing through heavy seas or traveling down-river on the *African Queen.*

"Black ducks," I said one lunchtime. "After my run this morning I scared up a pair on the swamp. They scared me up, to be more accurate. Maybe they'll nest here. Do you suppose they're the same ones those duck hunters were after last fall?"

He said, "I'm convinced de Vere has got to be the real Shakespeare, but why has everyone ignored the facts? Just to keep the tourist money in Stratford?"

"You mean I paid homage at the wrong place—and *twice,* once with Virginia, once with you? The Bard's hometown isn't the real thing?"

"Maybe we should go back and see the right place. The Earl of Oxford's. Castle Hedingham, in Essex."

"Sure. We could take the *African Queen* across the Atlantic and live on nuts and berries when we get there. This afternoon, I'm going to start raking out the Briggs flowerbeds to see what's still alive, if anything, after all those trucks last year. Allegra would say that spruced-up grounds are a good selling point."

"Where are our maps?"

"Packed."

"Essex. Near Suffolk. We must have driven past."

"Or bypassed."

Now I began staying outdoors as much as possible, doing yardwork, gardening, taking walks. Maybe I could build a treehouse, move into it, and never enter Shelterfield again. Housewife, househusband, married to a house. The structural integrity is impaired. I pushed a log across the brook for a bridge to the forest. By late April, early May, the yellow-green world out here could drive me mad with its burst of Monet. I found yellow adder's tongue along the brook, and the mat of pine needles under the dizzy pines was pierced by millions of Solomon's seal unfurling. Up the mountain I discovered a long waterfall as deafening as oncoming traffic into whose path I wanted to throw myself. Even indoors I wasn't sane; "Hi, handsome," I said to the rose-breasted grosbeak whistling on the birdfeeder as I washed lunch dishes, his rosy breast a color from a childhood paintbox, "hi, handsome."

On his forty-first birthday, Jacob went to the hardware store in Meader Intervale. I expected him to return, if he did return, with one of the many tools he had thought aloud about a lot B.F., Before Funk. He returned with a snorkel. I said, "But the lake isn't warm enough for swimming yet!" He replied, "I'll be ready when it is." I gave him two packages of red bandannas.

Edna and Phil sent him a Cross pen and pencil set. Edna phoned and said, "Is Jacob too busy for me to wish him happy birthday? First place in my class, Ib, a trophy, and Dad, he come to the show with me! He didn't say a word as I was driving off to the show, he just all of a sudden jumped in beside me. Oh, Louise rented one of them new apartments in Exmouth, she's going to move when Eric's school is out, she'll be nearer the other children." I asked, "But has she found a job yet?" "I guess I'm going to plant tomatoes again this year, maybe they won't get stolen this time. Madeleine, you know, who works at the Pot o' Gold, she and Louise used to be friends in high school and seems like they was always putting each other's hair up in pincurls, Madeleine's sister, she got Louise a job doing alterations in the ladies' department of Exmouth Apparel. It's not a very big trophy, but I polished it up real good for the living room."

My inner-timer, I realized while frothy apple blossoms wrinkled to brown, was still set for June. The end of school. The end of the true year, just as September still seemed the beginning. Would that ever change?

With June there also came an end to the easy lives led by Shelterfield's woodchucks. If I was home alone, I simply chased them out of the garden I'd planted and replanted and replanted, learning the late season up here, the frosts. But if Jacob happened to be home instead of sunning and snorkeling at the Dinsmere Public Beach, he roused himself to take stern measures. His best vantage point was my typewriter window. Ever alert at the keys, I'd spot a cuddly blob advancing upon the lettuce and I'd say in the quiet but reaching-the-second-balcony tone I'd copied from his library voice, "Jacob. Woodchuck." Out of bed or out of his chair he would leap, and up the stairs he'd fly, .22 in hand, and stealthily lifting the window screen, over my shoulder he would commence to fire. As shells pinged off my desk, off my cowering head ducked into my shoulders, I wondered if writing under these conditions felt at all like attempting to compose in a kibbutz.

Caca Thibodeau discovered a different method of dispatching woodchucks. "I was pulling in my driveway," he boomed at Jacob, arriving in his pickup with a six-pack, apparently having already consumed another to celebrate, "and there was the biggest fattest sonofabitch you ever saw sitting straight up in the beans just daring me. So I put my foot to the floor, and I took off, and he took off, and I nailed him halfway across the garden, flatter than a pancake!" Jacob observed, "Must've torn up the garden some." "Some," Caca admitted.

All the dirt roads in town had recently been graded by Caca and his crew, to get ready for the summer people. Dinsmere girded its loins for the onslaught. And return the summer people did, houses and camps were opened, the local handymen were hustled out of their torpor to unclog drainspouts and mow lawns and put in docks, I met new faces in the post office where the mail went up later each day because of increasing volume, and in the now-crowded store Mr. Dobbins offered a wider choice in his meat case and began stocking buttermilk.

One morning during my run, I saw that the Crandall cottage was coming alive. Mrs. Crandall must have arrived sometime yesterday; from last summer I recognized the car with Connecticut license plates in the driveway—yet another Mercedes in Dinsmere! This was a gray Mercedes, perhaps to match the weathered gray of the cottage. What about a dog? Last summer we hadn't seen a dog here or, giving Shelterfield its noise-level tests, heard one. As I jogged past, to and fro, comparing my present wary curiosity with my dread last year of neighbors, no matching gray dog came tearing across the unmown lawn to devour me. Windows were open. From a rafter on the front porch hung a pot of pink patient Lucy; first things first. We hadn't noticed the old tennis court ever in use last summer, and this morning, with the sun just beginning to push through the mist, the forest seemed eagerly reclaiming the fence and clay, the way it would any unplowed field.

Late that afternoon, my work in the garden over for the day, I was reluctantly washing from my hands the tomato plants' yellow dust which smelled even more juicy-red than tomatoes in seed catalogs looked, wishing you could slice that smell into a June salad, when the Crandall Mercedes appeared in our driveway. Hastily drying my hands too soon, streaking the towel yellow, I opened the ell's screen door to a dowager wearing dirty painter's-pants and a T-shirt that, over her imposing bust, told a white lie: I'M NOT A TOURIST, I LIVE HERE.

"Your iris are lovely," said Mrs. Crandall, charging into the kitchen and bringing with her such an entourage of mosquitoes that introductions were momentarily postponed while we slapped and clapped as if in a frenzied folk dance.

"Thank you," I said. "I'm amazed they can still bloom after all the neglect, it's given me hope for the black-eyed Susans."

"Good hardy Dinsmere stock! How do you do, I'm Emma Crandall, you must be Isabel Wetherbee, I meant to stop last summer and never did. How are you folks managing a year later? May I take a look-see?"

Like Allegra—although, I reminded myself, Allegra was only related to the Crandall family by marriage—Emma Crandall proceeded to inspect Shelterfield. I tagged along from room to room, seeing the place anew again, hoping she wouldn't notice the feeling of a dead halt to the progress, saying, "I'm sorry my husband isn't here right now, he could explain the intricacies of what's been accomplished; yes, we heat the main part with wood, but we don't chop our own; no, we don't plan dormers; I'm not sure we can save the barn—"

Jacob arrived then, coming indoors barefoot, in wet torn-off Levi's, around his shoulders his orange-and-green-striped beachtowel sandy. He was already so tanned this summer that, I thought as I introduced him to Emma, he looked like a white-bearded beachcomber and/or a candidate for skin cancer. "How do you do," he said, shifting his snorkel to shake Emma's proffered hand.

She said, "Were you at the public beach? Too goddamned small, isn't it! The town should have acquired more lakefront way back at the beginning. Concern for the future is essential! Have you thought of running for selectman? Thankless job, I agree. Now, tell me what you have in mind for the barn. Lift it up, get new pinnings under it, restore it?"

Jacob went tongue-tied. Before I rushed to fill the little silence, I tried to see him as Emma Crandall did. To her, he wasn't on vacation from a library. But, my God, that's what he still was to me! No matter how many hammer holsters and red bandannas I gave him! I babbled, "The barn is caving in, don't you think it's too far gone or—"

"Aesthetics aside," Emma said, "it would cost you more to start over than to renovate. Such a pity about the Briggses' pigheadedness, if only they could at least have agreed on maintenance. Do you two play tennis?"

Jacob shook his head, and I explained unnecessarily, "We don't play games in general, and in particular we don't play together, not after we once in our younger days nearly came to blows during a darts competition. Which, incidentally, *I* won."

No rise out of Jacob.

"Probably a very smart policy," Emma said. "Our court is in utter disrepair, I haven't had the heart for it these past two years since my husband died, but one of my many projects this summer is to fix it up. Good to meet you both! And congratulations are in order, Mr. Wetherbee, your visible work is so meticulous I know that those invisible jobs like wiring must be also."

"Thank you," I said.

Emma said, "Take care," and left.

As I watched the Mercedes make its majestic exit from

our driveway, I asked Jacob, "Do you remember when it was that people started bidding farewell with 'Take care'? On the phone, too? How do these things start? At least we know the origin of your 'Bye-bye,' copying your grandmother." And then I couldn't help saying, "So it's this house now too, as well as your library, it's your present as well as your past that you can't talk about, make smalltalk about?"

He could have snapped his towel at me, in playful locker-room fashion. Or, being strangled himself, he could have strangled me with the towel. What he did was drop the summery strip of terrycloth on the floor, the way Phil always left his bathtowels in sodden heaps on the bathroom floor for Edna to pick up. Jacob asked, "You want to add anything about towel racks?"

"No."

"Huh? Come on, how about a bathroom door, you must have something to say about that and a bathroom wall, haven't you? Let's hear it, come on, let's hear it."

"Jacob, cut this out, I'm sorry." The phone rang. "Hello?"

"It's Miriam," Miriam said. "If you happen to be in the vicinity this afternoon, stop in for a drink, I'm moving tomorrow. Paul let me take the day off to pack which is really generous of him seeing as how I'm moving in with him."

"Be right over." I fetched my pocketbook, took out my car keys. "I'm going to Miriam's."

Jacob had switched on the kitchen TV, and there, as always at this time of day in this neck of the woods, was Merv. Jacob did not bid me farewell in any form.

So I drove over to East Dinsmere, past villagers on hands and knees in gardens, stretches of forest calming down from springtime to a steady green, the mountains deceptively soft, an abandoned mill as mossy as its millstream, a catbird perching on a trail signpost to snack upon a butterfly.

"Paul?" I asked as Miriam opened the ragged screen door of her early-Exmouth type of house. Suitable for impoverished teachers, though set off by itself hermitlike along a mountain's dirt road instead of on the outskirts of a residential neighborhood, it was a young-marrieds little house, jerrybuilt, and you knew that there would be diapers in the toilet. "Who's Paul?"

Miriam slapped at mosquitoes. She was wearing baggy Bermudas and a hot-pink poorboy jersey which looked to be the twin of one I'd had in the mid-Sixties in England. "Paul? He owns the Sidelines, chief cook and bottlewasher."

"Oh, yes, Allegra sold it to him."

"With misgivings. Vodka and tonic okay? Paper cups, I've packed the glasses."

"Everyone's packing or unpacking. I'm still packed."

In the sticky kitchen (surely there must be jam underneath a highchair, peanut butter, a puddle of orange juice on the floor), Miriam sliced a shrunken lime and said, "We were friends downstate, Paul and I, before I met your brother, and when Paul quit teaching and bought the Sidelines he tried to talk me into coming up here to work. Even though I don't ski, which would be the only reason a good waitress like me would take the job unless she was desperate. Well, I did come here eventually. And now, eventually, Lesley and I are moving to that Intervale house Allegra sold him. Lesley's there this afternoon, getting ready for her horse. We went horse-hunting this weekend—*anything* so she won't discover boys! She'll still visit Gay Blade, but the Lords will have to find another stableboy."

"Percy must be heartbroken."

"Ever seen Hannah in the kimono Flossie brought her?"

"Awe-inspiring?"

With a clumpy-sandaled foot Miriam stomped down the garbage in her pop-up garbage can. Handing me a paper cup, she asked, "Didn't Batch once mention that his wife has started a thrift shop?"

"I keep meaning to go there. Cheers."

"I've been sorting out clothes and I wondered if I could ask you to drop them off when you're next in Bridgeford. It would be kind of—you know, awkward for me. The stuff's in here."

Into the gimcrack bedroom I followed Miriam, who seemed much more likely to buy her clothes at a thrift shop than to sell them. But I shouldn't be in here! I was the baby sister! Yet as she began rolling up a heap of clothes on the bed as though starting the base of a snowman, I realized that no longer was I a member of her family nor she mine, so I inquired, "Did Batch say why he left Nicole?"

"Who knows? He talked about the artificiality of his sales route, but he never said his wife didn't understand him. I gather you're aware that since February he's been winding his self-winding watch elsewhere."

"Uh, yes."

"I think for a while he was thinking of buying the Sidelines. Not that Paul would have sold."

"Buy the Sidelines?"

"And if the north country ever got stranded without mozzarella again, he'd have his secret sources. Has Jacob heard there's an opening next fall for a librarian at Intervale Regional?"

"There *is?*"

"Done. This bundle is my stuff, this is Lesley's outgrown, whatever Nicole can get for it will be welcome."

"My mother says she takes one-third the price."

"It'll still help, every little penny. We're expanding." Miriam carried the bundles into the living room, plopped them on the shedding plush sofa, looked around for her paper cup, tracked it down amongst the cartons in the kitchen. "Yes, cheers. I've spent far more thought on this shacking-up decision than I did deciding to marry my husband. Ex-husband."

"Batch was a detour?"

"I suppose," she said, collapsing into a dinette chair whose blotched chrome and ripped plastic seat reminded me of my chairs in the laundry cottage. "Paul made his own detours, too. Packing! Moving! It's worse than working during a Super Bowl. You're wondering how, if teachers hated what I did, Paul and I ever got together in the first place."

"Love conquers all? Even for an In-Service Training Specialist and a—what did he teach?"

"Social studies in mini-courses. He also coached skiing, what there was of it downstate."

"He didn't mind mainstreaming?"

"He was planning to leave teaching anyway, as soon as he'd saved up enough to finance a restaurant up north. I don't blame the teachers, who would want to waste their time after school attending my workshops, and the last thing they wanted to hear about, much less learn about, was mainstreaming fucked-up kids into their classrooms. They didn't finally get to me, not the teachers. Not the administrations, either. And I liked going from town to town to hold those workshops, not being trapped in a classroom. I had a mission, I persevered. But what happened was, one day I was talking with one of my deaf kids and I started laughing at him. I couldn't stop. Then it happened again and again, deaf, hydrocephalic, you name it, I couldn't stop laughing. I still can't. Show me a cripple, I break up. Luckily, they're fewer and farther between in restaurants, and I can get another waitress to take that table." We heard a car, and rising wearily onto her sandals she looked out the café-curtained window. "Oh, God, here's the couple I'm subletting to, they're going to be coming in the back door as I go out the front."

"Funny, when we moved here I never thought I'd be ready so soon to move again, but I envy you. Good luck, stop by when you're up this way, I'll see what Nicole can get for the clothes."

"And don't you forget our onion rings!"

Leaving, gingerly embracing the bundles, I nodded to the callow probably-not-marrieds who were lifting cartons out of the rear of their rattletrap jeep which was one of those vehicles allowed in a studied manner to rust and disintegrate, as were certain of Dinsmere's Mercedes population.

I had Le Car, I thought, driving away; I had my emergency twenty-dollar bill in my wallet, a VISA credit card, an Authors Guild Hertz card, and Miriam and Lesley's castoff clothing. How far could I get?

Braking at Shelterfield, I heard shots. From the driveway I couldn't see the garden. I sat rigid in the car until the noise stopped, telling myself it was not an explosion of acetylene, telling myself that you don't fire five times if you're blowing your brains out.

Then, heart in mouth, I raced indoors.

Jacob came downstairs carrying the .22. "He got some lettuce before I got him."

"I'll replant." Glimpsing the beachtowel hanging on the clothesline which ran from the ell to a pine, I plumped the bundles onto one of the cartons containing kitchen cabinets. "Miriam says there's a librarian opening at the Intervale school."

After a moment, he propped the rifle in its corner by the back door. "So?"

"So they probably want a Media Generalist. For Alternative Learning."

"Figured that out, did you?" As he went past the telephone, it rang. "Hello? Oh, hi, Allegra. You're *where?* At Exmouth Realty? Co-broking?"

What a simple emotion relief can be, so easy it's almost negative!

When Jacob turned to me his face was taut, unsmiling. "Great, but just a second, I'll check with Ib." He lowered the receiver. "Allegra heard of an Intervale family, they have to move to the Exmouth area, and she took them down and showed them our place. Didn't tell us first, didn't want to get our hopes up. She has an offer of forty-six five. Okay?"

"Okay with you?"

He raised the receiver. "It's fine with us, Allegra. Go ahead and 'finalize.' "

The July morning was hot and rainy, as stifling as a sickroom, reconfirming my theory that summer is a hallucination. Sweating, at last I found a parking space.

Nicole and her partner, Jane Tilton, the daughter of Dorothy's shy but intrepid friend, Pris Patterson, had settled on Potpourri for the name of their thrift shop, located just outside the urban renewal in the part of Bridgeford's Main Street still frankly a mill-town downtown. Lugging Miriam's clothes and Jacob's, I hiked along the sidewalk until I reached the Potpourri's window of plastic iced-tea spoons, sleeveless blouses, five-and-ten vases and figurines; as I entered the stuffy room which was crammed like a trunk I tried to remember what this storefront had once been: a coffee shop killed by Dunkin' Donuts, or a jewelry store moved to the mall?

"No," I said to brown-wren Nicole, discovering her perched on a stool behind a counter, caged by garment-district clothing racks of galvanized pipe, "it used to be a millinery shop, didn't it? Chez Rochelle?"

Nicole was sorting tags, slipping them into numbered envelopes. "Welcome to the Potpourri. We've got some hats too, over on that shelf. Did you ever buy a hat at Chez Rochelle?"

"No, but Dorothy did."

"I bought my going-away hat there."

Sister of the groom, I had been a teenage bridesmaid in daffodil organdy; I could remember that little hat of hers, navy blue, with a dainty stiff veil, grotesquely adult. Setting the armload of clothes on the edge of the counter, I asked, "Jane isn't working today?"

"We swap days. I'll be finished in a minute."

Below the hat shelf were shelves of flowerpots shaped like puss-in-boots and swans, old meat-grinders trailing strange attachments, Barbie dolls offering their own used clothes. I'd hoped to do business with uninvolved Jane, not with my quasi-erstwhile sister-in-law. Driving down here, while the car radio's irritating music was interrupted by supermarket ads for hot-dog-roll specials and by an incorrect hay-drying report, I had belatedly realized that this was going to be just as embarrassing for me as it would have been for Miriam, if not more so; before, I'd only worried about how Jacob would react to my suggesting we sell his schoolclothes and then about what his reaction might mean. He'd said, "I don't give a shit." Well, that was a sort of decision, wasn't it? As was my delving into his garment bags, leaving him only a minimum of formal clothes for parties, weddings, funerals. But other decisions? The savings account replenished, I found I could sign my name again, so I had resumed my job as chancellor of our exchequer. And, emboldened, last night I'd mentioned to Jacob our original plan of investing in another house for him to restore, adding, "As your Earl of Oxford put it on one of Dorothy's samplers:

> The day shall not be up so soon as I,
> To try the fair adventure of tomorrow."

Jacob had replied, "Mortgage rates are hitting ten percent now. If they keep going up, it'll be like a rent stabilization act, you can't afford to move." I'd said, "Then let's buy before they go higher." He'd said, "I thought I could whip right through doing a house. I didn't foresee how depressing it would get." "Okay," I'd pursued, "do you want to stay here, unpack, putter along? What happens when the money from the Millsted house runs out? Do you get a—you know, a job?" This question caused no anger, no Friday Night Fight on a Monday; no answer, either. Silence.

I said to Nicole, "How's it going, how's business?"

"Looks like we have more sellers than buyers, doesn't it, though actually the turnover is fairly fast. Especially the knickknacks."

"The knickknacks sell like hot cakes?"

"Yes, odd in these hard times." Nicole pushed aside the tags and envelopes, reached for a sales-pad and Miriam's clothes. "But I understand your hard times are over? Batch told me you've sold the house."

"Not a moment too soon. We were down to our last sou." Or our last thousand dollars, O shuddering stomach!

"You and Jacob must be overjoyed."

We should be. Yet there was no joy in Mudville. I said, "You've got to come up sometime and see the place, you and the kids. Their summer jobs, though—where is it Kate's working this year, Camden? And is Melissa back at the Lollipop Village? You and Davy then, how's his new day-care? Dorothy said he—"

"Are you being discreet, or don't you know that I've finally gone ahead with the divorce?"

"You have? Wonderful, high time!"

"Dorothy didn't call you?"

"When did you tell her?"

"A week ago. Now, our system here is, we itemize each article of clothing along with your price suggestion—these aren't your size, are they?"

"I'll be damned. Dorothy didn't tell me. How did she react?"

"I've been trying to remember what Virginia looks like. You little girls, we were always tripping over you. I've been trying to remember her when you were in high school, and I know I've seen her since then, at your folks' at Christmas-time or somewhere, I know I must have. Blonde, I'm sure of long blonde hair. Straight spine, isn't that what I mostly remember?"

"A dancer's carriage. Christ, Nicole!"

"Don't be upset. In one of my courses—"

The door opened, and a tall thin black woman came in, whisking rain off her natural linen sundress creased by driving. As I wondered if she might be a first for Nicole, I realized she was Stella.

"It *is* you," she said, hurrying past racks of slinky evening gowns and upside-down men's trousers while I gaped. "I thought I saw you coming in here but it took us ages to find a parking space."

"My God!"

On the brink of hugging, we clasped each other's hands, laughed, oh-for-heaven's-sake hugged.

"Stella," I said, "this is Nicole Pierce, my sister-in-law—well, yes, my sister-in-law, are you keeping your married name?—and Nicole, this is Stella Morrison, we met in England, what are you doing in Bridgeford, how many years has it been, how on earth did you recognize me!"

"Thirteen years," Stella said. "I recognized you because

you were walking. You weren't hauling a shopping bag full of Brussels sprouts, but I'd have known you anywhere." To Nicole she explained, "Ib here got me walking more miles than I ever did before or since," and then, startled, she pointed at the wall above a shelf of handbags, covered candy dishes, ceramic puppies, a waffle iron missing a cord.

There hung a little framed sampler which, when I last saw it, had still had its home near the coat-hooks in Dorothy's kitchen, having lived there forever. It said QUONDAM FRIENDS SHOULD NOT BE FORGOT. Tracking down "quondam" to "former" had been a childhood lesson in a dictionary too heavy for me then to heft.

"Appropriate!" said Stella, and I looked at Nicole.

"Yes, from Dorothy." Nicole shook out Miriam's rick-rack-trimmed shirtdress. "She brought it in yesterday, either for my house, she told me, or to decorate the store. I told her for crying out loud, she's still everything she always was, including the grandmother of my children—whose clothes *are* these, Ib?"

"Oh, they should have a separate slip, for a Miriam Holt, she's a Dinsmere friend who doesn't get down this way often, they're her clothes and her daughter's. Stella, you didn't even leave an address! Where did you go?"

"Miriam H-o-l-t?" Nicole asked, writing. "Do you know the prices she wants?"

"South Carolina, home." Stella held up lengthy pinky fingers. "Did you notice my nails? Remember how sorry I used to feel for you because you had to keep your nails so short for typing your stories? I've been a typist thirteen years."

I said, "Miriam told me to ask you to get whatever you can. Are you playing tourist in Bridgeford? Isn't it like us foreigners in England, the summer people in Bridgeford? Where's Amy, is she with you?" I stopped, remembering how Stella and Ed hadn't traveled in England, reeling at the thought of all the terrible fates that could have befallen a child in thirteen years.

"Would you believe I've just moved to Portsmouth?"

The door opened, the lid of the trunk. Two women came in, more middle-aged than Nicole and Stella and I were yet, their blouses tucked into polyester slacks over stomachs sticking out shamelessly, as if they were deliberately flaunting figures lost in childbearing; what the hell better excuse not to bother doing sit-ups? They caught sight of Stella, mimed forgotten errands, beat a hasty retreat.

I floundered, "Portsmouth, New Hampshire?"

"Pease Air Base there. I've remarried, I was a June bride though I didn't learn my lesson the first time, he's in the Air Force too. But an officer! And Amy graduated from high school this spring, this fall she's going to college in Boston to study broadcasting, can you believe it? Now you, what have you been doing, whatever happened about your writing, are you living in your hometown? I remembered you talking about Bridgeford and the lake, that's why I told Walt we had to swing in here on our way to Montreal."

"A postponed honeymoon? And you've left him sweltering out in the car?"

This struck us as hilarious, and she said, "But I opened the window a crack! Don't worry, he's getting some more film, in an air-conditioned store."

"Now these," Nicole said, her solemnity suddenly reminding me of Sebastian's comment about Miriam's, "are these Jacob's clothes? Sized and priced, I wish all our clientele were as neat as you, but winter suits and jackets aren't the right season, Ib. We're still mostly selling summerwear."

Unable to imagine returning to Shelterfield with those clothes, that decision, I asked, "Could you store them then, until fall?"

"We'll put them on sale anyway, if Jane agrees, seeing as how it's you. Batch quit his job, you know. Like Jacob."

I stepped backward into a rack of amputated little dresses, party frocks for female toddlers.

Nicole said, "Didn't Dorothy tell you? He's getting his real-estate license. He'll do well in that, I'm not worrying about child-support payments or—"

Tactfully Stella interrupted, "I've got to be going."

"So have I," I said. "Nicole, thank you, I'll call you, love to the kids."

Outside, we found the rain had stopped. Puddles on the street were streaked with oily rainbows.

Stella said, "I'm parked over that way."

"I'm down that way. Addresses," I added, reaching into my pocketbook for scrap-paper and pen. "This is mine, up in Dinsmere—and, come to think of it, here's my name. I married that librarian I met just before you moved onto the Base. Could you maybe detour for a visit on your way back? What's your name, address, phone number? Does your new place have a big enough stove? Wait'll you get a load of the stove arrangement in our house!"

"When you came back to the States, did you have to learn to cross the street again? After learning to look to your right in England so you wouldn't be run over?"

Pocketing addresses in pocketbooks, we contemplated this downtown, remembering a High Street.

I said, "Whenever I see a goldfinch I think of the lemon curd tarts that the breadwoman sold from her van."

"We'll stop by if we've got time before Walt has to get back. If not, I guess you must know the way to Portsmouth?"

Quickly now we said goodbye and parted, and as I got into my car relieved of those schoolclothes and drove off along one-way streets out to the road to the lake, I thought of driving not through this soggy muggy morning but through the cool sponge of an English fog, my headlights searching for the cat's-eye reflectors in the center line, the foglamp of an oncoming car large and yellow even a long distance ahead. If Jacob would finish the basic repairs and do some cosmetic work, we could sell Shelterfield, take the money from that sale and the sale of the Millsted house, and go live in Mousehole, the fishing village of my youthful story, until the loot was gone. We could dine on morgy brath and starry gazy pie.

But after Mousehole had come Porlock, a name synonymous with rude awakenings.

Nature-Friends Family Park was enclosed by a high board fence painted circus colors. Locking my empty car in the busy parking lot, I entered, treading wet paths. After many rundown years of whispered maltreatment of its animals, the zoo had been bought two years ago by the present owners who had refurbished it, so the interior was as spanking bright and innocent as the fence and you were lulled into forgetting that its healthy-looking inhabitants could not leave of their own free will. There was no way, however, to deodorize the smell.

In addition to the array of buildings and cages for more exotic creatures, the Park attempted to live up to its name by providing a small deer park bordered by enclosures for other native animals; at this deer park's cyclone fence, beyond the otter pool, I saw Dorothy pointing out to a group of little summer-camp boys the plaque on which were mounted two pairs of antlers.

"—shed every year," she was telling them, not tiredly singsong but as if for the first time in her zoo-guide career, her striped shirt and denim wraparound still crisp. "No, it doesn't hurt the bucks any more than losing a tooth does, but they don't have an Antler Fairy to leave them a dime under their pillows. Why, Ib!"

The little boys, I realized, were wearing an updated version of the jerseys and shorts in Jacob's camp photograph. Yet instead of the S for Sachem Camp on Jacob's chest, these jerseys bore a K.

I said, "I've finally been to Nicole's shop, I brought down some clothes. She told me she's—" I hesitated, knowing Dorothy wouldn't want a divorce overheard even by this band of midgets. "She's getting things straightened out."

"Oh, did she tell you about that cleaning woman she's hired?"

Amongst the trees, the browsing deer appeared and disappeared, slowly, quietly, dreamily. I said, "I don't think I mentioned how Batch took an interest in a Dinsmere realtor last winter. A woman, a real-estate *woman,* not a lady realtor. I'm getting awfully sick of people being so scared to call a woman a woman that they're using 'lady' all the time now. I gather Batch must have just been learning a new trade, not courting. I haven't heard from Virginia lately, have you talked with her mother? Is Virginia teaching summer school?"

One of the little boys asked, "Don't the lions eat the deer?"

Dorothy said, "Call it what you will, Virginia is going to be one too. She's studying for the real-estate exam. I don't know," she blurted, "I might as well divorce your father, everyone else is!"

"Virginia and Batch are going to be partners? Where? In Concord? Well, why not, almost the entire population of New Hampshire is selling real estate, the more the merrier." Giving Dorothy time to recover herself.

"Did you stop here because something's wrong?"

"Just to say hi."

"That was nice of you, dear."

"Dear!" the kids cried. "Dear deer!"

Dorothy adjusted the neck of my T-shirt and turned back to her charges.

Out on the lake road again, I drove past the crowded Lollipop Village whose miniature storybook cottages reminded me today of the gatehouse at Clopton Park. My niece Melissa was working there, in the gift shop where the Mother Hubbard cupboards were full of lollipops. In which Bridgeford tourist trap had I worked my seventeenth summer? Oh, that had been the summer of the Milkpail Parlor, at least until I quit.

Good God, Gary's old studio, the ice-cream stand, was gone! It had completely vanished since I'd last taken this road, obliterated by a spreading condominium which seemed to be made of fake barn-boards. No monument remained to the pot-throwing of either of us.

But farther up the lake I came to his boathouse studio and noted that he too was getting his share of the tourist business brought out by this brightening rainy day. Women were stepping from cars, smoothing skirts, slacks, admiring a flowerbed of blossoming plants in his pots. Did the child-bride have a green thumb? The Stud's Studio. I gave it a Dinsmere wave as I passed by.

Last winter, driving back from my earring visit, I had dawdled. Now, despite the limpid lake and the leisurely weather, all at once I wanted to rush home. Furious at the summertime stop-and-start traffic jams, the crazy Massachusetts drivers, the exhaust fumes floating on waves of heat that seemed thicker than the steamy asphalt melting beneath my tires, I fought my way north along the Indy, through a Meader Intervale nearly immobile with out-of-state cars and recreational vehicles, until I could turn off onto the Pequawket Road.

It was indeed noticeably cooler up here in the mountains, a reminder of why the old summer cottages had been built. Two tilting sailboats on Lake Pequawket indicated sturdy breezes.

The sampler of Dorothy's that had most scared the hell out of me was the one in the upstairs hall near my bedroom, hanging over the tall blanket chest Jacob had copied years later; its stitching read:

When This You See
Remember Me.

I'd left Jacob asleep, so I expected at the most he'd now be in the shower. Getting out of the car, unsticking my Levi's from my ass and the backs of my legs, I heard a whining sound. Indoors, I discovered him in the dining room all dressed, in his own Levi's and T-shirt, standing at the table saw, cutting a board.

I decided not to comment on such a flurry of activity. Instead, when the noise died I said, "You'll never guess who I met at Nicole's. Stella, from England!"

"And you'll never guess where I found the finials. In the pantry in a box of tools I haven't needed yet."

"For Christ's sake." I crossed to the bedroom, and there on top of the ugly old bureau were the two pineapples. "Well, I certainly didn't spoil my reputation for not being able to find anything."

"Emma Crandall phoned. She's got a bathroom floor rotted out from a sweating toilet, she wondered if I'd come have a look at it after lunch. Asked me to give her an estimate on taking up the toilet and fixing the floor. I thought I'd put together this tool carrier so I don't have to lug my whole toolbox along on jobs."

Carefully I asked, "Would you like lunch outdoors for a change?"

"How about on the barn steps? I'll be goddamned if I'm going to let that barn get the better of me—"

The phone rang.

"Hello?" I said.

"Ib," Dorothy said, "you're home, I just wanted to tell you before you hear it on the radio, I'm joining the posse. Little Horace has escaped again and this time he took a baby elephant with him!"

Ruth Doan MacDougall was born and grew up in Laconia, New Hampshire. She is the author of seven other novels, including The Cheerleader, Aunt Pleasantine *and, most recently,* The Flowers of the Forest.